THE SECRET BILLIONAIRE

Book One of The Surway Fortune

Teymour Shahabi

PageWing, LLC
NEW YORK, NY

PageWing, LLC
New York, NY
www.pagewing.com

Publisher's Note: This is a work of fiction. Names, characters, places, and incidents are a product of the author's imagination. Locales and public names are sometimes used for atmospheric purposes. Any resemblance to actual people, living or dead, or to businesses, companies, events, institutions, or locales is completely coincidental.

Book layout adapted from ©2013 BookDesignTemplates.com.

Cover design by Kerry Ellis.

The Secret Billionaire/ Teymour Shahabi. -- 1st ed.
ISBN 978-0-9978760-1-7

Contents

With profound gratitude, this book is dedicated to anyone reading these words.

June 24, 196...

At nine o'clock yesterday morning, following ninety days of fruitless searching, billionaire industrialist and businessman Lyndon Surway was officially pronounced dead. Mr. Surway was last seen by members of his staff departing from the main airplane hangar of his estate a few minutes past eight in the morning, flying alone aboard one of his aircraft. His last recorded words to the command center crew of his hangar were: "Clear skies and mild winds. Perfect visibility, or as perfect as I could hope, for as long as I can tell. Gentlemen, I wish you a thorough enjoyment of this fine day." Nothing unusual was noted in his language or behavior.

The late Mr. Surway often took his plane out with no stated destination. But this time, he failed to return at the customary hour of six in the evening. As no word had been received from him, the kitchens were advised that he would likely dine outside. At ten o'clock on the following morning, when there was still no news of Mr. Surway or his aircraft, the Steward of the House alerted the municipal, state, and federal authorities, and a search began for the missing magnate. But no airport, hotel, hospital or inn within fuel's range of the estate could provide any information. Dozens of interviews bore no result. Countless journalists and detectives rushed in from every corner of the country, but none of them could unearth a single clue regarding Mr. Surway's whereabouts.

Not even the Steward could guess where Mr. Surway had gone. On the morning of his disappearance, Mr. Surway had only told him: "My day is free and so am I."

Fifteen infantry troops were dispatched, with over a hundred hound dogs, across more than two hundred miles of hills and valleys surrounding the town of Spring Forge, where Mr. Surway lived. The infantry and the dogs found nothing. The Air Force then loaned eighteen jet-powered aircraft to continue the search. The Navy joined the effort with five ships, sixteen helicopters, and four submarines to scour the coastal regions, islands, and ocean floor within flying range of the Eastern Seaboard. Again nothing was found. Finally then, a large-scale search was conducted through the grounds and the buildings of Surway House itself, led by seven hundred volunteers from Spring Forge and other towns throughout the valley. Still they found nothing. Yesterday marked three months since Mr. Surway's disappearance. The aircraft was legally declared lost, and its owner deceased. Mr. Surway, estimated for each of the past twelve years to be the wealthiest man in the Western Hemisphere, leaves behind no known relatives.

At three o'clock yesterday afternoon, Mr. Surway's attorney arrived from the City to disclose his late client's last will and testament. The following lays down the words of the will, as written by the late Mr. Surway himself, and as read before the main representatives of his estate and business interests in the Great Hall of the House:

"[...] As I would find it particularly offensive not to be invited to my own reception, I ask that you kindly refrain from organizing a funeral ceremony for me. If you insist on honoring my memory, you may quietly toss a sip of your drink into a plant at the next party you attend (assuming the wine is decent, forgive me for saying so). I promise to do my very best to drink it and to thank you.

Having settled what I ask of you, now to the matter of what I shall give. From a designated trust, opened at the Metropolitan Savings Bank in the City exclusively for this purpose, I hereby grant every member of my House and business staff, including every person working for an entity of the Surway Corporation and its subsidiaries, an annual gift equal to twice the amount of the individual's current yearly salary, to be paid out in full on January 1 of each year from now until the end of the individual's life. In addition, to every member of my House and business staff, for every child born before this day, I leave an incremental yearly sum equal to the individual's current salary, to be paid out in full on January 1 of each year until the end of the child's life. There isn't a single person, among the many men and women whom I have had the privilege of living and working with, who doesn't deserve these sums and much more. And if there is, then I deserve at least this penalty for my poor judgment of character.

As for the remainder of my assets, I leave the entirety of my holdings, my property, and all my interests to my dear friend Lucian Baker, with the sincerest expression of my gratitude and best wishes. To him I bequeath my stake in every business across the Surway Corporation and its subsidiaries, as well as my ownership stakes across all other investments domestically and overseas, including but not limited to farms, factories, lands, corporations, and trusts. To Lucian Baker I also leave the estate at Surway House, along with all the possessions held therein, including but not limited to the main buildings and gardens, along with the numerous collections housed therein, including but not limited to the paintings, sculptures, statuary, weaponry, jewelry, gems, silverware, glassware, porcelain, precious metals, historical artifacts, aircraft, boats, cars, stables, rare books and manuscripts, common books and manuscripts, wine cellars, wardrobes, musical instruments, and maps. Finally, to Lucian

Baker I leave the entirety of my financial assets, excluding the trust set up for the members of my House and business staff as described above. To him will accrue any income from my stock and bond portfolios, my commodity holdings, and my real estate investments held domestically and around the world, along with any and all other funds held under my name or any business that I own. Most importantly, Lucian Baker will be the sole beneficiary of all my cash assets, whether held at hand in Surway House or in any financial account held in my name. It is my privilege to leave this inheritance to Mr. Baker as a token of my genuine friendship and heartfelt thanks."

Since the reading of the will yesterday afternoon, the desperate search for Mr. Surway has turned into a frantic one for Mr. Baker. As of the writing of this article, several individuals named Lucian Baker have been officially identified within the greater population, but none among the late Mr. Surway's personal and business relations. Inevitably, the news has begun to spread among the public. Conmen and imposters keep every telephone ringing across the editorial floor as I write. Certainly the search for the legitimate Lucian Baker will put an end to all their claims before the week is over.

The fortune to which Mr. Baker is entitled is almost as difficult to grasp as Mr. Baker himself. Indeed, by our independent calculations as well as official accounting records, the magnificently generous trust that the late Mr. Surway left for his staff members and colleagues amounts to pennies in comparison with the remainder of the legacy. After all taxes and duties are paid, Mr. Baker will remain the largest single inheritor of a fortune in the history of financial recording. And yet, to the bafflement of all accountants, bankers, and advisers currently engaged in the Surway estate, and even the late Mr. Surway's attorney, the entirety of the cash assets left by the deceased appears to have vanished with Mr. Surway himself. Aside from some pocket change left in a drawer of the desk in his bedroom, no money at all can be found either in the House or in any bank account. It has come to light that no single individual or professional firm has had access to the full amount of the fortune in at least a dozen years. As most of our readers know, this is not an uncommon or alarming practice among managers of tremendous wealth. But as a result, none of the distinguished lawyers and financiers who have built their careers upon the Surway fortune can now explain where his personal cash holdings have gone. Taken on their own, these holdings are estimated to be worth as much as the fifth largest bank in the country. But the only certainty as of the writing of this feature, according to every reliable source, is that none of this money can be located. While the search for this fortune continues, the remainder of the late Mr. Surway's assets, including his property and all investment holdings, are now safely held in trust for Mr. Baker.

In accordance with the wishes laid out in the will, no funeral ceremony has been planned, although the people of Spring Forge joined members of Mr. Surway's staff and various businesses across the Surway Corporation in a candlelight vigil last night before the main gates of the estate. As of this morning, the servants remaining on the premises are busy closing down the House. They have decided to do so in memory of their honored master, until the hour, undoubtedly near, when his heir will appear. We will be certain to report any developments in this story as soon as they arise. Until then, our thoughts and prayers are with the late Mr. Surway, and the many men and women in whose remembrance he lives on.

On the ground floor of the House, in a corner of a courtyard where cows and chickens had once lived, there was a round, empty room. No one had ever used it as a room. No one, even at the time when its bricks were scrubbed clean twice a week, had ever entered it in the middle of the night, because the room was an oven—a wood-fired oven. This oven, like the House, had been abandoned decades ago. In the darkness and the cold, no trace remained of the blazes that had once burned there, or the loaves, baguettes, muffins, scones, buns, croissants, and pies that had once puffed and turned golden brown there. The floor of the oven was slatted with iron bars. There was a space underneath the slats, hardly tall enough to crawl in, to clean out spills from the oven through a grate in the wall of the House. The shape of a man, outside the House, dropped over this grate. The oven that had been still for decades screeched with the grinding of screws. The man pulled the grate free and crept out of the night into the deeper blackness of the House.

He crawled through the space underneath the oven, seeing nothing, until the air felt thin and close. He then pressed up his back against the slats of the oven floor above him. He felt his spine crunch, and his lungs threatened to burst, but he continued to push upward. The metal over his back gave way and a square of slatted floor slid aside. He raised himself to his full height. He groaned and the echo jarred him. It was the only sound in the House. He glanced up at the ceiling, his eyes adjusting to the paler shade of darkness above him, and he found the tunnel of silvery light that he was looking for.

There it is. He smiled. *Other ovens have hoods. The Surway House oven has a chimney.* Suddenly he was struck by a coincidence he hadn't thought of. He cocked his head. It was both startling and funny. *Could this oven have anything to do with Surway's will? The name's Lucian* Baker *after all.* He wondered and grinned. Then he steadied himself again and carried on with his task.

He reached into the pouch sown into his jacket for the wire rope he had used to climb over the fence of the estate. He twirled it at his side to gather force and cast it up into the chimney as far as he could. He felt the grapple scratch against the stone and slip down. The rope slackened in his fist. *Catch, catch, catch*, he muttered to himself. Just as he was about to jump aside to dodge the grapple, the wire tautened again. He felt its tightness through the warmth of his glove. He chuckled out loud.

"Bet you didn't expect anyone to find this passage, did you?" he whispered. There was nobody to hear him. How long since anyone could have heard him in the House in the middle of the night? Forty years? Fifty years? He tried to recall the history. He thought of Surway's disappearance, but he waved the thought away. He began climbing the rope.

Slowly he pulled himself up the oven chimney, towards the white, gleaming circle of the moon in the sky above. Then he noticed another gleaming circle above him, much closer and much dimmer. It drew nearer with every tug on his rope, slipping off the surface of the sky. He recognized it before he reached the grapple of his rope—a mirror tilted against the wall. It was murky with decades of soot, but it could still reflect the moon-light down a second passage that broke off diagonally from the chimney. His grapple was hooked into the opening. It wasn't a secret passage, but its existence was a secret—it was the light well of a secret passage.

"If there's room for light, there's room for me," he said. "Good thing I've been staying away from bagels."

He reached his grapple, gathered his rope, flung it down the light well, and skidded down to the bottom. This time, he al-lowed himself a moment's contemplation.

He was standing in the middle of one of the many secret pas-sages that ran through Surway House, hidden tunnels that were rumored to riddle the entire estate. The stories of these passage-ways, of hidden chambers and trapdoors, had gone from hearsay to myth in the long years since architects had first designed the estate. During the construction of the House, the whole town had buzzed with the rumor of confidential maps that no two workers could share. People had spoken of a small army of engineers who talked to no one, and whom other workers sometimes saw at the entrance of the site, but never inside. These engineers had come and gone, and no one knew their names. During the four years of construction, even the builders hired from the town had signed endless clauses of secrecy; "as complicated as a Surway House labor contract" became a classic saying in Spring Forge. Many of these builders could still captivate their grandchildren around the fireplace by talking about the time they had spent toiling on the construction site, "when your dad was a little boy and you could still see the markings for half the roads that were torn down to build the House." "What about the secret passages?" grandchil-dren inevitably asked. And the reply came just as inevitably, with a smile: "Your grandmother would kill me if I told you anything." But lethal grandmothers weren't the only reason grandfathers gave no answers. Nobody knew the answers, or knew anyone who still did.

But decades can break men's secrets before they wear down walls. The man in the tunnel had memorized every detail in the secret plans, at least for the part of the main building that rose around the kitchens. Still, he could hardly believe that he had actually penetrated the legendary hidden network inside the House. He looked right and left, and he saw the tunnel disappearing past other light wells in both directions. *Left*, he remembered, and he set off down the passage.

He walked past rays of moonlight and gable windows through which he could look out over the gardens. He walked down little stairwells, through crossroads, under terraces and over bridges, each time recording his progress against the plans he had memorized. It was of utmost importance that no map, no blueprint, not even a written set of notes ever be found on his person. But his memory didn't fail him. On and on he went past all the signs he had anticipated. He could glimpse into the House all around him through openings in the secret passages. He could peer into courtyards, galleries, ballrooms, and corridors, over staircases and balconies where kings and queens would have felt small. He could look through the holes of missing eyes in painted ceilings, through two-way mirrors and hollow statues, and across the branches of chandeliers as big as elephants. But nothing stopped him on his way.

He reached a gap that looked down into the entrance hall of the House. He gazed into the famous room below him, and when he saw the moonlight pool into the fountain that he had seen in so many pictures, now empty and dry, he couldn't hold back a sigh. On the central landing of the double staircase at the end of the room, there was a white marble table. He could almost see the day's mail on top of it, just waiting to be picked up by the Master.

"Now there's a proper entrance hall—no hidden passage required," he said wistfully. But immediately he shook himself. "There's no right or wrong way into this House, as long as you find what you came for."

He shut the curtain over the window and continued on his way.

Finally he reached a wall. He had known that he would come up against it, and he knew it wasn't a wall. He placed his fingers over it and felt the reassuring scrape of canvas.

The painting.

Lightly, gently, almost quivering from the softness of his effort, he pressed the fingers of his right hand against the tight wall of fabric that formed the back of the painting. The painting didn't move. He tried again, clenching his fingers into claws, but still the canvas resisted. Then, suddenly angry at the back of the painting, at the secret passageways, and at his own deferential silence in the enormous House where no one lived anymore, he let out a cry and shoved both of his palms into the canvas. Immediately the painting swiveled and he tumbled into the room on the other side.

He got up. The darkness in the room was softer than the blackness of the passages. At first, he could see nothing. Then his eyes adjusted. Unlike the gloom of bread ovens, chimneys and tunnels, it was a darkness he knew already. It was the comforting, familiar darkness of nighttime in a house. Moonlight trickled in from a gap in the heavy drapes over the windows. He looked around him. Objects were solemnly displayed against the walls, some more curious than others, an old cap, a cane, a foreign-looking steering wheel, a handful of coins. On a stand by itself, he noticed the leather frame and plastic casings of a restaurant menu. He vaguely remembered the name of this room from the plans he had learned. He mouthed it in silence. *The Memory Room.*

For a moment, he was almost interested in its mysteries, in the life whose story it told. But all of a sudden he jumped. His eyes had fallen across something infinitely more precious than all the knickknacks around him. On a table in the middle of the room, resting on a silver square of moonlight, was a small white letter, folded in half. He could hardly breathe. He stepped over to the table.

Etched in golden script on the top fold of the letter were the initials *LS*. He picked it up with a trembling hand. There was a single line written inside:

A few steps more to the end of your journey.

He stared at the words, unable to let go of them. He felt the goal in his hands. Then, unhurriedly, lowering the letter, he lifted his eyes beyond the table. He saw a painting at the back of the room. He didn't even realize that he hadn't noticed it, the painting of a man in royal armor astride a horse. The man's outstretched hand pointed to the drawing of an elaborate structure, some fantastical city or fortress, held by two smiling women on the other side of the painting. Like the man on the horse, the two women stared back at the viewer.

"A few steps more," the man repeated, and he took a few steps towards the painting. Did the man on the horse look like Lyndon Surway? In the darkness and his excitement, he neither knew nor cared. The structure in the drawing was shown from above as an intricate maze, in which tangling pathways all led to a small square in the middle. The entire painting seemed to converge upon this point. The man's eyes focused on it. Was it possible? Was he only imagining? He wondered. Slowly, irresistibly, he raised his hand and trailed the edge of his thumb against the surface of the painting, circling around the little square at the center.

He let his finger graze the square, and he felt hundreds of minuscule hairs bristling down the curve of his neck. He was right. He hadn't imagined it. The square stood in relief from the rest of the canvas. It was a button hidden in the middle of the painting.

"...to the end of your journey," he whispered.

He took one long, soundless breath, looked one last time at the smiling man on the horse, and pushed his thumb down on the button. As the painting lifted over him, he felt his mind puffing out of his head. He even thought he saw one of the women widen her grin as her face swooshed past.

A new room opened before him, an octagonal stone room. It was only big enough for one person. There was a table in the middle, with another letter on top of it. He picked up the letter. There was no trembling left in his fingers. On the top fold in golden script, he saw the initials *LS* once again. He read the words inside. His chest tightened with joy.

And now you reach your journey's end.

Instantly a metal barrier shot down from the ceiling behind him. Blinding white lights began to flicker down the length of the room. The canvas that opened into the secret passageway swiveled shut. The flicker of white lights spread down the stairwells, through the hallways, across the ballrooms and over the balconies, flashing their alert to the gardens outside and the night beyond. And the man's screams of terror and anger were silenced by the blare of alarms throughout the House.

CHAPTER ONE

The Brandow House

Andrew Day woke up two minutes before the alarm clock was set to go off. He woke up from a dream in which he was sitting astride a lion on the roof of a moving train. He could still feel the throbbing fur beneath him and see the forests of pines rushing by when he remembered the room where he had fallen asleep. It was the first time he had woken up there. Before yesterday evening, he had never been in this room, in this house, in this town, or even on this side of the country. He had looked forward at night to seeing it all in the morning.

He sprang from the pillow, leaned over to the window alongside the bed, and yanked it open. The white wooden frame was surprisingly heavy. *Everything is so old.* He found the notion wonderful. The air rushed in from outside and flooded the warm hollow of the sheets, smelling of cropped grass and rainy roads. He had never known grass to smell like this. Where he had lived before, it was high, coarse, and a little droopy, yielding to every blow and tug. But it was also free and endless, and it ran away insensibly to the slopes of purple mountains that rose from the haze in the horizon. The grass here was divided by fences, and every blade stood on alert. And the mountains here were lower, so that it was harder to say where they began, and there was no horizon to be seen. The closest thing to a haze was a dimmer shade of blue in the shadows of the trees around distant houses. But the road beyond the front yard of this house was wide and clear, and it rolled in both directions towards places he had never seen. He rapped his knuckles on the ledge in excitement and hopped out of bed.

There was a mirror on the door of the wardrobe in the corner of the room. He caught his reflection in his T-shirt and boxers. Shifting to one side, he ran a hand through his messy hair.

This is it. He pulled the door of the wardrobe open. He had been told that everything would be arranged for him in advance; everything would be set for his arrival. But nothing had ever been arranged or set for him before, and he half-expected the wardrobe to be empty. And yet a pair of navy pants and a white shirt sat there waiting for him, pressed and folded on the shelf. His first reaction was to run his fingers over the shirt, to find out what fabric felt like before it had ever been worn. For a moment, he hesitated to pull it off the shelf. When he finally put it on, the coolness of the cotton spreading over him reminded him of the open window. He pulled up the pants, so crisp and straight that he thought he could never sit down in them. Then he put on and fastened a braided belt that had been left beside the pants. On the other side of the wardrobe hung a tie and a blazer. The tie was red with diagonal navy stripes—*unbelievably preppy* was his thought. He swung back the mirror, not just because he needed his reflection to tie it, but also because it was only the second tie he had ever worn (the first had been a gift from a schoolteacher when he was eight), and he couldn't wait to see himself wearing an adult-sized tie.

So this is what a high school freshman is supposed to look like. He couldn't help smiling at his own image. He then took the final piece of the uniform out of the wardrobe, the navy wool blazer that he hadn't dared to acknowledge before. There were other clothes in there, warmer and more formal clothes, but he didn't need them yet; the blazer was for every day. He put it on. It closed around him like a blanket, a jacket, and a suit of armor all at once. But just as he was drawing his arms together, he noticed two letters sown over the inside pocket. Two initials. *Someone else's initials.* He chuckled and gave a shrug. *At least it looks new.* And indeed it looked newer than any other jacket he had ever worn. Stitched over the right breast was the crest that had stared down at him since the moment he had opened the wardrobe: the red dragon of Saint Clemens, the emblem of his new school. He tightened his fist in the cuff as if holding the dragon's leash.

The bathroom was across the hall. In these new clothes and this new house, the tiny distance was a ravine. He took a few breaths on the bedroom threshold, shook his hands at his sides like a pianist, whispered "Here we go," and stepped outside. A few minutes later, face washed, breath fresh, fingers wet, and his hair almost flat, he strode into Mr. and Mrs. Brandow's kitchen.

"Good morning," he boomed. No one had ever taught him proper manners, but his instinct dictated two rules for the Brandow house: always walk as quietly as possible, and always greet everyone as loudly as you can.

Mr. Brandow, whom no sound could startle, looked out from behind his newspaper. He was about sixty years old, a handsome, gray-haired man who spoke little and smiled often. He had a serene, assured expression that made him look like a ship's captain surveying calm waters, or a retired captain remembering them. Professor Paul Brandow taught biology at the nearby university, as Andrew had read in the letter he had received from Saint Clemens. "Botany," the professor had corrected with a smile when they had first met last night (and Andrew still couldn't tell if that had been a joke he didn't understand). They had exchanged few words since then, even at dinner. But already, by morning, Andrew understood three things about the man: that Mr. Brandow was uncommonly quiet with everyone, even his wife; that Andrew was fond of him from the start; and that the man was also fond of Andrew, in his quiet way.

Laura Brandow had an older face and a more youthful energy than her husband. She looked just short of busy enough to be a mother, and she wasn't small enough or round enough to look like a grandmother, at least from Andrew's impression of what mothers and grandmothers looked like. He had read that she worked at the laboratory in town, and years of analysis, studied decisions, and impartial discoveries had given her an air of understanding the exact measure of everything. From the moment he had met her, Andrew could see her calm intelligence in her eyes. He could hear it in her questions and her laugh. Intuitively he had known that she loved her work, her husband, and all the science held inside their two heads. And when she had poured tea into his cup after dinner and swept her hand over the tablecloth's wrinkles, it had been clear at once to Andrew that this all amounted to a love of life. *Two scientists*, he had told himself when he had first read the letter. The thought was somehow reassuring. He repeated it to himself as he stepped into their kitchen on the first morning of his new life. But as he sat down at the table, stilted in his new pants, he wondered whether he would ever feel comfortable enough to call them Paul and Laura, as they had asked him to do.

"Good morning," said Mrs. Brandow. The pan she held on the stove smelled so delicious that for a fraction of a second, Andrew considered never breathing out again.

"You look so handsome! Do we know each other well enough for me to say that? The size is perfect. They said they'd leave all the clothes you'd need up there, but I was worried nothing would fit! Paul, see how nice his blazer looks."

"Yes." Mr. Brandow nodded, flicking his newspaper in approval.

"The pancakes will be ready in one minute," she went on. "Do you like pancakes? Blueberry today."

"Ye-es," Andrew stammered. He couldn't remember the last time he had eaten pancakes. But he was quite certain that he had never eaten anything that smelled this good.

"Paul and I like to have pancakes in the morning," Mrs. Brandow said. "I hope that's all right. We're too old to worry about eating too healthy—and you're too young! There's coffee, tea and orange juice on the table. Is there anything else you'd rather eat in the future?"

"Thank you," Andrew replied. "This is perfect."

She smiled and turned back to the pan.

"Did you sleep well? Did you get some good rest? I couldn't tell you the last time someone slept in that bed. It was certainly before our time! Was everything all right in the yellow bedroom?"

"Yes," he said. "Everything was perfect."

He wished that he could ask her and Mr. Brandow pleasant morning questions of his own, but he couldn't come up with anything. And because he couldn't think of anything else to do, he served himself a glass of orange juice.

"First day at Saint Clemens today," Mr. Brandow said to no one in particular, as if reading a headline from his paper. He smiled at Andrew again, turned the page and cleared his throat.

Andrew had never seen Saint Clemens. But the road from the train station to the Brandows' house had passed by a large black gate, and on top of it Andrew had recognized the red dragon he had seen on every letter from the school. There were two ways to enter this gate. For one hundred and ninety-nine students in every incoming class, the way in was to be born into one of the few families wealthy, illustrious, and well-connected enough to secure attendance at the most expensive school in the country. But for one and only one student, there was another way in, marked only as *excellence*. And for that one and only student, attendance was free. This scholarship for a single student had been set up many years ago by an anonymous gift to the school; the only stipulation was that the gift's mysterious donor could decide who received the scholarship. Each year, the search for a Saint Clemens Scholar sent ambitious students, overambitious teachers, and dementedly ambitious parents into a frenzy of competition. Students freighted paintings, sculptures, and even multilevel cakes into the office of the dean of admissions. Student virtuosos playing the piano paraded on flatbed trucks in front of the gate. Orphans on remote continents signed letters explaining how applicants had saved their lives. But so far, every year, every application had been rejected. Every year, until this one. Last spring, as incredulously reported in the pages of the *Spring Forge Gazette*, and then the *Metropolitan Times*, and then in newspapers all over the country, a boy had been accepted from an obscure middle school in the rural Northwest, to attend Saint Clemens for free. That boy was Andrew Day.

His teachers and friends back west had known too little about Saint Clemens and the scholarship to fathom his accomplishment. They had only understood that Andrew was leaving to go somewhere faraway and important. This vaguely suggested that he had always been different from his peers. Without a doubt, he was distinctively intelligent, and everyone liked him, but did he rise above every other student in the country? In truth, if they had known how unreachable the honor was, his teachers and friends might have found it a bit excessive for Andrew—and secretly, so did he. But they didn't know much about Saint Clemens. He was an orphan, and all his life he had been moved around from one school to the next by authorities that barely had faces and names to him, and for whom he was just another face and another name. And so, no one had celebrated his success. No one had cared enough to understand it, or understood enough to care.

But the Brandows had been thrilled. Only they had been as excited as Andrew. Their greatest wish had always been to have children; they had never had any of their own. They had moved into this house specifically for this reason. It was the oldest house in the neighborhood, and it belonged to the scholarship's donor, whom the Brandows had never met; he managed it anonymously through the "Saint Clemens Scholarship Trust." And the terms of the lease dictated that, whoever else might rent out the rest of the house, the yellow bedroom upstairs was reserved for Saint Clemens Scholars. Each spring since they had moved into the house, the Brandows had been the only people in the world as anxious for the results as the applicants and their parents. And each year, they had come away just as downcast. They had almost come to accept that no child would ever live in their home, and that everything they did and had was for the two of them alone. They had even come, it appeared, to look like each other as they grew old together, their big blue eyes pouring into each other in the absence of anyone to inherit them. But one day, last spring, they had received a brief letter topped with a red dragon, giving them a name they had never heard before: *Andrew Day.*

Mrs. Brandow's pan almost bounced up from the weight of all the love she poured into Andrew's plate with his pancake.

"Thank you," he managed to get out before attacking his breakfast.

"Did the police sirens wake you up last night?"

Andrew, his mouth full, shook his head.

"Oh good!" Her genuine relief was as sweet to him as the pancake. "It's all over the news. I bet it's going to be the talk of the lab today. And the university. And Saint Clemens even! It's on the cover of the Metro Times!"

Andrew glanced towards the paper in Mr. Brandow's hands, but the top of the front page hung over the headlines. The boy went on eating. The first break he took was to follow Mrs. Brandow's recommendation to pour some syrup over his pancake. The second was to notice the two sets of blue eyes staring at him. He looked down. His plate was empty.

"We have more," said Mrs. Brandow, though he knew the only other pancakes were the two on their plates. They hadn't touched them yet.

"Thank you very much," he said. "But I'd better get going or I'll be late."

He got up noisily from his chair and wiped the syrup between his mouth and his chin.

"Would you like me to take you?" Mr. Brandow asked. "My first lecture doesn't start until this afternoon."

"No, thank you, Mr. Brandow."

"Paul," the man interjected.

"Paul," Andrew repeated.

"And Laura," Mrs. Brandow added with a smile.

"And Laura."

"Would you like to borrow a bike?" Mr. Brandow asked him.

"No thank you," he replied.

He never liked to borrow anything and he loved to walk. He picked up his backpack and made his way towards the door. As he reached down for the knob, he swung around one last time and said,

"Thanks again for breakfast. That was the most delicious breakfast I've ever had."

And he stepped out into the morning. He had always enjoyed looking at maps, and he had spent much of last night in bed studying the town and the roads that led from the mountains to the river. He knew exactly where to go.

CHAPTER TWO

The Way to Saint Clemens

No matter where he goes, no man can ever feel like a stranger with the taste of pancakes in his mouth. Andrew walked down the sidewalks of streets he had known only as lines on a map, and already he felt that he was in his own neighborhood. The houses he saw on both sides of the street, which were older and more tightly packed than those he was used to in the Northwest, weren't just houses in his eyes; they were the homes of his new neighbors. They belonged to people who knew the Brandows, who knew Saint Clemens, and who might even know who he was. He felt that all he had to do was knock on any of the carved and colored doors he passed to be invited to a second breakfast. He wanted to lean over the flowerbeds by their thresholds. He wanted to twirl the wreaths around the peepholes and peer into the windows on both sides. He wanted to jump up and smack the flags that hung above the doors and shake hands with the trees in front. Breathing in a season he had never seen, thousands of miles from anywhere he had ever been, he let in a feeling that came to him sometimes, the feeling that perhaps he wasn't completely by himself in the world, that perhaps someone, somewhere, was looking out for him.

He had first heard of Saint Clemens last September, in the cramped brown office of the principal from his last school, on a painfully hot afternoon.

"It's on the other side of the country," the man had said, running a finger along his sweaty collar. "A private school, a very good school."

The principal couldn't stop looking down at the letter, as if digging for more to say. Andrew could tell that the man knew no more than he did. The letter only said that Saint Clemens offered a merit-based scholarship to a single individual for grades nine through twelve ("A full ride," the man had said, lifting his eyes from the letter). Middle schools across the country were encouraged to nominate their most exceptional students for admission.

And then he had added, reading directly from the page:

"It has come to our attention that Andrew Day, currently an eighth-grader in your institution, has demonstrated such a level of excellence as to merit close consideration for this award."

The words had sounded so formal and lofty that neither Andrew nor the principal could find anything to say after them. The man had turned the letter over and pushed it in front of Andrew across the desk, as proof. Obviously he hadn't nominated Andrew. Neither of them had any idea who could have. No one at that school had ever even heard of the scholarship. And yet there the letter was. Sitting in the stifling office, Andrew had read it and reread it in silence over the wheezing of the battered fan. Soon he knew every word on the page, and his eyes had been left to admire the thick, slightly tan paper that the principal's damp hands hadn't rumpled. Andrew still remembered staring at the red dragon on top of the page, standing on its hind legs, claws drawn, spouting fire.

Andrew had always felt that great things lay in store for him. Ever since he had been old enough to comprehend that most children had parents and that he did not, he had instinctively believed that his fate was different, that he needed to be more and do more than everyone around him. So far, the path in front of him had been interwoven with everyone else's path. But things would change. In time, his path would gradually turn aside, unnoticed by anyone else. And then one day, all of a sudden, his destiny would veer off course entirely. And everyone would know then that he had been marked for something different. But he had no idea what that was. Surely it knew him already and lay waiting for him, silently whispering his name, slowly drawing him near though he couldn't see where it waited.

And then this letter had arrived. It came from a grand, mighty, remote place he had never heard of. It had found its way through mail pouches, cargo holds, and moist principals' palms. And it called him out by name, as frank and direct as a postcard from an old friend. *Demonstrated such a level of excellence*, the letter had said. How had Saint Clemens found him—even found out his name? This couldn't be just a matter of good grades. Something, somewhere, that had long waited for him, that had known him all his life, had finally decided to call out for him. Something, or someone.

Andrew had known immediately after reading that letter that he would ultimately win the scholarship. Months went by. He wanted the answer to arrive; he wanted it so urgently that he was angry at each day that passed without it. But he instantly forgave all those empty days when finally, one spring morning, he opened his mailbox at school to find the red dragon baring its claws on top of a thick, heavy envelope. He opened it and read the first few words, and he was so excited that he ran out of the building and down the street. But he wasn't surprised. He felt that keen eyes were watching him, and that they would want him to look surprised, even if they knew he wasn't. The *Office of Admis-*

sions had sent the letter, but the letter also stated that the *Anonymous Donor of the Saint Clemens Scholarship* had approved his acceptance; and he recognized those watchful eyes hidden inside the word *Donor*. He had felt them watching him ever since that day in the principal's office, perhaps long before that day, perhaps all his life. The feeling grew as spring led to summer and as summer passed.

And as he walked down the roads of Spring Forge towards the river that morning, he felt watched, more closely, more carefully than ever before. When the houses on his path started to spread further apart and move back from the street, he began to feel uneasy. Soon the gaps between them were so wide that he could see the pale blue rise of the mountains behind them. He jumped at the rustle of the wind through the leaves. He swung around to catch shadows in swaying hedges. The sudden, faraway rumble of an unseen car made him start. The sound rolled away and died, and he realized there were no other cars and no more houses on the street.

He took a shortcut through a stretch of road he had seen on the map. A few steps down the shortcut, he stopped and turned around. He thought someone was following him. But there was nothing behind him except the empty road he had just left. A wall of stones ran alongside it, surmounted by trees. He kept going. Almost immediately he stopped again.

For a few seconds he couldn't move. He felt his heart bursting from his chest. There was a man standing in front of him. *No. Not a man.* It was only *the shape of a man.* An old wooden shop sign left on the side of the road. The figure of a chef. It wore a chef's hat and an apron, but the face was a mirror. Andrew stared at himself in it. A pair of hairy hands stuck out of the sleeves holding a tray. Andrew could still see the faded loaves painted on the tray. He could still read the worn letters underneath them that said,

What's mine is yours

Andrew laughed. *New rule,* he said to himself. *You're only allowed to jump like a little girl if you come across an actual person.*

He went on walking down the road. Soon, he heard the rumble of a car drawing near. Seconds later he saw it, a long, black limousine skimming down the street at the end of the shortcut.

That could be you one of these mornings—if you make it as a gangster before you graduate.

Another car drove by. This time, it was a silver sports car, headed in the same direction as the limousine. He turned into the street and watched the glistening machine roll away, followed by a vintage convertible. Then came another luxury car and another, forming a procession through the town.

Must be an auto show. But it wasn't an auto show: it was the start of a new school year at Saint Clemens.

Lucky I didn't borrow Mr. Brandow's bike.

He walked beside the cars along the bright houses and brick buildings that lined the main street of Spring Forge. He looked alternatively at the stately vehicles on his left and the shops on his right. And as the windows of the shops were spilling over with flowers, cakes, and signs that said *Hello students* in giant handwritten letters, and those of the cars were all tinted, he decided to keep his eyes on his right. The town came to an end and the sidewalk turned into a path. Finally, he had no choice but to cut across the trickle of cars to the other side of the street and step into the pedestrian entrance at the side of the Saint Clemens gate. He glanced at the red dragon spitting fire on top of it, and he peered at the tinted windows passing by. A steady thud sliced through the air above the trees. He looked up in a swirl of dust and saw a helicopter flying over the gate.

My classmates. Let's hope they like me.

The thought made him stop. He felt the need to pull himself aside. He stood under the trees, on the edge of the movement and, it seemed, of time itself. He was angry at himself for feeling intimidated. He hadn't come all this way to meet his fate, but to make it. He had been looked after and led, directed from one place to another without a say since he was born. Now at last was his chance to get out. Now was his chance to make his way. He didn't know why and how he had been given this chance. He didn't know what made him special, what made him unique. But he would go forth and seek it out, and from it he would make his destiny. He started again down the driveway, his path beautiful in the morning light through the shadows of the elms, alongside the parade of magnificent cars. And as he went, he corrected his thought:

Screw that. Let's hope I like them!

CHAPTER THREE

A Special Introduction

The road split at the end of the driveway around a circle of grass. There was a fountain in the middle where water rose and fell without a sound, as if fearful of disturbing the students all around. On the other side of the circle stood a large redbrick building striped with gleaming white columns. Over huge navy flags that hung vertically from the columns, the red dragon fluttered. Beyond the roof, Andrew could see the tips of gothic towers and the tops of enormous elms. He walked around the circle to the front steps of the building, where a small group of students stood gathered around a table.

"Hello freshmen! Good morning freshmen! Calling out to all freshmen!" cried a young man behind the table. "Come pick up your badges before you step into the Hall!" Andrew took his place at the back of the line. Before he had stepped close enough to glimpse his name among the rows of badges on the table, the man called out to him:

"Good morning sir freshman, from all of us here at Saint Clemens! Last name please."

"Day," Andrew said.

"What's that now?" the man said, cupping his ear and leaning towards him.

"Day," Andrew repeated as firmly as he could over the voices of the crowd.

The man looked to be in his twenties, but he was more awkward in his gray suit than any of the teenagers milling around him in their uniforms. At the sound of Andrew's name, his eyes almost lifted him off the steps like helium balloons.

"Mr. Andrew Day, sir, delighted to meet ye! Our very first Saint Clemens scholar here in the flesh. It's an honor, sir. I am Jesse McGallender—I'll spell that for ye someday, sir—descendant of the Scottish lairds, lords of the highlands."

He gave this introduction with a caricature of a Scottish accent, but Andrew wasn't sure if he should laugh. The man then gave him such a vigorous two-handed handshake that Andrew felt a sprain in his shoulder. A few impatient freshmen in line behind him began to scowl at the delay. But since most of the upperclassmen yelled out a friendly greeting to the man behind the table as they leapt up the steps, none of the other freshmen said anything.

"As for yer badge, Mr. Day, sir," Jesse went on, "here it is, of course, not to be mistaken for anyone else's."

After coiling in the air for momentum, his hand swooped down over the corner of the table to a badge that stood apart from the rest. A purple ribbon was pinned to it, proclaiming in shiny silver letters: *Saint Clemens Scholar*. Andrew took it from the man's hand with a groan.

"You wouldn't happen to have any scissors, would you, Mr. McGallender?"

The man hunched over with a grin. "I'm afraid I don't, Mr. Day, sir, but nonetheless, greetings from Saint Clemens. I hope ye enjoy yer time here. And please sir, I ask ye from the bottom of my heart, call me Jesse."

Before Andrew could rejoin that no one had ever called him Mr. Day before, the man had moved on to other students, greeting, bobbing, and twirling his fingers among his badges. Every few seconds, he stopped helping the students in front of him to yell out his announcement across the crowd or to shake hands with one of the upperclassmen rushing by. Andrew observed that they all called him Jesse, and they were all delighted to see him. Reluctantly pinning his badge on the right breast of his blazer, he trudged up the steps of the building.

He stepped into a broad wood-paneled room. The arches of tall windows rose into the vaulted white ceiling above him, and through their panes he could see the swinging branches of trees peering in. At the front of the room, a man wearing a red-and-navy bow tie and a red-and-navy pocket square stood facing the audience, his hands behind his back. His bushy black eyebrows stood at attention high up on his forehead, and an obliging smile was plastered on his lips. Students gradually filled the hall up from the back to the middle, leaving the front empty until there were no more seats left behind. But the man appeared to take no offense at this arrangement. He gazed at the room proudly, as if the students deserved a prize for where each of them had sat. Occasionally he glanced at the door and gave a particular nod of approval to one of the newcomers straggling in. But unlike Jesse, the man received no greetings in return.

On the occasion of one of his glances across the room, he noticed Andrew—or rather the purple ribbon on Andrew's chest—just as the boy was trying to wriggle his way down one of the rows. Their eyes met, and Andrew thought he noticed a slight curl on the edge of the man's smile as he motioned the boy to come forward. He dropped his backpack and walked up to the front of the room. By time he turned around, the hall was completely full, the students' chatter had died down, the doors were closed, and all eyes were turned to him. He stretched out his hands down the sides of his body not to yank the purple ribbon off his chest.

"Young ladies and young men of Saint Clemens," the man said, in a voice that would have resounded in a smaller room, "good morning. For those of you who don't know me, I am Mr. Clare, principal of this school, and I am delighted to meet you. For those of you who do know me, I am ecstatic to see you again. To all of you in this room, I wish you a spectacular new year as members of our institution."

Andrew tried not to stare at him too closely. He had been anxious to meet the principal. Perhaps the man could answer the questions that Andrew couldn't ask anyone else, the questions that no one else could answer, not even the Brandows: who had chosen him as the Saint Clemens Scholar, and why? But the principal had apparently forgotten Andrew standing awkwardly beside him.

"Our new school year has begun on a spectacularly beautiful day," he continued. "I hope it sets the tone for many triumphs and joys here at Saint Clemens for all of you."

A wrinkle crept over his forehead without any effect on his grin.

"Some of you may have heard about last night's incident on the outskirts of our town. And without a doubt, even those of you who weren't here last spring have heard about the unfortunate events here in Spring Forge a few months ago. It's my pleasure and my duty to assure you that your security continues to be our chief priority here at Saint Clemens. Our staff and the Spring Forge police have been working tirelessly and in close collaboration to ensure that you have nothing to worry about. Our campus and our town have never been safer. We simply request that you stay away from the cordoned-off section of town, around Civic

Square, and any areas under investigation farther up towards the mountains, near the perimeter of the House."

Andrew glanced around at his schoolmates, but their faces were all blank. The man went on, the wrinkle brushed off his brow.

"In a moment, you will begin the next chapter of your educational journey as you leave this hall for the start of your adventures across campus. But first," and suddenly Andrew felt a twist in his stomach, "I wanted to give a special introduction to a particularly distinguished new member of our community. Here is someone who might never have thought he would be standing here someday, someone, in fact, whom in all likelihood nobody had ever encouraged to even aspire to be standing here someday. But someone who by dint of hard work, good will, and sheer, plucky resolve, made it all the way to this hall to be among us today, here in our school where we open our doors to him at no cost for the duration of his studies. And for this, we thank the astonishing generosity of his scholarship's donor, who will remain anonymous. Here on my right, arriving straight from the other side of our country, having beaten out over eight hundred applicants—a record year—from across our nation and around the world, is our very first Saint Clemens scholar: Mr. Andrew Day!"

And he opened a palm out towards Andrew, though he barely glimpsed at the boy. His eyes, his grin, and his eager attention were fastened to the audience in front of him. Andrew tried to smile through his embarrassment. Dozens of vacant eyes rolled in his direction, sharpening for an instant with a prick of interest. A few hands managed a lifeless applause. Andrew didn't realize that no one expected him to speak until he opened his mouth.

"Hello everyone."

There was no response.

"It's great to be here, straight from the other side of the country, like Mr. Clare said." He looked at the principal with a hopeful smile. The man's face showed disgust and consternation.

"And also, like he said," Andrew struggled, wondering when vomit would take over for words, "it really is a beautiful day outside."

A few more stares shifted towards him.

"Have a great year, everybody," he said, and he pulled back from an invisible microphone.

A few claps flittered across the room again.

"Thank you," said the principal, drilling his eyes into Andrew's face before returning to the audience. Andrew stepped down from the stage and settled into his seat as the address resumed. He looked around him to make sure that no one was paying any attention to him anymore. He noticed a boy and a girl sitting across the room by the wall. They sat straighter in their chairs than everyone around them, though they were as obviously bored as everyone else. And while they waited for the moment to pass, with a stillness that was almost as disrespectful as impatience, it struck Andrew that they were the two best-looking people he had ever seen. He had never noticed hair or skin before, but he felt that the girl belonged in the kind of magazine where dreams of hair and skin are manufactured. The boy who sat next to her seemed more careless; his disheveled hair made his blazer look like pajamas. Immediately as he saw him, Andrew, who had never been within a hundred miles of a game, thought of polo.

He tried to read the names on their badges (which were blissfully devoid of a purple ribbon), but he didn't dare to look hard enough. In addition to being exceptionally good-looking, they were also unmistakably cool, a trait that looks the same everywhere in the world.

At last, the principal's speech ended, and the room came to life in a din of yawns and rustling blazers.

CHAPTER FOUR

A Full Plate

Andrew was afraid that he would lose sight of the boy and girl if he walked out of the room too fast. But the press of students surging from the hall soon carried him out. There was no pausing outside the door; the man who had given him his badge stood directing traffic in the hallway.

"Find yer table by last name and grab a schedule! *A to F* on my left, *S to Z* on my right. *G to R* right here in the middle! Find yer table and grab a schedule! Oh, hello again Mr. Day!"

He spotted Andrew in the throng.

"Mr. Day, sir, ye'll be under *A to F*, right here on my left."

Andrew wanted to answer that he didn't need any special assistance. But instead, he only said,

"Thank you, Mr.—"

"Jesse," the young man replied. "Jesse McGallender—but just Jesse, sir, please. Now, if ye'll excuse me..."

And he went back to yelling across the hallway, to lead a process that was only complicated and hectic because of himself. Students who had frowned and yawned all morning began to smile when they saw Jesse, and their smiles spread to Andrew's face. Walking away, he glanced down at the schedule of events he had picked up, which broke down every hour of the day ahead.

Suddenly he remembered, and he looked around him. But the boy and girl were nowhere to be seen.

No moment of Andrew's life had ever been as strange as the three hours that followed. The errands laid down in his schedule took him all over the lawns and monuments of the Saint Clemens campus, but none of them made any sense. His first stop required him to rest a foot on the stirrup of a horse while he smiled for a picture. Immediately after, he was directed to a tent where a man in a plaid cap measured his arm for a golf club. When this was done, he ran over to a cloister overlooked by a gigantic tree. There he met a tiny woman who handed him something warm to drink that smelled like grass. While he did his best to keep it down, she asked him to close his eyes and tell her his biggest hopes, his biggest fears, and the three main questions he wanted to address during his time on earth. "There's no wrong answer," she kept telling him, but Andrew was terrified that nothing he said would make her let him go. Next, he arrived at a marble terrace jutting out over the river, where he found a man wearing a paper mustache as a bowtie. Seven other freshmen were sitting around him in a circle. Over the twenty-five minutes that followed, Andrew learned each of the other students' animal cry (off the cuff, he gave his own as mammoth), and he joined them all in a pledge of trust, clinched forever in a secret handshake. The only thing he couldn't remember, as he walked away, was anybody's name.

All morning he raced, across courtyards and lawns, over quadrangles and hallways, under ivy-draped towers and murmuring treetops, past the cookie stands along every path, through the stages of his schedule. He met coaches, counselors, therapists and instructors who were so serious about studying the students that he wondered if anything else could be taught at that school. He stared into the eyes of every person he met, to look beyond the

politeness and the stiffness, to see beyond the ceremony of intro-
ductions. And every time, he wondered: *Does this person know me?*
Does this person know why I was chosen to come here? Do they know
what I'm expected to do here—what I'm expected to become here? Has
this person known me all my life?

But each time, in every pair of eyes, he saw only the eagerness
of an adult coming upon a promising new student, a student
wearing a purple ribbon that guaranteed good grades. He also
peeked into the faces of his fellow students. He tried to figure out
if they were as bewildered as he was by the activities of their
morning, if they shared his opinions about things, about Saint
Clemens and life in general, if they were interesting and warm, if
they might become his friends. But their faces were as unhelpful
as those of the adults. When finally the bells of the chapel rang
noon, he felt nothing at all but an exhausted confusion. He
looked down at his schedule to confirm that it was truly and officially time for the only thought left on his mind—lunch.

For the first time all day, he felt that it would be improper to
rush. He ambled to the dining hall without even looking at his
map; he was aware of its location by instinct. Standing by itself in
the middle of campus, the building had the appearance of a medieval house overgrown with ivy, struggling for air through stained
glass windows and a multitude of chimneys. Andrew felt it growing taller as he walked towards it, looming larger than the trees.
When he pulled the door open, arching his back with the effort,
he realized that this dining hall wasn't supposed to be from the
Middle Ages, but from a fairy tale about giants.

The building truly did have magical properties—as soon as he
picked up his tray in the serving area, he was a giant himself.
Every station was attended by a staff member not much older
than himself, wearing a white apron and a white hat emblazoned
with a little red dragon. Andrew passed them one by one, and he

filled his tray with a serving of roasted pumpkin, a rhubarb-and-broccoli pie, a side of caramelized onions, a helping of zucchini with walnuts, a double order of mushroom tortellini, a small bowl of mozzarella skewers, a side plate of mini crab cakes, and a half-dozen spring rolls. His tray was so heavy when he picked it back up that he could feel his veins sticking out in his sleeves.

Just don't drop it, he begged himself as he turned a corner to carry out his food. But then he lifted his eyes, and he saw what lay ahead, and the tray almost slipped from his hands. He had seen only the cold appetizer section. Before him, in multi-colored, many-splendored succession, lay the hot appetizer counter, the salad buffet bar, the sandwich bar, the pasta station, the pizza counter, the burger stand, the hot dog stand, the rotisserie and grill, the sushi station, the Indian station, the Mexican station, the Chinese station, the Korean barbecue, the oyster bar, the deli, the Turkish station, the bakery and pretzel stand, the cheese stall and the vegetable juice stand. Craning his neck to look further into the next hall, he glimpsed pyramids of fruit, rainbow-colored rows of drinks, and, sprawling beyond them in a mystical, luminous recess that stretched out beyond seeing, the cave of desserts. But there wasn't even space left on his tray for a cup of water. He cheered himself up by thinking of all the lunches that lay ahead, and he sternly made his way out of the serving area. When the woman who swiped his ID looked over his tray, he almost apologized. But she only smiled and said, "Such healthy choices!" before wishing him a wonderful day.

He stepped into the dining area, which was resonant and vast under the beams of the building's roof. There was a large double door across the room that led outside. It was a beautiful day, as the principal had said, and he carried his tray out to the terrace. The tables there were crowded, especially those overlooking the lawn. But he spotted an empty seat at the best table of all, in the shade of a slanting oak. On one side of the table sat two athletic-looking boys. On the other side, next to the empty seat, sat the boy and the girl from the morning's address. Andrew walked over to their table and sat down.

CHAPTER FIVE

Cameron and Olivia

"Hello," he said.

The girl, who was leaning far over the table and leading the conversation, paused for a second and turned her beautiful hazel eyes at him.

"Hi."

And she went on talking to the others.

"But if *someone* knows where it is," she said, "then *everyone* knows. Or at least, those who really want to know, those who really *need* to know, can find out. If only a single person in the world knew where it was, then how would that person keep it safe? By storing it in a safe somewhere, or in a vault—in some place where it couldn't be stolen, right? But who would design that safe? Who would protect it? Who would make sure that only the right person can access it? *Those people* would know. And then it would be *their* secret too. And do you think *they* would keep it from the police, from the press, from the lawyers, from the bankers, from the tax administration? There's no such thing as a one-person secret. Not where that kind of money is involved. No way—take my word for it."

While she spoke, Andrew noticed that no one else at the table still wore a name tag. As he dug his fork into one of the mountains of food on his tray, he discreetly reached across his chest with his other hand, unclasped his special badge, and buried it in his pocket. The girl stopped for a moment to let her audience absorb the truth of her words. She planted her fork into a meatball on someone else's plate. *Polo player*, sitting next to her, leaned over her towards Andrew.

"Olivia," he told her, "there's someone new at our table."

She fell back in her chair.

"Hi," the boy continued. "I'm Cameron. And this is Olivia."

He reached out and shook Andrew's hand. The two boys sitting across from them muttered a greeting without introducing themselves. The girl said nothing but only stared at the newcomer.

"I'm Andrew," he said.

"We know who you are," she replied with a smile, jabbing her fork into a sweet potato wedge on Cameron's plate.

"So tell me," she said, eyeing Andrew with an air of mischief, "who did you know to get in here?"

"Olivia," Cameron broke in, "that's not right!"

Andrew was glad for the interruption, until Cameron added, "It's *whom* did you know."

Olivia rolled her eyes and groaned.

"Don't mind him," she said to Andrew. "He thinks he's better than everyone else, and for all the wrong reasons."

And what would you *consider the right reasons to be?* Andrew wondered.

"But seriously," she went on, "how did you end up at Saint Clem's?"

"I have no idea," he said. "I received a letter of nomination, I sent in my application—right before the deadline—and a few months later I had an acceptance letter in the mail."

"Ha." She gave a nod of contemplation and reached for a mini muffin from the other side of the table. There were more empty plates stacked on top of her own tray than Andrew would have thought it could carry.

When the mini muffin was no more, she turned to him and resumed, apparently finished with the subject of Andrew himself:

"We were just discussing the break-in at Surway House last night."

Andrew's stare made her fine golden eyebrows rise in disbelief.

"You don't know the story?"

He shook his head.

Cameron rose forward with a magnanimous air.

"You can't expect him to have heard the news when he's just getting settled into this whole new life."

Shifting his gaze from Olivia to Andrew, he said,

"Someone broke into Surway House last night, apparently looking for the money."

"It's the third time this year," Olivia interjected.

"Yes," Cameron repeated, "the third time."

"Looking for what money?" Andrew asked.

This time, even Cameron looked incredulous. Even the two stocky boys on the other side of the table, who hadn't looked in Andrew's direction since they had first shaken his hand, turned round eyes on him.

"You haven't heard of the Surway fortune?" Cameron asked.

Andrew shook his head again.

Olivia, in what Andrew already understood to be an extremely rare occurrence, was speechless.

"What's the Surway fortune?" he asked.

As everyone else at the table was too stunned to reply, Cameron answered, as matter-of-factly as if Andrew had asked about the weather.

"Lyndon Surway was a very famous man, an industrialist, one of the great businessmen of the twentieth-century. He used to live in an incredible house here in Spring Forge—one of the biggest houses in the world. If you've had a chance to drive or walk around the north side of town, up towards the mountains, then you've probably seen the walls of his estate running along the back roads."

Andrew remembered the row of stones that he had seen on his walk to school. He aligned it in his mind with the edge of the large round area in the northeast corner of the map he had examined last night. He squinted at the thought.

"That can't all be one person's property. That area's as big as the town itself."

"It's bigger," Olivia rejoined. She had bounced back completely from her momentary shock. "Actually, it's so big, the Surway estate, that he had to buy up the land across a whole chunk of Spring Forge when he started to build it. He bought one house after another, empty lots, random parcels of land, everything in his way, until he owned entire roads to himself, and he could reconfigure them or raze them down and build over them as he liked."

"If you go around the edge of his property," Cameron followed, "you can see old roads that used to keep on going towards the mountains, back in the days before Surway. But he cut them off to make room for the grounds of his estate. He even rerouted the city's sewer system, which runs from the mountains to the river—he redirected the sewers to pass around his property."

"Things were a lot less involved in those days," he continued with a smile, waving his hand as if turning back the overcomplicated decades, his hair fluttering over his head. "If you had enough money, you could redraw town maps, rearrange drainage pipes, slice up roads, rename them, shift them around."

"Well," Olivia interposed, "it depends on what you call *enough money*. When he died in the sixties, Lyndon Surway was thought to be the wealthiest man in the Western Hemisphere."

"How did he die?" Andrew wondered.

"He disappeared, flying one of his own planes," she said.

"And what happened to his fortune?"

Her eyes widened and glinted.

"That's the mystery—no one knows. When Lyndon Surway disappeared, all his cash went missing with him. His investments were all intact, as well as a trust he had set up to take care of his staff. But the rest of his fortune was nowhere to be found. There was no trace of it anywhere. Nothing in his bank accounts, or anywhere in the House—nothing. All that cash, just gone."

She snapped her dainty fingers in the air. Cameron leaned forward.

"That's only *part* of the mystery," he said. "You see, Lyndon Surway left a will. His attorney surfaced it when Lyndon Surway was declared dead, after he had gone missing for weeks. In the will, he left all his fortune, the House, the estate, his businesses, his investments, all his cash, *everything*, to a single person."

Cameron stopped, glancing at Olivia, hesitating.

Finally, after a few seconds, Andrew ventured,

"His wife?"

Cameron stared into his eyes before answering.

"He never married. He didn't have a family. He had no relatives at all in any direction. He was an immigrant who came to this country with nothing and no ties to anyone."

"Then who was it?"

Andrew turned to the two students across the table. Their eyes were riveted on Cameron, though Andrew was sure that they already knew the story.

It was Olivia who finally answered.

"To some unknown person who's never been identified, who's never come forward, who had never appeared in any of Lyndon Surway's records before—somebody called Lucian Baker."

Silence fell over the table.

CHAPTER SIX

The Visitor

Andrew gazed out over the grass towards the hollow where the river flowed. He couldn't see it across the lawn, but he knew it was there, between the slopes on either side. He followed it with his eyes as the valley widened beyond Spring Forge and bent along the dented bank, before turning for good into the mountains in the north. After a moment, he asked,

"What happened to the House all these years?"

"It's still there," Olivia replied. "Nothing's been added or removed since the day Lyndon Surway disappeared."

"In the beginning," Cameron said, "in the first few weeks and months after he was gone, the servants continued to care for the House, as if they expected the Master to walk in through the front door at any minute. They kept on polishing the silvers and washing the windows. The flowers were watered, the hedges were trimmed. Those who grew up around here say that after the first few days of the search, once the shock had come and gone, the people of Spring Forge started to forget that Surway was gone at all. They chose not to believe it. The dozens of people who worked on the estate, the gardeners, the maids, the manservants, the bakers, they all kept on going to work every morning, as if nothing had changed. And everyone outside could still see the chimneys smoking on the roof every day. The horses were paced outside the stables every morning. The lights kept on shining in the windows. The ovens kept on burning."

Again, there was a silence.

"And then what happened?"

"Then," Cameron continued, a shadow coming over his face, "just like the search for Lyndon Surway, the search for Lucian Baker came to an end. Of course, there had been hundreds of impostors descending on Spring Forge, claiming to be Surway's heir. Some of them even had the last name Baker—it's not *that* uncommon, obviously—and there were even a few real Lucians. But not a single one among them could prove a tie to Lyndon Surway. They were all just trying to turn a crazy coincidence into the biggest jackpot in history. The search had extended around the country, around the world, but no one legitimate was ever found."

"It actually became a fairly common name for people born that year," Olivia added with a grin. "Parents started naming their kids Lucian Baker—just in case."

She reached for an apricot forgotten behind a bowl on a tray across from her.

"And so the servants began to leave the House," Cameron went on. "Many left Spring Forge altogether, and the enormous estate was abandoned."

"Not *entirely* abandoned. Tell him about the visitor," she mumbled from behind the fruit.

"Surway had left a bit of his money in a trust for the people who worked for him," Cameron said. "Well, it wasn't just a bit of money: it was enough so that none of them ever had to take another job again. It was the only other gift he left in his will, but it was nothing compared to the missing fortune for Lucian Baker. Out of gratitude, or simply out of loyalty to his memory, the servants and some of his business partners pooled together a part of that money to take care of the estate until the return of the rightful owner. They never even shut off the electricity! Every year, on the anniversary of the original Master's disappearance, the Spring Forge City Council organizes an extensive cleanup of the entire residence with that money."

"Tell him about the visitor!" Olivia cried. "About the *man in the window!*"

"I'm getting there," he told her, motioning her to be quiet without turning his eyes from Andrew. "That's the only day of the year when the gate of the estate is unlocked, and the great door of the House is swung open."

"And people just go in and clean the House?" Andrew asked.

"Yes. They don't change anything else in the House. The first few years, some of the volunteers snuck away and tried to look for the missing fortune. But they all came back empty-handed. Nowadays, people just leave everything as he left it. I've heard there's even an undelivered letter on the table in the entrance hall—it's been there for decades! No one's touched it, even though hundreds of volunteers sign up every year. It's like a holiday for the town of Spring Forge. People sell T-shirts and mugs, volunteers come down from all over the country, schools take the day off. People call it 'Surway Day.'"

"When is it?" Andrew asked.

"In the spring. Although, this past year—I'm sure you heard what happened in Civic Square earlier this year."

"Of course he did!" Olivia interjected, though Andrew had no idea. "Tell him about the man in the window!"

Cameron blinked and let out a sigh of exasperation. Raising his hands to form a barrier against Olivia, he said,

"Every day of the year, except that day, the House is completely deserted. No one can enter the estate. The gate is closed. No
one can set foot in the House, except..."

Olivia's eyes opened wide, her mouth buried in the last of the
apricot.

"Someone's been seen inside the House," Cameron blurted
out.

Andrew stared at him in silence.

"Someone's been seen?" he repeated after a moment.

Olivia nodded.

"People have seen a man walking past the windows at night,"
Cameron continued.

"A man?" Andrew echoed. "What does he look like? What
does he do?"

"No one can say. No one can talk about it calmly, let alone
provide a proper description. Witnesses just claim they've seen a
man through the windows of the House. At that point in the story, they usually break down."

"Has anyone taken a picture of him?"

"No. There hasn't been any other evidence of anyone in the
House."

"Well," Olivia corrected, "except for the break-ins."

"That's right," Cameron said. "The break-ins. Three of them
this year."

"And not a single arrest!" Olivia exclaimed.

"And not a single arrest." Cameron shook his head. "Every
time, the police make it to the House within minutes of the alarm
going off. Eleven minutes last night, I read in this morning's paper. But every time, the intruder gets away. No one knows who
he is, or even if it's just one person."

"Could it be the man who's been seen through the windows?"
Andrew asked.

Cameron shrugged.

"There's no lead, no suspects. We have absolutely no clue what's been going on in there."

"Stupid local police," one of the two boys across the table muttered. "As useless and corrupt as the boys down in the City."

Suddenly he gasped. He raised himself against the back of his chair and shot terrified eyes at Olivia. The other boy and Cameron were also staring at her, their faces tight with anticipation.

A cold, hard expression was set on her face. She returned the boy's look, lowered her eyes, and picked up a glass of water. No one said a word as she drank. At last, Andrew broke the silence.

"Whoever it was last night, looking for the money in the House, was wasting his time—the money can't be there."

They all looked at him.

"Lyndon Surway wouldn't have left his fortune in the House," he went on. "If he thought vaults and banks and safes and all the traditional security techniques weren't solid enough for his money, then there's no way he would have left it all in the most obvious place in the world. Besides, his estate, from what it sounds like, is probably worth a record-breaking fortune on its own. I bet there are priceless paintings in there, statues, precious objects... What if something happened to the House, like a fire? Would a meticulous, brilliant businessman keep that much wealth all in the same place? That wouldn't make any sense. It's pointless to search in the House. The money's got to be somewhere else."

Olivia looked down, her cheeks sharpening as she puckered her lips.

"I like my theory better," she said.

"What's your theory?

Instead of answering, she fixed her eyes on his face and asked,

"You'd seriously never heard of the Surway fortune?"

"No."

"I was expecting more insight," she said as she rose from her seat, leaving her tray on the table, "from the person with the one trait that no one else has at this school."

"I'm not that smart," Andrew grinned, metal creaking around the table as the three other boys stood up from their chairs.

"I meant poor," Olivia said, and she walked away without another word. Strolling behind her and the other two, Cameron turned around with a smile.

"It was nice to meet you!" he yelled out before disappearing into the dining hall.

Andrew finished eating on his own. He didn't get up when he was done, but sat looking across the lawn without moving. It wasn't until a woman in a white uniform had defeated his efforts to help her clear the table that he determined it was time to leave.

The rest of his day passed in a blur. He went back to following his schedule across campus, quietly passing the hours in tree-appreciation strolls, study-habit seminars, a quick tour of the menagerie, and a guided introduction to the gym and spa. But nothing could clear his mind, not even the white oak, the achievement ladder, the red panda or the cedar-wood steam. His thoughts kept returning to Cameron and Olivia. He had never met anyone like them, in any school he had ever known. The students in other schools, no matter who they were—the slackers and the chess wizards, the rebels and the cheerleaders—always asked Andrew where he came from, or how old he was, or sometimes what he went by (the answer was never Andy or Drew but simply Andrew). For the first time in his life he was surrounded by people who simply didn't care. Would it be acceptable for him to look for Cameron and Olivia at future meals? Had they been rude to him? Had they been friendly? *Come to think of it, I didn't ask anything about them either.*

The afternoon came to an end. Walking by himself along the diagonal path that cut across the main lawn to the front of campus, where the day had started, he paused and looked around him. One last time, he scanned the quadrangles within sight for the two of them, *Polo Guy* and the girl who had called him poor. But neither of them had been in the A-F group. Their schedules were different from his, and he hadn't come across them since lunch. He went on walking.

As the light reddened and faded around him, his thoughts gradually turned to their conversation at the table, to the story that appeared to hold such interest for people who found nothing interesting. Who had Lyndon Surway been, and what had happened to his fortune? Had he known, when he had decided to build his personal kingdom on the slopes of these mountains, clearing entire roads from his path, that someday children going to school down by the river would spend their lunch breaks wondering about his treasure? Was that what he had wanted? Was that what he had planned? And who was Lucian Baker? Where was he hiding? Why had Surway chosen him, and where had he gone? Was there really someone inside the House?

These questions drifted through his mind as Andrew walked out of the gate, under the emblem of the red dragon. Suddenly he stopped. On the other side of the road, a man stood staring at him. Andrew had never seen him before. He had short, ruffled, graying hair, and a short, bristling, graying beard. He wore a long, black overcoat that was too warm for the weather. He stood alone by a tree at some distance from the gate—Andrew could have easily missed him altogether. For a second, their gazes locked. Andrew thought he glimpsed a smile on his lips. Then the man turned around and walked away.

CHAPTER SEVEN

Herman Hoss

Sixty miles down the river from Spring Forge, where the water flowed with surging speed through the harbor into the ocean, there rose in the middle of the City a tower that stood tall, mighty, and monumental even against the forest of towers that stretched around it in every direction. This was the Hoss Tower. And while there was no sign of the name *Hoss* anywhere on the building's spire, the chiseled lines across each of the massive doors on the ground floor met in a giant letter *H*. The doors of the elevators slid shut in a letter *H*. The arrows of the clock in the lobby shot from a letter *H* raised in its center. The top panel of each of the double doors that led out of the lobby was grooved in the shape of the letter *H*; each of the painted warrior gods lining the high, pale blue ceiling reached across to the warrior next to him in a sinewy letter *H*; and, though few people had ever noticed this, the rows of stone squares that spread through the floor of the ground level, wherever they touched, formed a perfect letter *H*. Going up the floors of the tower, every rail post of every stairwell gave one half of a letter *H*. The indented parapet of every terrace perpetually repeated the letter *H*. The capital of every column made the letter *H*. The casement of every window was the letter *H*. And in the largest room at the farthest end of the top floor of the tower, behind weighty doors of sculpted bronze, the last and the heaviest *H* of all was the furrow in the brow of Mr. Hoss himself.

Without a movement, without a sound, he sat alone at his desk, his face buried in his hands. On one side of the room, the portrait of his father looked down at him from the wall. He had thought of having the painting removed when he had first taken this office, but then he had changed his mind. He came from a long line of illustrious men who had all shared the same few names. But gradually, over the years since his father had died, all the *junior*'s, *son*'s, *successor*'s and *the second*'s had dropped from the headlines, and he had become just *Herman Hoss*, as his father had before him. And when at last there were no brothers left to extend it, no sisters left to dilute it, or cousins left to claim it, the entire world had agreed that he alone stood for the name. He had become simply "Hoss," a single syllable that the universe recognized. It was then, and only then, that he was content leaving his father's portrait on the wall.

Slumped over his desk was the day's *Metropolitan Times*. He had hardly touched it. For years now, since they had reconciled with him, its senior editors were in his employ, not officially, but through bribes that kept them closer than any salary. He had barely even glanced at the headline, and yet it scrolled over his mind as clearly as if he had written it.

Third Break-in at Surway House; Intruder Escapes Again

He relaxed his eyebrows and smiled. Lowering his hands over his desk, he looked at the limp bundle of printed pages. *No wonder they call articles "stories."* He rose from his chair.

The newspaper had printed the lie he had dictated. The police had carried out the scheme he had directed. Last night, the phone had rung a few minutes before midnight. Even before picking up, he had known the news would be bad. The man in the House carried no phone, no device of any kind that could be tracked, and there was no way, if he had accomplished what he had been sent to do, that he could have found a way to call so quickly. The phone call couldn't come from him. There was no introduction, no greeting, from the man on the line.

The man had only said,

"The alarm has gone off."

The first time Hoss had heard these words, months before, he had almost laughed. They had sounded so mundane, so trite, so *small*, the stuff of a suburban burglar's nightmares, the dread of a teenage shoplifter at the mall. And yet there had been no other words to convey the situation. *The alarm has gone off.* The momentous miscalculation; the persistence of the secret; the abject squandering of intelligence and labor and time; the counterstrike of the House, the biggest House in the world, silent and treacherous, only pretending to sleep in the night; and, most painful of all, the slipping from his grasp of the largest legacy in history, the biggest prize on earth—all of this in a few words that could just as well apply to a set of earrings or a pair of sneakers. The first time, the words had sounded like a joke. The second time, just a few weeks later, they had repulsed him. The third time, last night, he had sensed them before hearing them. He had learned to respect their dissonant candor. Hearing them for the third time, he had almost greeted them like a friend. *The alarm has gone off*, he recalled once again at his desk. The search had failed again.

There was little to be afraid of. There would be no trouble *from* the police. The call had come from the police. It meant that they would have to drive over to the House, their own sirens blasting, with reasonable haste, taking no more than ten to fifteen minutes to arrive. The chief of the local department would come across the trespasser, trapped like a raccoon, somewhere near the northeast gallery. One of the chief's men, carrying a chainsaw, would slice across the metal bars, the armored door, the length of rope—whatever was holding the trespasser captive this time. Then the trespasser would be let out. The police would officially leave the house empty-handed. The public would be fed some nonsense, some explanation for the sounds and the lights in the night. And the man whose mission hadn't succeeded would never be heard of again.

Hoss stared out over the City through the glass wall of the room. The bars and arches of steel between the panes drew a great circle in the middle, like the eye of a zeppelin, from which Hoss liked to watch the world. Though there was little more in his enormous office than his desk of marble, inlaid with bronze and tortoiseshell, and the curving sword displayed on the wall, it was one of the most beautiful rooms in the City. But the only colors there, besides those of the sumptuous carpet on the floor, belonged to the sky. The portrait of his father beside the door was always in the shadow somehow, whether the door was open or closed. And the wall across the room from the windows was bare—or almost. There was a window in that wall as well, one more window, but it gave no light. It was an old window with a frame of stone set against the wall like a mirror, majestic and ancient, seemingly lifted out of some castle never to be opened again. And though the wall of the room was white, behind the glass panes of this window there was only blackness, as if it were always night on the other side, even when sunlight streamed across the room. Hoss turned his back to it as he leaned over the round glass that looked outside.

The trespasser in the Surway House had never seen Hoss. He had never even touched the actual plans he had been instructed to memorize. He would never know whom he had worked for.

And even if he had found out somehow, by now the question of what he knew no longer mattered. But this didn't satisfy Hoss. It bothered him, it nettled him, that the man in the House—who was, after all just some unlucky hardworking man, and a thief of some skill—should be punished, should be disposed of, for something that hadn't been his fault. Injustice wasn't the issue for Hoss. Rather, what had happened offended his sense of logic, of cause and effect, of the determined, dependable chain between a force and its consequence. Hoss himself was nothing but force—consequence running loose teetered his understanding of life itself. The failure hadn't been the trespasser's fault. The blame lay within the plan that the trespasser had been taught, the instructions he had been ordered to follow. And the man behind that order would never be punished.

So it wasn't the northeast gallery. It had seemed so promising. It had made so much sense. *Goddamned Surway.* He sighed. *Goddamned*—he forced himself to say the name in his mind, halting for a second before the sound—*Lucian Baker.* Where was he? Who was he? Did he know where the treasure was hidden? Surely he couldn't have found it yet. Surely he couldn't have lifted it out of hiding. The House was still uninhabited. If the heir had come already, if he had taken hold of the legacy, certainly he would have reopened the House. The flow of money, going wherever, coming from wherever, would have rocked the financial markets. The banks would have known. The banks would have told Hoss. The world would have found out. Besides, Hoss had sent Lucian Baker a message in Civic Square, this last Surway Day. No one had responded. Lucian Baker hadn't come forward. No, the fortune still lay hidden. There was nothing standing in Hoss's way, in the way of the mighty Hoss, nothing but a booby-trapped house, an uncooperative mound of stones. And yet he was powerless. All his assaults had proven futile. Battered with disappointment, he let his gaze roll down the spires, bridges, arches and walls of the City before him, the City that they called the New Rome. His thoughts wandered with the hundreds of minuscule lives that he saw swarming below.

Who are they? He wondered. *What are they? What are they made of?* As his eyes roamed on top of the countless pairs of shoes that beat the pavement below him, hundreds and hundreds of feet below his window, he considered their lives. Where was each of them headed? Where was every man running, with such haste, such oblivion? What was the golden object at the end of each path that justified this rustling, hustling, and hurtling through the day? How big was it? How much was it worth? And inevitably, as he gazed down at them, Hoss felt dizzy with the difference in scale between what he pursued and what they pursued, what he sought and what they sought. If any one of them knew what Hoss coveted, if any one of them had a chance at a crumb of what he wanted... Any one of them would suddenly stop dead in his tracks. Any one of their lives would immediately lose all meaning. Hoss could cross distances with a glance, from where he stared at them, that the dots of their feet could hardly cover in a day. And yet, Hoss asked himself as he watched them milling about, did they run any more slowly than he did? Were their legs any less tired? Did they want what they wanted any less than he did? And were they any less certain of how much they wanted it?

The line of his square jaw was reflected in the window. From a corner of his eye, he could make out the shade of his hair in the glass. It was only just beginning to turn gray, like the overcast sky. No, it wasn't the trespasser who had failed. It was himself. No one else was to blame. He lightly nodded his head against the glass. For him there would be no consequence. As always, there was no risk for Hoss at all, even if the call last night had ripped a hole in his gut. It wasn't danger. It was defeat. The craving rose from the pit of his stomach to his throat, as it always did when he felt a limit to his power. The thirst for violence clenched his fingers, tightened the veins on his hand. With his last look at the crowds, he felt his foot lifting to stomp them.

He sat down. He reached for his pen, having resolved to do the one thing that always calmed him down, the only thing besides inflicting pain. But then, as he leaned over his desk, his eyes fell across another bundle of folded pages, crinkled and forgotten underneath the *Metropolitan Times.* For a few seconds, he struggled to focus on the printed words. *The Spring Forge Gazette.* The local paper that he read and maneuvered, that he *controlled* in order to keep a watch over what was read and discussed in the town and around the House. He read the top headline:

Man Seen Inside of Surway House

He groaned with contempt. Again that story of spooky sightings. But no one could have entered the House. No one outside of the three break-ins. And no one had come forward after Civic Square. *People are all morons.* The paper was a week old. He rounded his fist to pound it, but he held back his arm. His fist landed with a tap. He drew a breath, and he thought of the sword behind his desk. A rush of desperation and thirst swept through his head, tasting of blood. He felt his eyes drawn to the old window against the wall. Instead, he looked down again, and he lighted on another headline:

A New Year Starts at Saint Clem's:
Preparations Underway for the Annual BnC Ball

It was just a glance from there to the final story on the page:

Civic Square in Final Cleanup Stages after Surway Day Incident

A pale grin rose on his lips.

"Well, *if* Lucian Baker is in there, then maybe this time around we can draw him out."

He didn't even realize that he had spoken those words out loud. He flattened the crumpled paper with a wave of his forearm as if he were sweeping away midges, or the tiny people on the street. Then he rolled the paper up, wedged it under his arm, and stood up.

CHAPTER EIGHT

The Oldest House in the Neighborhood

When Andrew walked into the Brandow house, his mind was swimming with thoughts of new schoolmates, lost fortunes, endless food stalls and empty mansions. He was also out of breath, because he had run most of the way. Now that he was back, now that he was safe, he could admit it to himself—the man outside the school had spooked him. He could laugh about it now. He could call himself a sissy. But when he closed the door behind him, he rested against it for a moment to feel it shutting out the world outside.

He poked his head into the living room and the kitchen to exchange a quick greeting with Mr. and Mrs. Brandow, and then he climbed up the stairs three at a time. The doorknob of the yellow bedroom felt warm in his hand. He paused and closed his eyes. *Made it through the day.* In the bliss of the moment, his head fell gently over the door. He took a deep breath and went in.

He saw himself in the mirror on the door of the wardrobe. As twilight turned to evening outside the window, sharpening the light of the lamp on the bedside table, he stood looking at himself, surveying his blazer, his shirt, his tie, and his pants. He tried to learn what he looked like. Hundreds of other students in uniform couldn't make him look any less strange to himself. The tie around his neck and the dragon on his breast still looked like beautiful props. He was still posturing and examining himself when the sound of Mrs. Brandow's voice rose from downstairs.

"Andrew, dinner!"

He was so startled that he didn't even think to take off his blazer. He had picked an enormous flower for Mrs. Brandow at school. He had been so gentle that it was still plump and round when he pulled it out of his backpack. But picturing himself holding it as he stepped into the kitchen made him feel like a clown—he threw it out the window before running down the stairs.

Mr. Brandow was just unfolding his napkin over his lap when Andrew tumbled down into the opposite chair. The man burst into laughter, immediately followed by Mrs. Brandow when she turned around from the stove.

"We get it—you look spectacular in your uniform!" she cried out.

"I'd also keep my work clothes on if I looked that good in them," said Mr. Brandow in a chuckle that made his frame bob.

"It's a good thing you don't," Mrs. Brandow replied, with a smile tenderer than any compliment.

And before Andrew could drape the blazer over his head in shame, Mrs. Brandow reached a mitt over his shoulder and lay down a steaming chicken pot pie on the table. One glance made Andrew forget everything else. He tallied up the meals: blueberry pancakes for breakfast, appetizers for lunch, and cookies throughout the day. This dinner would complete the best day of eating in his life. As he picked up his fork, he promised himself to eat slowly and make room for conversation.

"What did you think of your first day at Saint Clemens?" Mrs. Brandow asked him. "How was it?"

"Good!" he replied, trying to amplify the word by widening his eyes.

"Did you like it? What were some of the highlights of the day?"

"It was great!"

He didn't know what else to say. His eyes fell on the plate. "This food is really excellent Mrs. Brandow."

"Call me Laura," she laughed, and she looked down at her own plate with a smile.

"The day was good, really," he went on. "A lot of interesting activities that I'd never done before, like getting outfitted for my fencing suit, or feeding watermelon to a family of lemurs."

Mr. Brandow snickered as he ate.

"I wouldn't want to be the one in charge of impressing those kids," said Mrs. Brandow.

"Or impressing the parents who pay for it all!" said her husband.

"It's all pretty incredible, all the resources they have," Andrew went on. He still couldn't say "we." "I'm pretty sure I came in and out of more buildings today than there were in the whole town I used to live in."

"It's a beautiful campus," Mrs. Brandow said.

"And I learned a lot about the local area too," Andrew added, raising his eyes from his plate to observe the effect of his next words. "Like the Surway mystery."

"Ah yes, another break-in!" Mr. Brandow exclaimed, wiping his mouth with his napkin. His blue eyes twinkled. "Every town in the valley is talking about it."

"Yes, the ongoing Surway mystery," his wife mused. "It's sort of like our Loch Ness Monster here in Spring Forge."

Andrew evaluated his next question carefully before he spoke.

"I heard some people have seen a man inside the House..."

The only reaction was a slight arching of Mrs. Brandow's eyebrows.

"I suppose any Loch Ness Monster comes with sightings," she said. "I've never seen anything, but then again I haven't been near the House in years."

"Where were you last night shortly before midnight?" Mr. Brandow asked her with a smirk.

"Unfortunately, just looking after you, as always."

"Is the House close to here—the building itself I mean?" Andrew asked.

"Oh yes. It's only a few minutes' drive up the road going into the mountains. I always drive right past the main gate on my way to the farmers' market."

"So you *have* been near the House recently," her husband continued. "She's constantly lying."

"I would love to see it," Andrew said.

"It's a shame you just missed it," she replied, leaning forward on her elbows. "If only you'd been here a few months ago, in the spring, you could have volunteered for the annual Surway Day cleanup!"

All at once, her expression changed. She exchanged a somber glance with her husband. Andrew instantly remembered something he had heard over lunch, and during the principal's address. About an incident in Civic Square. His curiosity prevailed.

"I'd be very interested in checking it out... I might try to sign up next year."

Neither of them made a reply. Andrew thought they should all change the subject, when suddenly he heard himself blurting out,

"What do you think will happen to the House? Will anyone ever live there again?"

Mr. and Mrs. Brandow looked at each other and sighed. No one had ever warned them that children, and teenagers especially, ask unanswerable questions.

It was she who replied,

"I can't imagine that someone's just going to turn up someday and move in as Surway's heir. What, so that person just never got around to it all this time?"

Suddenly, the thought of the mystery overtook her. In spite of her, the thrill rippled her eyes.

"You know they never found the deed to the House?"

Andrew stared at her, bewildered.

"They never found it," she continued. "They went looking for it in the county records, after he was declared dead. It wasn't there. To this day, it's never been found."

Andrew looked down. A chill ran across his shoulders. After a moment, he asked again,

"So what do you think will happen?"

She shrugged once more, and considered before answering. Finally she said, her gaze wandering off, the sketch of a smile on her lips,

"I think someday, when the time is right, someone, somewhere, with some kind of power and authority, is going to realize that this House is more than just a piece of record-breaking real estate. Surway's universe, his era, is gone, but he created something beautiful that he left behind. We are fortunate to have it, and the world, in time, will find the proper role for it. All we need is someone who can make something intelligent out of something fortunate."

Though he couldn't say why, Andrew knew that he would remember these words. He drew in a breath and cast down his eyes. Then he asked,

"Did either of you know Mr. Surway?"

A sudden burst of laughter pushed Mrs. Brandow deep into her chair.

"How old do you think we are?" she asked as she laughed. "The man disappeared decades ago."

Andrew felt his face burning.

"Did you grow up around here?"

"Yes, I suppose we both did," she said as she recovered. "But no, neither of us knew him."

"Laura's just being modest," Mr. Brandow said. "The lab she works in is still technically a part of the Surway Corporation. So really, you can think of him as Laura's boss."

"Yes," she chuckled. "I was such a precocious child that he became my mentor in my first six months on this planet, when he and I overlapped."

"She was always at the top of her class," Mr. Brandow confided in Andrew. Then, with no less pride, "This house actually goes back to the Surway days. It's the oldest in the neighborhood. You can see that it's a little bit wider, a little grander, than all the other houses on the block."

"You can tell from the little columns around the front door," she added, "underneath the balcony."

"No other house in the neighborhood has columns," Mr. Brandow said. It hardly mattered whether he was teasing or not— he was unable to speak of either his wife or the house without affection.

"It's also set back from the street," he continued, "because it has a tiny bit more land. All the other houses were built in the eighties and nineties, but this one dates all the way back to the first half of the twentieth century. It goes back to the Surway days, and even further."

He took a gulp of water and a rascally look came over his face.

"You can ask Laura all about it. She actually built this house."

Mrs. Brandow had long ago given up rolling her eyes. He turned to Andrew.

"How did you find out about the Surway story?"

"Over lunch," he said. "I ate with a few other freshmen who were talking about it."

Mrs. Brandow's eyes jumped. Finally the question that had been burning on her lips all evening, even hotter than the chicken pot pie, could come out.

"Did you make any friends?"

Andrew shrugged.

"I had a fairly long conversation at lunch with a boy and a girl who were pretty friendly."

"What were their names?"

He pretended to dig into his memory for a few seconds, and then he said,

"The girl's name was Olivia."

Mr. Brandow's eyes opened wide.

CHAPTER NINE

Powerful Children

"Olivia Gladys?" Mr. Brandow asked.

Andrew stared at him curiously.

"I didn't find out her last name. Maybe?"

The man smiled.

"Did she mention anything about her father or the City at any point?"

"Not really," he said. But then he added, after a few seconds' consideration, "I did notice something strange. One of the other students at the table made a comment about how useless the police were in the City, and I got the sense that she was deeply offended for some reason. She glared at the guy, and no one said a word."

Mr. Brandow clapped his hands.

"It *is* she," he said. "That's the daughter of Mayor Gladys. I did read that she was starting at Saint Clem's in the fall. Nicely done, sir! Homing in on the daughter of one of the most powerful men in the country—in the world—on your first day at school!"

Mrs. Brandow frowned at her husband.

"Paul," she chided softly, "you're making him sound so calculating. Besides, I don't think there's a table anywhere on the Saint Clemens campus where that wouldn't be the case."

Andrew's awareness of current affairs was hazy. He had always lived in places where nothing ever changed, and he had grown up without parents—adults who would watch and discuss the news. But even he had heard of Mayor Gladys, the billionaire businessman who had become a legendary politician. The man who famously had *the guts to follow his gut* had gone from building one of the largest fortunes in the country to governing the most powerful City in the world. And Olivia was his daughter.

"What is she like?" Mrs. Brandow asked. "She looks like a model in all the pictures... Is she nice?"

Andrew squinted as he pondered the question.

"She's not *unfriendly*," he said at last, "but I don't think she's very interested in what goes on inside of other people."

He flushed as he remembered her calling him poor, until he was certain that Mr. and Mrs. Brandow could read the word on his cheeks.

Mrs. Brandow wondered, her fork hanging in the air,

"I wouldn't want to be that poor boy who made the comment about the City."

"And not all the corruption is Gladys's fault," Mr. Brandow broke in. "Though God knows there are things I disagree with him about. It's just that the City has..." He stopped, searching for words. "Mighty enemies."

He gave his wife a severe glance and looked down at his plate.

Mrs. Brandow shook her head slowly, took a bite from her fork, and quietly said,

"It certainly can't be easy being her. Her childhood wasn't rosy all the way."

"What happened?" Andrew asked.

"She lost her mother at a very young age, to cancer. She must have been no more than two or three years old. And her father never remarried. She's his only child. And he came from nothing, you know. That's why he's so passionate about opening up our society to anyone who wants to come here and work. He wants everyone to have the same chance as he had. I'm sure he spoils her rotten. But I can't imagine it's always been an easy battle to fight—the two of them versus the world."

Andrew lowered his eyes, when Mrs. Brandow asked in a brighter voice,

"Did you make friends with anyone else?"

"Yes," he said. "A boy who was with her—Cameron."

"That must be Cameron Renfrowe!" she exclaimed as she ate, hiding her mouth behind her napkin. "Mia Renfrowe's son. Of course! They're good friends from the City, and I heard he was coming to Saint Clem's. Mia and Mayor Gladys are famously close... Their kids must have practically grown up together!"

"Who's Mia Renfrowe?" Andrew asked her.

"Oh she's wonderful," Mrs. Brandow said with a mooning smile. "She's a famous socialite, from a well-known family in the City—the Wimbleys, from the Wimbley bank."

"When I was a kid," Mr. Brandow said, "they were still the second biggest bank in the country. They've merged a few times, but I bet they're still doing pretty well. And I suppose Mia's father is still the biggest shareholder."

"Yes, yes," Mrs. Brandow waved her hand over the boring intrusion, "but Mia was always a bit of an intellectual, a bit of a rebel in the family. She was incredibly well-read for the time, and she was friends with all the cutting-edge artists in the City. She went to all the scandalous parties—she was notorious when I was in my twenties. She was also a legendary beauty... There were always rumors of her going into acting or modeling. You should see the pictures of the clothes she used to wear. Even today I don't know how many celebrities could get away with that kind of wardrobe! She was wild. And every eligible bachelor in the country was after her. But she ended up marrying this Renfrowe character, to the shock and disappointment of everyone around her. He was a handsome, good-for-nothing playboy—a high-society heartthrob—and he left her the moment they had a child."

"Why did she marry him?" Andrew asked.

She raised a shoulder.

"Bad taste in men I suppose. Guess love is the only taste you can't refine."

"Don't you know it," Mr. Brandow chimed in.

"That son was their only child," she went on, "your classmate Cameron. He grew up without a father. No doubt Mayor Gladys is a better role model than a man who spent the last fifteen years partying —or should I say gold-digging—in Europe! Although I hear he's mostly in Latin America now..."

"Emerging markets!" Mr. Brandow chuckled. "My wife is a fountain of knowledge, and her insights come in many varieties."

She turned impish eyes to Andrew and said,

"I'm always here if you have any questions."

"I have a few," Andrew ventured. "What happened to her, to Mia Renfrowe?"

She sighed.

"What happens to all women who are too unique for men to appreciate. She's aged beautifully, gracefully. She's still stunning, but in a more serious, regal way, and she still doesn't give a damn what the world expects of her. For one thing, she doesn't seem to have any interest in remarrying. She does precisely what she wants to do, and these days that's mostly charity work, and some academic research.

"Did you know," she went on to her husband, "that she frequently lectures on economics at the University in the City? She also serves as independent advisor on several of Gladys's Action Committees."

"I'm sure," he rejoined, "that charity work and lectures are all that keeps her looking stunning at her age."

Mrs. Brandow let out a groan.

"No one asked for *your* tips on aging gracefully."

Both of them laughed.

"Olivia Gladys and Cameron Renfrowe..." she reflected, still smiling. "I imagine they must be among the celebrities of your class."

"That's my boy," Mr. Brandow said, giving him a high five that made Andrew grin through the next three bites.

An abstracted look descended over Mrs. Brandow's face.

"I wonder, what's it like to go to school with such powerful children?"

"It's easy and fun," said Mr. Brandow, "just like going to school with any other kids!"

He then cast a long gaze into Andrew's eyes.

"Don't be afraid of anyone," the man told him. "You're better than the whole lot of them. There isn't a single one among them who stands an inch taller than you do. And you're going to have lots of fun getting to know them, and they're going to have lots of fun getting to know you."

Andrew smiled and shrugged. But he absorbed every syllable as Mr. Brandow went on,

"Just give it a few weeks and you'll be best friends with all those kids. I guarantee it."

Then he leaned into Andrew's ear and concluded,

"When it comes to school, always listen to me. Laura was always a nerd."

"And you were always the cool kid?" she asked, one eyebrow raised.

"Actually I was."

Looking at him and then checking his wife's expression, Andrew knew it had to be true.

"Then again," Mr. Brandow considered, crossing his hands behind his head, "I ended up marrying the school nerd."

"Best damn thing that ever happened to you," she said.

Andrew had never climbed a staircase more slowly. If Mrs. Brandow hadn't insisted on cleaning the dishes without his help, and if Mr. Brandow hadn't looked so peaceful reading his book in his armchair, Andrew would have stayed downstairs a bit longer. He might have sat down at the empty table in the kitchen or on the rug in front of the fireplace, and simply stared at them and listened to them, quietly imbibing their happiness. He could have watched them for hours, trying to learn from them what it was like to be cared for over a lifetime. But there would be many more nights. The time had come to go upstairs.

Once in his room, when he finally took off his uniform, his thoughts turned again to Polo Guy and "Poor" Girl—Cameron and Olivia. Now he knew where they came from. He knew their last names, and he knew what people who didn't know them said about them. Did this make him more nervous to see them? And how would *they* behave when they saw *him*? Would they wave at him from their table? Would they greet him by name? Would they remember him at all?

In spite of all these questions, Andrew fell asleep right away. The day had been too dense. He slept and he dreamed, but he didn't dream of Olivia, or Cameron, or ivy-covered gables or red dragons. Instead, his spirit hovered over a curve of ancient stones, past a soundless stretch of grass, and onto the side of an enormous grey mountain. Only this wasn't a natural mountain. As he peered in the dream through the mist that shrouded the earth, he distinguished lines in the stone. Columns and balconies took form. Crags became terraces, and spikes turned into spires.

Cornices appeared, parapets, bridges, towers and domes, a magnificent city crystallizing into the distance. And then he noticed an opening in the stone, a single square of light that was a window. And in the window, there was a man, with cropped, graying hair and a spiny, graying beard, dressed all in black, staring back at him.

CHAPTER TEN

A Surprise

Whatever he may have dreamed of, Andrew opened his eyes in the morning thinking only about pancakes. He wondered, as he took his seat at the kitchen table, if he could ever go back to a life of breakfasts without them, or without the Brandows themselves. From now on, his days would begin with sweetness and warmth. When he stepped out of the house in his school uniform, the motion of pulling the doorknob behind him felt so natural that he clenched his fist to hold its memory.

He didn't take the previous morning's shortcut but he still arrived at school a few minutes early. Not knowing what else to do, he reached into his backpack and dug out the plastic folder he had been given the day before. He leaned against a tree and looked through it, just in case he had missed anything: the morning's schedule, starting with strategy class; a map of campus, with a list of important phone numbers; a letter from which he had peeled off his Saint Clemens ID (with a picture of his face squished like a pumpkin); a booklet on how to use the Saint Clemens library system and other academic resources; an assortment of colorful flyers inviting him to various upcoming campus events; and a handful of brochures for useful student services in Spring Forge, including a pet-friendly spa, a hair and style consultancy, and a helicopter transit service (*I'll have to make some calls after class*, he said to himself and laughed).

He was about to shut the folder when he noticed something he hadn't seen before—a white card stuck between two flyers. He pulled it out. The card was thick and bordered with silver. On the front, there were only three letters:

BnC

He turned it around. Two words were engraved on the back:

Get ready.

He flipped the card back and forth a few more times, but there was nothing else on it. He shrugged. If he had to *get ready*, then he would find out in time.

He dropped the card back in the folder when the letter that had held his ID caught his eye. One sentence took up the bottom half of the page:

To be used for cardholder's mailbox

He felt a skip in his chest. He was *the cardholder*. And he had just a few minutes left. He shoved the folder back in his backpack and ran over to the main building.

Mailboxes, it turned out, were lockers equipped with card readers, spread along the floors of a large atrium on one side of the building. Other students were milling about when Andrew came in. He walked past them as he looked for his number, and he found his mailbox in a corner at the end of the ground floor. *Don't get too excited*, he warned himself. *There's nothing waiting for you in there.* But he couldn't help the quiver in his stomach when he heard the locker's latch disengage and the metallic door popped open.

For a few seconds, all he could do was gape at the shiny rectangular box that lay slanting across the locker, too big to lie flat. A silver ribbon was tied around it. He inched closer to the locker and reached a timid hand inside.

A little envelope slid over the glossy surface of the box and fell to the floor. Andrew considered picking it up, but he couldn't wait—he opened the box first.

Inside, he found a black leather-bound notebook. He leafed through the pages, breathing in their woodsy smell, and he found a postcard slipped in the middle. It showed the Saint Clemens campus seen from the mountains on a sunny day. But there was more inside the box. There was a pouch, as tight and trim as a roll of quarters, made of some luxurious hide Andrew didn't know. He pulled the zipper open, and he saw that it was filled with new pencils and markers and all manner of school supplies. He peered again into the gift box. There was one more object propped against the side, a heavy cylinder of brushed metal. He slid a fingernail down to open it. There was a purple fountain pen inside, embossed with a red dragon. This he didn't touch. He wondered if his hands would ever be clean enough to pick it up.

He remembered the envelope on the floor. He lay down the box in the locker, as gently as if he were setting down the last egg on the planet, and he picked up the envelope. There was nothing written on either side of it. But inside of it, there was a card. It was a thick white card bearing only the words, beautifully handwritten:

Enjoy your first day!

It took him almost a minute to take in these words. When at last he looked up, the atrium around him was deserted. He reached back into the locker and grabbed the box in one arm. Not trusting it to be left alone, not trusting it in his backpack, he hurried away clutching it to his chest. This was the largest, most expensive, most astounding gift he had ever received.

Who had sent it to him? He first thought of the Brandows, the only people in the world who seemed capable to him of unbounded, unreasoning kindness. But he crossed them off just as quickly. This wasn't their style. It was too dainty, too shiny. And he had just seen them over breakfast—no one could hide a surprise that well. No, it couldn't have been the Brandows. Then who? He never received gifts from anywhere; he never received gifts from *anyone*. As he stalked through the hallways, he went back in thought to his childhood. He tried to journey back over every acquaintance he had ever made, every neighbor and friend, and all the relatives of his friends. But nobody came to mind.

Suddenly he knew. He must have known all along, since he had first glimpsed the box in the locker. The *person* must have sent it to him. The person who had nominated him for the scholarship, the person who had led him to Saint Clemens. It must have been the person who had secretly watched him all his life, who had waited for him, and who had quietly marked the time, year after year, for the unfolding of his destiny. Hustling to his lecture, Andrew could feel his heart pounding against the hardness of the box.

He arrived in front of the lecture hall. The door was closed. Strategy class had started. A man in a suit stood outside the door. He smiled at Andrew, offered him a small bottle of water, and asked,

"Would you like a fresh towelette?"

Andrew didn't know what a towelette was—fresh or otherwise. He shook his head. The man opened the door and held out his arm to show him in. Andrew walked in and the door closed behind him.

The room was dark. At first, Andrew could see nothing but a line of lights on the floor. He followed them to an empty seat at the end of the last row. He took off his backpack and sat down, and he glanced around at the few faces he could see staring back at him in the darkness. Polo Guy was one of them. The boy waved, and Andrew flicked two fingers to his head in reply. Poor Girl, sitting next to Polo Guy, didn't turn around.

The stage in the front of the room was a giant grid, pulsing with an electric hum. Two of the squares in the grid were lit, one blue and the other red. The hues they cast across the room were the only colors in the hall. One student stood on the blue square, and another on the red square.

"Will you accept the move?" asked the professor, a long man standing outside the grid. His expansive black beard was the vengeance of all the strands that would never grow again on his head.

"Yes," the student on the blue square replied with a faltering voice, and he moved diagonally to another square. The square he had left went black, and the new square turned blue. A collective sigh of relief, more felt than heard, rose from the room.

Andrew lay his box down on his desk and opened it, reaching first for the little black pencil case. He had no idea of what was happening on stage, but no mystery was too thick for his new instruments. He grabbed a pencil and hefted it in his fist. It felt as strong as a wooden staff. He bounced the ball of his index finger over its point when he noticed the hand of another student a few rows down. The hand was drooping over the side of a desk, and a pencil dangled from its fingers—Andrew's pencil. There was also

a notebook on the desk. The hand holding the pencil had drawn a
vortex of doodles inside it. It was the same leather-bound notebook as Andrew's. He glanced at the next desk, and he spotted the
pencil sharpener from his pencil case. On another desk he saw
the box lid, and on another, the silver ribbon. On the edge of
another desk, stripped of its cap, forgotten and left to dry, was
the purple fountain pen he had been afraid to touch. Andrew's
eyes then drifted to the end of the front row, at the center of the
auditorium. There he recognized, over the rim of a trashcan,
shaded red in the glow from the stage, a little white card bordered with silver. He could just discern the words from where he
sat. *Enjoy your first day!*

The student on the blue square made another move. But this
time, though the square he had just left faded into blackness, the
one he landed on didn't turn blue. It flickered in white flashes
that blared across the room, before vanishing with a crash.

So it wasn't a gift at all. The box hadn't been meant for Andrew. A surge of sadness came over him. His eyes fell to his box,
and now he could see nothing inside of it but countless days
without mail, several years of empty lockers, nameless cards and
hollow milestones as far as he could imagine—a life made of lone-
ly years, celebrated for nothing and with no one. He slowly
breathed out. Then he sat up straight in his seat, pushed his
shoulders back, and opened the box. He pulled out his new pen.
He lifted out his leather notebook, turned over the cover, and on
the top left corner of the first page, right below the words *If lost,
please return to,* he wrote down his name: *Andrew Day.* There was
another line, labeled *Reward.* Without hesitation, he wrote: *Gratitude!* Then he thought about it for a moment and added: *+ 1 dollar.*

He traipsed behind some of the other freshmen to his next
class, *Shade and Depth,* without saying a word. He entered a build-

ing that looked like a Roman temple past another attendant handing bottles and towelettes. Andrew took one of each and stepped into an auditorium that was as bright as the previous one had been dark; sunlight flooded the room through the glass dome of the ceiling. On the stage in front, two men wearing black suits stood on either side of a painting. The painting showed a naked woman, seen from behind, looking over her shoulder at the audience. A note stated in block letters at the bottom of the frame: *ON LOAN.*

Andrew took his seat. Instead of a desk, he faced a blank canvas mounted on an easel. Looking down, he found a box of new brushes and untouched paint tubes under his chair. Polo Guy and Poor Girl sat next to each other a few rows down, but this time neither of them looked back. For a few minutes, nothing happened. Students hushed in anticipation of authority. Finally the door opened. Principal Clare entered the room and walked up to the stage, where he waited politely for the students to direct their eyes at him. As he watched him smirking in front of the class, Andrew discovered that he had instinctively decided not to ask the principal about his scholarship—decided, in fact, not to go near him at all. The man took a small bow and said,

"Good morning students, and apologies for making you look at me when you were expecting to see great art. I have an announcement to make."

The audience stared at him in silence.

CHAPTER ELEVEN

The First Day

"I'm here," the principal said, "to apologize on behalf of Professor Singer"—pronounced with a French accent—"who, we just found out, was wandering around the school zoo last night looking for inspiration, when he apparently had a most unfortunate encounter with the baboon colony. I'm told the baboons used his own paints on certain parts of his body to make him look more like one of their own. He's currently recovering at the infirmary, but he should be back in top form by tomorrow. Regrettably, this means your lecture will need to be adjourned to next week."

A tremor of joy ran through the audience. In all the principal's words, the students had heard only that an hour of class had disappeared, and that somehow they had baboons to thank.

"We will try our best to extend the loan of this week's artwork before returning it to Paris," the principal went on, as the two men in black lowered a drape over the painting of the naked woman.

"But more immediately," the principal said, "this means at least one free period before your next class, and maybe two depending on your schedules. I respectfully request that you spend that time in quiet study in the library. For those of you who are new to our institution, members of the campus staff are waiting outside to show you the way."

These words deflated the students' elation. But the principal was anxious to regain the crowd's favor, so quickly won and lost. He blinked, took a breath, and began again in a new tone,

"In cheerier news, I hope you're all as excited as I am for the annual BnC ball on Friday night. By now, I trust you've all had enough time to prepare. It seems like only yesterday when we sent out the first invitations to your families, early in the summer. But the big night is almost upon us!"

Andrew, who didn't remember receiving anything over the summer, looked around at the other students. A buzz of anticipation rose across the room. The principal smiled broadly.

"This year's event promises to be our most spectacular yet," he said. "And I can't wait to see what each of you will bring to the occasion. Mr. Cavanaugh," he turned to a sleepy, sullen student balancing his foot on a box of paint in the last row. "I can't wait to see a new generation of the well-known Cavanaugh showmanship. People around here are still dazzled by the impression your father left in his day."

The junior Cavanaugh wheeled a stocky fist in the air without lifting his eyes.

"Miss Ahmer," the principal called out to a beautiful, olive-skinned girl in the front row. "I'm sure people all over campus have been wondering what treasures you've brought with you this fall from your family's collections across the ocean."

For her only reply, the girl gave a majestic nod.

"Miss Hansler," he said, "your mother has already warned me: you can tell her that I'm ready."

The girl thus addressed hardly raised her eyes from the curlicues she was drawing on her notebook. But Andrew thought he caught a wrinkle of pride down the corner of her mouth.

"And Miss Gladys, and Mr. Renfrowe," the man turned to the two students. "I can anticipate nothing less than Mayor Gladys's famous perfectionism, and Mrs. Renfrowe's legendary elegance."

Cameron smiled politely, but Olivia's face showed no expression. The principal's gaze then swept across the room, scanning the audience for other illustrious children. His eyes fell on Andrew.

"Mr. Day," he intoned, his voice suddenly broad and hard. Andrew met his stare.

"I trust you'll be able to join us," he said. It was a statement that admitted no reply. "Feel free to come as you are, or as comfortably as you'd like."

A malicious thought sparked in the principal's eye. His head teetered slightly. "I'm afraid your scholarship doesn't cover such expenses," he said. And he gave a little laugh.

Andrew kept his eyes on him, forbidding himself to look at the faces turned in his direction, forbidding himself, as he felt a sting at the base of his eyelids, to look at Cameron and Olivia. The principal turned back to his audience, clasped his hands together, and said,

"Without further ado, I invite you all to spend the next part of the morning in the library. As I said, please do not hesitate to turn to our staff for assistance. Apologies again for Mr. Singer's lesson, and I will see you all looking your finest at the BnC ball."

With these words, he loped off the stage and out of the auditorium, as row after row of slumping bodies stretched and straightened. Andrew waited until all the other students had filed out of the room. Then he stood up, all alone in the vast white lecture hall, and he walked to the door. There was no one left outside. Even the staff members were gone. He dug his hands into his pockets and stepped out of the building. Without thinking, he let his legs carry him to the front of the campus. He wasn't

even conscious that he might be doing something wrong until he
heard his name, his last name, across the lawn.

"Mr. Day!"

He turned around to see the young man who had given him
his badge and his schedule the day before.

"Good morning Mr. Day," the man said in his Scottish accent,
which Andrew was convinced would sound ridiculous to anyone
in Scotland.

"Good morning—"

"Jesse," the man finished for him, reaching out to shake his
hand. "The name is Jesse."

"That's right," Andrew remembered. "Jesse McGallender?"

"Indeed, Mr. Day. But only Jesse, I do ask ye."

Andrew smiled weakly, and the man gave him a curious look.

"Where are ye going? Can I help ye get somewhere?"

"I was just going," Andrew mumbled, "to get some breakfast."
And he poked a thumb in the direction of town.

"Oh I see," Jesse said with a thoughtful dip of his head. "Then
there's something I need to tell ye." He clamped a hand down on
Andrew's shoulder, and the boy felt the grip of trouble. "I know
the best place for waffles in the whole valley. In the whole country! And I promise I'm not biased. Now I mean no disrespect to
our wonderful cooking staff here in the dining hall, but if ye're
ever looking for a *serious* breakfast..."

"It's all right," Andrew interrupted, hunched over with relief.
"I don't think I have enough time now anyway."

Jesse nodded. He considered Andrew quietly, before asking,
"Is everything all right?"

"Yeah," Andrew shrugged.

Jesse sighed and cast down his eyes. Then he stared off into
the distance.

"Well, I'm sure glad yesterday's over," he said. "And soon the whole first week will be behind us forever. It's a lot of busy nonsense, trying to get a whole new year going."

Glancing sideways at him, Andrew observed again how awkward the man looked in his suit. The clothes weren't too tight or too big for his body—his body itself was a problem that no suit could fix. He had the unhinged shoulders, the gangling arms, the swinging knees, the tottering toes and the tapping feet of a little boy, all trapped in a grownup's clothes. He almost seemed to be making the best of a costume. In that, Andrew thought, the two of them were alike.

"I won't disagree with you," the boy said, turning away towards the river. "I sure can't wait for this whole week to be over. This week and that BnC ball at the end of it, whatever that is."

Jesse looked at him, opened his mouth, and changed his mind. He lowered his eyes.

"Don't worry about the ball."

"It's not just that," Andrew said, mostly because he didn't want Jesse to talk to him in that tone. "I get the sense that everyone around here is just a flag-bearer for some wealthy dad or some famous family or some major business empire. It's not the most comfortable place to be for someone with no heritage."

Jesse's eyes widened with reproach.

"Don't ye ever go talking about not having a heritage," he said, his voice suddenly sharp. "Everyone's got a heritage, and it's got nothing to do with money. Why, I bet ye'd think McGallender was the lowliest name ever pronounced around this campus, but I'll tell ye it's the proud name of an ancient Scottish tribe! There isn't a clan in all the highlands whose fathers didn't tremble at the name. Even our emblem was enough to make free men bend a knee: the McGallender hand clutching arrows. And I tell ye that the pride of that emblem is worth more gold in my heart than any dad and any family and any business that anyone at Saint Clemens has ever known."

And when he drew up his fist around an invisible sheaf of arrows, Andrew couldn't help but smile.

"That's amazing," he replied. "Certainly the best heritage I've ever heard of. But you see, I don't even have parents. There's no one behind me to pass things on. Even this stupid blazer is a hand-me-down from someone I've never heard of. It has some other person's initials inside."

And he pulled on the jacket to show the two golden letters stitched over the inside pocket. But Jesse kept his eyes on Andrew's face.

"There is no Day heritage," Andrew muttered, and he let his hand drop from the blazer.

"That's even better!" Jesse exclaimed. "Everyone here is important because of something great that someone in their family started a long time ago. Well, ye get to be that person—ye get to start it all! There's no such thing as an old family or a new family. People are all people; all of humanity's the same age on this planet. But ye get to start a heritage, and someday some lucky kid named Day will get to parade in here with a limousine and be greeted all over campus like royalty, and all over the world like a celebrity, because of something *you* did. Ye see, you're the first Day!"

Andrew looked into his eyes and smiled. Jesse slapped him on the back and said,

"Come on, it's only morning. A lot of exciting things ahead."

And without another word, he turned around and walked back in the direction from which he had come. Andrew watched him trundling into the distance, shrinking back into the tapestry of ivy, stone, and oak. Then he turned around and set off down the long, shaded driveway, through the gate and onto the road.

Jesse's words followed him as he went. They reminded him that nothing was settled yet for the first Day, that everything was still possible, and the thought gently lifted his footsteps. He was fairly sure that he wasn't allowed to leave the campus in the middle of the morning, but no one stopped him.

He walked towards the town center, and as the school grounds came to an end at his side, he began to breathe more freely. He wandered down the main street of Spring Forge, peered into the clutter of antique shops and glanced over listings in the windows of real estate agents. Through the window of an old-fashioned soda shop, he came upon Polo Guy and Poor Girl. They were sitting at the marble counter, their cheeks hollow around the straws of their milkshakes. Polo Guy saw him and waved. Poor Girl stuck out a foamy tongue and winked. Andrew laughed and walked away. *So much for library period.* He walked for a full block before he realized he was still smiling. Perhaps the two of them could become his friends.

He paused by an old souvenir shop at the end of the block, as if he might wear out the happy thought if he kept on walking. The main street came to an end a short distance away. The rest of the town was cordoned off with yellow tape. On the other side of the tape, he could glimpse the bell tower of an old church. Around it, the chimneys and gables of the street gave way to treetops and flagpoles. Andrew recognized the proud spire of a bandstand at their center. The farthest thing he could see was the broad white pediment of some official building across from the church.

He turned back to the displays of the souvenir shop. Mindlessly, he began to spin a rack of old postcards on the sidewalk. Round and round, he saw pictures of old Spring Forge, black-and-white photographs of the valley, faded prints of abandoned mansions.

Suddenly he stopped. He turned around slowly, the rack still whirling in front of him. Standing a few steps away, under the awning of the souvenir shop, so close that the spinning of the post cards seemed to ripple his hair, was the man in the black coat. He seemed to recognize Andrew. He gave a curt, formal nod, turned around the corner of the block, and disappeared.

CHAPTER TWELVE

Instruments and Ornaments

Back at school, when lunch time came, Andrew had no appetite. The thought of all those rows of new faces made him queasy. He decided to skip the meal. Instead, he ambled across the lawn to the music building where his next class would take place.

As soon as he walked into the lobby, the young woman at the front desk smiled at him and said,

"Good afternoon. Do you have a reservation?"

"N-no," he answered.

"No problem."

Her smile didn't break. She turned to a large notebook that lay open in front of her.

"And which instrument were you interested in practicing today?" she asked.

He was lost, not just for words, but for thoughts.

"Which…" he mumbled after a moment, "which instruments are available?"

"Let's see," she said, looking down the columns of her notebook. They were all empty. "Would you prefer percussion instruments, winds, strings, keyboard instruments, or anything electric?"

Andrew dug his chin into his hand. The woman kindly turned the notebook towards him, so that he could read the full list. Not a single instrument had been reserved. One by one, he contemplated trying his hand at the bass, the violin, the triangle, the maracas, the cymbal, and, for the allure of the name alone—he had no idea what the instrument might look like—the timpani. He had almost made up his mind to go with the bagpipes, perhaps in homage to the McGallenders and to the hills they had terrorized, when he realized he had only twenty minutes left before class (he determined that he would have to spend at least half-an hour with any instrument to make the woman think he knew what he was doing).

"Please come back anytime," the woman said as he bumbled an apology. Eighteen minutes later he was back, flushed from a brisk walk around the lawn, so winded that he had almost turned into bagpipes himself. He found his way past the woman to the wood-paneled auditorium reserved for music appreciation, and he took a seat in the last row. A professor with long white hair and a brown tweed suit took the stage, swishing invisible tails behind him as he walked.

But he wasn't alone on stage. And when he began to play music, he didn't push a button. Ninety performers played the music behind him, because there was a live symphony orchestra at the front of the auditorium, and he directed their strings, bows and drums with a wave of his hand.

One student in the middle of the room shouted over the music:

"Can you play that part again?"

The professor turned around, nodded, and led the orchestra back to the start of the melody.

"Not there," the student yelled out. "A bit further."

Again, the professor stopped and resumed a few bars later.

"Nope, a bit before."

Over and over the student jerked the orchestra backwards and forwards, giggling when the teacher looked away.

"Play the *other* bit," the boy kept saying, "the part from *before*."

And Andrew was astounded to see the professor oblige every time, leading all ninety musicians to skip and stop and continue as the student demanded. But Andrew also noticed that the man wore a strange little smile all along, as if the joke in reality was on anyone who couldn't hear the magic that happened on stage.

The music still played in Andrew's chest when he stepped out of the building and onto the plump grass of the lawn, when a voice called his name. It was Cameron.

"Hey," the boy said with a grin, as if they were making fun of something together. "We missed you at lunch."

Olivia shuffled behind him, her face screened by an enormous pair of shades. She was obviously looking at Andrew, but she didn't greet him.

"I had something to do," he answered. "And I'd already eaten."

"Well if you found anything good to eat in town, let us know," Olivia said, dragging her little shoes a few steps closer. "A milkshake is hardly a substantial breakfast."

"Especially with this one digging her straw into other people's," Cameron added.

"I thought the whole point of ordering two different shakes was to share them," she said. She raised her shades over her hair and looked away at nothing in particular. She and Cameron always seemed to go from one place to another with the tranquil, indifferent air that people have in old portraits.

"Hey," Cameron ventured, "you're going to the BnC ball on Friday night, right?"

"Sure," he said, unable to think of an alternative answer.

Cameron nodded, before adding,

"Don't listen to Principal Clare. He's an idiot."

"He's a suck-up, is what he is," Olivia broke in. "This job is his chance to brownnose famous rich people through their kids. It makes me nauseous."

And as if to seek a remedy, she reached a hand into the jingling mess of her purse.

"I think you mean *nauseated*," said Cameron.

Her hand shot out of her bag to her forehead.

"You know, Cameron, it really doesn't matter how good-looking you are if you're gonna be this lame."

Cameron smiled, and the blood rushed so heavily to his face that his head fell to his chest.

Wearily, Olivia turned to Andrew and said,

"Clare probably sees you as his only chance to be a regular jerk of a school principal and get away with it. The scholarship's donor is anonymous, and he's already given as much to Saint Clemens as he's ever gonna give. So there's nothing more to gain from being nice to you. And you're just taking up space among all these other students whose parents could buy and sell the principal."

Andrew couldn't tell if she meant to be nice. He had already gathered that he would often feel this way around her. The three of them started walking.

"But don't let him stop you from enjoying the night," Cameron said, "or this whole place in general."

"Of course not," Andrew shot back, a little gruffly.

"You don't even have to go along with all the shenanigans," Cameron said.

"I know."

"Seriously," said Olivia, "you don't even have to do the whole BnC thing. If you feel like going, just show up as you are. There are no rules. No one will care."

"Totally," Andrew shrugged off.

"It's not like your goal is to be BnC King anyway," she continued. "The whole thing's just a dumb showoff circus."

Andrew couldn't contain his curiosity any longer.

"BnC King?"

Cameron and Olivia stared at him as they walked.

"Yeah," Cameron muttered after a few seconds. "BnC King and Queen... That's not why you would go anyway. No one cares about that."

"Sure," Andrew replied. "So lame."

"Completely," Cameron said.

But Andrew needed an answer.

"I don't even know how it works, exactly—the whole BnC King and Queen selection process..."

"It's so dumb," Olivia said. "People cast their votes all night for the best B and the best C. The totals are tallied up and the winners are announced at the end of the night."

"The best B and the best C?"

"Yes."

He resolved that if he were to be friends with them, then he would have to be honest. He stopped walking and asked, in as clear a voice as he could summon:

"What's a B and a C?"

Neither of them paused. Olivia responded with no surprise in her voice.

"It's a jewelry contest, when you really think about it. The *B* is for girls. It stands for brooches. And the *C* is for boys. It means cuff links."

Andrew left them on the way to his next class. *Cuff links.* Two quick clattering syllables. They sounded vaguely mechanical, sprinkled with sawdust, faintly reminiscent of latches and lanyards, or of the interlocking leather straps that hitch the harnesses of horses. *Cuff links.* The term rang in his head like the clapper of a bell. *Cuff links.* How did he even know what they were? But there was a far more important question. Where in the world was he going to find *cuff links?*

The rest of the day disappeared behind this thought. He could sometimes hear the afternoon screeching and blowing behind it. But all he had to do was sit at the back of the class in front of the pencil case and the notebook from his mailbox. All he had to do was glance towards the front of the room every now and again. (He didn't even need to write anything else—beyond his name and the reward of *gratitude + 1 dollar*—in the notebook). Nobody minded him. Nobody interrupted the conversation in his head. All his classes seemed to end before they began.

When he turned the key inside the lock of the Brandow house, he couldn't have said where the past few hours had gone. When he took off his blazer in the yellow bedroom, he didn't have a clue about the weather outside. But sitting down at dinner with the Brandows, he was completely alert. The two of them were his only hope. He couldn't ask them to buy him a pair or even to loan him the money. But surely Mr. Brandow must own a set, and surely he wouldn't mind lending it to Andrew. All Andrew had to do was ask. But Andrew hated to ask. He hated to request and he hated to borrow. All his life he had asked for little and he had been given little. Now that, for the first time, others were giving to him without his asking, he hated to ask for anything at all. And so he kept on delaying the question and eyeing them in silence. He smiled at their jokes and he praised Mrs. Brandow's cooking (as sincere as they were, the compliments tasted false in his mouth). He felt so gloomy that he even helped himself to more broccoli over potatoes.

Suddenly Mrs. Brandow exclaimed,

"I just remembered—big night tomorrow!"

He dropped a fork into the serving dish, and he fished it out with an anxious hand.

"The first big formal event of the year, right? It's all over the *Gazette*, like every year. Paul, I hope you didn't throw away the latest copy."

Her husband shook his head without meeting her eyes.

"I'll look for it after dinner—they describe all the preparations," she said. "But anyway we'll hear all about it from our own participant! How exciting!"

Andrew's lips were glued shut. Almost immediately Mrs. Brandow added,

"The two of us also have plans tomorrow night!" She stared at her husband in disbelief when he showed no response. "We have the back-to-school wine-and-cheese over at your department!"

The man's head fell into his hands.

"All right you big baby," she said, "don't act like you have anything better to do on a Friday night."

"How about staying at home with my lovely wife?" he answered, flashing a mischievous grin at Andrew.

"Oh, such a big baby," she repeated, and her husband looked at his napkin with a smile.

Turning to Andrew, she said,

"But if we're not home when you come back, there's always food in the fridge in case you're hungry."

She added with a chuckle,

"I'm sure they'll have *some* food over there, but nothing that could beat my kitchen."

The three of them laughed, and the subject of the following night was laid to rest. After dinner, Andrew went upstairs and threw himself over the bed.

He jumped from his sleep in the middle of the night with a sudden thought. He looked out the window. The moon was shining outside. It was three o'clock in the morning. He raised a hand to his forehead as if to rub the painful thought away. It had just struck him, in the clearness of a dream, that today was Friday.

The day of the ball.

CHAPTER THIRTEEN

Friday

Some nights bring solutions; others take them away. Andrew stepped out of bed on Friday morning utterly convinced that the chance to ask Mr. Brandow for cuff links was gone forever. What might have been acceptable over dinner one night in advance was totally unthinkable, inadmissible, on the day of the event. Not even Mrs. Brandow's pancakes could cheer him. He hurried out of the house as fast as he could.

Again, he arrived at school early, and again he let himself fall against a tree in front of the main building. *Cuff links.* Since there was no chance of finding them in a gnarl of the tree at his back, he decided to go visit his mailbox again.

He touched his card to the reader and the door swung open. He was no longer allowed to hope for mail. After yesterday's disappointment, he had promised himself not to get excited, and he almost succeeded. But there was something in the locker.

There was a stiff, glossy bag, a purple gift bag overfilled with tissue paper. He tried to rein in his curiosity before he looked inside the bag. From the corner of his eye, he noticed the same tissue paper spilling out of a nearby trashcan. *Good. Now I know where this stuff goes.* And he pulled out the bag.

The first thing he took out was a white card. It was bordered with silver, exactly like the one he had found yesterday. Once again, the front of the card bore only three letters: *BnC*. But on the back of the card, in much smaller font, was written the following note:

We look forward to the honor of your presence at the 87th Annual Saint Clemens 'Brooches and Cuff Links' Ball starting at 7 p.m. on the River Lawn. Members of our staff will be waiting to escort you and your guests from the fountain starting at 6:45 p.m.

Above an engraving of the red dragon, the card was signed:

With our most scintillating regards,
The Saint Clemens School

Underneath the dragon was a small map showing the trajectory from the campus gate to the river. Along the bottom edge of the card was printed:

No guests allowed without proper identification

Looking inside the bag again, Andrew found a lace pouch filled with tiny white eggs that turned out to be candy, all marked in silver: *BnC*. They were hard as rock and overly sweet, but Andrew ate every one of them. Then he noticed a miniature card tied to the silver straps of the gift bag. In the calligraphy that he was starting to know well, the card told him:

We can't wait to see you shine.

He pushed the locker door shut, but suddenly he held it back. He lowered the gift bag in his hand to the floor. There was something else inside the mailbox, something that he hadn't seen behind the bag. He opened the door wider. All he could see was a black box the size of a pack of batteries, streaked with gray scuffs. He picked it up. It felt fuzzy beneath his fingers. He opened it.

There were two little circles in the box, two little metallic crests. The edge of each circle was fashioned into a belt with a buckle. And in the center of each circle, there was a fist clasping a sheaf of arrows.

Andrew stood staring at the cuff links without moving. As light as they were, he felt the tiny jewels in his palm dragging down his arm. They tightened the breath in his lungs. They strained the edges of his eyelids. No gem in the world could weigh more than what he held then in his hand.

Of course, he couldn't accept. He knew that if Jesse owned another set, then he wouldn't have loaned the McGallender cuff links to Andrew. Jesse was giving them up for him, and Andrew would sooner miss the BnC ball—miss every Saint Clemens event for the rest of his life—than accept. He made his decision, and he breathed a sigh that was almost entirely free of regret. Then he closed the box and buried it in his pocket.

He passed Jesse on the lawn later that morning. The man was hurrying in the opposite direction with a pile of papers under his arm. Before he had a chance to speak, Andrew reached into his pocket and pressed the box against Jesse's stomach.

"Thank you," he said. "That's the nicest thing anyone's ever done for me."

"Are ye saying ye're too good for the McGallender arms?" Jesse asked with a grin.

"I'm definitely not too good, but I can't accept."

"Come on," the man said with a tilt of his head. "Ye're not really going to say no to this, are ye? This is yer first big Saint Clem's affair. I promise it would make me happy."

He still hadn't touched, hadn't even glanced at the box Andrew held against him.

"But then what would you wear?"

Jesse replied with a laugh,

"A *real* man wears his shirt cuffs loose and dangling."

Andrew laughed as well, but then he grabbed Jesse's free hand and placed the little box inside it.

"I can't accept really. Besides," he lied, "I already have my own."

And he strode away without another word.

"Oh, great!" Jesse cried out after him. "I bet they're nice!"

Looking over his shoulder as he walked, Andrew yelled back,

"Not as nice as yours!"

At his next lecture, he saw Cameron. The unusual intentness in the boy's eyes reminded Andrew of Jesse's expression on the lawn. It made him nervous. Had Cameron also figured out his problem? What if he also tried to help the poor scholarship kid with no cuff links? Andrew dashed out of the classroom the moment the lecture ended, without even saying hello.

To avoid running into him at lunch, Andrew packed a sandwich from the dining hall and walked down to the river. Enormous white tents had been raised all along the water. He wandered into the first tent, strolling past rows of white tables and silver chairs. The sight of the preparations, of the hidden details that none of the other guests would see—the wires running under the floorboards, the fire extinguishers under the tables—was oddly soothing. He stepped out on the other side.

He ate his sandwich on top of an outcrop of rock that rose out of the water along the bank. The babbling stream rushed from the mountains down the valley that wound past Saint Clemens, past Spring Forge, and past a hundred other places to the City and the sea. For a long time he let his gaze rest over the water, until the workers who were setting up the tents finished their lunch break and returned.

Principal Clare made one last announcement that afternoon. It was during archaeology class. Andrew and the other students were bent over their shovels in a sandbox where the professor had buried Phoenician artifacts from the school museum, "to instill a thrill of discovery." Andrew ran a sore hand over his forehead and looked up to find the principal staring over the class with a manic grin.

"My archaeologist friends," he said at last, when the last student had stopped excavating, "in just a few hours, I expect that each of you will have left the priceless treasures of past millennia for the choicest jewels of today. Festivities will begin at 7 o'clock sharp, and, as always, we will declare this year's BNC King and Queen right at the close of the event—at midnight. Please remember that you and your registered guests will need to show proper identification to attend the ball. Saint Clemens is tremendously excited to see you and your parents, for those of them who are able to make it, in your BnC finest. We cannot wait for you to dazzle us."

Andrew wondered if the reference to parents was another jab at him. He started shoveling again before the principal had left the stage. But the principal, in fact, hadn't noticed him until that moment. At once he added,

"And in the event that *any of you* has any last-minute shopping to do, I'm happy to inform you that the luxury stores in the next town over are usually open till ten."

Andrew carried on digging. The principal had almost left when the shovel of a curly-haired boy rang against the bronze of a buried bowl. The remainder of the lecture became a celebration of the breakthrough.

At last the afternoon drew to a close. Andrew was about to walk up the path that led to the gate when a voice called him back.

"Andrew, wait!"

It was Cameron again.

"You coming tonight?" the boy asked him.

"Of course!" Andrew said. "I'll see you there!" And he turned into the driveway before Cameron could say another word.

Walking down the main street of Spring Forge, Andrew thought he remembered seeing cuff links in a shop window. In the distance, he could glimpse the yellow tape that closed off the street, and beyond it the church and the trees, and the pediment of the official white building. And perhaps because his mind was so occupied with other things, the thought suddenly struck him: *Civic Square.* This was the place where something had happened, something bad, though he still didn't know what. For a moment, the notion drew him out of his head. He became aware of police officers standing along the street, one on every block, all the way from Saint Clemens. He had never seen them there before. They paid him no attention as he passed. *All part of the BnC show.*

He continued down the main street, glancing at the storefronts on both sides, peering into doorways and bay windows. He stopped in front of a small brick building on a corner. Across a weathered wooden sign over the second floor, he could make out the word *Press*, followed by the subtitle *Fine Clothing for Men.* Each of the two mannequins in the window wore a pocket square, a vest, a metal clip across his tie and a scarf around his neck, one green and the other red, the perfect colors of Christmas. He couldn't see cuff links, but this was the store he had been looking for. He went in.

There were two things the store wanted every visitor to buy: its apparel and its atmosphere. Andrew wondered if any of the oars, pennants, athletic photos and battered books that lined the brick walls were for sale. But he couldn't see the one thing he wanted. The red dragon on his blazer beckoned the sales clerk from behind the counter.

"May I help you?" she asked, leaning forward over clasped hands.

"Sure—do you have cuff links?"

"Certainly," she said, and she led him to a glass case near the register. Arrayed in orderly pairs, ten sets of cuff links stood at attention. Andrew barely looked at them. He focused only on the tiny upturned cubes that stated their prices.

"Were you looking for any style in particular?" asked the woman.

He shook his head.

"I'm just browsing."

"I'll be right here if you need me," she said before returning to the register.

Andrew stared at the glass display. The cheapest pair in the case was eighty-nine dollars. *About a hundred*, Andrew thought. It was an ugly little circle of needlepoint, stitched with the face of a bulldog. He swung his backpack around and pulled out the leather notebook and a pencil. The first page was dedicated to his name and his reward, but the next page was blank. He wrote down *100*. Then he screwed up his eyes, bit the back of the pencil, and put down another number above the first: *300*. This was the amount his scholarship provided for school supplies through the end of the semester. In his first two days of classes, he had already been asked to purchase about two hundred dollars' worth of books. He had four more subjects for which the first class hadn't met yet. And then, on top of any books that would come out of those, there would be supplies for all his schoolwork. There would be binders and rulers, colored pens and paper—maybe even a second notebook. He squinted at the two numbers on the page, trying to figure out the right arithmetic. But he already knew the answer. No calculation was needed. He simply couldn't afford to buy cuff links. He couldn't afford anything in the store. The clammy thought slid down the collar of his shirt, when someone standing behind him suddenly spoke.

"I wouldn't get those if I were you."

Andrew turned around and saw the man in black.

CHAPTER FOURTEEN

The Man in Black

The man's eyes shifted back and forth between Andrew and the glass display before settling over the cuff links.

"No," he said, shaking his head, "this set is definitely not worth your while."

Of the countless questions that whirled in Andrew's head at that moment, he uttered the simplest one.

"Why not?"

The man shrugged.

"Look at it," he said, squinting at the bulldog. "He looks so ugly, so dumb. It's just a very stupid cuff link."

Andrew looked down into the display case again. This time his eyes moved up from the price to the item itself, and he realized the man was right.

"They're..." he attempted, "they're the least expensive."

The man gave a thoughtful nod.

"I didn't think anyone at Saint Clemens knew that word."

Leaning forward, he added in a lower voice, discreetly pointing a thumb towards the register,

"*She* might disagree, but I think it can be a useful word every once in a while."

Andrew glanced back at the sales clerk. Because of his uniform, and, more importantly, the presence of the man beside him, she was compelled to smile, but he knew she was becoming impatient.

When the man spoke again, even more quietly than before, Andrew thought he caught a grin underneath his beard.

"I bet all the people who work here have read every book in this store. Twice."

Secretly cocking his head at the antlers on the wall, he added,

"They read them every night after bringing in their trophies from the hunt."

Andrew looked down at the red dragon on his own chest.

"Were you... were you at Saint Clemens, as a student?" he asked.

"I was," the man replied. He crossed his arms, staring abstractedly at the display. "I spent a few years there."

And then, with a shake of his head,

"Don't misunderstand me—I was just as spoilt as the rest of them. But there weren't that many among us who were actually *bad*. Maybe one or two."

He turned and looked at Andrew.

"How do you like it over there?"

The boy shifted from under the man's gaze. He saw that he was still holding his notebook over the display case. The numbers *300* and *100* stared back at him unhelpfully. He shoved the notebook into his backpack and zipped the bag shut.

"I've only been a student there for three days."

"Right in time for tonight's festivities then?"

Andrew made no reply. The man lay down his hands over the glass case and said,

"I don't know what your impressions are, but I wouldn't judge too quickly. Things always change—or at least the way you perceive them."

Andrew remained silent. For a few seconds the two of them stood there without speaking, their eyes idling over the display. Suddenly the man drew himself straight, his hands sliding off the glass, and he asked,

"How is your living situation?"

"I don't live on campus," Andrew answered.

The man laughed.

"Does *anyone* at Saint Clem's live on campus? Calling a set of cuff links expensive is one thing, but a Saint Clemens student actually living in a dorm? Now *that* would be something."

Andrew screwed up his eyes in thought. It struck him for the first time that he had no idea where his classmates went when he left school in the evening. He had no idea where they straggled from in the morning. He knew there were dorms scattered throughout campus. He had come across their stately towers in his travels through the school. But he had never heard their names. None of the tours on his first day had included them. No student had ever mentioned them. He felt curiously comfortable turning to the man and asking,

"Don't the other students live in dorms?"

The man's eyebrows rose.

"Students have dorm rooms, but I don't think anyone lives in them. I don't think anyone's *ever* lived in them. Back when I was a student, the rooms in the dorms were used for storage, or as guest accommodations. I guess I must have slept in mine once or twice when there was a blizzard, and a couple of times when I had early morning exams."

"So where did you live?"

The man considered.

"Different places over the years. The Charles, the Inn at Spring Forge, the Randolph, an apartment on Main Street, a shared house on the river—I'm sure the options haven't changed much. Some of the more energetic kids had lodges up in the mountains, up by..."

He paused, looked at Andrew, and turned away as he finished, "Up by the House."

A moment later, he resumed in the same offhand tone as before,

"And inevitably there were always a few students who chose to commute from the City, or from one of the other towns in the valley. They would come to school in their yachts or in their helicopters in the morning... But how is *your* living situation?" he asked again.

"It's perfect," Andrew replied, realizing that he hadn't answered the question the first time—that he had never talked about the Brandows before to anyone. "The people I'm living with might be the best two people in the whole world."

The man smiled. He said softly with a bow of his head, "Good."

Another moment passed without a word, until the man took a deep breath and propped up his fingers on the edge of the case. Once again he was tall and forbidding.

"I still don't think these are the cuff links for you," he said.

His sudden laughter startled Andrew.

"Then again," he said, "I can only watch. You're the one who has to act. But I'm sure you can find much better ones out there."

For a few minutes, for the first time since yesterday afternoon, the thought of cuff links had faded from Andrew's mind. As he remembered them, his eyes fell to the floor. The man cast a tired glance around the store.

"They do have some good things for the colder weather. It's almost time to start bundling up."

Suddenly the doorbell chimed. The man jumped. His eyes flashed with alarm. A plump woman walked in. She took a few steps and the sales clerk sprang in front of her. Andrew and the man watched the two of them, transfixed, until a quest for belts took both women deep into the second room of the shop. Still the man didn't move. Andrew turned and met his eyes. He pressed a hand on Andrew's shoulder and gave a hard, opaque smile. Then he set off towards the door. And because standing alone in the store was even more unnerving than standing there with the man, Andrew followed him out.

On the sidewalk, he turned to Andrew one more time. After a pause that was oddly long, he reached out and shook the boy's hand. Andrew felt a creeping obligation to introduce himself. But if he had to give the man his name, then at least he would give him only his first name.

"I'm Andrew."

He urged himself to tighten his hand in the man's grip.

The man dipped his head and replied,

"You can call me Elder."

Then he let go of Andrew's hand and walked away. He had gone only a few steps when he abruptly turned around and said,

"You didn't need those cuff links for *tonight*, did you?"

Andrew didn't answer, but he felt his eyebrows clench.

"Relax," the man added with a grin. "I have no intention of buying them for you. I wouldn't buy them for you if they were the only remaining set of cuff links in the world."

His expression softened. He shuddered, dug his hands into his pockets, and said,

"It really is getting cold."

As if talking to himself, he gazed at the sky and added,

"It's going to be a clear night tonight, with a full moon."

Andrew looked up, but it was too early to see the moon. The problem remained.

"Do you know where else I could go to find cuff links?" he asked.

The man stared into his eyes with no expression. Then he said,

"You said you live with other people, right?"

Andrew nodded.

"In some kind of house?"

Andrew nodded again.

"Just look in the house," the man said with a shrug. "There are always cuff links in every house."

And he was gone without another word.

CHAPTER FIFTEEN

Square One

Evening descended over Spring Forge as Andrew walked away from the main street. He recognized some of the cars streaking past him from the first day of school, only two days ago. Their headlights seemed to try to scoop him up as he went, to roll him up and waft him back to Saint Clemens where they were all headed. To him, the cars carried the fragments of another civilization across the darkness, fragments of a world that was both small and tremendous, an alliance of isolated islands in the night. He had learned enough about this world from his first few days at Saint Clemens to guess the smell inside of every car, the blend of leather and perfume that he came across wherever girls took off their jackets. It was usually accompanied by a tinkle of jaded voices and a clink of accessories. He heard the sounds in his head over the silence of the road.

He tried to picture the parents in the cars with their children. Would they look like parents from TV shows? Would they look like kings and queens in movies? Where were they coming from? How long had they traveled? He tried to picture the places where they lived, the palaces and ranches, the penthouses and castles, the garden-topped towers in the heart of the City. He tried to imagine the excitement in every car. He could feel it coursing through the engines. He could almost hear every passenger's pulse, the patter of fingernails against windows, the nervous urgency that spread down to the shoes that pressed on the gas. It was a universal excitement; he could even hear it in the trees. It murmured across their leaves and swelled the breeze in their branches. It seeped under his soles and rushed from his toes to his chest. Even though he was going in the wrong direction, going back to square one, it bubbled in his veins. The moon appeared. As the man had said, it was full, and there were no clouds in the sky.

I'll just ask Mr. Brandow. There's nothing wrong with asking—it's what people do. I'm sure he has cuff links, and I'm sure he won't care. Why should I be scared? Mr. Brandow said so himself: "Don't be afraid of anyone." He told me himself.

With each step, the words grew more secure in his head. *I'll just ask Mr. Brandow. It's no problem at all. If only every problem had such a simple solution! "There are always cuff links in every house." That's what the man in the black coat said.*

By the time he turned the corner into the street where the Brandows lived, he was so convinced he had found cuff links that he wasn't even sure he still wanted them. *What if they don't look good?* But then he chided himself. *You ungrateful jerk. Mr. Brandow's a cool, classy guy and you know it.* He opened the front door and strode into the living room.

"Mr. Brandow?" he called out. But there was no one in the room. The armchair where Mr. Brandow drank his glass of bourbon in the evening before dinner was empty. Andrew walked over to the kitchen. The lights were off. He paused. "Mrs. Brandow?" he asked. But no answer came.

"Mr. Bran—" he began, thrusting himself up the stairs, when suddenly he stopped. He slammed his hand on his forehead. He had completely forgotten—the Brandows were gone. Mrs. Brandow had mentioned it over dinner: the *back-to-school wine-and-cheese*. He mouthed the name of the event as he crumpled down over the steps. Then he stopped moving altogether. Several minutes passed before he reached for the railing again, drew himself up, and lumbered up the stairs to the second floor.

He collapsed on his bed without taking off his backpack. The weight of his books pushed his head into his pillow. He felt the warmth of his breath pooling over his face. When he turned his head towards the window, the world outside was a perfect black. He lifted himself up on his hands and sat on the edge of the bed. On the other side of the room, his reflection stared back at him from the mirror on the wardrobe. His eyes shifted around the glass. He began to look at the wardrobe itself. He stood up and took a few steps towards it. He reached for the knob of the wooden door and pulled it open.

There was a dark navy suit hanging in the corner, next to an immaculate white shirt. He had seen them there before but had never worn them. He lifted the sleeve of the shirt to his eyes. For the first time that day, he started laughing.

All this time torturing yourself over cuff links, it never occurred to you that you needed a special type of shirt. His laughter faded in a sigh. *At least you have that.* But then his eyes widened. A new idea made them glimmer. *They wouldn't have left this shirt for me unless they had also left...*

His eyes shot down to a shelf at the bottom of the wardrobe. There was a small box without a lid on the shelf, with a wad of red and navy fabric inside it. *A Saint Clemens bowtie*, he thought, as if checking off a list. He set a knee to the floor, and he peered into the shelf. At the back of the shelf, a rectangular opening had been cut out of the back of the wardrobe, revealing the wall of the room. The outline of a square was carved into the wall. But Andrew didn't see it. There was only one thing he could see: a little clasp of gold at the back of the shelf. He picked it up. When his fingers closed around it, he felt the elation surge through his arm like new blood. *Cuff links.*

No. *Cuff link.* There was only one. A single buckle of gold that was sculpted into the shape of a lion. It stretched out its paws and lifted its head like a sphinx. *One.* Andrew needed two. He held it in his hand and considered. Suddenly he remembered the hole in the back of the wardrobe. *The other cuff link must have fallen through it.*

He dropped his other knee to the floor, set the cuff link back on the shelf, laid both of his hands over the cold, grainy wood, and looked under the wardrobe. But the bottom shelf was too low. He couldn't see anything, not even with his cheek pressed against the floor. He stood up, picked the cuff link up again, and set it down on the bed. Then he closed the door of the wardrobe, clamped his hands around its corners, and pulled. Slowly, with a creak, the wardrobe swiveled away from the wall. He drew himself up again, stepped behind the wardrobe, and looked down. This time he saw it.

CHAPTER SIXTEEN

In Search of Something Lost

He stared at the bottom of the wall behind the wardrobe, his heart still battering from the effort of pulling it aside. But the seconds passed and the battering went on, and he could feel the rest of his body growing limp around it.

There was no second cuff link on the floor. There was nothing at all on the floor, except for the circles imprinted by the wardrobe's feet over the years. But Andrew's eyes were fixed on the wall. The shape of a small square was cut into the plaster over the floor, with a black metal ring in the center. It was a door. Andrew could feel the rasp of the metal ring against the palm of his hand without touching it. It was a doorknob, and it sent a tingle from his shoulder to his knuckles down to the little bones at the bases of his fingers. His muscles moved without asking him. His arm rose and pulled on the ring. The door swung open.

There was nothing behind the door, nothing but another wall just a few inches behind the first. But there was no floor underneath. The wooden floorboards of the room stopped at the door, leaving a short empty space, just wide enough for hands to reach into. Andrew lowered his fingers into this opening, gripped the edge of the floor with both hands, and pulled. The floor shifted. The floorboards underneath him were loose. He spread his feet apart, grabbed the edge of the floor once again, and pulled. The loose section of the floor came free. A hole opened beneath him. A narrow spiral staircase went down into the hole.

Andrew stared into the opening. At first, he did nothing at all, except pull on the side straps of his bag, which was still on his back. *It's only one step. Just a single step. One step at a time.*

And at any step you can turn back.

He wavered a foot over the first step, a stone ledge so narrow that it could hardly hold his shoe. The second step was a bit wider. The third step curved out further into the hole. *The other cuff link must have fallen down there.* But he knew he no longer cared. One step at a time, he began to descend.

The staircase soon closed in around him. The steps behind him became a ceiling over him. The light that came from the room grew dim and wispy. It weakened and dulled with every step that he took, until finally its paleness leveled off. Only then did Andrew realize that the light from the bedroom had stopped reaching him altogether. The only light he had now, which was only just enough to show him the next step, came not from above, but from around him, from tiny diagonal shafts dug into the wall. It also occurred to him, with the same thought, that he must have gone lower than the house itself, that the secret well of stone between the rooms of the house was now carrying him underground. Strangely, he felt relieved. It seemed to him that he could breathe better, that he could almost stretch out his arms. The rooms, the other houses, the world itself no longer crowded around the round wall of the staircase. There was no longer anything around him but stone and earth. He reached the bottom of the stairs.

He stepped out into a tunnel and brushed against a wall at his side. The wall swung behind him and fell shut. He turned around and ran his fingers over it. It was a door that had closed behind him, almost without a sound. But it had no handle.

Andrew fell back against it. He would have to find another way out. The tunnel would lead him somewhere. There was no reason to be afraid. He closed his eyes and breathed. He promised himself that he wasn't afraid. He opened his eyes again and looked around him.

The tunnel lay deep beneath the earth. On either side of him, Andrew could see broken rays of moonlight that sifted down through rocky openings in the ceiling. How far had he gone beneath the house? And how far had he gone *away* from it? Where had he gone? And where *should* he go?

He turned left. He hadn't taken a full step before he stopped again. There was a white arrow on the ground. Time had scuffed and grayed it, but it was still brighter than everything around it. The arrow pointed in the opposite direction. Andrew shrugged. *Why not?* He turned around and started walking down the tunnel.

He reached a crossroads. There was an old metal sign nailed to the wall on the other side. He raised himself on his tiptoes, screwed up his eyes, and read the inscription carved across it:

WIDENER ST

The indication meant nothing to him. He didn't know of any Widener Street in Spring Forge, or anywhere else. But there was another white arrow on the ground, and it pointed in the direction of the sign.

He nestled his chin in his hand. *Two minutes down Widener Street. And not a minute longer. Then, if you haven't found the way out, you can turn around and try the other direction. Two minutes.*

But Widener Street intersected with Storrow Lane, which cut across Johnston Street, which turned into Winthrop Drive. The white arrows kept guiding Andrew. They assured him, at every turn, that he could find his way back, that he was just a few steps away at any moment from the last arrow behind him. He kept on going. Somewhere in the tunnels, a shaft of moonlight made him stop. It shone over his whole face, so much larger than the rest that he almost shielded his eyes. He looked up into it. The shaft was obstructed with boulders and branches that hid the tunnel from above, but there was just enough space in between them to clamber up to the surface. He looked over his shoulder and crossed his arms.

No need to look behind you anymore. Now you know your way out.

The arrows would mark his way back to this shaft, which would lead him outside. His gasp of relief was as loud as laughter. But he also felt something else, something even more powerful than relief. From that moment on, he was free to explore the tunnels as far as they would take him. He filled his chest with the air that dribbled down the shaft. It was a crumbly, ragged air, thick with a powder of stone and soil. But he felt as if he were standing on top of a mountain. He turned his back on the path behind him and continued down the tunnel.

On and on he walked through the maze of tunnels beneath the roots of trees. Gradually, imperceptibly, the path sloped deeper into the earth. The air smelled wetter and tasted more bitter in his nose and mouth. It became harsher in his lungs. Tunnel after tunnel, the shafts of moonlight stretched thinner over his head. They became tatters and cobwebs of light that only layered the darkness instead of breaking it. Sometimes the air expanded, he could hear it purling in the distance, and he knew then that the space around him had widened and that he was passing through underground valleys and plains that he couldn't see. Soon he could no longer make out the words on the metal signs. He began to disregard them altogether; they were of no practical importance to him anyway. But he couldn't stop. And because he couldn't explain where he was going, or why, he stopped asking himself. On and on he went, as long as he could still glimpse the white arrows on the floor, as long as they continued to point him forward. Nothing mattered but the white arrows, and the white arrows went on. And so he kept on going, until finally he felt a soreness down the back of his right arm, and he leaned against the wall to rest. Only then did he realize that he had been walking with his right arm extended in front of him, as there was no longer enough light to see ahead. His head drooped over his chest. He lowered his hands to his knees to catch his breath.

He stared down at his feet and squinted. *Nothing.* He opened them wide and scrunched them up again. Still nothing. The floor at his feet was completely black. The wall in front of his face was also black, as were his hands and his arms, as were the ceiling and his body and the way to the left and the way to the right. Everything was black. He couldn't see anything at all. He shuddered. *The white arrows.* He could no longer see the white arrows.

He bent down to the floor for something to see, anything at all. There was nothing. His eyes showed him only shades without size, without shape, without color and in every color, shades that existed only inside of his head. Outside of it there was nothing. He looked up again and looked down again but still there was nothing. He looked left and he looked right, and this time there was no gasp left in his chest. Which way had he come? *Which way to go back?* A new sensation rose in his body that felt liquid and melted his ribs.

Something. He glanced at it, but there was nothing. He looked away.

Again, *something.* He looked again. And again he could see nothing. He looked away. It was visible only if he looked at something else—he could see it only from the corner of his eyes. But it never moved. It could run away from his stare, but he could catch it. It was still, and it was less black than the darkness. It was pale. It was a tinge of gray. It could have been white. He walked towards it. Walking sideways against the wall, groping his way along the stone with the palms of his hands, he fixed his eyes straight in front of him, at the nothingness before his face. He could spy the pale shape on the floor drawing closer, inching towards him, sliding slowly towards the soles of his shoes. At last it vanished under them. He looked down. He knew that he was standing on top of it. He stepped aside and caught it. *A white arrow.* He breathed out. For a moment he didn't move, his hands gripping the wall as if the ground might open beneath him. *A white arrow.* He was safe. He could find his way back. He began to sidle away from the arrow, still holding on to the wall, when a sudden thought made him stop. The arrow wasn't pointing ahead of him or behind, but *to the side.* He turned around.

He couldn't see the new tunnel that extended in front of him. All he could see was the end of it—not even the end—only a trace of blue light, so faint that he could have imagined it. But the trace had a direction, an angle. It came from the corner of another tunnel where there was light.

No, Andrew commanded himself. *Don't even think about it. If you keep on going the way you came, eventually you'll make it back outside. No more exploring.*

But his eyes remained fastened on the blue light.

There's light in that direction. There could be an even closer exit, a shortcut back into the stairwell...

He knew that what drew him to the blue light wasn't the hope of an exit, or a shortcut, or even the blue light itself. It was the arrow, the clear, unmistakable white arrow that he was certain lay waiting there, on the other side of that corner, though he couldn't see it from where he stood. Again, he implored himself.

Don't even think about it. He was still pleading with himself when he took the first step.

Halfway down the new tunnel, he stopped and made a promise to himself. *That's the last white arrow you go after. Even if the next arrow is made of electric blue lights flashing your name. That's the last one, understood?* And he nodded in the dark, so firmly that he was dizzy. He steadied himself and went on.

There indeed at the end of the tunnel was the white arrow he had expected, gleaming in a ray of blue light. Andrew smiled. He almost kneeled down to pat it. Then he looked in the direction the arrow showed him. He drew himself upright and rested a hand against the wall. He had reached the end of the maze.

He was standing on the threshold of a room, a large square room glowing with curls of blue light waving over the walls. The floor of the room was strewn with rocks, but its ceiling was a sheet of water. He could see the moon shimmering through it. He gaped at its light without moving. Then he understood. The ceiling was made of glass. He was standing beneath the river.

A glass pillar rose in the middle of the room. Because it was open to the river at the top, it was filled with water—a bottle of moonlight. Andrew approached it and lay a hand over the glass. He felt that he was touching the river, and he couldn't tell if it was cold or warm. Then he looked around him. Three of the room's walls were made of polished stone. But the last wall was a cliff of craggy rock, made of the same rock that lay scattered over the floor. This wall and the floor seemed to be the only remnants of an underwater cave that had been fashioned into a room. Andrew looked up again. The wall of rock didn't rise all the way to the ceiling. It came to an end a few feet below the glass. The opening at the top of the wall was the entrance into another passage that led away from the river.

Not *away from the river*, he corrected himself. The passage was meant to flow *into* the river. He could see, standing on tiptoe, that the passage was made of arching bricks. *The old sewage system. It used to flow into the river. Before it was re-routed by—*

His mind went still. He looked back again at the white arrow that pointed to this room. It was the final white arrow. He had arrived at the place where all the arrows led. He turned his eyes again towards the wall of jagged rock at the end of the room. His eyes ranged over it, assessed it, considered it. *Well, you promised not to follow another* arrow. He stepped over to the foot of the wall.

For a few seconds he tested his grip on the rock and pressed as hard as he could on his foothold. The surface of the wall was solid. He began to climb. He pulled himself up from one crag to the next, breathing the dank, gritty smell of the rock against his face, feeling the curls of the water's reflection over his back. He threw an elbow out over the crest of the wall and lifted himself to the top. He landed on his knees, and he drew himself to his feet. He could have reached out and almost touched the ceiling of glass beneath the river. But he didn't. He pulled on the side straps of his backpack and turned around.

The old sewer stretched before him. He lay a hand on the surface of curving brick. It was warm, like an enormous animal made of clay. He felt dimly that it was aware of him but couldn't speak. Again, he thought of the arrows. The arrows had led him to the room beneath the river, but the room itself was empty. The only thing he had found in the room *was a way up to the sewer.* He stared down its length. The moonlight through the glass ceiling behind him cast a feeble glow down the passage. On and on it went, as far as he could see. Where did it end? The thought kept rolling down his mind. *The arrows pointed to this.* But the sewer had been abandoned for decades. A chill blew over his back. He stiffened against it, told himself that it was the cold from the river. He would go no further down the passage.

But there was an opening to his right, a round hole in the brick wall. A slope of rugged rock, the same rock as the wall he had scaled, trailed down beyond it. He took another step and peeked into this hole. He could see nothing. He turned around and looked down the sewer again. He took another step. The ground at his feet was rubble. It shifted. He tried another step, and this time he tripped. He steadied himself by clutching the teeth of the broken wall.

"Enough is enough," he said out loud, and he flinched at the sound of his own voice. *Time to go back.* He placed one faltering foot in front of the other, swiveled himself around the edge of the hole, kicked back another foot, and slipped.

CHAPTER SEVENTEEN

Benjamin

He pitched into the hole. He tumbled down into the darkness, rolled over the stone, and landed on his stomach against a flat, hard surface.

He raised a hand to his forehead. He felt a whirling in his skull. It settled as he rubbed it. Without opening his eyes, he examined his body for pain. He felt no sensation at all except a dull, crumpling ache throughout his bones. Or was there something else? Yes, there was another sensation. It was a smell. It was a smell that he knew, a thin, acrid smell that he could recognize, though he had never noticed it before. He opened his eyes.

A familiar face greeted him. Benjamin Franklin. *Poor Richard.* The nicknames floated back through his brain. *The First American.* The Founding Father. *Benjamin Franklin.* Andrew lifted himself on his elbows. He turned over the floor. Other Benjamin Franklins. More Benjamin Franklins in every direction. He then noticed another sensation, a soft, striping press across his arms, his legs, his elbows, and his knees, hard and flat against his clothes. He jumped up and took off his shoes. For lack of a place to drop them, he kept them in his hands. The entire floor that he stood on was made of green blocks of paper lined in perfect rows and columns. On each of them was the framed image of Mr. Benjamin Franklin, looking out over the three simple words: *One Hundred Dollars.* Money. Andrew sniffed back the salty, damp, slightly acidic smell that poured into his nose. *The smell of money.* The floor that he was standing on was made of money.

He looked behind him at the slope of rocks he had fallen down. A faint light spilled over them into the room, just enough for him to see. But he was too stunned to realize that it was different from the moonlight that fell in shafts across the tunnels, that it was a quiet blue glow made by man beneath the earth. He looked down again at the floor. Each of the bills at his feet was lined with little paper bands, one on each side of Benjamin Franklin's face. He gently set his shoes down on the floor, on top of the money, and he ran his fingers over one of the bills. He let his hand slide into the space around it. His fingers dug down. When he pulled them out again, they were holding a stack of bills.

He looked up and down the room. Its surface was an unbroken plane of hundred-dollar bills, except for the hole left by the stack in his hand. He lay down the stack at his side, stood up, poised his backpack over his knee, and pulled out his notebook and pen. He opened the notebook to the second page and uncapped the pen with his teeth. There was nothing on the page except for two numbers he had written down earlier, one on top of the other: *300* and *100.* His hand paused in the air. He looked down once more over the rows and columns of bills across the room. It was then, and only then, that the reality of the wealth around him began to take shape in his mind.

He knelt over the floor again, and he peered into the gap he had just made. He reached into it a second time and pulled out another stack of money. He eyed it, turned it in his hand, thought of brushing a finger down its side like a gambler, but he worried that he might damage it somehow. He set it down on top of the first stack. He reached down again and pulled out another. Then he looked down into the hole. Again Benjamin Franklin stared back at him from the bottom, from the bottom of the well of money, watching him, observing him without focusing, without the trace of a squint, following him with his inscrutable eyes whenever Andrew moved. The stillness of those eyes struck Andrew as a challenge. He dug out a fourth stack, and a fifth one, and a sixth one. One after the other, he pulled out the packs of money, unconsciously measuring their height against the disappearance of his wrist, then his forearm, and then his entire arm into the floor. He was almost shoving his shoulder into the hole, the side of his face pushing down against the floor around it when suddenly he lurched back with a cry. His fist had slammed against something much harder than paper. The impact had struck a low, metallic ring under the floor that seemed to throb in his knuckles.

He sat back, shaking his hand, and he glanced at the piles of money he had scattered around him. The gap he had made was just a dent in the floor. He looked at the stacks he had pulled out, and he tried to gauge the number of bills in each stack. But the numbers dribbled out of his brain. Every calculation blurred and faded from his mind.

He rested his hand over his knee. What had he knocked against at the bottom of the hole? Was it the bottom of the room? Was he sitting inside of a gigantic metal vault? He stared into the hole, and his mouth fell open. The object he had struck wasn't the bottom of the room. It wasn't a continuous plane. It was separate from other objects, to its right and its left, above it and below it. And immediately Andrew knew that there were rows and columns of this new object underneath the bills, and he also knew that there were more levels of this new object underneath this new level, and more underneath those, and maybe even new levels of new types of new treasure underneath those. He forced his mind to focus, tried to fasten his thoughts on this new type of object he had hit. Andrew had seen bills before, even hundred-dollar bills, but this he had never seen. And yet he knew what it was—he had always known exactly what it would look like. It was a bar of gold, as heavy and dense, as solid and hard, as he had always imagined. And if he could only raise it out of the hole, he knew it would be just as shiny too. He let himself fall back. He could feel the money growing warm beneath him, under the seat of his pants. Then he whispered out the words, too loud to keep in his chest, almost too astounding to say out loud.

"The Surway fortune."

He folded his arms around his knees. The scale of the secret tightened his knuckles. *The lost Surway fortune.* He rocked slowly back and forth, no longer looking at the treasure. A shudder crept over his spine. Was he the only person who knew where it was? He felt short of breath, as if he couldn't fit the entire secret inside of himself. Then the chill on his back turned to ice. What if he wasn't the only person? What if *someone else knew?* What if other eyes, like Benjamin Franklin's but sentient and reasoning, had seen him—were watching him now? He lowered his face between his knees. *No.* No one else could know. No one else in the world besides him. Who could have known the secret and kept it buried all this time? Who could have known where the fortune was and left it untouched? No. He was the only one in the world. No one else had found it. No one else had claimed it. Not even Surway's own heir, that mysterious man with the unidentifiable name, that man who had never come forward, who had never been tracked, whose shadow was lost across the decades, like the shadow of Surway himself. What was his name?

Andrew became as still as a statue, as if to block himself from remembering. *No.* That man had never come. The secret was

Andrew's alone. Again, he looked out over the room. He felt that he must do something, that he must say something, as if the fortune were another person that he didn't know how to talk to. After a moment, as there was nothing else he could think of doing, he unclasped his knees and stared down again at the bar of gold in the hole. Something in the sight of it stirred the haze in his head. Forgotten corners of his mind began to wake up. The tint of the gold, the sheen of it, the shade of it, seeped into his eyes, wafted over his memory, trickled in and took form. *The lion.* The golden cuff link. Andrew sprang up. *The ball.*

He looked in front of him. His consciousness of the great wide world above the surface of the earth flooded back to him all at once. The evening wasn't over. There were still a few hours left. And he knew his way up—his way out. Another fact drifted into his mind, a vague remembrance from another age. Someone, sometime, somewhere nearby and far away, had told him something that he could almost hear again, something about luxury stores in a neighboring town that stayed open late. His eyes fell again over the floor of cash at his feet.

He knelt down and began to grab the stacks of money around him. One by one he dropped them back into the hole, as gently as he could. The first one made a resounding slap against the gold. The second one gave a fat thud on top of the first one. Little by little the pile grew back up to the original floor of the room, each pack quieter than the one before. At last there was only space left for one final stack, the first one he had dug out. Andrew looked at the small gap in the floor, picked up the last stack at his side, more money, by far, than he had ever held in his hands, more money, many times over, than he ever held to his name. He cast one final glance at the dent in the floor, wedged the stack of bills down the waist of his pants, and stood up.

Then he spoke out loud into the silence.

"Let's go get ourselves some cuff links."

CHAPTER EIGHTEEN

BnC

The card given out to every student that morning had stated that members of the staff would be available to escort the guests to the river starting at six forty-five. But the carriages had begun to line the road in front of the fountain around six. Their silver-and-navy frames, marked with red dragons and upholstered with red velvet, had been opened like jewelry boxes at five forty-five. The white horses before the carriages had been flicking the red and navy plumes on their heads since five-thirty. The drivers in white livery had worn red dragons on their chests since five o'clock, sharing a schedule with the footmen who held open the carriage doors. The fountain had begun to practice its new height—as high as the flag on the main building's balcony—around four, just a few minutes ahead of the surrounding arches of water. The carriage path across campus had been swept clean at noon. The silent security guards on each side seemed to have appeared out of nowhere. And the scintillating trees above them looked so different with their lights on that it was hard to believe they had stood there long before Saint Clemens.

But the stars of the night, both above and below, began to show themselves at seven. Their preparations shamed those of the school. Nothing could sparkle over the jewels worn by the guests. Nothing could be more elegant than the young ladies' dresses, and the bow ties of the young men. Soon the sound of horse hooves rose as high as the music. Soon conversation grew louder than both. There was much to talk about by the river, but every conversation began (and a good number ended) on the same subject: brooches. One young lady wore a ruby-encrusted parrot, another a golden octopus speckled with emeralds. One drew gazes with sapphire eyes in a peacock's feathers. Several others carried fireworks of pearl. The young men's cuff links were admired less openly. They were assessed quickly over hand-shakes and one-armed hugs. They were saluted with casual compliments that went unacknowledged. But beneath their coolness, the young men were just as anxious as the young ladies. And they fidgeted with their cuffs and they calculated their waves as they went roaming through the party.

Colorful monuments of food rose under the tents by the river. Servants carried platters of champagne for the adults and pointed disappointed students to fountains of cider, where non-alcoholic bubbles poured down pyramids of glasses. The dance floor was outside, along the water, under crystal chandeliers that floated among the trees. The music was mixed on the deck of a yacht.

Andrew came out of his carriage and gave one final tug of his jacket sleeves over his wrists. His suit felt rigid and tight. He had never worn anything so black before, as black as the night beyond the party. But he also knew, as he stood upright, that the suit was the perfect size and the perfect color, and that nothing had ever fit him so perfectly. He knew that simply by wearing these clothes he could never go back to being the person he had been only a few hours before, the person who had had no idea that tuxedos were different from black suits. But still, he was nervous. He realized with shame that he was terrified. Trying his best to feel the way he looked, he urged himself to start walking. One final thought crossed his mind. *Don't be afraid of anyone,* Dr. Brandow had told him. He pushed back his shoulders and stepped into the tent.

At first he didn't recognize anyone. *I'm sure no one can recognize me.* The thought gave him comfort. And those he passed only looked at his wrists. His hands made his first impression; the rest of him didn't seem to matter. But then, after seeing his cuffs, girls started smiling in his direction. The boys gave slight nods. A few of them frowned and turned away—they were the most flattering of all. He strolled through the tent trying to determine what *he* should look at, what he should do among those glances, when suddenly a hand slapped on his shoulder. He turned around and saw Cameron. The boy's eyes were round with excitement, and they hadn't searched for Andrew's hands yet.

"You made it!" Cameron said, and he released Andrew's shoulder to give him a handshake. He looked even more natural in his tuxedo than he did in his school uniform. His hair was brushed to the side—not quite combed over, but for once it wasn't disheveled—and Andrew wondered if perhaps the brochure-perfect polo player he saw every day was, in fact, just the sloppy version of Cameron.

"I just got here," he said with a smile, and his eyes landed on Cameron's right hand. The cuff was gleaming with an old-fashioned race car; the driver's helmet shot rays of blue light. Cameron looked at Andrew's hand in return, and his big eyes grew even wider.

"Wow," he blurted out. "These are phenomenal."

Andrew wore a bow tie of silk around his neck, and two made of diamonds on his wrists. His handshake slowing to a halt, Cameron leaned over Andrew's hand. The hand didn't move, but Andrew flinched. He had started to prepare a lie, on his way, about borrowing the cuff links—he suddenly realized that he had never settled on whom he had borrowed them from. But fortunately no one at Saint Clemens was used to thinking about how anyone got anything. When Cameron looked up again, his smile was even brighter than before.

"Come on," he said. "Olivia's over there."

"Over there" was a moving point. It was the jostling circle of boys that trailed around Olivia across the party. Andrew could make out the top of her head among the tuxedo backs bobbing around her. As Cameron approached the circle, the other boys drew back. He pulled Andrew in with him and tapped Olivia on the shoulder.

"Olivia," he yelled out. "Look what I found on my way to get drinks!"

There she was, Polo Guy's friend: Poor Girl. She wasn't wearing a brooch, or at least anything like what the other girls were wearing on their chests. Instead, some form of light was spilling over her shoulder, twinkling as she moved. Andrew couldn't explain what it was. It looked like a fringe, like the shoulder piece of a military officer, but it was entirely made of diamonds. She cocked her head, raised an eyebrow, and gave Andrew a weary smile, as if he had annoyed her for years but she had somehow decided to give him one more chance. She turned to Cameron and said,

"So does this mean no drinks?"

Aside from her dress and her jewelry, she looked exactly as she always did, which was to say perfect.

"Let me see," she said when no one replied, and she lowered her eyes to Andrew's hand.

Her second eyebrow rose alongside the first.

"Not bad," she said after a moment. Her eyes returned to his face. "Who knew? Turns out expensive things suit you."

Suddenly she gasped.

"My father's arrived!"

She turned to Cameron.

"Come! Let's go say hello."

And without another glance at Andrew, without another word to him or any of the other boys, she took Cameron's hand and loped away. Her retinue of tuxedos wheeled around her down the tent. Andrew remained where he was, wondering as always, and against his will, what he must do to make sure the two of them would talk to him again. He drifted to the nearest table when a familiar voice called his name.

"Andrew!"

"Jesse!"

Beaming, he gave the man's hand a vigorous shake.

"You look unbelievable!" he said as he scanned Jesse's costume—he wasn't sure if he could call it a suit. It had the top of a tuxedo, but no pants. Jesse was wearing a kilt, and three leather tassels dangled from a metal pouch on his belt. Greetings, side hugs, backslaps, and shoulder punches rained down on him from all sides as he stood before Andrew.

"I can't believe you were going to loan me your clan's cuff links—when you were going to wear this!" Andrew burst out.

"Now there, Mr. Day," Jesse answered, and as he raised a hand in objection, his jacket sleeve slid back to reveal the brass arrows and fist that Andrew knew already. "This is yer first BnC ball, and I get to do this every year. It would only have been fair. But there was no need to loan ye anything—ye look like the emperor of the world! And besides—"

He didn't finish his sentence. His eyes had suddenly noticed the glinting bow ties on Andrew's wrists. When he spoke again, his Scottish accent was more garbled, more burbling, than Andrew had ever heard it.

"Mr. Day" he muttered, and he gently lifted the boy's hand to his face. "These are unbelievable."

Andrew grinned sheepishly.

"Why, these are the finest cuff links I've ever seen!"

He began to nod, as if making a firm and important resolution to himself. Looking up into Andrew's eyes, he said,

"We need everyone here to see these. We need everyone here to look. I think ye might have a real chance at this, Mr. Day—a real chance with these tonight."

Andrew shook his head. His hands darted into his pockets.

"I insist, Mr. Day," Jesse went on, lightly tapping Andrew's chest. "Ye could be crowned BnC King at midnight. That wouldn't be bad for yer first week at school. I think it can be done, sir. With these here tonight it can be done."

Andrew tried to protest, until Jesse added,

"Ye don't have to do anything. Just let old Jesse McGallender take care of it. There's less than two hours to go before midnight anyway."

And as he stepped away from Andrew, he said,

"Ye'll be a scholar *and* a king, Mr. Day."

The boy laughed.

"I still think yours are nicer," he said.

Jesse smiled and disappeared into the crowd.

CHAPTER NINETEEN

A Campaign

Whether or not he had old Jesse McGallender to thank (or to blame), as Andrew wandered through the party, he noticed more and more eyes swooping down on his cuff links; and when they shifted up to his face, they seemed to have caught some of his cuff links' sparkle. The feeling these glances gave him was different from anything he had ever felt. It made him unfamiliar to himself. He stepped out of the tent onto the narrow pathway alongside the river.

All alone, he thought gratefully. He pulled down on the lapels of his jacket and straightened his back. He cocked his head, rehearsed his smile, and turned around when he suddenly fell headlong against a pair of black pants. He hit the ground with his knees. The damp stone along the water smacked his skin. A hand reached down to help him, but it drew back as Andrew was wiping his pants. When the boy looked up to apologize, the man was no longer there.

Great. Now I'm clumsy and rude.

He pulled himself up to his feet. At least his suit was fine. He could barely make out the spot where the fabric clung to his knees like cold plaster. He looked again for the man, but the pathway was empty in both directions. The cold along his legs made him shudder, and he hurried back to the party. In his haste to get back in the tent, he almost stumbled again into someone else standing by the entrance. This time, he saw the person's face. It was Principal Clare.

Of course, the man wore Saint Clemens cuff links. But he was also smoking a cigar, or at least keeping one soggy between his lips. Andrew knew that this cigar was the *C* in the principal's BnC. This was his jewel, his accessory, his chance to rise above the glittering children around him and to glow in front of their parents—or just to remind them, as he flashed his teeth at their feet, that he was also part of the party. He didn't hide his surprise at seeing Andrew. Without civility, without subtlety, he dragged his eyes down to Andrew's wrist. He took a puff of his cigar, as if to make the exertion more bearable. Then he saw the boy's cuff links.

His eyes opened wide. They flared and flamed, redder than the end of his cigar. The cigar itself drooped from his mouth, held in place only by his saliva. He looked up again at Andrew, his eyes vacant with shock. And then, something else rose inside them, a question, an indecision. Should he start being mindful of this boy? Was *this* someone to keep an eye on, to be aware of, someone to whom he should start showing respect? Andrew could almost read the doubt in those eyes. But no. Even mercenaries have their principles. Even lackeys have their pride. Andrew might have been the school's first Saint Clemens Scholar, but he was also its first nobody, and to treat a student like a nobody made the principal feel like somebody. So what if the boy had managed to wrangle some expensive accessory for one night? That didn't change who he was. The man took another puff, and his eyes dulled again behind the smoke. He gave Andrew such a disdainful sneer that his cigar almost fell out of his mouth once and for all. Then he said,

"Glad you were able to join us."

He dropped his pudgy hands into his pockets and strolled away.

Andrew followed the top of the man's head as it bent and bowed across the crowd, dipping left and right for curtseys and fake laughs. As he watched him, the muscles of his own face relaxed. His frown thawed into a smile. *Thank you,* he thought. *Now I actually want to win this thing.* He clenched his fingers over his wrists, and he pulled the cuffs down so hard that the fabric almost tore. *Rip the shirt if you have to. You won't need it after tonight.*

That moment transformed Andrew's night. He began to swagger through the party. He flashed his cuff links like cameras, as if everyone should see them, smile at them and greet them, as if they had the power to capture the night and make it live forever. He stretched out his arms across tables, over platters of food, around columns of flowers. He joined toasts he didn't understand and cheered for jokes he hadn't heard. He scratched his neck. He smoothed his hair. He stroked his chin at every turn. If there had been apples, he would have juggled. And as he dropped his cuff links like business cards, he also introduced himself. He joined conversations and entered groups. Soon, without knowing it, he was accomplishing the goal that should have been, that might have been, the entire purpose of BnC. He began to make friends.

He was surprised to discover that he could be pleasant among these people, and that they could be pleasant as well. He came to realize that their boredom and their ornaments were only fancier versions of those of every teenager he had ever known, including himself. He started forgetting that handshakes were opportunities to flourish his diamonds. He started feeling that tearing himself away from conversations was even more difficult than joining them. After about an hour, a funny notion struck him as he walked—it had taken three bow ties, one made of silk and two made of diamonds, for him, who had never worn a bow tie before, to finally feel like himself in this new place.

Smiling in secret at how timid he had been, he continued to make his way through the party, eager to talk to everyone. At one point, he felt so secure that he even ventured to the dance floor, by the edge of the water. But once he arrived there, his feet refused to go further. Not even bow ties made of diamonds could drive him *that* far.

Back inside, his eyes found Cameron and Olivia across the tent, still the closest thing he had to friends among the students of Saint Clemens. He was just about to stride over to them, and maybe even wrap an arm around Cameron's neck and plant a kiss on Olivia's cheek, when suddenly something stopped him. He couldn't take another step. The circle of her admirers had also widened (but not broken), leaving a ring of space around her for the first time. She and Cameron were talking to a middle-aged, wiry man who nodded calmly as they spoke, his hands folded in front of him. He wore a tuxedo like everyone else, but it was oddly imperfect—a little wrinkled, as if worn too often. And yet he didn't look too common for the event. Rather, it seemed that the event itself wasn't uncommon enough for him. The detachment on his face, as he stood listening to Cameron and Olivia, made him look too important for any suit and any setting. While he heard what they said to him, it was clear that he also heard other things, honors and demands that he couldn't shut out, not even on this night. "Mayor Gladys," Andrew whispered to himself, and he was surprised to discover how well he knew the man's face, from newspapers and television, and even, it appeared, from the softer features of his daughter. A woman stood next to him, majestic and tall, wrapped in a red shawl, so thin that the purse in her hand seemed to weigh down her arm. And yet the gems on her hands, around her neck and on her ears appeared to have no weight at all, enormous though they were. Her name floated back to Andrew from the folds of his memory. *Mia Renfrowe.* Cameron's mother.

The sight of Olivia's father and Cameron's mother, with the two children between them, was almost unbearably complete. Andrew had to remind himself that Cameron's father had left him and his mother, and that Olivia's mother was gone. But seeing people his age with their parents always paralyzed Andrew. Nothing made him feel more out of place than another student's family. He took a few steps back and lost himself in the crowd.

As the minutes scuttled on towards midnight, servants holding silver platters began to pass among the guests. Following the other guests' example, Andrew reached onto one of the platters and picked up a red-and-navy pen from the vase at the center and one of the white cards that were fanned out around it.

There were two columns on the card: *BnC Queen* and *BnC King.* He tipped the back of the pen into his mouth and peeked around him. A man was flitting through the crowd, leaning into groups and nodding with authority. Every few seconds, he glanced in Andrew's direction. At one point, he discreetly gave Andrew a thumbs-up down by the pocket of his kilt.

Andrew looked at his card again. In the left-hand column, he wrote *Olivia Gladys.* And on the right-hand column, without a second's hesitation, he put down *Jesse McGallender.* Then he strode over to the table at the end of the tent where the woman from the music building was collecting the votes. Andrew checked the time. It was almost midnight. He exchanged a smile with the woman, cast his card into the ballot as she crossed his name off the list, and walked away.

As far as I'm concerned, he declared to himself, crossing his hands behind him, *tonight was a success. One of the best nights of my life.* His eyes flickered as he meandered through the tent. *I can't wait to tell the Brandows.*

But the evening wasn't over yet.

Parties tend to narrow, to focus over time. Soon the night had been simplified to a single person, a single name. *Olivia.* He could hear it, he could glimpse it, he could almost smell it throughout the ball. It seemed to waft over the fragrance of the flowers. No one competed with Olivia. The fact that her jewel was the most extraordinary of the night didn't seem to matter—she could have won wearing a cabbage on her chest. By chance, she came to stand next to Andrew, and he saw in her eyes that she knew all this better than anyone else.

"They're counting the votes," she said in a tone that didn't warrant a reply.

The music by the river stopped. The last remaining dancers shuffled into the tent. Andrew noticed that the mounds of food on each table had been cleared away.

"Almost time for bed," she added with a yawn. She seemed so tired that even her followers had decided to give her some rest. Andrew turned away, to stop staring at her.

The woman at the ballot finished counting the votes, straightened the last bundle of cards in a neat stack on her table, and carefully wrote something down on a sheet of paper. Then she placed this sheet of paper into the gloved hand of a man in tails. The man carried it to a podium at the center of the tent, where Principal Clare stood waiting. Silence descended on the crowd.

CHAPTER TWENTY

Midnight

"Honored guests," the principal began, raising his head just high enough to see the audience as he bowed. "I'm very grateful that we have only a minute left before midnight, because an hour wouldn't suffice for me to thank you for your beauty, your elegance, and your gracefulness tonight. This has been an extraordinary evening, and I say to all of you, come here from near and far, on behalf of myself and the entire Saint Clemens institution, thank you."

He cast his eyes down to the piece of paper the man in tails had just given him. He looked up again, and what was most striking in his face was that it hadn't changed at all. It wasn't surprised. It wasn't joyful. It was no more animated or bright than it had been a moment before. His eyes ranged again over the audience. For once, those eyes seemed sated by the sight.

"And now," he began, and a shudder of anticipation ran through the crowd, "in just a few moments, midnight will ring on our eighty-seventh annual Saint Clemens 'Brooches and Cuff Links' Ball."

Applause erupted through the tent.

"That hour, as you know, marks both the end of our event and the crowning of this year's BnC King and Queen. In just a moment, I will ask a young lady and a young man from the beautiful assembly I see before me to put on yet another jewel, the last of the night: the BnC crown."

He trailed his hand majestically over two red-and-silver crowns resting on velvet cushions in front of him. The applause redoubled across the tent, cresting in hoots of excitement. Andrew looked beside him at Olivia, who stared at the podium with no expression. But she was no longer yawning.

Men in tails pulled open the wall of the tent behind the principal. As the towers and courtyards of the campus appeared in the distance, illuminated across the darkness, the applause rose even higher, as if given the space to stretch.

Andrew took a breath. He dropped his chin on his chest. *Am I actually nervous?* he asked himself. *Am I crazy enough to hope for this thing?* He tried to let the cries of the students around him drown out the thumping of his heart. He glanced at their faces, and he felt their exhilaration sweeping him up.

The principal extended his hand, and his Saint Clemens cuff link gave the crowd a final wink. Then he took a theatrical look at his watch and said,

"My dear guests, please join me in listening to our bell tower across the lawn for the twelve strokes of midnight. The end of our evening together comes now."

And with a precision that made Andrew wonder if the clock took its cue from the man, the first stroke of midnight suddenly pealed across the night. Immediately after, roaring over the crowd's applause, thick jets of flame shot over rooftops across the school, streaking the night with blasts of red. Andrew felt a cry of delight rasp in his throat. All around him, the cheering and the yelling threatened to rip off the roof of the tent. With every stroke of the bell, followed each time by a new burst of fire, Andrew's heart pounded harder against his chest. With every leap of the flames, his head grew lighter on his shoulders, until he felt there was nothing left of his body but a pair of hands that couldn't stop clapping. He looked up and saw the moon, full and bright, which had moved across the sky, and it was hard to believe that it was the same moon he had seen on his way back from school, the same moon he had seen everywhere in his life. The bell went on ringing, one stroke for every hour—*six, seven, eight*—until another sound broke over the clamor—*nine, ten*—the sound of the principal's voice—*eleven*—stretched to a yell:

"And this year's BnC King and Queen are..."

Twelve.

Another blast of flames shot through the night. Only this one was closer, so much closer, that Andrew felt the heat whip his face. He saw the faces around him glow red. The cry that had continuously lifted from his throat pitched to a scream. Then everyone screamed, and everyone ran.

He looked for Olivia. She was no longer there. He turned around and his saliva clotted in his throat. He felt the tips of his hands begin to tingle.

The tables in front of him were on fire. Great bulbs of flame flared in place of the flowers. The chairs around them were all empty. The principal stumbled between them groping helplessly before him. All the others in the tent were running, and their screams were even louder than their cheers had been. They ran like wild beings, grasping at one another and vaulting over chairs, and they glanced at the flames with the eyes of beasts.

But one man in a tuxedo stood still inside the tent. His right hand, raised high into the air, held a torch. There was a mask on his face, a delicate, horrible mask painted gold. The blank eyes of his mask turned to Andrew, and a coldness slithered over Andrew's body. It froze him by the edge of the fire. His mind went numb. All he could think of were the fire extinguishers that he had seen earlier that day, under the tables, which nobody would use. But then he heard his name.

"Andrew! Come with us!"

He turned around and saw Olivia being carried out of the tent under a bodyguard's arm. He sprang after them.

The air outside washed over his face. He began to see clearly again. In front of him, on the lawn, men and women ran in every direction. They shrieked as they ran. They cried out for people lost and found, people who could tell them where to go. But there were others among them. There were other men wearing masks, masks like the one Andrew had seen in the tent, and those men didn't run or call for anyone. Without screaming, without moving, those men stood among the rout, outcrops of wax and gold. They bore lifeless, sculpted faces. They wore the masks of wailing kings, laughing monks and hysterical pirates. They wore crowns and drooping hats, or gladiator helmets with no mouth holes. But they all had eyes. And they began to reach for women's heads and to tear the necklaces from their necks. They clawed the gems out of women's hair and yanked the bracelets off their wrists. They clutched at men's watches and cuff links. They gripped the girls by their throats and tore the brooches off their breasts, ripping shreds off their dresses.

Andrew remained by the entrance of the tent. He considered rushing back inside. But the fire was growing, creeping outward from every table. It twined around chandeliers, consuming their little candles. Andrew didn't move.

A blast made him look back. A cone of flames rose over the river, sending billows of packed smoke into the bluer black of the sky. He could hear shatters of glass inside the boat where the music had come from.

He caught sight of Olivia and her bodyguards. They were standing on the grass by the river. The bodyguards spoke quietly into their earpieces, muttering things Andrew couldn't hear. Olivia stared around her, the edge of her hair damp against her forehead. A word leapt out of her throat with no direction.

"Daddy!"

She had no idea where her father was.

Andrew looked down at his knees, as if to parse his own instincts. He was crouching in the grass. He straightened himself and ordered his mind to focus. The water was impassable. The tent at his side was on fire. And the masked men on the lawn were gathering closer. A few of them carried torches. One of the men wore the mask of a frowning Caesar. Andrew couldn't see his eyes, but all of a sudden he knew they had noticed something. The man paused almost imperceptibly. The golden laurels over his face tilted by a fraction of a degree in Olivia's direction. Across the shadows and the rays of the flames, he had seen the diamonds on her shoulder. He began to quicken his pace. His haste spread to the men around him. They turned to him and followed his stare, and every one of them saw Olivia.

Low to the ground by the burning tent, Andrew knew no one had noticed him. He commanded himself to be still.

The bodyguards around Olivia bent their knees. They drew together in a backward huddle, closing their circle around her. Then they stopped moving. Everything was still around them, everything except for a mace topped with a ball of spikes that the man in the Caesar mask carried. He rammed it down over the head of one of Olivia's bodyguards. The bodyguard ducked, hooked his leg behind the man's knee, and toppled him to the ground. But another man leapt over the first man's body. Blades jutting out of his glove sliced the air. Olivia screamed. The bodyguards in front of her charged forward as the golden faces descended upon them.

But one of the bodyguards didn't fight. He clutched Olivia in the crook of his arm. Without a sound, he carried her alongside the water. Suddenly he stopped, threw his head back, and almost fell. The sound of Olivia's scream made him firm again on his legs. The man in the Caesar mask had stood up. He had hurled his mace at the bodyguard's face. The bodyguard ran a hand over his forehead, over the tips of his eyebrows, and looked at his fingers. Andrew couldn't see if there was blood. The man gently unrolled Olivia from his clasp, pulled her softly behind him with the same movement, and dug his heels into the wet grass in front of her. He fixed his eyes into the hollow stare before him. The man in the golden mask picked up a torch. He waved it once, and the bodyguard gave a twitch. He waved it again, and the bodyguard made no movement. But the third time, the man in the mask spun the torch sideways, away from the bodyguard, reaching as far back as his arm would go, and then, with a force that seemed to twist the mask itself, he thrust it against the side of the bodyguard's head. The head gave a plunk and a splatter of blood before the bodyguard collapsed to the ground. The man in the mask cast his empty eyes over the man lying on the grass, looked up again, and saw Olivia quivering alone against the edge of the river. Her face was glowing in the light of his torch, and diamonds showered down the slope of her shoulder.

CHAPTER TWENTY-ONE

Flames in the Dark

Andrew crouched by the entrance of the burning tent without moving. There was no air. There was no time. He knew that his only asset was the clarity in his mind.

No one had noticed him yet. But there was nowhere he could go without being seen. There was only the tent behind him. He heard the rumble of the fire. He breathed in the wood of the burning tables. He knew there could be no one left inside. But the fire still hadn't reached the wall of fabric.

He kept his eyes on Olivia, and he saw the man in the mask leaning into her face. Andrew's body bypassed his thoughts. He dashed into the tent and grabbed something. Only when he smashed it over the head of the man in the mask did he recognize that it was a chair, and that his hand stung from the heat. The man toppled to the ground. All Andrew could think was that the man's hands were uncovered—they were the only uncovered part of his body. And they were normal hands, the hands of a person, harmless, at rest, with skin just like Andrew's, and even their own set of cuff links. Andrew looked up, and he saw the other men in masks fighting Olivia's bodyguards. There was nowhere to run. The boat on the water was sinking, and the sight of the slanting, blazing hull horrified him more than anything he had seen. He turned to Olivia and took her hand. Then he leapt with her into the tent.

The heat throbbed against his eardrums. It pricked his eyes and the back of his throat. He felt his stomach melting. He glanced at Olivia. The only indication of fear on her face was a slight crease of her eyebrows, as if she were watching bad weather in the distance. He thanked her in his head for being calm. He squeezed his fingers around her hand and looked around him. A few steps from where they stood, a flaming tablecloth swayed manically like a pendulum in the draft. Andrew lunged for it and pulled. The cloth swept off the table and tumbled in a sheaf of sparks. The heat smoked off the plastic surface of the table and floated away. He looked over his shoulder at Olivia.

"Come on!" he shouted, and he pulled her behind him. The two of them vaulted over the table, and she jumped down on the other side to an opening that faced the lawn. But an odd sensation held Andrew back. He slipped and fell over the table. His first movement, before getting up, was to look over his shoulder. A man in a golden mask stood inside the tent. He had come in behind them. His mask was a howl of laughter below the miter of a bishop. He held something long and thick in his hand with a sharp projection at the end like a hammer. He lifted it to the fire, and it lit. Andrew was paralyzed.

"Andrew!" cried Olivia.

But he couldn't move, lying on his back over the table. The laughing bishop stepped forward and strode onto the table. He stood over Andrew. The laughter on his mask seemed to melt into a real smile. He pulled back his arm, and the burning spike of the hammer disappeared behind his body. Then he swung the hammer down. Andrew reached under the table and hurled the fire extinguisher against the spike. The explosion blasted him to the ground.

The man was no longer on the table when Andrew looked up. He couldn't see the ground on the other side. He slapped a hand over his chest to steady his cough. Olivia reached down for his hand and pulled him up, and the two of them ran out of the tent.

"This way!" she whispered.

They slipped into the shadow of a tall, wide edifice on the edge of the lawn. They crouched behind a hedge and scurried to the end of a stone path alongside the building. Vaulted windows behind them showed a soundless world of books, undisturbed and endless. Andrew peered out through an opening in the hedge.

He stared at the burning tent. He looked for the laughing bishop. But no one came behind them. Fire flickered in the distance, over treetops and rooftops. Horses crossed the lawn, no less terrified, no less lost than the people they had carried. They raced without their riders, flopping their red-and-navy plumes, searching for a land of silk and diamonds that had burst into flames. The last masked man that Andrew and Olivia saw had the beard of a Greek god. Standing at the front of a carriage, a golden trident in his hand, he tore across the lawn and disappeared into the darkness. Then the lawn was silent.

Andrew turned to Olivia, and he saw the empty fabric over her shoulder.

"Did he take your..."

He didn't know what to call her jewelry. He hardly knew what to say at all.

She turned around, reached into her pocket, and pulled out a fistful of diamonds like a pile of beans in her hand.

"*Of course* not," she said. She wasn't whispering anymore. "I had to take it off."

He couldn't tell whether she was smiling when she added,

"I certainly know a thing or two about drawing attention to myself."

He turned again towards the lawn. For a few minutes, the two of them stared out into the night without speaking. Then he remembered a question that had bobbed around his head for the past few days.

"Is this what happened in Civic Square?" he asked without looking at her.

"On Surway Day this year?"

Her eyes remained fixed on the grass beyond the hedge.

"Yes," she said. "They were men in crazy costumes, carrying firebrands and weird, ancient weapons. They torched the square in front of the courthouse, right in the middle of the day. They burnt down the courthouse, too. And then they disappeared. The police never caught them. No one knows where they came from. I wasn't there. I wasn't even at Saint Clem's yet. Nothing like that had ever happened on campus."

Andrew could feel the tightness in her breath beside him. Distant sirens began to blare across the silence.

Suddenly she said,

"Last time, when this happened, there was also a message—words that followed."

Andrew looked at her, bewildered.

"A plane flew a message in the air after they were gone," she explained.

Andrew was just about to ask her what it was when abruptly she added,

"They also didn't attack people last time. They started the fire and ran away, but they never laid a hand on anyone. There were a few injuries in the commotion, from people trampling one another to get away."

She cocked her head in the dark.

"It was just really bad luck for those people."

Andrew said nothing. He looked away across the lawn. He could hear her watching alongside him. He could hear the unspeakable, unthinkable question inside her. The words slipped out of his mouth.

"I'm sure your dad's all right. We would have seen him if he'd stayed behind."

She made no reply and continued to stare through the gap in the hedge. The siren drew nearer. It multiplied in different directions. Andrew realized that he was cold, and the forgotten sensation reassured him. He let the feeling wrap around him like a raspy blanket. He heard a movement at his side, and he turned to find Olivia's big eyes fixed on him.

"I voted for you as BnC King, you know," she said. "I thought you had the best cuff links of the night."

Andrew felt a flush hotter than any flame on the lawn. He knew what he must say, but it sounded too obvious. She already knew what he would answer. But then she spoke again:

"Don't tell Cameron."

She was smiling when she added,

"I'll tell him myself."

She chose precisely the moment when he chuckled, when his head was bent down, to say,

"And thank you for rescuing me."

He looked up again and met her eyes. Only then, when he had nothing else to say, and he knew that the only alternative was silence and that nothing he said could be worse, he replied,

"I voted for you too."

She didn't thank him. She didn't look at him or pretend to be surprised. She didn't even pretend to be flattered. She only turned away and said, returning one obvious fact for another,

"I know. So did I."

One o'clock came. The bell tower that had rung the twelve strokes of midnight rang once. A drizzle began to fall. Perhaps it had already been falling for some time. It wasn't enough to wet them, but it made the air colder. Andrew started shivering inside the stiffness of his suit. The lawn in front of them was deserted.

CHAPTER TWENTY-TWO

The Words That Followed

All at once, Olivia stood up. Her face was bright in the moon-light. "Daddy!" she called out, and she reached out for Andrew's hand without looking. She pulled him up from the ground. The two of them ran down the stone path. Their hands parted as they raced past the library and onto the lawn.

A group of people walking across the grass stopped and turned around.

"Olivia," Mayor Gladys cried as she dove into his arms. A groan choked in his throat. His grip fastened around her and he pressed a hand on top of her hair, and then he lifted her into the air. The formidable Olivia Gladys rose several feet off the ground, where he held her for a few seconds. He dropped her back on the grass and looked into her eyes.

"Are you all right, my darling? Are you hurt anywhere?"

"No," she replied, shaking her head. "I'm all right."

She clenched her arms around his neck. He gently brought her hands down in front of him, and, without letting them go, he turned around to the men behind him.

"Olivia, my darling, I want you to take a good look at a hero here tonight, at a man who almost gave his life trying to protect you."

He stepped aside to reveal the bodyguard who had tried to save her, and who had been clubbed by the man in the Caesar mask. The bodyguard's forehead was wrapped in a bandage that was stained with blood above his left ear. His left cheek was swollen, pushing his left eye shut. But the tip of a smile tried to climb over the swelling, and the one eye he could open shone for both.

"Roger!" she cried out, dropping a kiss on his cheek before clasping her arms around him. "Thank you," she whispered, her voice muffled against his shoulder. A woman stepped around him and draped a red scarf over Olivia. The girl turned around and her eyes opened wider.

"Aunt Mia!" she gasped, and she took the woman's hands in her own. "I'm so glad you're all safe."

There was a flash in her eyes.

"Where's Cameron?" she asked. "Is he all right?"

The woman raised a knuckle to her eyes as she answered,

"He's all right, my darling. He's safe, back in town. He wanted to stay and look for you but I urged him to go."

Olivia threw her arms around the woman, who almost fell back. Then she squeezed the woman's hand, turned around, and said,

"There's another hero here, someone who rescued me and took me to safety. His name is Andrew Day, and he's my classmate. He may have saved my life tonight."

Everyone turned to Andrew. No one had noticed him before. Even Andrew had forgotten himself. Olivia's father strode over to him and clapped a hand on his shoulder. Andrew's first emotion was relief—he was still wearing his tuxedo and his diamond cuff links. But the mayor paid no attention to what he wore. Instead, he gave Andrew the firmest, slowest handshake the boy had ever received. And then, still gripping his shoulder, gazing deeply into his eyes, the mayor said,

"Andrew Day, I've never said these words to anyone the way I'm saying them to you. Thank you. From the bottom of my heart. If there's ever anything I can do for you, anything at all, consider it done. I owe you everything I have. Olivia is everything I have."

His hard, steadfast voice, so secure that it seemed to raise a daylight of its own in the night, gave a crack. From the corner of his eyes, Andrew saw Cameron's mother smiling. The mayor released his hand, nodded and turned around, his hand still clamped on Andrew's shoulder.

"Principal Clare," he said "from now on there are *three* children I want you to think of as my responsibility. You will be personally accountable to me for their safety and well-being for the duration of their stay at Saint Clemens. Two of them are Cameron and Olivia, as you already know. And the third is Mr. Andrew Day."

The principal's face poked out between the shoulders of the bodyguards. Traces of his obsequiousness still twitched beneath his fear, like a worm that has survived a shoe. His eyes obediently shifted to Andrew. But there they narrowed. Somehow color returned to his face. The boy understood then that neither the terror of the attack, nor Olivia's rescue, nor even the mayor's authority, could overcome the loathing the principal felt towards him. The man was only able to mutter,

"Well done, Mr. Day. Thank you for Olivia's safety."

Andrew knew this might be his only opportunity to ask the principal a question.

"Do you know if Jesse is all right?" he asked.

The man gave a smirk, the only smile he had left.

"Mr. McGallender's safe and accounted for," he said with a dip of his head. By the time he had finished the sentence, he was done looking at Andrew.

All of a sudden, the mayor's anger burst.

"I still don't understand how this could happen! Wasn't the ball supposed to be heavily guarded? Didn't you assure all of us that security would be tighter than it's ever been?"

The principal lowered his gaze and bumbled a few unintelligible words. When he was able to pick up his thoughts, as well as his eyes, he looked up and said,

"We had everyone's identification checked at the campus gate, and then again at the fountain. No one could have entered without showing proper identification."

"Then who were those people?" the mayor shouted. "They were all on the guest list I suppose? Who checked their identifications?"

"It was the Spring Forge police force, Mr. Mayor," the principal said. The blame on his shoulders smothered his breathing. "Those men must have gotten past them somehow, entered the party, and hidden their weapons and their masks until midnight. Once inside the school grounds, they wouldn't have been differentiable from guests. We were working closely with the Spring Forge police to ensure the security of the event."

"A fine job you all did," the Mayor said.

The principal hesitated, casting glances around him.

"We need to take this up with the Spring Forge police department," he said at last. "The school wasn't responsible for—"

"*You* are responsible," Cameron's mother broke in, her voice a wedge of glass. "For everything that happens here. Responsible for all our children. That is the one thing here tonight that *is* clear."

The principal lowered his head again.

"Mrs. Renfrowe..." he mumbled, and was silent.

He didn't move until she lifted her chin and turned her eyes towards Mayor Gladys. Then the mayor said,

"Evidently something went terribly wrong here tonight, something that has to do with the safety of our children. We've entrusted their safety to you, and that is the most precious thing that any of us could ever entrust to anyone else in the world. Mark my words, Principal Clare, Saint Clem's is what it is because of people like us sending our children to you. And if we don't feel that they are safe here, if we don't feel that you're taking proper care of them, then no amount of prestige or tradition or fancy amenities is going to keep this school afloat. Understand?"

"Yes, Mr. Mayor."

"Now," the mayor said, "it's obvious that there's a gross lack of competence within the local police department. But it's not my job to babysit whoever's in charge of this town. I have a major city to run."

At these words, Andrew, who had never met the mayor before, who had never even seen the City itself outside of movies, felt a swell of pride in his chest. He felt it as well in Olivia beside him.

"So you leave me no choice," the mayor went on, "but to station bodyguards from my personal staff to keep an eye on this campus at all times. And on the village, too. This is what I need to do to protect our children."

Olivia frowned. She must have felt all this time that some annoyance was bound to come of this night. No one knew what the principal's face showed. The man had never been so close to touching his toes. Then came the mayor's final words.

"As both an elected official and a father," he said, "you make me sick."

The lawn was silent. The air was so still that Andrew could hear the clouds begin to roll off the valley. He looked around him. The drizzle had stopped, and a cold wind blew open buds of ash. Moonlight broke the darkness. Olivia took her father's hand. Andrew felt a hand on his shoulder, looked up, and saw the beautiful face of Cameron's mother smiling at him. She didn't remove her hand as the two of them started walking behind the mayor and his daughter. Gradually the rumble in the sky, moving away, turned back. It grew more distinct, grew louder, took form and gained force as it drew closer over their heads. By the time they looked up, they all knew it was a plane.

It was a small, single-passenger plane, a shard of metal against the black sky. It cast a light on the words that followed, fluttering in the wind:

I WILL NEVER STOP UNTIL THE SURWAY FORTUNE IS MINE

CHAPTER TWENTY-THREE

Stories Told and Untold

Parents tell bedtime stories; journalists save them for the morning. Spring Forge awoke to reports of the *BnC Ball Blast-Up*; of the *Situation at Saint Clemens*; of the *Midnight Masquerade*. Young and old were consternated. The shopkeepers were shocked. The denizens were in delirium. Within minutes the furor spread to the towns around Spring Forge. The flames of disaster look like spotlights from a distance; soon the entire valley was abuzz. Some were downright delighted to see mention of a neighboring town in the news. By lunch time, across the country, just to know someone in Spring Forge had become once again a boast. The story, of course, was heard in the City. It wasn't even necessary to open the *Metropolitan Times* (or, more precisely, to flip it over and read the bottom fold of the front page) to learn of the strange, savage assault on the illustrious school down the river.

Some told the story more factually than others. Some people made it their own, expanded it, abridged it, and turned it into a thriller, a fable, or a farce. Some wailed, "Is there nowhere safe left in the world?" Others cried, "Do the police do nothing all day besides eating donuts?" Others yet declaimed, "This is a story of corruption that goes all the way to the top!" And others, still nearer the truth, mumbled, "The only thing we know for sure is that this is not the end of the story." And they were content to leave it at that.

But although there were as many different stories as there were people to tell them, every story ended with a question. For some, it was: how come the men were never caught, neither this time nor during the Civic Square attack? Others wondered: were the attacks related to the unsolved break-ins at Surway House? But one question inspired the most conspiracy theories by far: who was behind the attacks? Who was it who had twice written the same message in the sky—who had vowed never to stop *until the Surway fortune was mine*? It had to be someone powerful, someone important. It had to be someone with enough money to produce such madness. Was it someone famous that nobody suspected? Was it someone respectable and secretly insane? Soon the questions returned, once more, to the oldest question of all: what had happened to the Surway fortune? Some offered answers, but the questions never ended. By dinner time, every house within fifty miles of Saint Clemens could talk of nothing else—except for Surway House, where not a single word was heard.

Andrew returned to the Brandow house that night to find Mrs. Brandow sitting on the floor of the foyer. As soon as he opened the door, she rushed over to him and locked his neck in her arms. It took him a few seconds to understand why her face had looked so strange—she had been crying for some time. She kept his head in one arm as she closed the door behind him. Mr. Brandow's face, when he came in from outside a few minutes later, was even more haggard than his wife's. He was stuck on the threshold, dazed in the rectangle of the doorframe. There was a helplessness in his eyes that Andrew didn't know they were capable of. At last, Mrs. Brandow stepped over to her husband's shoulder and wrapped her arms around him. But he continued to stare at Andrew. Then he mumbled in a tone that would have sounded weak for any man, let alone Professor Brandow,

"I went looking for you."

Slowly he started to smile.

Andrew wanted to run up to their side. He wanted to enfold his arms around them and dig his head in between theirs. But his body wouldn't move. And in the end it made no difference. He read in Mr. Brandow's eyes that there was no need to do anything. The stillness of the house wrapped itself around them. The lamp wasn't used to shedding light over two o'clock in the morning, and it peeped into the darkness of the living room next door. Andrew wished he could have stayed there for hours, watching Mr. and Mrs. Brandow in each other's arms while the rest of the house and the world were asleep. But it was time for bed.

Once he was alone in the yellow bedroom, Andrew didn't change out of his clothes. He didn't dive into the pillow. Instead, he sat down on the bed. There were too many things to think about, and none of them would let him go. Was this what family felt like? And danger? And loyalty? He didn't know.

But there was also the other side of the night, before the attack, before the ball itself. There was the black and kaleidoscopic journey, straight and mazelike, below the earth. Andrew urged himself not to think about it, but he knew he couldn't stop. He knew he could never forget it, not if he lived another hundred years. He tried desperately to think of something else, but his mind kept being dragged back to the cave, as if something down there had tethered it. The memory was like a dream, a nightmare, and a hallucination all at once. He didn't dare to look at the wardrobe. He knew that it was standing there, causing no trouble where it stood. And yet he couldn't look at it. He felt that he would lose his mind if he did. His eyes fell over the clothes he was still wearing. He should take his suit off. It was a stroke of luck—

and a miracle—that the Brandows hadn't noticed it. But then he thought of the cuff links in his pockets. He couldn't touch them. He was too afraid. He thought the diamond bowties might knot themselves around his fingers.

But he couldn't be afraid forever. Nothing was broken that he couldn't fix. He would figure it all out tomorrow. All he had to do now was take off his fancy clothes, which were nothing, after all, but clothes. All he had to do was take them off and hang them up. It would take him just a few seconds to hang them up in the wardrobe. Then he would put the cuff links back in their case, and he would leave the case on the shelf below the suit. He would shut the wardrobe and go to bed, and tomorrow he would figure it all out. This was his plan, and he set to it immediately.

The wardrobe was hidden behind the open door of the bedroom. It wasn't until he had pulled the door shut that he realized the wardrobe was turned away from the wall as he had left it, and the hole in the floor was still open. The thought that the Brandows could have seen the hole, if they had only looked behind the door, was too much for him to face. He pushed the wardrobe back against the wall.

By the time he was lying between the sheets in his pajamas, he felt that everything was in its proper place. But what he hadn't figured on was that anything can happen when the lights are out. Wardrobes can open by themselves. Secret doors can spring out of the ground. When you can't see anything, the entire universe is an endless hole. And silence can sound like shrieking tuxedoes and howling tunnels. He didn't sleep a minute.

The next day was Saturday, one of those perfect Saturdays where there is nothing to do but nestle against cushions and sip tea, where unfolding a heavy blanket is labor enough for the whole day. There were two circumstances on that perfect Saturday for which Andrew was particularly grateful. The first was that it rained all day, one of those draping autumn rains that make every house feel like a treehouse. The second was that the Brandows didn't push him to talk about last night. They would wait until he was ready. All day they smiled and spoke softly. Over breakfast, they resumed their gentle joking. They asked him simple, inconsequential things, such as what he might like for lunch, or whether he might want to watch a movie. And as breakfast dragged into lunch, poked into dessert, and curled into tea time, they made no reference to the ball.

At last, as he was blowing over a cup of hot chocolate, peering down into the ripples under his nose, Andrew heard Mr. Brandow crack the newspaper in his hands. The sound nudged him and he said,

"Thank you so much for waiting up for me last night." His eyes darted from Mrs. Brandow looking up from her book to Mr. Brandow peeking out from behind his paper.

The statement was meaningless, and they all knew it, but it was the opening they needed. Mrs. Brandow closed her book, Mr. Brandow folded his paper, and Andrew started talking. He began in the red velvet seat of the carriage that had driven him from the front of the campus down to the river. He told them about his nervousness upon entering the tent and his joy when Cameron found him. He described to them the crunch of the chocolate crystals and the fragrance of the edible flowers. He told them about the fountains of cider and the mountains of berries, about the hovering chandeliers and the dance floor by the water. He described his conversations and the new acquaintances he made. The Brandows laughed with him as they listened, and they quietly marveled at the things he had seen. They tried to recognize celebrities among his memories, speculating about faces he couldn't name. At last, his account reached midnight. All three of them had almost forgotten the attack. The masked men made

Mrs. Brandow gasp. She slapped her mouth when he escaped through the burning tent. Mr. Brandow pounded a fist over his head when Andrew ran across the lawn with Olivia. But it was Mrs. Brandow who broke into applause when Andrew related the principal's humiliation ("I run into him sometimes at the pharmacy," she chimed in with a grimace). And she bit her lip in amazement when the mayor shook Andrew's hand—Mr. Brandow gave him a high five. She bit her lip once again and exchanged a glance with her husband before lowering her eyes to her cup of tea, when Andrew spoke of Olivia's gratitude. His chronicle came to an end, an end that all three of them knew, which had taken place just a few steps away in the foyer of the house. There was only one thing he never mentioned: the set of diamond cuff links he had worn.

Suddenly, Mrs. Brandow struck her cup down on the table.

"It just occurred to me—did you find everything you needed for last night in the wardrobe?"

Andrew swallowed and looked down. His hands withdrew underneath the table.

"Yes," he muttered.

"I wish I'd remembered to ask you beforehand!"

"It's all right," he said, "I had everything I needed."

"That's an understatement," Mr. Brandow broke in. "The boy looked like a movie star when he came back!"

Andrew smiled weakly.

"The thought of cuff links never even crossed my mind," Mrs. Brandow went on. "If only I'd had my wits about me, we could have shown you what Paul has, just to give you some options."

Mr. Brandow nodded.

"I was all set," Andrew replied. He would have traded his hands themselves for a voice that sounded natural. "There was a set of Saint Clemens cuff links in the wardrobe. They were perfect."

They were all silent. Andrew was certain that Mr. and Mrs. Brandow were curious. They wanted to see the cuff links. They were wondering what he had worn. They would ask him to go bring them down. But there were no Saint Clemens cuff links. There was a golden lion, by itself, in the wardrobe. And then there were diamond cuff links that cost more than a car. He would have to tell them everything—the diamond cuff links he had bought; the money he had spent; the treasure he had found. The silence continued. It expanded through the room. He kept his eyes fixed on his cup, his stomach clenched so tightly, his heart beating so hard, that he thought he was going to throw up. Then Mr. Brandow spoke.

"It's all right."

Andrew met Mr. Brandow's eyes, and he knew the danger had passed. Mr. Brandow raised his cup of coffee to his lips and said,

"I bet yours were cooler."

In the barely perceptible grin that lifted the corner of his mouth as he took a sip, Andrew knew he didn't mean it.

The hours went by, the rain went on falling, the gray light of day folded and shifted inside the house, and still Andrew kept his secret. And maybe because the Brandows had set such an easy example of leaving heavy topics aside, Andrew gradually stopped bringing it up to himself. He had made a vow to himself from the very beginning, even before he had left the cave. He would tell no one what he had found. The message in the sky over Saint Clemens had reinforced his decision. This was a secret that men were willing to fight for, to burn for—perhaps to kill for. The magnitude of his secret, the scale of it and the depth of it were more than he could conceive. He stopped thinking about it altogether.

He had never before had occasion to learn that secrets, like all stories, have lives of their own.

CHAPTER TWENTY-FOUR

A Delivery

Sunday morning was no sunnier than Saturday, but the rain had stopped. The day rose fresh and fragrant. The sky wouldn't pour another drop over the valley, so that all those who lived there could come out and see the glistening world it had cleaned for them. Andrew and the Brandows went to the farmers' market to buy lunch. They saw a sliver of sunlight edging out from behind the clouds, and they decided to have a picnic in the mountains. They ate alongside a spring. The water was so bright and brisk that Andrew rolled up his pants and dangled his feet as he ate. By the time lunch was over, the sun was shining over the valley, and it dabbed off the drops of water on his shirt.

Andrew hadn't thought of his secret all day. But forces can move deep in the mind, as in the ocean, without making a ripple on the surface. The moment the three of them came back to the house, he walked up the stairs, opened the door of the yellow bedroom, and made an announcement to himself. He was going to return the cuff links. He would return the suit as well, and the bow tie, and the shoes. He would get the money back. By chance—by magic—none of Friday night's handshakes, cupcakes and flames had damaged anything he had worn. The only money he would lose would be the cab fares. He would have to make up for that from his stipend. But he would return what he had taken. He would put the money back in the floor of the cave. He would leave it behind once and for all. And he would never tell anyone what he had done. He had never set out to find the fortune, and he would never go searching for it again.

His plan was settled. It was the right thing to do, the only sensible course of action. Or was it? Wasn't there something else he could do? Wasn't there something else he should at least consider? He could go to the police. He could tell the police everything. It wasn't too late. He could still go. He could explain to the police that he had found the fortune by accident, that he had discovered a hidden stairwell when he had been looking for a missing cuff link. No one would blame him. It wasn't too late. This could have been his best idea, his first idea, his only idea. And yet he hadn't thought of it. And as he thought about it now, he knew he would never do it. Why not? He wasn't a natural liar. He wasn't a deceiver, a boy with secrets. He had never had anything to hide from the police. But he had taken the money from the cave. He had taken it without asking, without thinking, without hesitating, all to look impressive for a few hours, in front of people he didn't know. Were people who did such things instinctively afraid of the police?

He wouldn't tell anyone, but at least he would return what he had taken. He would make it all right again. If anyone at school were to ask, he would say that he had borrowed the cuff links from a relative, from a friend, from a man in a black coat in a shop. He didn't need the diamond cuff links. He didn't need the money. He had never needed any of it before. He would leave it all just as he had found it. It was none of his business anyway. Clearly there were powerful forces at work, dark and dangerous forces that played with fire and wore masks. Perhaps the police themselves were involved, perhaps the town, perhaps the state, the government. Why throw himself into the line of fire? He had never meant to do anything wrong. No, he wouldn't tell anyone. If he went to the police, he would commit himself forever to their files and their folders, and to whatever maneuvers went on behind their doors. And he would never get out. And then there was something else.

If he went to the authorities, then the Brandows would be involved. He was certain that they knew nothing about the stairwell beneath the wardrobe, but it was hidden nonetheless inside the house where they lived. The house had been built long before they had moved into it. They had chosen it only because it could give them the chance to fulfill their only dream, the biggest wish in their lives: to have a child in their home, to take care of a child like Andrew. If he went to the police, then suspicion, danger and crime would come crashing into their home, through the door they had opened for him. No. He couldn't repay them like this, not within a few days of meeting them—not as long as he lived. It was for their sake as well as his own that he would stay away from the police. He would return the money. It was decided. But he wouldn't do anything else. The silence, the stillness and darkness would fall back once more over the mystery of the Surway fortune, where they had remained for so long.

He would have to go back to the cave on a school day. The Brandows would be at work. He would have to find his way in and out through the opening in the forest, the one that had led him out on the night of the ball. He had clambered his way up the light shaft to a hole in the soil, just a few trees away from the side of the road. He had scrambled out of the ground, drawn himself upright, and slapped the dust and the leaves from his clothes and his hair. Then he had stopped and looked around him. Only when he was sure that he could find the exact spot again had he stepped out of the woods. He had walked down the road. There was an intersection nearby, with a gas station and a diner. He had asked for a phone to call a taxi, and the gas station had pointed him to the diner. He had peered into the eyes of the men in the gas station, the woman in the diner, and the cab driver who had picked him up. He had wondered if any of them knew that just a bit further up the road, just a few trees from the road, lay the entrance of a tunnel to the biggest treasure in the world. But none of them knew.

There was no school on Monday. All weekend long, the news on television covered the attack, unveiling new details every hour. But the two most important updates were given early and never changed: no one had been killed, and all the attackers had escaped. Nobody knew who was behind them. But there was one more question that occupied Andrew more than all the others, and the answer was given to the Brandows over the phone. Classes would resume on Tuesday, even though much of the campus was under repair. Andrew stayed in the house all of Monday. The Brandows only went to work after lunch. Not once did it occur to him to peek into the hole in the floor or even glance behind the wardrobe when they were gone. He would return the money on Tuesday. And then he would carry on with his life.

But something did happen that Monday. Andrew didn't know about it, and nobody could have told him. A few dozen miles away, dozens of miles from the yellow bedroom, from the wardrobe, from the stairway under the house and from the tunnel under the earth, in the middle of the City, someone walked into the lobby of the *Metropolitan Times* headquarters (in a building named, in fact, the Metropolitan Times Building). This person wore gloves. It was an early autumn morning, but few people would have found the weather cold enough for gloves. And yet nobody took notice of this person. The woman at the security desk was overly busy. Once she was able to put down her phone

to find out who had momentarily cast a shadow over her notebook, the person was gone. But there was a thin letter-sized envelope on the marble counter in front of her. There was no
stamp on the envelope—it had been delivered by hand (or by
glove). There was no return address either. There was nothing at
all on the envelope except for a small white label in front. The
following address was printed over it:

To Mr. Gerald Watches
Managing Editor
The Metropolitan Times
- URGENT -

The woman barely raised an eyebrow when she read the label.
Urgent letters flooded her desk at every hour of every day for
every editor in the newspaper. Few of them, it's true, were addressed directly to Mr. Watches, but almost none of them ever
contained anything that was actually urgent. She looked again
across the lobby, and she only saw the usual scuttle of journalists
between cups of coffee at their desks and cups of coffee outside.
And so, without another look, she tossed the envelope into the
metal basket marked *Editorial Floor* (whose designation had in
fact been inaccurate for several decades, the editorial staff having
grown over the years across a dozen different floors). She knew
the boy would sort the letters out. It was only nine-thirty in the
morning. At ten o'clock sharp, the boy—the latest intern from the
mailroom (one of the most competitive jobs in the City)—would
arrive to pick up the morning basket; and all the letters, the rumors, the exclusives and the scoops that had piled up since the
woman's bagel at seven o'clock would find their ways across the
building through the honeycomb of writers' desks. She gave the

envelope no further thought and returned to the other activities of her morning.

She was just about to get up for lunch, almost exactly one minute before noon, when the elevator doors drew open, and a flurry of people with notebooks and tape recorders swept across the lobby to her desk. There were also photographers among them. Worse yet, there were members of building security. Worst of all, there was Mr. Watches himself.

The questions shot breathless and blaring until Mr. Watches silenced them all, sweeping down an X in the air with his hands. Then he asked her the question himself, because there was, in fact, only one question.

"Do you know," he asked (*too good to say hello and read the name off my name tag, jerk,* she thought), "who delivered this envelope this morning?"

Wearing gloves of his own, he presented to her the thin envelope addressed to himself, rumpled along one edge by the passage of a penknife.

She didn't know. She hadn't seen the man.

"Was it a man?"

She couldn't be sure. He never spoke.

"Did he talk to anyone else?"

Not to her knowledge. He hadn't left anything else or done anything else. He had only dropped the envelope on the marble counter and disappeared.

Much slower and noisier, much more troublesome than he had been, the journalists eventually left the lobby. They had no clue. Even the fact that he had worn gloves was something they discovered later, once they scanned the security videos. He had also worn a hat. Not a single feature, not even his hair, could be discerned from the footage. The head was completely obscured by the rim of the hat. No one could even state confidently that the person in the videos was a man. It could have been a woman of above-average height.

In the early afternoon, Mr. Watches sighed, cracked a smile, slid a cigar into his mouth, and lit the tip. (Twenty years he had been told, "It's a non-smoking building." Twenty years he had replied, "I keep'em for special occasions only.")

"Well," he turned to the crowd in his office, the full editorial staff, crammed over cabinets and bunched into chairs, pressed against window blinds and over bookshelves, but still leaving an empty circle several feet around his desk. "We may not have the end of the story, but we certainly have the start. And everybody in journalism knows that all you need is a start."

He took one puff of his cigar and added,

"No need to tell any of you that this is one hell of a start."

His gaze swung around to a bottle of scotch in the corner of the shelf behind his desk. He hesitated for a second, and all the members of his staff held their breaths. But *No*, he said in his head. *Now isn't the time for celebration. We have a long day ahead.*

It turned out to be one of the most accurate predictions of his career—none of the journalists slept that Monday night. But if somehow, on the following morning, Mr. Watches had been given supernatural sight; if his eyes, looking out the window, had been able to pierce through the buildings all around; if they had been able to look across the City, down the valley, across the country and around the world; if they had been able to see the wonder in his readers' eyes, as each of them came across the front page of his paper; then, on that following morning, the bottle on his shelf would have surely been put to good use.

CHAPTER TWENTY-FIVE

Today's Front Page

Not far from the Metropolitan Times Building, inside another tower, one that carried not the name of a newspaper but his own name, Herman Hoss gazed out over the City. The day was cloudy. His own reflection was drawn over the pale canvas of the sky. But his face wasn't somber that morning. On that Tuesday morning, he was smiling. Slowly he nodded at the words that came out of the young man sitting on the other side of his desk. But Hoss wasn't listening. The young man was a promising new executive, no doubt an accomplished, hardworking youth. And even if he wasn't, even if the words he spoke were garbage, even if the decisions he made were disasters, there were dozens, hundreds of other men and women in the building to ensure that no damage came to the business. The young man, of course, was talking about the business. Inside of Hoss's office on the top floor, there was only ever talk of the business. Never, ever a single word about the *other matter*. And the business was always well. Hundreds, thousands of people in the building had fought their entire lives through school exams and grueling jobs to be where they were and to make sure that the business was well. One of the secrets of his life that Hoss guarded most closely was that the business didn't need him. It was only out of courtesy that he even nodded as the young man spoke.

How wonderful it was, Hoss thought, to have reached a point in life where he didn't need to listen to anyone else ever again? A quiet laugh, imperceptible to the young man across his desk, drew the corners of Hoss's mouth. And just as Hoss didn't need to listen to know that the business was well, he also didn't need to say anything, or do anything, to know what the young man would tell everyone after leaving his office. Simply because the chairman, the chief executive, simply because *Mr. Hoss himself* had been quiet and polite, the young man would say, "Mr. Hoss is so nice; Mr. Hoss is so charming; Mr. Hoss makes it so incredibly easy to talk to him; Mr. Hoss makes you so comfortable; Mr. Hoss is so calm; Mr. Hoss is so evidently the most even-tempered, most collected, most confident leader in the entire City." And on that cloudy Tuesday morning, nodding slowly in front of his window, Mr. Hoss really was.

But he wasn't naturally even-tempered and collected. He wasn't one to trust others without listening. Much to the contrary. The business perhaps, could be trusted on its own. Half the necks in the City were craned from morning till night to keep watch on its progress. There was nothing for Hoss to do. The only task expected of *his* neck was to wear the Hoss tie smartly, to keep it smooth and unstained at the center of everyone else's gaze. It was hardly even his business. It was a business that he had inherited. By the time he was born, his father and his grandfather had driven enough cleverness, money and might into the business to ensure that it would keep on going indefinitely, and that it would keep on growing as it went. In fact, the relentlessness and ambition that he, the younger Hoss, had displayed since he was a child had almost been considered strange. He could have spent his entire life swimming in wealth without ever doing a day's work. But he had shown the fierceness of someone born hungry. It was more. It was a savagery that had frightened him in the beginning, when he had started to understand what it was, and what *he* was, which the rest of the world would never know. At first, he had unleashed all this savagery into his work. He had done more for the business than his father could have expected, perhaps even more than his father could have done. But that hadn't been enough for the younger Hoss. For many years now, none of it had been enough. He no longer cared about the business. What had dominated his mind and his spirit for many years now (*how many exactly?* It seemed a lifetime, more than a lifetime) was the *other matter*. The *other* business. And it was this other business that drifted before his eyes as he gazed out the window. It was this other business that made him smile on that morning and feel as calm, charming, and collected for once as he appeared.

The attack on Saint Clemens had been a success. Not in terms of progress on the Surway fortune; not in terms of publicity, which had no worth; not for the jewels the men had stolen (although there was no harm in keeping the men happy, if such baubles were a fortune in their eyes). No: the chief benefit of the attack had been the balm on his own emotions. He had felt broken since the last break-in, which had failed once again. But on the morning after the incident at Saint Clemens, he had woken up rested and refreshed. Most marvelous of all: he had actually slept. He had tired himself out with play. Besides, the attack had answered a question he had needed to answer. If someone had come back for the fortune, if someone had stepped into the House, as witnesses claimed, then that person would have come forward since Friday. The violence against innocents would have called him. The message behind Hoss's plane would have drawn him out. But no one had come forward. The attack had taken place on Friday night. Today was Tuesday. No one had come. As

always, the reality was obvious. It was also reassuring. Those
who believed implausible things were idiots.

He grinned, and he didn't even hide his grin. It had all been
done perfectly—it had all been so *neat*. No one had been caught.
Aside from a couple of higher-ups within the Spring Forge police—those who had secretly let the men in—no one was involved. Not even the media's collaboration had been required
over the weekend. Hoss had sat back in his chair, like everyone
else in the country, and discovered the coverage in the newspaper
only yesterday, on Monday. He had enjoyed coming across the
story as a reader. The report had made him smile. He remembered how amused he had felt, almost proud, to see the journalists piecing together the facts using only their own devices,
unguided by coercion or misdirection. He had read it while
drinking tea. In the section where they linked Friday night's incident back to the attack in Civic Square, earlier in the year, he had
almost dipped his head in greeting, he had almost murmured
"How do you do? Oh yes, me again!" All in all, it had been a remarkably tidy affair. *Neat* was the word that kept coming back in
his mind. *Too neat?* It was almost as if something had been missing, something that would have made it perfect, not just successful—something that would have made it *beautiful*. Something that
would have made him not just appreciate the attack, but even
revel in it and savor it. Something that would have spilled not
only ink, but also...

Stop! he commanded himself. It was the irrational thought. It
was the *savagery*. There was nothing he could do about it. But it
was the lack of logic in the feeling that bothered him. It was no
different in this regard from other people's enjoyment of music
or a specific food. It was only more uncommon, which made it
more curious, and Hoss didn't like the idea of an uncommon,
illogical feeling, a curious feeling, especially since it was a feeling

that he couldn't control. And so he might allow himself to feel it, to act upon it, to relish it, but he was never allowed to *think* about it. If it was something that worked independently of his mind, then he would leave his mind altogether out of it. Perhaps it was this very aspect of it that made the feeling so delicious to Hoss, when the thought of it was so displeasing. It was the possibility of escaping from his own head, from his own implacable head that never rested. Yes, perhaps the attack on Saint Clemens could have been a tiny bit less neat for his liking, but he wasn't going to spend any time thinking about that, just as he wasn't going to think about how sunny it had been on Sunday afternoon, and how much he would have preferred another one of those cool, gray, rainy days that he loved so much in the fall.

He realized that he couldn't remember what the young man looked like. Hoss turned around. There it was, that candid face, as eager and optimistic as Hoss was detached. There was that earnest face, almost handsome in the way of World War II soldiers, when all good-looking people were slightly stout. Suddenly, a wild thought shot across Hoss's mind, the thought of slapping the man's face as hard as he could. He imagined the young man's shock and the immediate silence in the room. He saw redness mounting over the young man's cheek, the only movement on his blank face. He saw the eerily unshaken hair, with too much gel in it to budge. He started to feel the burn in his own hand. What would the young man say if Hoss smacked him all of a sudden, in the middle of a sentence? Hoss felt the onset of a giggle.

He spun back towards the window, clasped his hands behind his back and stretched himself on his tiptoes, so that the young man couldn't see the shiver of laughter down his frame. He let it out in coughs and nods. *What fun!* Hoss gazed at the buildings and all the little people behind all the bright windows. He felt a momentary fondness for the entire world. The giggle subsided and his smile remained. His good humor spilled out in a happy sigh. Wasn't life beautiful after all? He had almost forgotten, over the past few weeks, that he loved life and that life loved him back.

There was a silence behind him—a pause in the young man's words. The last sentence had ended with a rise. It hadn't been a question, or Hoss would have heard it. From the sound of it, from the echo of the sound, Hoss knew what it had been: an attempt at being finished. A request for his approval. He turned around again.

"Thank you," Hoss said, and there was no need to wipe off his smile. "Your reputation is well-deserved. That was exceptionally helpful." And as he shook the young man's hand, Hoss stared into his eyes with all the molten laughter left in his body. He knew that those words, that gaze, and that vigorous handshake would appear in every conversation the young man would have that week, at every meal, over every cup of coffee, until all the people around him would start rolling their eyes. Hoss knew it from the young man's face, better than the young man knew it himself. By the time Hoss sat down in his chair again, the young executive, whose name Hoss didn't remember, was at once both infinitely dear to him and worthless.

Hoss shot a loving glance towards the long curved sword displayed behind his desk. It was a beautiful sword, designed to be held with two hands, and it rested in a case along the wall, but not directly behind him, so that anyone sitting across his desk could see both the blade and his face at the same time. The sword was always curved, but today it seemed to smile. It was the only clue to his true nature that could appear in this room. There was also the old window set against the wall in its frame of stone, but that window showed nothing.

The young man peeked at the sword, and then his head made a slight movement towards the wall, in the direction of the old window. He must have been giddy, to allow himself to ask,

"Mr. Hoss—if I may—what is that window over there standing against the wall? It's very beautiful."

Hoss smiled. He knew he looked magnanimous as he answered.

"It's an heirloom. From an old home."

And as he turned again towards the wall of glass, he could almost hear the young man thinking, *it must have been a very grand home.*

The young man got up, and Hoss heard the door closing behind him.

But suddenly it opened again.

"By the way, here's your mail if you want it—I just grabbed it outside your office."

"Thank you," Hoss replied without looking back, and he heard the fat sheaf of paper plop down on his desk. He heard the young man walking away again. But the young man turned around one last time, drunk with confidence—because the two of them were so close now—and he said,

"Crazy stuff about that Surway business on today's front page."

Hoss gave a chuckle that would provide the closing detail in the young man's chronicle of their meeting. Then he heard the door shut for good.

Hoss fell in his chair. *That Surway business on today's front page?* His heart was pounding. The *other* business. The business he truly cared about. The newspaper sat on top of his mail. Was there really so little going on in the world that the *Metropolitan Times* was dedicating a second cover story to the Saint Clemens attack? But that had been at the *bottom* of yesterday's front page. How could the same story have not only survived into the next day's edition, but also been promoted to the top of the cover, to the front page itself? Hoss felt a chill creeping over his arms. He leaned over the desk, turned the newspaper around, and directed his eyes to the headline.

At first it made no sense to him. He often struggled with headlines. Their language was too fragmentary for his mind—he was too exact for all the missing articles. He left off the headline and let his mind scramble through the words below. *Decades after... tycoon's last will... fortune left unclaimed... unexplained disappearance...* There! He struck the page with his index finger. A break. A shift from one paragraph to the next. The paragraph before had regular margins. The paragraph after had a deep indentation, which continued down the page. He re-read the first two paragraphs, before the indentation. A letter. The newspaper had received a letter. An anonymous letter. The indented part was the letter itself, reproduced in its entirety on the page. The full, anonymous letter. No, it wasn't anonymous. *Letter was handdelivered... could not locate the sender...* But the letter was *signed.* Hoss's eyes darted across the words, over the lines and the columns to the end of the letter. His heart battered his chest. His breath came slow and wispy. He read the signature at the bottom. He stood up again and sat down again. He tightened his grip on the newspaper's edges as if to keep himself from collapsing on the floor.

CHAPTER TWENTY-SIX

The Letter

Below is the full letter as it was published in the *Metropolitan Times*:

> To whom it may concern (which should, in fact, be nobody at all),
>
> It is difficult for me to tell if the polite thing for me to do, at this moment of my life, would be to introduce myself. And if the answer is yes, then it is even more difficult for me to know, as I am writing, how to go about introducing myself and to whom. It seems a bit silly, in reality, a bit stodgy, to speak of introductions when I know that my name is most likely familiar to you, to anyone who may be reading this letter. In fact, I should be the one wondering who you are, on the other side of this letter, you and all the others who have been speaking my name for so long (though less and less frequently over the years). Let us then agree, whomever you may be, wherever I may have been, to meet here on this page as old acquaintances, even perhaps as old friends, and to leave the ceremony of introductions behind us.
>
> I have been far away for a long time. But I wasn't so far, and I wasn't gone so long, as to be unaware of the extraordinary gift left to me by the late Mr. Lyndon Surway several decades ago. On the contrary, most likely I would not have gone so far, and I would not have gone so long, if I had not known of the gift that was left in my name. It is

*evident to me now, so many years after I left, that it was this gift that
sent me away and even kept me far away. Let me explain.*

*I knew Mr. Lyndon Surway. I didn't know him well, or at least not
as well as you might suppose. But now I understand that I knew him
better, or at least he knew me better, than I suspected at the time. I was a
boy when he died. I heard that my name was in his will. I could hardly
recognize my name when I heard it. I was usually called by a nickname—I wonder how many people would have even known upon hearing of his will to think of me. The name in the will sounded like such a
grownup's name, such an important man's name, as if Mr. Surway
were addressing one of his peers, someone of his own age and stature.
Perhaps, at the time, all of you who heard my name pictured someone
much older than I was, much wiser, more accomplished, more deserving
in every way of the tremendous legacy Mr. Surway left behind. To tell
you the truth, that's what I would have imagined as well: a figure far
removed from the boy that I was. Funnily enough, what I imagined at
the time was much closer to what I am today, in appearance at least, if
not in wisdom or achievement (both of which, it turns out, age is surprisingly powerless to impart).*

*I was only a boy then, as I said, and at first I was convinced that I
had understood the letter wrong, that I had misread it or misinterpreted
it, or perhaps that Mr. Surway had known someone else who shared my
name, someone far worthier than I was, someone he had known much
better. But in the end I came to accept the incomprehensible, inconceivable truth: that the largest inheritance in recorded history had been left
for me alone.*

*Now, I say that I knew Mr. Surway. We met a few times. I used to
ride my bike in the field right outside one of his factories. One day he
was there, and we talked. I saw him again a few times, during breaks
from my bicycle in the shade of his enormous factory. We had a few
conversations. I wish I could say that he had given me guidance for life
during those conversations. That is what one would expect from such an*

eminent man, and it seems disrespectful of me not to remember any such wisdom. But he was never my mentor—at least he never tried to be. The few times we met, Mr. Surway barely gave me any advice at all. He talked to me as an equal, as if I had been his age or he had been mine, or more exactly as if no age or distinction existed between us. In fact, we talked mostly about me, about school, about the future, about what I was planning and hoping to do with my life. I was by no means a poor student, but I can't imagine that I said anything especially impressive. I was mostly an average, happy child, with no particular passion for geometry or biology or a hundred other things that I didn't learn then and that I don't know now. And he was Lyndon Surway.

But since then I've heard more than once that he spoke with everyone the way he spoke with me. He didn't consider himself an example to anyone, and he always asked more questions than he answered. It strikes me now that he always talked to everyone as if the person who stood to benefit the most from the conversation was himself. It took me years, long past his death, to comprehend this, and many more years to realize that he didn't do this out of guardedness or humility, or even courtesy. Rather, it was his natural curiosity, towards all people and all things in the world, that drove him to learn from everyone at every moment. And it was this same unquenchable desire to know and understand, the same curiosity that made him ask me about my life, that enabled him to build one of the greatest empires in the history of business. And for everything he learned from all the people he met, he was genuinely grateful and genuinely glad. You see, what few people remember now, when his name has become a marker for a fortune that has become legend, is that Lyndon Surway was a great man, even greater than the magnificent life he led.

Now he is gone. I am left with his gift and his memory. I am not so ignorant or so oblivious as to say that the latter is the more precious of the two, but I feel more protective of it. I am more worried of losing it. Maybe it's because I am getting older myself, because, while I am still not entirely an old man, I am now closer to the time when I will meet Mr. Surway again on the other side than to the last time we met. Everybody knows that there are worlds inside of our memories. But perhaps one needs to age in order to understand the frailty of these worlds. Mr. Surway, however, also left me his fortune. And, as strange as it may sound, I was never afraid of losing that. I knew where it was, I knew that it was mine, and I never much doubted that it would always be there for me. I was still a child. And so I left.

I went away. I didn't know at the time for how long. I never even articulated to myself that I was going away for a long time. If someone had told me then how many years, how many decades I would be gone, I would have thought the notion was crazy. I would have thought it was a plan for a far greater adventurer than I. I simply left without thinking, without looking back, and, to be honest, without looking ahead much either. I left school—a choice I recommend to no one, though among all the abrupt decisions I ever made, that might be the one I regret the least. I left my hometown and everyone I knew. I didn't have a proper family like other children. I had no concept of what it meant to miss people, or of people missing me. I left with nothing but a bag of clothes and a vague promise to return. The bag of clothes showed some (inaccurate) sense of the time I would be gone; the vague promise gave none. I set sail on a passenger liner for Europe.

I omit the specific destination not because it is a secret, but because I didn't have a particular one in mind; and it seems unfair to give it any more significance now than it had for me at the time. The only thing I will allow myself to clarify at present, though it was obscure to me then, is the reason I left at all. Even now, the best I can do is try. Why sail away when the life I was leaving behind was perfectly fine; when there was nothing I was particularly anxious to sail towards; when any dreams I might have had of climbing aboard a ship were no more desperate, no more urgent, than those of any other boy my age? In fact, why go away at all, when I had suddenly received, without any expectation, a far greater treasure than I could ever hope to find at the ends of the earth? Perhaps no one can understand my answer, or my attempt at an answer. Perhaps I wouldn't understand it myself if this had all happened to someone else. But I will try to remain as close to the truth as I can.

I was never an especially ambitious boy. I had hopes and goals that were admirable and reasonable—perhaps even a bit too reasonable. No part of me yearned for greatness, or felt that greatness was my due. And then Lyndon Surway named me his heir. I was designated, in an instant, the sole possessor of the largest fortune in the country, perhaps the world. All of a sudden, in just the time it took for me to understand the words, I had reached something that only the most wildly ambitious of boys could hope to attain in a lifetime. This made me consider, for the first time, that I could become something other than what I had always been. It wasn't the thought of his wealth that took hold of me then—Mr. Surway could have left me a hundredth of his fortune or a hundred times more, and I think my reaction would have been the same. Rather, it was the thought of becoming something else, anything at all. For the first time in my life, I glimpsed infinite possibility, perhaps the greatest treasure that anyone can behold on this earth. Suddenly, I discovered that I could be someone else, that I could be anyone. But I also sensed that as soon as I claimed the inheritance, then my life would forever be bound to the astounding fortune I had been given. I knew that I had to leave, right at that moment, if I was to have any hope of ever living at all. I felt like a boy who opens his door one morning to find that his house has been moved to the top of the world's highest mountain. I worried that there was nowhere left to go. And so I left.

Where did I go all these years? I went everywhere. No, that's not correct. Twenty, thirty years ago I would have said that I went everywhere, and I would have meant it. But I've traveled enough over the decades to know that the world is much bigger than everyone says. We bump into the cousins of our cousins among the neighbors of our neighbors, and we say the world is small. But there are oceans beyond our neighborhoods, and we all have brothers throughout the world who look nothing like us. There can be places beyond places and eras after eras in every one of our lives. The earth is so much larger than people give it credit for, just as our lives are so much longer than anyone admits (though I would never say too long). Or maybe it's the colorless, changeless lives that pass quickly. Mine has been filled with color and movement, and it has felt ecstatically long. There were a few places where I stayed a long time, or at least where I started to feel that I had stayed a long time, because I had grown used to the sights and sounds and smells there, and to the people that I knew there. And my habits there seemed to have become my existence, and I woke up without surprise, without confusion, without questions, on the mornings when I woke up there. But even then, I knew there were still other places, other sights, sounds, and smells as yet unimagined, other people, other mornings. And so I never stayed in any one place for more than a year or two. I continued on my way. There are so many lives to be lived on this earth—so many times more than there are days in our lives. In all my travels, the one type of person whom I could never respect is the one who complains of his life and does nothing to change it, the one who always thinks he needs more money or more freedom to do so. Mine has been rich beyond belief, and I never spent a cent of Lyndon Surway's fortune to make it so, when all of that fortune was mine. The only fair grievance belongs to those whose time runs out too soon. That is the only resource that can never be replenished. Everything else is in our hands, even if our hands are empty. We are everything we feel, and every feeling in the world is free. I never had much money with me (however much I may have had in name). I didn't touch Lyndon Surway's wealth. But his inheritance drove me to discover the thousands and millions of ways in which every single minute of our lives can be spent. Perhaps this was the greatest part of his gift. Did he suspect what I would do? Did he know I would go away, once I found out about his will? Sometimes I like to think so. But *most often I prefer to think that he was too generous to form any plan for me at all.*

But now I am back. I have returned to the country of my birth. I won't bore you by describing how much everything has changed since my childhood; other accounts have done so much better than I could (as would many of you who are now reading these words). I have come back to claim what is mine. There is no reason to stay away from it any longer, now that I have already lived enough for several lifetimes without it. In fact, I am in a hurry. There is a reason for me to send this letter right away. There is a reason for me to step out of the shadow not within a few weeks but within a few days, within hours if possible. The news has reached me of the horrible actions that have been taken in relation to the Surway fortune, of terrible things that have been done either to draw me out into the light or to seize the fortune in my absence, or just to rage in frustration against the continued emptiness of Surway House. It is sad to see such barbarity and greed endure when so much else in the world is transformed with the decades. But as it is so, I can no longer keep my silence. I can no longer carry on with my travels while the perpetrators of such acts go unchecked and unaddressed. And so, to the insane, broken minds behind these deeds, and to anyone else who might care to know, I hereby come forward and declare that Lyndon Surway's heir has arrived, that the fortune isn't lost, that it was never lost, or even forgotten, but was simply laid to rest for my return. Soon I will go and take possession of it. The money will flow, once again, through every channel of the financial system across this country and around the world. There will be no mystery about it, no secret. The ripples of this enormous wealth will wash widely and loudly over every market on the globe. And soon I will take up residence in Surway House. It has remained uninhabited for too long. The great House will be lived in once again. Water will rush into the moat and fill the lake that has been dry all these years. I will restore it to its former splendor, which the years, it appears, have done little to fade.

I am taking the liberty to deliver this letter to the Metropolitan Times *in order to send it to as many people as possible at once: to people who may have cared about the mystery of Lyndon Surway's legacy, to people whose lust for it may have turned into a sickness, and to anyone who may simply be curious for a bit of regional history. It seems self-important. It seems vain, especially for someone who has never said or done anything in public. And yet, ridiculous as I may appear in my own eyes at this moment, I know the mighty paper will publish this letter, just as I know that its editors will verify, with the attorneys in charge of the Surway estate, the copy of the property deed for Surway House that I am enclosing in the envelope as proof of my claim.*

I had refused to start with an introduction. Perhaps you will forgive me if I end with one. I am very excited to meet you all. It feels good to be home.

Sincerely yours,
Lucian Baker

Hoss's eyes paused over the printed signature. His mind stood still before it, as if he would never read another word; as if he must suck the entire universe out of those letters; as if there were nothing left for him to do but tick down the seconds while he stared, like an old clock beating time in the last room it would ever know. Then he saw the words that came after. They were from the editors of the newspaper.

The staff of the Metropolitan Times *has confirmed the authenticity of the enclosed copy of the property deed (not shown here) with the lawyers designated as executors of the late Mr. Surway's will. As this is a genuine copy of the deed, which was never released to the public, we currently have no reason to doubt the authenticity of the letter reproduced above. So far we have not spoken further with Mr. Baker, nor*

*have we met him in person. We look forward to sharing the latest up-
dates as the story unfolds.*

With these words the article ended. Hoss's eyes darted back to
the signature at the end of the letter. The symbols began to lose
meaning. The sounds attached to them dissolved, and the echoes
that had rung for so long in his head fell silent.

After a few minutes, he stood up from his desk and looked
outside. The sun had come out. In his mind, it felt like the beginning of a day, or the end of it, anything but the bright, clear noon
that it was. Hoss wasn't sad. He wasn't angry. He simply stared
out of the top floor of the tower that carried his name, and for
once he wasn't thinking or feeling anything at all. He sat down
again, and he mechanically reached for his pen, just as he had
done on the morning after the last break-in had failed. There was
only one thing left to do, and he dimly planned it before starting.
He pulled open his desk drawer and drew out a clean sheet of
paper. He took off the cap of his pen, lifted the tip above the
page, and let it hover there a few seconds. No word came out. His
eyes turned to the old window set against the wall. Vacantly,
slowly, he raised himself off his chair. For a moment he stood
behind his desk without moving, his eyes fixed on the silent stone
and the lightless glass of the ancient window. When he shut the
cap back on his pen, he felt the snap through the bones in his
palm. He set the pen down and walked over to the wall.

He grasped the old window's metal handle. He turned it to the
right, then twice to the left, then once again to the right, and
twice again to the left. Each time, the metal creaked, either in
pain or in assent, until it stopped in a resounding roll. Hoss felt a
deep, quiet tremor somewhere far beneath his grip. Then he
pulled the handle down, clanking the teeth of unseen gears, and

out towards himself. The window drew open. The wall behind the glass panes was black, but there was a vertical slit down the middle, as well as a hole on each side at the height of Hoss's eyes, which had been hidden behind the bars of the windowpanes. He looked in through the holes. A ray of red light skimmed over his pupils. The wall swished open and he stepped inside.

CHAPTER TWENTY-SEVEN

Beneath the Tower

Down, down the height of the tower, the elevator went. It had no buttons of any kind. Only one man could ride it, and that man was Herman Hoss. If he entered from below, then it went up, and if he got in from above, then it went down. When it went down, it passed through the many levels of the Hoss Tower and continued below them into a place that was like the elevator itself—without indication, without escape, and commanded by Hoss alone.

The elevator opened. Hoss stepped out onto a circular balustrade that looked down over an empty marble hall. He stopped in front of the railing and drew in a deep breath. The air was stale and thin, and yet he expanded his chest with it. Already he felt better. The elevator was fast, but the journey still lasted over a minute. It was a minute he always enjoyed. It was a minute-long greeting, a cleanse, before he arrived underground, deep under the bustle of the Hoss Tower and the City. And when he stepped out at last, the close air and the round wall always felt like an embrace.

A curving stairway led to the floor below, whose white marble was tinged with a red glow from beyond the room. But Hoss didn't go down. He walked along the railing to a double door opposite the elevator. It was a heavy wooden door, and the keyhole in the lock was as big as a fist. But the key he pulled out of his pocket was tiny. He pushed it into the key hole. A square of red light appeared on the door plate, then turned green. He pressed his thumb over it. The lock made a beep followed by a clatter, and he opened the door.

It seemed like nighttime when he entered the room, because there were no windows anywhere. One side of the room was occupied entirely by a fireplace, tall and wide enough to walk in, blackened by years of smoke. On the opposite wall hung an enormous painting depicting the coronation of Napoleon. But the wall in between them, at the back of the room, was covered in books, hardbound and venerable books so musty that they seemed to breathe. As the door swung shut behind him, Hoss walked over to this wall. He reached out for one of the books without needing to look for it: *One Thousand and One Nights*. He pulled out the spine and took a step back. The bookcase whirred up to reveal a smaller room behind it, bathed in a soft light that glowed from the edges of the ceiling. There was nothing in this room but a table and a leather chair. A large binder was placed on the table, left open in front of the chair. Hoss sat down. His eyes fell over the pages cased in plastic protectors. He rested his gaze over the blueprints of the Surway House. He closed his eyes and exhaled.

The plans were still his, the legendary plans of the Surway House, the only plans of the secret passages left in the world. No other copies survived. He was certain of it. He had made certain of it. He had spent years of his life and troves of his wealth for these brittle, smudged pages. Much violence had been committed on their account. But now they were his, and no other version would ever be made. He looked at them. He had watched them for many hours. He was always watching them. He watched them with obsessiveness, with concern, like his very own golden eggs. He watched them as a stern father might watch his children, with shaded tenderness. There was no blessing or gift in life that he would have watched over more closely. He rested his hands over the plastic protectors, and he let his skin breathe in their warmth. The binder was still open to the page that showed the tunnel in the oven, the promising tunnel that had proven useless. It didn't matter. Hoss forgave the stolen pages, just as he felt that they forgave him. He wasn't asking them for information. He wasn't asking them for anything. He had come simply to be with them. He only wanted to feel them beneath his palms. He had longed for them from the glass-walled expanse of his office. He breathed out again. The sight and touch of something that he had fought for steadied his heartbeat. He began to feel like himself again. He glanced over the pages, and logical thoughts began to take shape in his mind.

The letter couldn't have been from Lucian Baker. It was too much of a story, too much of a tale. It was too flimsy to break a decades-long silence. Its content was nothing but shadows—coherent, convincing shadows, but immaterial nonetheless. They told the *story* of a man, not his life. Beyond this story, there were no details, no facts, not a single point of reference. Where had the man been? Where had he lived? He hadn't even given the destination of the first ship he had boarded. There were no country names, no years, no markers of time or place anywhere. Why? This man was presenting himself to the world. There was no reason to hide anything, to scatter the traces of his past. Why be so vague? Why keep so much behind the curtain, when he had deliberately announced himself on the biggest podium in the world, the front page of the *Metropolitan Times*? Why not provide any real information? Hoss knew the answer—so that no one could substantiate it, so that nobody could check it. Where had this person met *Mr. Surway? In a field outside of a factory?* Surway had factories everywhere. And when? The letter only said *as a boy.* Would Lyndon Surway leave his entire fortune to a boy he barely knew? Where had this boy gone? *I went everywhere,* said the letter, which, in terms of verifiability, was exactly the same as going nowhere.

It was all a story. A compelling fable. The person who wrote *I* was not a person, but a character. As he remembered the letter, as he assembled sentences back together, whole sections of it in his head, Hoss realized that this wasn't the expression of someone's mind. Rather, it had been written for *other people's minds,* a story crafted for the public that the *Metropolitan Times* would serve to spread. It was a trick Hoss knew well. For years, he had used the newspaper's pages for his own messages. He had filled them with his own tales and become an expert in disseminating lies. He knew how to mold a narrative such that it fit neatly into the public memory, in precisely the manner that was most advantageous to himself. Most importantly, most usefully, he had perfected the art of fashioning the semblance of truth without ever giving details. And he could recognize this craft in the letter he had read. He could spot its devices and techniques. And beyond the broad voice that said *I,* he could hear another voice, one that was squeaky and low, like the voice of a mouse, one that was barely audible in his own head, and that he knew no one else would hear. It was the voice of a liar, whose name was written nowhere.

Hoss sat back in his chair and wrapped his hand around his chin. Who was this person? Where had he come from? Where had he gone? The end of the article said that no one at the newspaper had met him. This much had to be true—the paper wouldn't overstate its own ignorance. Of course, Hoss would follow up with the paper's editors. He would find out everything they knew. But he was almost certain that the author was still in hiding, at least as of the time of publication. Who could the author be? Where had he been all this time?

There had always been impostors. The first few had appeared on the very afternoon the will had been read, all those decades ago. They had arrived only a few hours after the attorney had first pronounced the name of Lucian Baker in the Great Hall of the House. They had started by preying on the attorneys themselves, followed by Surway's social and professional connections, followed by the acquaintances of those connections, followed in the end by the most faithful and least loyal connection of all, the one who is acquainted with everybody and yet is nobody's friend—the press. But none of those impostors had been successful. Soon the only type of prominence the press was willing to give them came in scraps of sad humor. At last, even those jokes had ceased to entertain, and therefore to circulate, and the impostors, over the years, had fallen off the pages of the papers. None of them had made the slightest impression on the public. None of them had commanded even a morning's respect in the news. As Hoss had grown up and grown aware of current affairs, of Lyndon Surway, of his fortune, of its mystery, of the name of Lucian Baker, and of the maddening, unrelenting, unconquerable desire inside of himself, he hadn't once felt threatened by a competitor. He hadn't once felt that someone else was closer to the fortune than he was. Not once, until today. He leaned over the table, and he pressed the tips of his fingers over his temples.

What was it that made this letter so remarkable? What was it that had pushed it past the hundreds of other scoops and the thousands of other tips, past the countless other events in every corner of the world, to the front page of the newspaper? The answer lay in the editors' text at the end of the article. Hoss remembered it exactly. *The staff of the* Metropolitan Times *has con-*

firmed the authenticity of the enclosed copy of the property deed (not shown here). He looked up and his eyes drifted away. A smile of admiration tucked into his cheek without his noticing. How had this person acquired this deed? It was reported missing from the county records when Surway was declared dead. No one had ever found it. Like the rest of his fortune, it had simply disappeared, as if it had never existed. How could this person have it? How was it possible? Hoss's memory had absorbed the text of the article word for word. *As this is a genuine copy of the deed, we currently have no reason to doubt the authenticity of the letter reproduced above.* Again he fell back in his chair, and he folded his arms over his chest.

Could this man truly be Lucian Baker? Was it possible? Hoss could barely formulate the thought to himself. To him, Lucian Baker wasn't a name. It wasn't a person. It was a title that came with the prize he was after. So far, nobody had come closer to it than Hoss himself. Nobody, he knew, could be better equipped to reach it. And nobody, he was certain, could want it as much as he did. For most of his life, he had accepted as an objective truth that no one else would ever have it, that the fortune would belong to him, Herman Hoss, or to no one at all. What had tormented him all those years was the thought that he may not find it. He had never envisioned that someone else might find it first, that there could even be a Lucian Baker, a real Lucian Baker.

That had all changed this morning. Now there was another contender. Now there was a real menace, far more powerful and obscure than the mystery and self-doubt that Hoss had contended with before. For the first time in his life, in the history of the Surway fortune, there was someone else in the world, someone hidden, someone unknown, who was close to taking hold of it.

He felt a burning at the bottom of his eyes. He drew himself forward, narrowed his stare on some invisible object that lay far into the distance. *Close to taking hold*, the thought echoed in his mind. But the fortune wasn't taken yet. The author's letter had written so himself. *Soon I will go and take possession of it.* It wasn't too late. The fortune was still untouched. Did the letter's author know where it was? Was he already on his way there? Was he looking at it, reaching for it, grasping at it even now, while Hoss sat gazing over ancient blueprints in a secret chamber underground?

Hoss recoiled at the thought. No. The fortune was still safe. If the letter's author could have seized it within hours, or even days, then he would have done so before sending the letter. The person was close to it perhaps. Hoss was almost certain the person was close. But the fortune wasn't taken, or the letter would have said so, the newspaper would have said so. The fibers and fluids around Hoss's bones would have said so.

His eyes descended again over the blueprints in his hands. What about the House? Had this person gone inside? The letter's author had found the deed—did he also have the key? And how big of a step was there from the House to the fortune? Was the fortune inside the House? Again, his eyes drifted over the secret, silent plans. Why did they have nothing to say to him? Could there be more secrets beyond these tunnels, beyond these swiveling paintings and sliding walls? What else could the plans show him? What else could pen and paper say? He let his thumb skip down the dividers along the side of the binder: *Main House, Main Gardens, Additional Buildings, Open Lands*, and *Spring Forge and Local Area*. And to see them all so reticent, so unyielding before him, after all the time he had known them, only heightened his respect for them and for the mystery they guarded.

He looked up again and focused. There had been a rumor in Spring Forge. People had seen a man in the House. People were idiots. They were impulsive. They were quickly impressed and easily hysterical. But they weren't all crazy, and they weren't liars. What had they seen that could have looked like a man? Could it have been the letter's author? Could it have been...

The burning mounted over his eyes. His eyebrows drew tighter. He slammed the binder shut, closing it for the first time since the break-in through the oven. He rolled up his fists and stood up. He slipped out of the secret chamber and heard the bookcase slide down behind him as he strode to the door of the windowless room.

CHAPTER TWENTY-EIGHT

The City Without a Sky

Hoss took the stairs down to the marble hall. He entered a corridor on the other side. The marble went on beneath his feet, and the red glow that tinted it grew brighter as he walked. Some of the doors on each side of the corridor were half open, but most of them were closed. No sound came out of the half open doors, but groans, muffled shrieks and colored lights leaked out of the closed doors. Some of the lights were blue and some green, but most of them were a heavy red that became denser as he went, until it seemed to stream through the corridor itself. Gradually the marble at his feet became rough. Soon the floor and the walls on both sides turned to stone.

By the time he reached a crossroads, he was no longer in a corridor. He was walking over cobblestones through the square of an underground city, a rowdy, nocturnal place lit by crooked lampposts. The air didn't flow except to carry whimpers and damp smells. There was no moon or sky or ceiling—there was nothing above but a perfect, unbroken black. He passed other people on his way, staggering women in lace dresses and quiet men in strange costumes, Roman soldiers, French revolutionaries, pirates, sailors, and Tudor princes. And as Hoss passed between them, they respectfully bowed their heads.

He recognized each of them, and every one of them knew him. They were his army, his clan. Anyone observing their grim society would have called them his gang. Those who belonged to it were the most dangerous people in the City. They were the artists and aristocrats of its criminal population. They had found their way through misery or ambition to the outskirts of Hoss's kingdom, to smaller crime dens and lesser villains. Hard work and luck (either good or bad, depending on perspective) had led them higher into wrongdoing and lower into the underworld, all the way to the gates of Hoss's community. Finally, after years of felony, through evil triumphs and hateful friendships, the best of them—the worst—would arrive in this place, the underground city where Herman Hoss ruled, and in which he was even more powerful than in the City above.

Together, these men and women, or rather the derailed attempts at men and women that had rolled down into this darkness, were responsible for most of the violence in the City. And because they were all mad, or mostly so, even their everyday lives were gruesome. With the wealth they all plundered, and all the resources Hoss possessed, they were free to live in his underworld in whatever manner they liked. They had no laws beyond his will, and their imaginations were rank, like underground weeds. Their existence, therefore, was a form of reverse masquerade, where they could be precisely the demons and oddities that they had always felt themselves to be. And when they ventured outside, it was part of their revenge on the world that the way they looked was almost as horrifying as the things they did.

The police knew that they existed and that they were organized into some sort of community, with different families and factions within it. The public lived in fear of them and of the brutal tragedies they arranged, sometimes with a purpose, more often for no reason. But they went unpunished and unchecked.

Hoss was too powerful. The network of his corruption was too deep. The chains it bound around the City were too strong, and they held it captive in terror. But though the City could feel those chains, no one knew they were held by Hoss. Above the surface, among the people who worked for Hoss without being officially in his employ—the lawyers, the bankers, the police agents and the city workers—and even among those who *knew* they worked for Hoss—the reporters, the magistrates, the crooked politicians and business leaders—not a single person knew of his kingdom underground. Those who suspected him of bribery and fraud were astonishingly few, so consummately did he cover his tracks. But even among those who did, no one would have accused him of violence and murder. It's true that some people did hold certain hypotheses about the man. Some conjectured that the brilliant leader of the Hoss conglomerate was far more powerful than anyone knew, and far more vicious than anyone thought. But those people were conspiracy theorists—every public figure inspires a few. Only underneath his Tower was Hoss acknowledged for what he was, and it made him feel more fearsome, more revered, even more majestic below the ground than in his office above the City.

The might he wielded underground was different. He didn't fraternize with the inhabitants of his underworld, but he cared about them in his own way. Because they all saw him as he was, he didn't look upon them with contempt. He had his favorites among them, and some were almost his friends. He had his most trusted generals and his shrewdest counsels. But his will held more authority down there than the entirety of government above. There was no rule, no defense, no mercy against his pleasure; and his pleasure was simple and often bloody. Therefore, none of them lifted their eyes as he passed through the alleyways.

None dared to step across his path. And he didn't have time to lay a hand on any of them as he went through the dark city.

He walked past noisy taverns and silent gardens, past sagging stairways and mangled statues. If he had paused to look into any of the houses on his way, he would have seen more people in strange costumes, in weird homes that matched their clothes— Roman pleasure houses, medieval dungeons, pirate inns and courtly salons. But Hoss never slowed down.

He arrived in front of a house on a quiet street. It was a pretty house, set back from the pavement, with a little balcony upstairs supported by columns around the front door. No sound came out of the house. The door was closed.

He knocked, waited a second, turned the knob and went in. He stepped into the parlor of an elegant Victorian home. A fire burned softly in front of a tufted red armchair. At the foot of the armchair, a beautiful young woman in a flower-patterned dress sat on a cushion staring at the flames. A man sat reading on the armchair, running his hand over her hair. This man kept a perfect mustache, and he was never seen without a bow tie. He hardly ever spoke. In regard for this mustache and his bow tie, and for the tail coat and the top hat that he always wore when he left the house, everyone called him the Gentleman. The young woman at his feet was his daughter.

The daughter's eyes jumped when Hoss entered. With a turn of her head, she looked at her father. The Gentleman laid down his book, open to the page where he had stopped, on a little table at his side. Then he turned his face to the visitor.

Standing just outside the glow of the fireplace, Hoss took a glance at the young woman. Then he fixed his eyes on the Gentleman and said,

"I need your help."

CHAPTER TWENTY-NINE

Breakfasts Large and Small

Even before the appearance of the day's paper, that Tuesday morning was lively in Spring Forge. It was the day when Saint Clemens was set to reopen, after the events of the previous Friday. Andrew woke up early, even earlier, in fact, than he needed to. This was the day he was going to return the cuff links and the clothes he had bought. This was the day he was going to return the money to the cave. The thought had jostled in his head all night, poking into his dreams. Finally it had shoved his eyes open, and he was forced to accept that he wouldn't fall asleep again. He pulled himself up on his elbows and looked outside. The world was a dim gray blue. It was a little before seven—his favorite time of day. He always loved the way it smelled, in any place he had ever been, cool, misty and serene. He decided to get up and leave the house.

He tiptoed into the kitchen, which was brighter in the first light of morning than he had ever seen it. The Brandows were still asleep. There was no coffee on the counter. Andrew held his breath. There was no sound at all in the house. Even the kettle, which had the busiest schedule of all in the Brandow house, was still asleep in a corner by the stove. Andrew savored the thought of the two of them sleeping upstairs. He breathed in their silent nearness like a mug of cocoa. He pulled out a little piece of paper from the notepad on the counter and wrote,

I had to get an early start at school. Sorry to miss breakfast! I'm sure my entire day will be rough as a result.

He left the note on the table, promising himself that it was the last time he was lying to them (and only the beginning was a lie anyway). Then he grabbed an apple from the basket on the counter and slipped out the front door.

There was nowhere for him to hurry to. The thought of returning the money had hustled him out of bed, even pushing out the prospect of pancakes from his mind. But the brisk morning air made him think clearly. There wasn't enough time before class to get the money back and return it to the cave, and he didn't want to carry all that cash around with him at school. Most importantly, the stores probably weren't even open yet.

His BnC clothes were in his backpack. He had folded them as neatly as he could into their shopping bag and shoved it inside. The cuff links were also there. Somehow, standing still with all that treasure on his back didn't seem secure. He started walking down the street.

He stopped at a crossroads. Straight ahead, the road went on, winding through the sleepy neighborhood down to the main street of Spring Forge. But another road cut across. It led to the main street as well, but there were no houses alongside it. *The shortcut.* There was no reason for him to take it, especially on a morning when he had more time than he needed. But there was something else down that way. There was the wall, the round wall of stones that encircled the Surway estate. He stared down the road. He could glimpse the stone wall behind a drooping golden tree just a few steps past the crossroads.

Two things made him choose the shortcut. One was his fear, or rather the shame of it. The other was the little trash can that stood a few steps down the shortcut, beckoning softly under the sway of the golden tree for the apple core in his hand. He walked over to the trash can and slammed the core inside. Then he tightened the straps of his backpack, looked down the empty road, and set off.

A minute later, he reached another intersection. The curving stone wall unrolled into the distance down the back roads of Spring Forge, all the way, he assumed, to the gate of the estate. But his path lay to the left, down an empty street he had taken on the first day of school. He wanted to keep on following the wall, but the cuff links and the suit on his back strapped him in place.

Another time. He gazed wistfully down the wall. *Just return the money today. After today, you can go on all the crazy adventures you want for the rest of your life.* And he turned left towards the town.

Suddenly he jumped. A man stood beside the road, looking straight at him. No, he realized. It wasn't a man. *Once again.* He breathed out. He chuckled in embarrassment. Bending over his knees, he lulled his heartbeat back to normal.

And you wanted to walk all the way to the Surway House. He stared at his feet. *You magnificent weirdo.*

It was the old wooden shop sign that had startled him the last time, on the morning of his first day. There, on the side of the road, stood the chef whose head was a mirror, and who held a tray that said,

What's mine is yours

Andrew sighed. Something in the ragged lines of the kindly message and the faded drawing of the bread loaves made him long for the Brandows. Surely they were awake now. Strangely, his mind turned to the flower he had picked for Mrs. Brandow on his first day at school. He should have given it to her, instead of throwing it out the window. He felt a sudden yearning to sit with them in their kitchen and warm his chest with a cup of tea. His legs ached to run back. He could have stayed in their house all morning. He could have missed his first class and asked them for a note. He let the fantasy roll out in a sigh.

Just get yourself to school, crazy pants.

He came out in the middle of the main street a few minutes later.

The town was prettier than he had ever seen it. It had dried itself from the weekend's rain with the crisp, crimson blanket of fall. But there was also another change. There were men in black suits walking up and down the street. One of them passed him by, and Andrew caught sight of a wire looping over his ear behind the stem of his shades. Avoiding the man's eyes, Andrew remembered Mayor Gladys's promise. The mayor had deployed his own bodyguards to protect Saint Clemens and Spring Forge. Andrew went on for a few blocks before he dared to look again over his shoulder. Suddenly a door was flung open behind him. Cameron's face poked out.

"Hey man," the boy called out. He was smiling. "Come in and join us!"

He held open the door as Andrew followed him into a little coffee shop furnished with couches and plush armchairs. The air smelled of coffee, cider and cinnamon. Walking in, Andrew was delighted to realize how cold it had been outside. Olivia waved at him from a brightly painted table in the corner.

"Good morning," she said as he took his seat in front of her. There was a fullness to her voice that made him feel even warmer. Cameron sat down in a chair next to her.

"Good morning," Andrew echoed. "What are you guys doing up so early?"

Huddling over the table with the two of them, he found it difficult to keep himself from smiling.

"We're having breakfast," she said. "We *love* breakfast. As a matter of fact, every night when I go to bed, I'm so excited to get up the next day that I can't tell if I'm passionate about life in general—or just breakfast."

Andrew looked down at the enormous plate of French toast with bacon in front of her, which was about to spill over onto a second plate filled with hash browns. In front of Cameron was a bowl of oatmeal topped with berries. The rest of the table struggled to accommodate the two biggest cups of tea (*or bowls?*) Andrew had seen in his life. A dangling newspaper was held in place by Cameron's cup.

"How've you been—since what happened?" Cameron began.

Olivia raised her arms.

"Let's not talk about anything dark," she said. Turning to Andrew, she added gently, "Unless you want to."

He had no choice but to shake his head. She gave a gratified nod.

"So what would you like?" she asked him.

"Nothing," he said. "I just had breakfast."

"Are you sure?"

"Don't worry about—" Cameron attempted.

Andrew met his eyes, and for a second the humiliating offer hovered, unspoken, on Cameron's tongue. Andrew's thoughts turned to the cuff links in his bag, and to the cash he would soon have in their place. But Cameron shrugged and looked down without finishing his sentence.

"No thanks, I'm all right," Andrew said.

His answer appeared to satisfy everyone.

Olivia turned to Cameron.

"I still don't think this is the place."

"We've been looking for the perfect breakfast in town," he explained to Andrew. "This place might be better just for coffee." His eyes descended into the creamy oats in front of him. "That said, I am sure loving this oatmeal." Looking up again, his face more serious than Andrew had ever seen it, he said,

"I really love oatmeal. I have it for breakfast every single day, and I can never get enough. I can't stop thinking about new topping ideas, with different types of nuts and dried fruit—I'm obsessed with it."

"I love oatmeal too," Olivia chimed in, digging a spoon into Cameron's bowl.

"Olivia!"

"What? I thought we were doing family style. You know, small plates—sharing. That's what we always do."

"How the hell is anything in front of you a *small plate*? No one orders oatmeal family style. And you know what? No one orders burgers or ice cream family style either. Since when do you even like oatmeal? Aren't you worried there might be something healthy in there? Like *fruit*?"

"What are you talking about?" she replied. "All I eat is fruit. If I ate any more fruit, you'd have to peel me."

And she casually returned to her French toast and bacon.

Soon the time came to leave. Andrew shifted the table towards him so that Olivia could step out, and the movement sloshed the tea at the bottom of Cameron's cup. Cameron looked down and remembered the newspaper pinned under it.

"Do you want my copy of today's *Metropolitan Times*?"

Andrew shrugged.

"You should check it out. Remember that mystery about Lyndon Surway we told you about? There's a crazy story about it on the front page."

And he slapped the newspaper over Andrew's chest.

CHAPTER THIRTY

Long and Short Distances

Andrew urged himself not to look at the newspaper in his hand, the newspaper that had the *mystery about Lyndon Surway* on the front page. Was the discovery of the treasure in it? Was the *dent* in the treasure? Was *Andrew*'s name in it? He reached into his stomach, into the balls of his feet, for the strength to keep his eyes in front of him. The three of them paused on the sidewalk outside the coffee shop. Andrew looked at his friends, and he felt the pavement closing in around his legs. Cameron and Olivia were staring at him. Instantly, he was certain that they knew what he was thinking—that they knew what he had done. But then Olivia put her shades on and drowsily gazed around her.

"I suppose this is where we part ways," she said with a yawn that made her hand look tiny when she covered it, a few seconds late.

Andrew was lost.

"Aren't you going to class?"

She shook her head over the final stretch of her yawn.

"My first class isn't until ten."

"So, why did you wake up so early?"

"I told you," she answered without expression. "I *really* love breakfast."

Andrew burst into laughter. His stomach unclenched. His toes loosened. Cameron and Olivia didn't know.

"What are you going to do between now and class?" Cameron asked her.

She took another look around her, and this time she noticed one of her father's bodyguards across the street. She wore enormous dark sunglasses, but shades made of granite couldn't have hidden the roll of her eyes. She turned back to the two boys and said,

"I might just go shopping around here."

Andrew wondered what she could shop for on the main street of a sleepy village on a Tuesday morning—the nearest options were antiques, stamps and money orders, and the free sighting of a stationed fire truck. But before anyone could make a reply, she tossed out a "See you later" and strolled away.

Andrew started walking with Cameron towards Saint Clemens. His hand was wrapped around the newspaper. He could feel the unseen words pressing against his skin, burning their tiny letters into his fingers. But he couldn't read them. He had to wait until he was alone. He tightened his grip until he heard the paper crease.

Another anxiety came over him as he and Cameron walked in silence. What if the two of them had nothing to say to each other without Olivia? Class was at least another twelve, fifteen minutes away. What if they had nothing to talk about? The only sound between them since she had left was the tapping of their shoes.

Suddenly Cameron spoke.

"That was incredible, what you did on Friday night. You saved Olivia."

Then he added in a lower voice,

"Thank you, for doing that."

If there was a better answer than what he came up with, Andrew would never find it.

"No problem," he said.

They went on without talking for a few more blocks, until Cameron broke the silence again.

"So," he began, "how are you liking things?"

"How am I liking— what?"

"You know," the boy continued, waving his hands in the air. "Everything. The school, the town, the people... How do you like it here?"

Andrew shrugged. It struck him that through all the adventures, mysteries, and surprises of his short time in Spring Forge, he had never once paused to ask himself the question. He counted the days since he had arrived. The number made him stop on the sidewalk.

"I've been here only ten days," he muttered, more to himself than to Cameron.

He started raising his fingers to count again when he remembered the newspaper in his hand. He carried on walking.

He had first stepped out onto the platform of the Spring Forge train station less than two weeks ago. It had been less than two weeks since his fear that Mr. Brandow wouldn't be waiting there—that Mr. Brandow didn't actually exist. Two weeks ago, Andrew had never seen this side of the country. He had never seen any place that looked like Spring Forge, or anything that looked like Saint Clemens. He had never known anyone who might have known anyone like Cameron or Olivia, or like Jesse McGallender. He had never known that there could be people like the Brandows. Those few days, on this side of the train, had been more packed than the entire existence he had left behind on the other side. *Rich* was the only word that he could think of, rich with emotions and events. But the word then made him think of something else, something that tinkled and twinkled at the bottom of his backpack and on the cover of the newspaper, something that was buried in a cave beneath the earth. It was something so humongous that the rest of the country, the rest of the world, the rest of his life didn't seem large enough to contain it. He spoke again to hush his thoughts.

"I guess I like it a lot. Or maybe—maybe it's not so much that I like it, but just that it's become—" He searched for the word. "It's become reality. Really fast. Do you know what I mean? It feels like this is where I am, like this is where I'm staying. I always used to feel like I was nowhere—like anywhere I happened to be was just a stop on my way to somewhere else. But this place... this place feels different. It almost feels like I've been here for years. Almost as if I'd always been here, my whole life, even when I was thousands of miles away. Does that make any sense? I guess that sounds crazy."

"No—that's great," Cameron said, and there was just enough warmth in his voice to convince Andrew to continue.

"And the people are amazing. The people I'm staying with— the Brandows—they're the best people I've ever met. I can't believe how good they've been to me. I've never had—"

Suddenly he checked himself. He felt an uncomfortable glow in his cheeks. He had never intended to say so much, to reveal so much of himself. But it was too late to stop now. He had already begun the sentence.

"I've never had a family before," he said.

"That's great," Cameron said again, and though the words didn't mean anything, Andrew was thankful for the reply.

After a moment, he asked Cameron,

"How do *you* like it?"

The boy squinted into the distance.

"It's fine, I guess," he answered. Then, more solidly,

"I mean it's great. I have a bunch of friends here already from before, like Olivia, of course. The town's beautiful, and it's an excellent school. I've known the place, or at least I've known *of* it, for as long as I can remember. It's all great. There's really nothing to complain about."

Andrew had no idea what the words stuck inside Cameron's mouth could be. After a few seconds, Cameron attempted,

"I'm just..."

But there he paused, and Andrew wondered if the words were even harder to say than he had thought.

"I'm just really excited," Cameron began again, "to see what lies ahead for you. Forget about me. I'm fine. I'm doing great. I always will be. But you? You're a bit of a wild card, obviously!"

Andrew laughed. No one had ever described him as a wild card before, or a wild *anything*.

"What do you mean?"

Cameron grinned as he went on.

"It's clear that you're a huge mystery for everyone! You just said that you'd never been on this side of the country, that everyone you meet is completely new to you. Well, *you're* just as completely new to us! No one here knows anything about you, anything about where you're from, or what it's like over there, or where you're going, or what you're thinking. It's all a big enigma. Everything about you is a mystery. Where you've been, where you're headed, what goes on inside your head..."

"Usually not that much," Andrew snickered.

But Cameron countered, completely serious,

"That can't be true. You're the Saint Clemens Scholar. You must be brilliant. But even that's a bit of a riddle—how is your intelligence going to show itself? Are you going to be better than everyone else in every one of your classes? Or will you be too intelligent to function normally, among the rest of us regular kids? Are you going to get bored? Are you going to get lazy and slack off? Or will you be tempted to have too much fun? But forget about school—what about life? What lies ahead for Mr. Andrew Day, Mr. Saint Clemens Scholar, from the middle of nowhere? Who the hell knows?"

They passed through the gate under the red dragon and into the shaded driveway of the school.

"You could discover a talent that no one ever knew you had," Cameron went on, "that no one has ever looked for in you, not even yourself. Or you could end up living on the street if you wanted to—no one here's going to stop you. Or you could end up living on the street even if you *don't* want to, if that turns out to be your place in the world. But you could also become a tycoon. You could pull yourself up by your bootstraps. You could just get lucky, or be smart enough, or work hard enough and build a fortune from scratch, like Lyndon Surway himself! You could become a criminal mastermind. That could be your secret goal for all I know. Or you could become a crazy artist, or some wandering bandit, or some zany scientist. You could be any of these things and anything in between. And even if you landed somewhere in the middle, somewhere pretty normal and decent, say, as a banker or a lawyer, you would still have gone much further, you would have covered a lot more ground, in every possible way, than anyone else at this school. Everyone else here has had the whole future spoon-fed to them."

They walked around the fountain at the end of the driveway, past the main building where they had found themselves under the same roof for the first time just a few days ago.

"That's why all eyes are on you," Cameron said. "That's why it's so interesting to see what you're up to every day. There's never been another Saint Clemens scholar! You're the biggest mystery in town, since... since..." He screwed up his eyes, searching. "Since the Surway fortune itself!"

Once again Andrew burst out laughing. The reference didn't even jolt him. They stopped in front of the building where his class was about to start. Andrew realized that they were going to different places.

"What about you?" he said. "Your path isn't that straightforward either. You said that you're doing great, and that you'll always do great. But it's not entirely clear what *that's* going to look like. All you have is the base, the foundation. It's like the oatmeal that you love so much. You said so yourself—you can't stop thinking about new topping ideas."

Cameron chuckled.

"That's what you said!" Andrew went on. "Who knows what kinds of seeds and fruit and spices and nuts you could throw in there... You could even make savory oatmeal, for all anyone knows! You could make dinner out of oatmeal. There's no reason your future's any more predictable than mine. The only person who can ever know where you're going is yourself, and even you can't see much further than the next place your foot lands."

The smile that was never more than a few seconds away finally tumbled over Cameron's face, like the ruffled hair over his head.

"That's the best thing about you," he said to Andrew, holding out his hand. "There's so much excitement coming off of you that the people around you can catch some of it."

He shook Andrew's hand and disappeared to his own class.

Andrew was hardly aware of the newspaper in his hand as he leapt up the steps of the building two at a time. He dug himself into a seat at the back of the auditorium, leaving his jacket open on his shoulders like a blanket. Looking around, he saw a few of his new acquaintances from the ball—new friends perhaps—and exchanged a few nods. The professor walked onto the stage, and the class on speech and rhetoric began.

There was a curtain behind the professor. Grave and eloquent, she told the audience that there was somebody behind it. She said that it was somebody everyone knew, someone celebrated around the world for the clarity of her speech and the beauty of her elocution. It was someone to whom the whole class should be grateful. And now, the teacher asked, would anyone in the room like to come down to the front for a conversation with their guest? It could be on any topic of the student's choosing. The only goal was to speak with confidence.

Several hands shot up around Andrew. The teacher called out Miss Hansler from the other side of the room. Andrew turned to look as the tall, quiet girl stood up. He knew who she was. After only a few days, people were starting to talk about her as the best student of the freshman class. All eyes followed her to the stage. The curtain went up.

A gasp of wonder rose across the auditorium. Then applause erupted. Even Andrew could recognize the face grinning back at the room, one of the most well-known faces on the planet. Their guest was the most famous actress in the world. She beamed at the euphoric students and bowed her head as they clapped. Then she rose from her seat to shake hands with Miss Hansler. But Miss Hansler was as arrogant as she was intelligent, maybe even more so. The only thing in the room even more extraordinary than the actress's presence was Miss Hansler's indifference.

The student chose a topic that she seemed to know even better than her interlocutor: "success." The two of them began to talk. But when the actress spoke of her own beginnings, of the poverty she had overcome and the wretched home she had fled, Andrew felt that she was speaking to him, with words that Cameron had also used. And for an hour, he thought not about the cuff links and the cave, not about the newspaper in his bag, but of great, unknown things that he couldn't imagine yet.

The class went by quickly. By the end of it, Andrew was ready to face the newspaper. He pulled it out of his backpack on the front steps of the building. But then he checked himself. He looked at the time. He had five minutes before his next class. He stepped onto the lawn and walked over to a tree that cast a wide shadow over the grass. He leaned back against the trunk without taking off his backpack. Then he straightened the paper and turned his eyes to the front page.

By the time he looked up, over an hour had passed, and his next class had ended.

CHAPTER THIRTY-ONE

The Return

The rest of the day was a fog in Andrew's mind. The President himself could have attended all his classes and Andrew wouldn't have noticed. For Andrew, there was only one other person left in the world. No, it wasn't even a person; it wasn't even a man. It was a name. It wasn't even a name; it was a signature. *Lucian Baker*. The sound purled in his head. It rushed with a downward swoop and pooled at the bottom of the first name, *Lucian*. There it paused for a moment's breath before springing across the last name and dissolving in a coil: *Baker*. And just as the signature was no longer a name, the sound itself no longer had any meaning. It was just a noise, a vibration, both a murmur and a din that filled the bones of his face with dread. *Lucian Baker*.

Where was Lucian Baker? When had he returned, and what did he know? Did he know where it was? Did he know that someone had found it? Did he know that *Andrew Day* had found it?

Andrew shuddered at his own name. He stopped pronouncing it in his head for fear that someone else might hear it. He added it to his unwritten list of unsayable things. With every passing minute, more of his life became unspeakable; more of the world became a hush. Only four syllables remained, syllables that, try as he might, he couldn't remove from his mind, syllables whose letters he couldn't peel off his eyes. *Lucian Baker.* The stickiest syllables of all time.

He could no longer see or hear anything beyond them. He didn't even notice the turn in the weather, the gray cast in the sky, which only mirrored the haze in his head. He was oblivious to the bodyguards on campus. He barely glanced towards the sections of the school that were closed off, buildings whose walls were black from the fires of Friday night. His mind was stuck with the cuff links and the suit in his backpack, pressed against the newspaper that observed them like a staring passenger on a train. He was hardly aware of where he was. He didn't seem to notice that history class had relocated among the vines of the indoor rainforest, or that philosophy was being taught under the gazes of the cows in the Saint Clemens barn. He avoided his classmates. He hung back from everyone around him, especially people he knew. He even hurried away from Jesse when he caught sight of him between classes.

But there was one encounter he couldn't prevent. Early in the afternoon, as he turned down a hallway, he bumped into the principal. The man locked his huffy, puffy stare on Andrew's face.

"Good afternoon, Mr. Day."

Even in his distraction, the boy cringed. Every time the principal said his name, Andrew felt the need to rinse it in cold water.

"Good afternoon," he answered blankly.

Immediately he knew the principal had something to tell him. The man didn't budge from his path, didn't shift his eyes from Andrew's face. Finally, he said,

"That was quite a performance on Friday night. It was highly accomplished."

Andrew answered without trying to interpret the words.

"Thank you."

But the principal remained where he stood, still blocking Andrew's way.

"You made your way out of the riverside through the burning tent, didn't you?"

"Yes," Andrew said.

"On your way out of the tent..." the principal continued, and he lowered his voice. For a few seconds he hesitated. He leaned over slightly closer to Andrew's face.

"On your way out of the tent," he began again, "did you happen to... pick anything up?"

This time Andrew made an effort to understand. He couldn't fathom what the principal meant. The only thing he could do was reach back into his memory and answer the question as literally as possible.

"No," he replied.

The principal nodded slowly. Then he leaned forward again, even more closely than before, so closely that Andrew felt his breath in his ear.

"You see," he said, in a voice that was almost inaudible, "out of respect after what happened, we have decided not to share the results of the BnC contest this year. So you might be thinking that you won. Well..." He paused again. "I just wanted you to know that you didn't."

Andrew felt a wave of nausea. It wasn't the disappointment of having lost. It wasn't even the manner in which the principal told him. It was the principal himself. It should have been easy to look up to him. He was a man of authority in a place of learning, tasked with teaching a lifelong lesson in respect. And to see his preoccupation with something so petty, to see him pitting himself for no reason against a kid, against someone a third, a quarter of his own age, filled Andrew with disgust. He found nothing to say in reply. He just stepped around the principal and continued on his way.

At last the school day came to an end. Andrew walked up the path to the campus gate without hurrying. There was no need to run. There was no need at that moment to do anything different from what he had done on previous days, from what he would do again and again in days and months to come. He would walk out of the gate and take a right down the road. He would follow it alongside the campus until the road became the main street. The trees would grow thinner, the lampposts would tighten, and houses and shops would replace the towers and lawns of Saint Clemens. But then, his path would change. At that point he would have to do something he had never done. It was only one thing, and he would have to do it only once. Somewhere before the turn that led up into the foothills where the Brandows lived, Andrew would stop. He would find a taxi. He would open the door and wiggle his way down the backseat, and he would give the driver the name of a place in the next town over. That was all he had to do. Once the driver started driving, all the other steps would fall into place. As Andrew passed through the gate of the school and came out onto the road, he didn't even think of the things that would happen next. They would set themselves in motion one after the other. They would roll on in their quiet momentum like the footsteps that carried him out of campus. He had told the Brandows that his day would be long. He had time. There was no reason to hurry.

In fact, the letter in the newspaper changed nothing. He had decided to return the money before he had read it, before he had known the letter existed. There was no reason to feel like a criminal. Perhaps there had never been a crime at all. He certainly hadn't hurt anybody, and he had taken the money only in a moment of need. Perhaps he had always meant, from the beginning, only to *borrow* the money. Perhaps he had struck a quick, unspoken deal with Benjamin Franklin, as well as the salesman at the jewelry store. Perhaps he had had an understanding with the tailor at the department store who had run the tape measure around his neck. Maybe he had always known that his sudden fortune would last only a few hours. Maybe he had considered it to be just a dream, just a few hours' escape from reality, the first vacation from himself that life had ever offered him. Who knows what had gone through his mind? Who knows what he was thinking right when he had wedged the last stack of bills into his pants? Perhaps he had known, at that moment, that he would later go back and replace it. Perhaps that was the reason his memory had precisely set down the location of the hidden entrance in the woods. Who knows? It was difficult to remember now what had been almost impossible to believe then.

But there was one image he couldn't erase from his mind. It wasn't something he had witnessed. Maybe it had never even happened. But he kept on imagining it as he walked, and it weighed him down with each step until he thought he couldn't go on. It was the thought of Lucian Baker in the cave. It was the thought of this other person, of the rightful person, finding his way through the tunnels to the treasure in the cave. Lucian Baker would see the dip in the floor. He would know money had been stolen. He would instantly discover that someone else had found the fortune, that someone else had been there first. And this notion of *someone else* in Lucian Baker's mind, of *someone else* who was Andrew, hobbled his feet as he went. To disentangle them, he started to run.

The sky was a brooding gray when Andrew stepped into a taxi to leave Spring Forge. It was barely a shade darker when he stepped into another one to come back. He no longer had the cuff links. He no longer had the suit. For the first few minutes, he was convinced that he was being followed. He was afraid to ask the driver to go faster. All his courage was consumed in looking out the rear window. But the shops soon disappeared behind him. He let his head fall back over the seat and closed his eyes. The return cab didn't drop him off on the main street. It took him instead to an intersection in the back roads of Spring Forge where there was a gas station and a diner. Andrew remembered them well, particularly the L-shaped diner, whose name he had learned without realizing it. He paid the driver, gave him two dollars extra, and got out of the car. He looked in through the window of the diner. He tried to breathe in the smell of coffee and toast, and the yellow, tired air that places have when they never sleep, like people. He wanted to plop into a stiff red leather booth, watch the day turn into night, and spend the silent hours staring at a plate of breakfast in a cloud of steam. He sighed. *Maybe tomorrow?* He turned around and began to walk up the sloping road towards the woods. The cab was gone, and the road was silent.

Andrew trudged up the road. The bag on his back was lighter than it had been all day. It had returned to its familiar droop. He could feel it in his shoulders. But there was a new weight in his pocket that dug into his leg with each step. He felt its denseness against his skin, bending slightly around his thigh, not so much following the line of his leg as clasping it. He was sore behind his knees as he carried the money up the road.

Then he stopped. He took a final look behind him and another glance ahead. The clouds were streaked with purple. The road was dark in both directions as far as he could see. The day had ended. All was still. A shiver ran down his back. *From the cold*, he thought. He stepped onto the grass and walked to a tree that was slightly bent. He had marked it in his mind, the night he had crawled out of the cave.

He laid his hand on the trunk. He screwed up his eyes and peered into the distance through the woods. A few steps from where he stood, a stub of rock poked out of the carpet of fallen leaves. Quietly, slowly, almost on tiptoe, he came to the rock, hunching against the crackle of the leaves beneath his shoes. He no longer felt the money in his pocket. The stack of bills had faded away, like the rest of the world around him. Even more silent than before, he bent down and touched a knee to the ground. He rested a hand on top of the rock and took a breath. Then he brought his hand to the ground, breaking the surface of the forest floor where he had covered it with leaves on Friday. He paused. He couldn't see his fingers beneath the leaves, but the tip of his middle finger gave a soft nudge into the earth. The soil crumbled away before it. There was a hole in the ground.

He commanded himself to stand up. He planned to look around him once again, to take one last look in every direction. But his legs wouldn't obey him. He could hardly move at all. And so the only thing to do, the only thing he *could* do, was reach further with his middle finger, draw his other fingers around it and drive them deeper into the ground. Down they slipped into the hole, and his wrist sank beneath the leaves. He pulled out his hand and swept off the soil, the needles, and the twigs where he had dug, and the hole in the ground stared up at him.

CHAPTER THIRTY-TWO

In the Cave

Andrew climbed down the hole. He felt himself shrinking as he went. His eyes narrowed at the darkness, his lungs withered at the dust, his limbs tightened into crooks and his fingers pointed into claws as he scrambled down like a badger. He landed in a crouch on the tunnel floor. He stood up, brushed the dirt from his clothes and looked around him. Light had followed him down from the hole in the ground. There it was, just a few steps from his feet, brighter and clearer in the twilight than he had seen it in the nighttime: a white arrow. It pointed left.

He passed the next arrow and the next one. Keeping his eyes on the ground, leaping through the shafts of light from the ceiling, he began to run. He lifted his eyes in between the arrows and saw the metal signs on the walls, the old metal signs engraved with street names, none of which he recognized from the world above. But the signs, he felt, could recognize him. They greeted him as he raced through their city, a city whose signposts and plan seemed to have been designed for him alone.

For him? Or for someone else. They had been planned for someone else, were meant to guide somebody else. Andrew had intruded upon them. He could see them only because there was nowhere left for them to hide, since the darkness, the silence and the earth hadn't been enough. They began to eye him with suspicion. They were helpless against him. Andrew ran faster so that he wouldn't face their reproach. He ran fast enough to silence his own thoughts. He hurtled from one tunnel to another, from one arrow to the next, until finally he arrived in the room underneath the river.

He was alone. There was no one else underground. He bent over, rested his hands on his knees, and caught his breath. As he straightened up, he felt every danger and dread float away from him with the waves that shimmered on the walls.

He passed the glass pillar filled with water and climbed the wall of rock at the end of the room. He reached the top so fast that he felt dazed. The glass ceiling of the chamber ended right above the wall he had just scaled. The sight of the river flowing over it was both soothing and dizzying. As soon as he could stand, he turned around. Comfortingly dark, the sewer stretched out before him, unfurling in his eyes as they adjusted to the gloom. But he couldn't see the end of it. Once again, the question stunned him. Where did it lead? Was he standing at the beginning or at the end? If the beginning of this passage was the room beneath the river, or the tunnel that led to the stairs, or the stairs beneath the house, or the yellow room at the top of the stairs, then where was the end?

Andrew clapped his hands over his ears. *No more questions.* He looked down at his feet. He would go no further. He would never go further. Wherever the passage began, wherever it ended, he knew that the center of the maze, and the end of his own journey, lay on the other side of the opening in the wall to his right. Down in that darkness was the core of the labyrinth. There was its heart, which went on beating day after day below the earth.

Andrew took a step towards the opening. This time he wouldn't slip. He lay down his foot among the rocks, holding on to the teeth of the broken wall. Then he straddled the opening and shifted his weight to the other side. He looked down and saw the slope of loose rocks that he had tumbled down the first time. A ceiling of rock slanted over it, so low that he could touch it by raising his arm. He couldn't see the cave at the bottom of the slope. He imagined in the silence that he could hear it. He sat down.

The danger was past. There was no one else in the cave, no one else in the passage behind him. The stillness around him, the silence in every direction, was complete. He had arrived at the treasure all alone. He lifted himself slightly and tried to sweep off the rocks from the floor under his pants. He sat down again and drew his knees to his face. He slipped his arms out of his backpack and pulled out the black notebook. Holding it in both hands, he stared at the cover. The black leather whirled in his eyes. A thought surfaced before him. It was the same thought, now fully formed, that had seized him unexpectedly at random moments since Friday.

What if he *didn't* return the money? What if he kept it in his pocket? He reached out towards the idea slowly, as if it were an animal that could bite. So what if Lucian Baker had returned? So what if the heir had found his way back to Spring Forge? What difference could a single stack of bills make to him, when there was so much more money in the cave, when there were so many more bills than any pocket in the world could hold? And this single stack of bills was more money, by far, than Andrew had ever held in his life.

The idea turned and shifted in his mind. What if he did keep the money—who would ever find out? How would anyone ever discover who had taken it? Maybe he could even hide its disappearance. Maybe he could go down to the cave and stuff paper underneath the bills to hide the gap. Or he could remove an entire level from the floor—he could multiply his treasure, a hundred times, a thousand times over, simply by shaving off the top layer of money and taking it with him. Then, not only would he hide his tracks—he would also gain the wealth of a lifetime. He would be richer than he had ever imagined. And who would ever find out?

The idea twisted and spiraled in his brain. It grew more entitled, more imperious. He squinted in the darkness. What if, instead of hiding, instead of making a criminal of himself, instead of falling from the cave's shadow into an even deeper shadow that he could never climb out of, what if he faced Lucian Baker? What if he fought him for the treasure? If becoming a thief was an option, then why not become a fighter? Wasn't it less shameful? Cameron had said something to him that morning, just a few hours ago, that it was all a big enigma, a giant question mark, that he could become anything at all in the world, an artist, a tycoon, a scientist or a felon. What if he became a nemesis instead, a foe to Lucian Baker? What if he became a contender? Andrew had been in Spring Forge less than two weeks. It had taken him less than two weeks to find his way to the treasure. Wasn't it natural, wasn't it only fair, wasn't it in the order of things, that he should at least stand his ground for what he had found, when it had taken his opponent several decades to come and claim it? If the treasure had been meant for Lucian Baker, then why had he abandoned it for so long? Why had Lucian Baker let the course of decades run by, past the turn of a century, past the springtime of his own life, when poor teenagers were out chasing their fortunes every day? Andrew gazed into the nothingness in front of him. The tightness of his stare lifted shades out of the darkness. The veins of his hands stuck out as he clenched the notebook.

There, in the gloom, in the sloping ceiling of rock in front of him, the blackness took shape. He had focused on it for so long, without knowing it, that the lines of the stones grew distinct. Maybe Andrew himself had penetrated their surface. Nothing around him was dark anymore. And then he recognized himself in the rock. He saw the shape of his own thoughts in the blackness before him. Suddenly he gasped. He realized what the treasure had done to him. He realized how far outside of himself it had taken him. The distance was longer than all the tunnels he had followed. It was wider than the entire country he had crossed. And although somewhere in the tunnels, while running, he had ceased to feel cold, he suddenly shivered.

Cameron was right—it was a big riddle. But only Andrew held the answer. He would become whatever he set out to be. He would make of himself whatever he wanted. And this tangle of darkness was not what he wanted. The bills in the cave, the stack in his pocket were only paper. They were sheets of paper that weren't addressed to him. There was an entire universe out there, far beyond the cave, far above this little chamber buried under forest and rock, a universe where innumerable paths awaited, where there were even more paths, uncountably more, than Lucian Baker had ever traveled. And all those paths were Andrew's. Let Lucian Baker have his own. The paths above all waited for Andrew, and the treasures they kept would make the entire hoard of gold and money in the cave fade into dust.

He sighed quietly and opened the notebook in his hands. From the faint light that spilled from the passage behind him, he saw his own name written on top of the first page, promising a reward of gratitude + one dollar. He flipped to the next page and saw two numbers jotted down. He was almost surprised to find that his handwriting was still the same. *300* and *100*. His school-supply stipend for the first semester, and the price, rounded up, of the bulldog cuff links on the main street. He squinted and counted in his head. It was a calculation he had already done over and over. It had four numbers, one for each of the cab rides he had taken—two trips to buy the cuff links and the suit and two more to return them. He pulled out his pen and wrote down the total on the page below the other two numbers: *89*. The same implacable total every time. By a stupid coincidence, it was also the exact price of the bulldog cuff links. He gave a humorless chuckle. He had spent just as much money buying and returning the diamond cuff links as if he had simply bought the bulldogs. He had lost as much money as if he had never found the treasure.

He tried to cheer himself up. *At least you got to be the most elegant person at the party for a few hours. You got to wear the best cuff links of all.* But then he remembered what the principal had told him. He didn't win. *Thanks for clearing that up, jerk.* He sighed once more and shrugged. Then he closed his notebook and got up. At least he hadn't done anything irreparably wrong. True, he had lost about a third of his semester's budget on cab rides, and he would never get that money back, but at least it had been his own money. At least he wasn't a thief. One last thought came into his head before he made his way down to the treasure. He had never had money before. For the first time in his life, he realized that he didn't want it. The discovery lightened his feet. He almost hopped down the whole way.

He reached the bottom of the cave, and the notebook in his hand smacked to the ground. He didn't hear it. He didn't even bend down to pick it up. He couldn't even feel the pummeling of his heart or the torrent of blood rushing from his face. He failed to realize, for the second time, that there was a pale blue glow in the cave that his presence had triggered. The only thing he could sense, the only thing he could see, was a small muted glint in the distance. It hovered faintly in front of him in a tiny metal mound dipping crookedly into the floor. He recognized it immediately. He even remembered, in his shock, that someone had asked him about it that day, though at the time he hadn't understood. He couldn't remember what he had answered. He couldn't remember what he had thought. For a moment, as he stood staring, he couldn't even remember where he was, or how he had arrived there, or why he had come there. The only thing he knew was that there in front of him, on the floor, poised over the gap he had left when he had taken the stack of bills, was the red-and-silver crown of the BnC King.

CHAPTER THIRTY-THREE

Without a Face

Andrew didn't have any dreams that night, but somehow he must have slept. He knew this as soon as the alarm clock rang on the windowsill, as soon as he opened his eyes: there had been a blankness, a silence on the other side of the blare. And his first emotion when he woke up that morning wasn't fear. It was grief for this place that he had lost, this empty land of sleep that had shut out his dread.

He ate breakfast with the Brandows as if nothing had happened. Of course he was terrified; there was nothing he could do to help that. But no good would come of showing his fear to those around him. No good would come of staring at it himself. There was no room in these events for any weakness at all. His body still obeyed him, and he ordered it to keep going as it had always done.

He ate his pancakes not too fast, not too slowly. He commented on how delicious they were (and they truly were, as always) not too eagerly, not too timidly, and he said a few generic things about the day ahead. He mentioned school and the weather. He knew exactly what to do. He felt that every movement, every word had been set down for him in advance. He felt that there were now two Andrews. There was the Andrew who felt and discerned everything, who plotted and shuddered as the hours went by. And then there was a second Andrew whose only responsibility was to keep the rest of the world from seeing the first. This second Andrew had arrived last night. He had delivered a plausible excuse to the Brandows for having come back so late (the story of an impromptu baseball game had also explained his dirty hair and muddy clothes). He had talked about the day's classes at dinner. And it was he who now raved about the perfect crispiness of the caramelized bananas (something the first Andrew enjoyed just as much, as quiet as he may have been). And as the minutes went on, Andrew had to recognize that he was deeply impressed with this second self who did a remarkable job of making everything seem normal. In fact, the only thing about this second Andrew that gave the first Andrew pause, that almost worried the real Andrew, was how easily he could hide the truth.

But hiding something from the Brandows—*No*, he had to be honest with himself if with no one else, *fooling* the Brandows—made Andrew unutterably sad. To see him happy at breakfast made them happy. They didn't poke or squint at the impression he gave. They only smiled at it without question; the morning sun promised a beautiful day. But the morning he showed them was a lie. And it terrified him to be all alone across from them, on the other side of a lie.

But he couldn't tell them his secret. He felt that telling them would mean involving them, and involving them might put them in danger. Nothing in the world could be worse. He needed to keep them safe, not only because they protected and cared for him, not only because, for the first time in his life, he wasn't the only person looking out for himself. There was another reason. There was a new emotion in him, another instinct that he had never known existed. He needed to keep them safe also because he was responsible for them, because they needed him just as much as he needed them. It was his duty to protect them, however he could, doing whatever he could, for as long as he lived. And this feeling, he discovered, could rise even above his fear, even above his desire to confide in them and ask them for help. As he gulped the last of his tea and wiped the syrup off his lips, he realized this new emotion was the only one he could be proud of. By the time he left their house, he was certain that they suspected nothing. And the thought of being strong for them gave him the strength to defy the rest of the world.

But he was still afraid. Someone had been inside the cave. Someone had noticed the gap in the floor. Someone had discovered the theft. Someone knew what Andrew had done and had known that Andrew would go back. Someone had waited for Andrew, someone who knew who he was. Someone had caught him. Someone was playing with him. One final thought always came back, the eeriest thought of all. *It was someone who had been at the BnC Ball.* It was someone who had seen the crown, who had been near the crown, who had picked it up and stolen it just as Andrew had picked up and stolen the stack of bills. Perhaps it was someone who had seen the diamond cuff links on Andrew's wrists. Perhaps someone had understood where they had come from—*what* they had come from. It must have been someone who had seen Andrew. The logical outcome of this thought trickled like ice down his back. It must have been someone *he* had seen.

Who could it be? Was it a guest he didn't know, some guest he hadn't talked to? Or was it someone he had greeted, someone whose hand he had shaken, someone whose smile he had smiled at? Was it someone whose name he knew? Was it someone even more deceitful than Andrew, an even better liar? Maybe it wasn't a guest. Maybe it was a man in a golden mask, one of those faces without eyes. The possibilities paralyzed Andrew. There were masks of gold and masks of skin. Under the black light of his fear, demonic shadows appeared beneath the faces he knew and the masks he remembered. It could be any face in the world. Andrew had no idea who it was. But the eyes in that face knew who *he* was.

He had never touched the BnC crown, but he felt it on his head. He felt it in his chest. It was jammed in his throat. It told him, like nothing he had seen, like nothing he had experienced since he had first heard of the Surway fortune, that he was now involved. It didn't matter that he had gone to replace the money. It was too late now. It was too late to disappear, too late to creep up to the surface of the earth. He was caught. The crown inside the cave was not like the letter published in the paper. The letter changed nothing. Nothing in it was addressed to Andrew. But the crown was a message for him. It was tipped over the dent left by the money he had taken. It was a keepsake from Andrew's ball, a memento from his theft. He couldn't pretend that it had never existed simply by looking away from it, simply by putting it away like the newspaper. The crown itself would continue to hover over his head wherever he went. The hands that had left it would reach out for him. The eyes that had seen it could still see him.

He had left the crown in the cave. Replacing the money had been tricky with the crown in the way. He had been afraid of touching it, with a brute, unreasoning fear. He had found it almost impossible just to approach the crown and bend over it, or even to look at it up close. His only choice had been to drop the money over the gap, as close as possible, letting it plop over the silver rim of the crown. Then he had climbed up the slope of rock without looking back.

But the crown still followed him. It had spied on him last night from the shadow of the wardrobe. He had known, lying in bed, that it would spy on him all night. He had known that even if somehow he managed to fall asleep, the crown would stay awake and watch him. It had snickered at him from under the floorboards at breakfast, so quietly, so sneakily, that the Brandows hadn't heard it. And it jogged alongside him behind the trees as he hurried to school, that gaze without a face, those red-and-silver eyes. He felt them following him into school.

CHAPTER THIRTY-FOUR

Without a Name

He kept to himself all morning, asking no more of the second Andrew, the outward Andrew, than a few waves and quiet hellos to people he knew. He avoided Cameron and Olivia, but they found him by chance at lunchtime eating a sandwich by the river. He winced when he saw them walking towards him from the lawn. He forced his face into a smile. But he found it stuck on his cheeks when he saw them smiling back. It was the first true emotion he had shown all day. By the time he could hear their footsteps, he was beckoning them over with his hand.

"We clearly think alike," Olivia said when she arrived at the edge of the water. "Maybe all three of us should be Saint Clemens Scholars."

She pressed her skirt behind her legs before sliding down to the grass beside Andrew.

"I'm excited to have all my food in a bag for once," Cameron said, sitting down between them. "Maybe this will keep your hands off of it, Olivia."

"Like a paper bag's going to stand in my way," she said.

Following a morning of frozen emotions, laughter felt like hot chocolate in Andrew's mouth. Olivia turned to him.

"It's a beautiful day to be out here, and it's so nice to get a break from all that talk going on in the dining hall. Everyone's going crazy over that Surway business."

Andrew flinched. He was glad the sun was in his face when Cameron asked him, flourishing a sandwich out of a paper bag,

"Did you read that article in the paper I gave you yesterday?"

"Yeah."

Though he couldn't explain why, seeming normal with Cameron and Olivia was considerably harder than with the Brandows. Gone were the first and second Andrew. With Cameron and Olivia, just being Andrew at all was always challenge enough.

"It's just my luck," Olivia said, lifting a plastic fork to her mouth from a bowl in her lap. "And I mean that as *good* luck."

She swallowed and continued.

"For decades the trail goes cold. Nothing happens in the Surway House or anywhere near Spring Forge, let alone at Saint Clem's. No one has even spoken the name *Lucian Baker* in years. I show up as a student and boom! Explosions everywhere, unexplained break-ins, unidentified figures in windows, menacing messages in the sky, anonymous deliveries to the newspaper..."

"Well, not exactly anonymous," Cameron broke in. "The letter came from Lucian Baker."

He looked at Andrew. It was Andrew's turn to say something, but the words were lodged at the base of his throat. Helpless, he took another bite of his sandwich.

Fortunately, Cameron went on.

"That letter has to be real. It must have come from Lucian Baker."

"We don't know anything for sure," Olivia said.

"But we do!" Cameron continued. "We have a copy of the property deed—the deed to Surway House! Now *that's* something you can't fake, not with the world's best lawyers double-checking and triple-checking everything. That copy is genuine. How could anyone but the real Lucian Baker get his hands on the real deed? It was never released to the public. It was never released to anyone! No one's seen it since it disappeared from the county records. Only the real Lucian Baker could have it."

"The real Lucian Baker," Olivia rejoined, "or whoever that person is, the person to whom Lyndon Surway left everything. Whatever that person's *actual* name is."

"You don't think that's an actual person's name?" Andrew asked. The thought had never occurred to him.

Olivia squinted as she considered. So deep was her reflection that she lowered her fork, still full of food, into her picnic bag.

"To me," she began, "it just doesn't *sound* like an actual name. It sounds phony. Obviously *some people* are really named Lucian Baker. But none of them was ever able to prove a legitimate tie to Lyndon Surway. Just think about it: if a *real* Lucian Baker, who was *really* tied to Lyndon Surway in some way, was actually alive in the world—anywhere in the world—then surely somebody at some point would have found him. An army of attorneys, journalists and detectives have been on this case for years, for decades, ever since Lyndon Surway disappeared. If there really has been someone with that name all this time, how come no one has ever found him? How is that possible?"

Andrew had no reply. At last Cameron ventured,

"The world is a giant place."

As no one spoke, he added,

"And you've got to remember: when Lucian Baker, or whatever his real name is, left the country, all those years ago, our access to information was much more limited than it is today. In those days, it was much easier for people to just fade away. And he could have changed his name since then. He could have changed it a hundred times over!"

Olivia nodded.

"I suppose that's possible," she said. "But you have to admit it just sounds like a code. *Lucian Baker.* It sounds made-up!"

"So what are you saying?" asked Andrew.

She leaned back on her hands and her hair fell off her shoulder.

"I'm not saying there's no Lucian Baker. There must be dozens of them in the world. But what I *am* saying is that Lyndon Surway never knew any of them. He never meant to leave anything to any one of them. He just picked a name."

She looked into Andrew's eyes, and for once there was nothing sly in her smile.

"I never told you my theory, did I? Well, here it is. I believe that Lyndon Surway intended to have an heir. Why wouldn't he? He was famous for his generosity. He did want *someone* to inherit everything. And he chose the name Lucian Baker for that person—as a code. But he disappeared before he could tell that person. And that person never found out. And so there really is—or was—someone out there singled out by Lyndon Surway as his heir. And there really is a hidden treasure somewhere. But the rightful owner never found it. And Lucian Baker doesn't know that he or she is Lucian Baker. That's been my theory all along."

After a pause, she added,

"I don't know how this *property deed* fits into it." Her voice managed to make the detail sound idiotic. "But I stand by my belief."

Andrew considered her words in silence. He considered the name—*Lucian Baker.* With his friends at his side, in the brightness of daylight, he was able to pronounce it in his mind for the first time since leaving the cave. *Lucian Baker.* He tried to rediscover it. He tried to sound out the syllables in his head as if he had never heard them. Was it a code name? Did it *sound* like a code name? Obviously there were real Lucian Bakers in the world. Everyone knew there were. But was one of them *the* Lucian Baker? Or was Lucian Baker a made-up name given to someone else? The question, then, to ask was not whether the name sounded real, but whether it sounded *fake*. Was it a name Lyndon Surway might have chosen at random? Was it a name he could have invented? Andrew struggled to answer. The name was embedded too deeply in his head. He couldn't rip it apart from all the notions and feelings it had rooted in his brain. *Lucian Baker.* He might as well have asked himself if *Andrew Day* sounded genuine. The name had blended into his consciousness. *Lucian Baker.* He must have felt *something* back when he had come across the syllables for the first time, only a few days ago. But the impression was gone. And as he wondered to himself, Andrew realized that he wished he had never doubted the name. He hoped that there was a reality behind it. He was already facing someone without a face. He didn't want to be left without a name.

"It's the Lucian part," Olivia went on. "Baker, fine. But *Lucian?* Who the hell is named Lucian?"

"Now you're just talking nonsense," Cameron said. "You said so yourself: there are lots of real Lucian Bakers out there. And there must have been a lot more in the mid-twentieth century. Names go in and out of fashion. I have a great-aunt who was born in the thirties. Her name is Gwendelaide."

The three of them burst out laughing; Olivia almost spilled her bottle of sparkling water all over her blazer. But great-aunt Gwendelaide didn't stay with them for long. Silence soon fell over their picnic, stirred only by the purling of the river.

After a while, Cameron said, mostly musing to himself,

"I'm actually a Lucian if you go back a few generations."

Andrew started. He turned to Cameron as if seeing him for the first time.

"What do you mean?"

"I'm a Lucian," the boy said again. "My great-grandfather's name was Lucian. Well actually that was his *last* name."

Andrew exhaled.

"So that's useless," Olivia said.

Cameron chuckled.

"Don't talk about my great-grandfather that way. *You're* useless. It's actually the side of the family that's from around here, just up the valley. All those lands alongside the river used to be the great country estates of the City's prominent families. My great-grandfather, who was in the tobacco business, owned half the mountain on the other side of Spring Forge, right past that bend. We still have pictures of the old family home in our photo albums."

"What happened to it?" Andrew asked.

Cameron looked down.

"The couple of generations that came after lost it all."

In a muted voice, he added,

"That was all on my father's side."

Andrew and Olivia said nothing. After a moment, Cameron resumed,

"What difference does it make anyway whether Lucian Baker's a code name? The point is that *someone* wrote that letter. And this *someone* holds a document from Surway's inheritance that everyone else thought was lost forever. Someone knows the truth, whatever his name is."

"Or *her* name," Olivia interjected with a raised eyebrow.

"Or her name," Cameron repeated, smiling.

A question was taking shape in Andrew's mind. He peered into the sunlight through the trees.

"One thing I don't understand," he began, so quietly that Cameron and Olivia leaned in closer. "Why would Lyndon Surway use a code name in his will? I could imagine situations where he might want to hide his own name under a pseudonym. But why create a pseudonym for someone else? Why create a mystery at all? He could have just named his heir and made sure that no one could dispute the inheritance. With so much at stake, why take the risk of using another name?"

Olivia nodded slowly.

"That's a good question. Why would you hide someone's name from the gift you're giving them?"

None of them could think of an answer.

"I wonder if we'll ever know the answer to the mystery," said Cameron. "Whoever this man is—sorry, this *person* is—I wonder if he really is going to take up residence in Surway House, like he says in the paper. Is he really going to come back and claim everything, after all those years? Somehow I just can't see it."

Suddenly he huddled closer and he lowered his voice, as if he could hide it beneath his previous words.

"People have talked about seeing a man inside the House," he said. "That sounds like too much of a coincidence. Could it be Lucian Baker? Could he be hiding inside the House?"

Instantly it made no difference that the midday sun was shining, that his shoulders were almost touching his friends', or that the whole campus was twittering around them: Andrew felt the color drop from his face. He looked down so that no one would notice.

At the same moment, Olivia declared,

"There's only one way to find out."

The two boys stared at her. They looked so determined not to understand that she had to add,

"By checking out the Surway House for ourselves, dum-dums."

CHAPTER THIRTY-FIVE

The Escape

Five o'clock rang from the great tower of Saint Clemens. Standing in front of the library, his hands folded behind his back, Andrew stared across the lawn towards the trees that hid the river. All afternoon, a thought had floated over his mind, surprisingly steady against the darker and weightier thoughts around it.

As he waited on top of the steps, he replayed his earlier picnic with Cameron and Olivia in his mind. They weren't the only ones, it turned out, worthy of a Saint Clemens scholarship: towards the end of their lunch, another group, also inspired by the beautiful weather, had appeared along the river. Andrew was vaguely acquainted with the newcomers. They had always been friendly to him. Though he was only half-sure of their names, he said hello to them in class. And everyone knew Cameron and Olivia. It wasn't surprising then that the new group had waved in their direction. But then something unexpected had happened, something that would make him feel inflated and light, like a balloon, for the rest of the afternoon. Olivia had called out to the newcomers, "Sorry, we can't stay!" And she had stood up with an urgency that had communicated itself without a word to Cameron and Andrew beside her. That moment had proven to Andrew beyond any doubt that Cameron and Olivia were the cool kids. Suddenly he had realized that he was also included.

The three of them had passed another bodyguard on their way back from the river. This time, instead of rolling her eyes, Olivia had stopped and turned to her friends. (*Please don't say anything rude*, Andrew had prayed in his head. *The bodyguard can hear you.*)

But she had only said,

"Are you both free at five? Why don't we meet in front of the library. We can help each other out with the reading. I'll see you guys at five?"

And since no one had ever said no to her, she had walked away to her class without waiting for an answer.

The echo of the bell dissipated over the lawn. The air slackened and turned chilly. Andrew looked out again towards the trees in the distance. There were no clouds in the sky, but a cool wind began to blow in from the river. He drew up the lapels of his uniform's blazer. His thoughts wandered to the red-and-navy scarf that he hadn't yet taken out of the wardrobe. The final stroke of the bell released a scattering of students from the buildings around the lawn. Among them he saw Cameron, his hair even more disheveled than before, looking more and more, with each hour, as if he had just fallen out of bed. He walked over to Andrew and shook his hand as he always did, no matter how many times they met in a day.

"You're ready to hit the books?" Cameron asked with a grin.

Andrew shrugged. He couldn't tell if the question was serious. It was a relief to see Olivia arrive almost immediately after. Both boys knew that every decision lay in her hands. She looked unusually earnest as she walked up the library steps. Another bodyguard stood at the corner of the building, slowly surveying the lawn.

Intently she said,

"Thanks for coming, guys. I hope you're ready for a long evening of study."

Her voice was so eager, so insistent, that it might even have caught the bodyguard's attention. Then she stalked to the door, the massive purse on her shoulder slanting backward in protest. Cameron and Andrew exchanged a dubious glance and followed her.

They passed through the turnstiles of the entrance into the silent, vaulted expanse of the reference room. Corridors of books surmounted by arches stretched in every direction around them. Olivia led them through the aisles without speaking. She seemed to know exactly where she was going.

They came upon the door of a little garden on the other side of the building, when Andrew wondered in a whisper,

"How well do you know this place?"

She paused. She turned around. And just before stepping out into the garden, before leaving the perfect quiet, she replied to him in the same voice as she might have used in a busy street,

"I *do* love reading, you know."

And she walked out.

The two boys came out behind her into a garden that overlooked the lower half of the campus down to the river. A fountain stood at the center in a patch of grass bordered by flower beds. There was no other sound but the crunch of gravel beneath their shoes. Even the water of the fountain was silent. There was no one else around them, no one sitting down on any of the benches along the path. Olivia stopped, stood on tiptoe, and peered out over the hedge at the edge of the garden. She gave a hum of satisfaction, turned to Cameron and Andrew, and motioned them onward with a jerk of her head. They followed her down a path on the other side of the fountain, between rosebushes and shrubs under a curved ceiling of leaves. They arrived in front of a fence. It was so low that they could have easily stepped over it, but Olivia drew tremendous gratification from lifting the hook on the door. She couldn't stop grinning when she pushed the door open and looked behind her at the two boys. But Cameron didn't smile back.

"Olivia, where are we going?"

She was confused.

"Are you serious?"

He made no answer. The puzzlement on her face turned sour. She lowered her eyes, tipped her head in Andrew's direction, and said,

"I don't know who you mean by 'we,' but *Andrew and I* are going to investigate the Surway House."

Andrew was amazed to hear his own voice before Cameron could reply.

"Yeah, Cameron, let's go."

For a few seconds, the only thing Andrew was conscious of was the jut of approval from Olivia's chin.

Cameron's eyes shifted from one to the other. They moved too quickly for either fear or excitement to settle over his face. But Olivia knew exactly how to read them.

She said with a tone of indifference,

"Taking a right after the fence will take you straight back to the dining hall. We'll tell you about it tomorrow."

Andrew took a step closer to Cameron and said,

"We can only do this if we all go together. It will be fun. And we won't actually go into the House."

Olivia broke in,

"Well, I'm not promising—"

"Come on," Andrew continued. "Nothing bad will happen."

And because he felt that his gentle encouragement was about to work, that Cameron was only a twitch of a muscle away from looking down the path on the left, Andrew added,

"Your next cup of oatmeal is on me."

The thought sparked a smile on Cameron's face. His forehead unwrinkled. His eyes turned bright again. The three of them glanced at one another, their mouths sealed up with grins. One by one they slipped through the door.

With Olivia at their head, they walked along the sleepy athletic fields into the woodlands on the north side of campus. Gradually the habitats of the school menagerie appeared above the trees, the bearded vines of the tropical jungle and the horny hilltops where the antelope lived. They crossed over the bridges of the campus canals, which wound through the botanical gardens all the way to the river. They peered into the windows of the boathouses, whose doors were all locked. Through the shadow, they glimpsed the boats that they had been told they could take out in the spring. They then made their way through the gardens themselves, through the islands of the arboretum that were shaped like the continents, and through the flower parks that smelled like different countries. The weather itself seemed to change as they went from one garden to the next.

Finally they arrived in a secluded vegetable farm, overrun with messy crops. A farmer's house stood at one end, as stout and hardy as the pumpkins that grew in front of it. There was no sign of anyone inside. Olivia stepped around the edges of the vegetable patches over to the fence behind the house. She rested her hands on the wooden rail and stared into the quiet forest beyond. When she looked back over her shoulder, she wasn't smiling anymore. Her silence made Andrew more uneasy than the stillness of the forest. He and Cameron walked up to her side.

She pointed into the woods and whispered,

"The road should be just a couple of minutes down this way."

There was nothing to say in response. She climbed over the fence, which was much taller than the last one, hopped down to the other side, and disappeared into the trees.

CHAPTER THIRTY-SIX

The Road

The woods were so thick that they couldn't see how close the road was. They had hardly gone a few minutes past the fence when they came out from behind a tree and found themselves on the edge of the pavement. For a second, the brightness of the black road almost blinded them. The concrete seemed to blaze with the joy of freedom itself. Giddily they set out.

They were walking in single file over the grass alongside the road, when Andrew asked Olivia,

"How did you know the way out of school—*that* way, I mean?"

"It's simple," she said, barely looking back. "The moment my dad said he was going to station bodyguards all over campus, I knew I had to get myself a map. And a detailed one, too."

"But why?"

The answer was obvious to her.

"How else am I going to sneak out of school in the middle of the day?"

Andrew could hear the grin in Cameron's voice behind him.

"Do you plan on *ever* going to class?"

This time she turned around.

"Only when I have nothing else to do."

They walked along the road, with no cars and no other people to slow them down or interrupt them, as if they were the only three people in the world. Soon they came upon a smaller street that rose in a winding slope towards the mountains, with a path along it where the three of them could walk side by side. They had gone a few minutes up this path when Olivia turned to Andrew and said,

"You must be so happy that we're friends now."

The words made him laugh.

"What's so funny?" she asked. "I'm happy too! But did you *expect* us to become friends?"

He considered the question.

"Did *you?*" he asked after a moment.

"Sure. You were obviously one of the more intelligent, one of the more interesting people around. And on top of that, Cameron thought you seemed cool."

Cameron kept his eyes on the ground.

"Yeah," Andrew felt compelled to reply. "I had a feeling we'd all be friends."

But then he remembered their first few encounters. He cocked his head.

"One thing I will say," he began. "It's funny how different people become once you get to know them. Even if I knew we were going to be friends, even if we all got along from the start—and we all found each other cool—it's funny how different you both seem now. It's only been a week or two, but you almost *look* different, you know? It's almost as if you weren't the same people as before. I almost have to make an effort to remember what you used to look like in the beginning."

He knew they understood him. But he didn't expect Olivia to ask,

"Are we *better* than those people from before?"

Andrew couldn't contain his smile.

"I wasn't too sure what to make of you guys."

He looked at his feet before adding,

"I had nicknames for both of you."

"Nicknames!" she cried out. "What were they?"

Andrew swallowed.

"You have to tell us," she insisted.

But his eyes were stuck on the ground. He forced himself to lift them to her face and said,

"Well, you were 'Poor Girl.' Because you called me *poor* to my face the first time we met. And Cameron was—"

He turned to the boy. Cameron was smiling just as awkwardly as he was.

"And you were 'Polo Guy.'"

Olivia howled with laughter. Her head fell back and she clapped her hands. Cameron, beneath his irrepressible smile, was perplexed.

"Polo Guy?" he mumbled.

"Poor Girl and Polo Guy," Olivia repeated, heaving. "We sound like superheroes—like a comic book! Poor Girl and Polo Guy... You should have told us from the start. We would have become friends *way* faster!"

And her laughter resounded up the silent road.

"Why Polo Guy?" Cameron asked.

"Well..." Andrew wavered. An uncomfortable grin was glued to his face. "You just had that kind of look, you know? Like you'd just come out of a polo match."

"How does someone look coming out a polo match?" Cameron asked.

Andrew waved his hands in the air. But then a better question occurred to him.

"Tell me this: have you ever played polo?"

The boy blushed and looked down.

"Not... *professionally*," he muttered.

This time the three of them burst into laughter, and the noise they made rattled the reddening leaves.

At last Olivia said, when she could talk once again,

"Poor Girl. That's got to be the funniest nickname anyone's ever given me. I can't wait to tell my dad."

Andrew's heart dropped. His voice suddenly blank, he said, "Please don't tell your dad."

"Relax. He'll think it's funny."

"No, Olivia, I'm begging you!"

But she only started laughing again, and there was nothing for Andrew to do but giggle in anguish beside her.

"I bet you have all kinds of nicknames for everyone at school," she said.

But no one else had captured Andrew's imagination as Cameron and Olivia had. He said nothing.

"Ooh," she pricked up, "I bet you have your own special code name for Evil Hamster too, your own special love code, probably something ending in *Hotster*, which is what Cameron calls her all day in his dreams."

"I do not," Cameron said. And for someone whose emotions were always so apparent, he remained surprisingly cool.

Somehow Andrew knew immediately who *Evil Hamster* was. Olivia gave him a suspicious look when she turned to him and said,

"Please don't tell me you're *also* in love with Eva Hansler in our class."

Offhandedly he replied,

"I don't see why anyone here should be in love with her."

"Oh please," she drawled out. "Because she's beautiful, and perfect, and she's the famous Hansler daughter, and she's probably the smartest kid in the class—well, after the Saint Clemens Scholar I suppose, it's too early to tell…"

Andrew chuckled.

"Perfect Miss Hansler," she continued, "always the first in every classroom, always turns in her homework on time, always has the perfect answer… Looks perfect in her uniform and beautiful at the ball, in her perfectly beautiful dress, with her perfect and beautiful mom."

She stopped. Her eyes darted to the ground. Her voice had dipped at the end of the sentence. The rest of it had been banter. The last thing was the only thing that Olivia was jealous of. And the sound of longing in her voice was more foreign in Andrew's ears than the most remote language on earth.

After a moment, she said without lifting her eyes,

"My mom died a long time ago."

A few seconds passed before Cameron replied, almost in the tone of a joke, throwing his hands up in a shrug.

"Well I practically don't have a dad."

"At least *I* have the greatest dad in the world." She gave a grin. "Subjectively *and* objectively."

It then occurred to Andrew that he had the perfect reply for them both.

"I don't have any parents at all. I'm an orphan."

Unexpectedly, incomprehensibly, Olivia began to laugh. She turned to him with an affectionate pout and said,

"No matter how hard we try, you *always* manage to be the poorest person around."

She went on laughing, and Cameron said,

"I guess that means you can still call me 'Polo Guy' if you want."

And before Andrew could understand how any of it could be funny, he started laughing along with them. Suddenly he had the giddy, dreamlike feeling that the three of them had cancelled every sadness from the world forever.

"You guys are great," he said without thinking.

Their laughter stopped at once. He glanced at each of them. Their chests were puffed out, and he noticed a slight strut in their steps.

They kept on walking up the street. They turned left and then right. The afternoon cooled down. The sky turned a heavier blue. Soon the sunlight came slanting through the trees. Still there was no car, no one else on the road. As he often did when he was walking, Andrew had picked up a stick from the ground. And as he always did when he carried a stick, he had started spinning it around with both hands like a weapon.

"Where did you learn to do that?" Cameron asked him.

"It's my staff," Andrew said without stopping. "I've been a master since before you were born."

Cameron smiled.

"I'd like to see you act this tough in front of a man with a real sword."

"I'd like to meet the man who'd try to take me down."

"You already have. I've been fencing since I was a kid."

"Settle down boys," came Olivia. "I could knock you both out with my purse."

Andrew kept his staff a while longer before tossing it aside, but towards the end he had switched to using it as a walking stick.

They must have gone nearly an hour from Saint Clemens when they came upon a wall that Andrew recognized. He had seen it several miles further down the valley. It was the curving stone wall of the Surway estate. But here, instead of the trees that towered over it where it passed near the Brandows' house, there was a fence above the wall; and the spikes of the fence seemed to rise higher than any tree. The three of them followed the road alongside it.

At last they arrived in front of the gate.

CHAPTER THIRTY-SEVEN

Boots

They stopped in front of the gate. Andrew wondered if even Cameron and Olivia had ever seen anything so imposing. But it wasn't the size of the gate that squashed the breath in his lungs. It wasn't the width or the height of it, though it seemed that it had been built for another species, for gods or giants who could peer above the trees. It wasn't the length of the avenue that unrolled behind it, in the shade of gigantic elms, or the curtain of sunlight in which the avenue appeared to end. It wasn't even the awareness of standing before the gate of Lyndon Surway's home, before the realm of the man whose mystery had entwined itself with his life. It wasn't any of these impressions. The reason for Andrew's shock was the pair of stone lions standing guard around the gate. He had seen them before. Or rather he had seen lions exactly like them. Or rather he had seen *one lion* exactly like them. He had never found the second cuff link.

Olivia pulled on the sleeves of her blazer and looked at the sky. Streaks of pink, shooting from the river, turned purple towards the mountains. She seemed to be addressing the clouds and the wind when she said,

"We made it. Here we are."

And she added for herself alone,

"I'd never seen the Surway House before."

But she wasn't satisfied. The chill around her and the gate in front still defied her. She cocked her head and declared in a louder voice,

"I *still* have never seen it."

Turning to Cameron and Andrew, she said,

"Come on, guys. We came here to see the House, not just the gate. We need to get a better look."

And she set off, as was her habit, without waiting for a response. Cameron caught up to her.

"Where the hell are you going now? There's no way we can get to the other side of the fence!"

He trotted backward as he spoke because she wouldn't stop.

"Of course there's a *way*," she replied. Then she broke into a grin. "But don't worry. Climbing over the fence is our *last resort.*"

And she carried on walking.

Andrew answered Cameron's nervous look with a smile, mostly to reassure himself.

They continued to follow the fence on the sandy path along the road. But the House remained hidden. The elms on the other side of the fence barred their sight. They all sensed, without saying so, that the trees would thin out. They were so hopeful for a clearing that they could picture it as they went, lying just beyond the shadow of the last trunk they could see. But the last trunk kept receding, and the curtain of trees kept on going beyond it, as silent and unhelpful as the empty road alongside.

All of a sudden, Olivia stopped. Her eyes were fixed on the ground. Neither Cameron nor Andrew could make out what she was staring at in the sand of the path. She brought a hand over her knee and crouched. The boys gathered closer. Their shadows mingled over her. She looked up into their faces. After a few seconds, she asked,

"What do you guys think?"

"What do we think of—?" Cameron began, taking another step closer, when suddenly she shouted,

"Cameron, stop!"

She jumped up and held out her arms.

"What the hell was that?" he yelled out.

"Don't step on it!"

"Don't step on what?"

"The footprint!" she answered in a whisper, as if just remembering the sound of her own voice. She glanced over both shoulders, gave Cameron and Andrew a significant look, and slowly lowered herself once more to the ground. The two of them mirrored her movement.

All at once, Andrew saw it. It was a footprint, unmistakable, elementary, like a picture in a comic book, a single elongated shape with a line separating the heel. Cameron asked in a muted voice,

"What kind of shoe is that? It doesn't have any—any *details*."

Olivia rolled her eyes. Not even whispering could soften her contempt.

"It's a *boot*," she said.

"A boot," Cameron repeated. And after a second's reflection, "So it's a boot. So what? People leave footprints every day on every path in the world. Some of them wear boots."

But he didn't dare to go back to his normal voice.

Olivia continued to study the print as if he hadn't spoken. It was Andrew who answered,

"But no one leaves footprints on *this* path."

Cameron and Olivia looked up.

"There's nothing along this road, nothing for miles in either direction, right? Nothing but the gate of the Surway House."

They stared at him without reply.

"Well," he went on, examining the footprint, "assuming that's the case, then there's really no reason for anyone to have come here recently—no reason other than..." His eyes turned to the fence.

Olivia's gaze followed his.

"It's not just the fact that someone was here recently—" she began.

"How do you guys know it's so recent?" Cameron broke in. "The print could go back several days, anytime since the last rainfall. For all we know, someone could have left it over the weekend. No one here's an expert in detection."

"No," Olivia rejoined, "but I'm an expert in *shoes*. That's how I know it's a boot."

Andrew wondered. He didn't know anything about footprints (unlike Olivia), but he could tell the mark was fresh. He knew that anyone could tell, even Cameron. The break above the heel was so thin that a puff of air would blow it over. Another hour or two, with a bit of wind, might sweep it out altogether.

"What's weird to me," Olivia resumed, "as I was saying, isn't just the fact that someone was here recently. It's that someone was here *on foot*. It's one thing to be *driving* by the Surway estate—you could get lost, or you could be curious to see what the gate looks like—but to be *walking* here, where there's nothing at all except the entrance to the House, where there's nowhere else to go and nothing to do..."

Slowly she stood up. There was another print behind the first one. It had almost crumbled away. And there was a third print behind the second one. She carefully stepped back and took a long look around her, from one end of the path to the other. Something in the distance caught her attention, on the grass beside the path, down the way they had come.

Her voice was low once again, even lower than before, when she said,

"The prints couldn't have gone back all the way to the gate or we would have noticed them earlier. They could be coming from that bush right over there, just to the right of the path."

She turned around and looked in the opposite direction.

"And they seem to be going..."

Cameron and Andrew followed her gaze as it traveled up the path.

Her next words could no longer be contained in a whisper.

"Let's find out how far they go."

She didn't walk away this time—she ran.

They didn't run for long; the footprints soon disappeared. Most likely the wind had scattered them away. But an enormous oak stood next to the path, just a step or two away. Andrew's eyes traveled up the branches. All their eyes did. They all knew that the top of the tree, glowing in the day's final brightness, must look out over the House.

Andrew turned to Cameron, whose face was fixed with apprehension, halfway between a prayer and a frown.

"That's one hell of a bowl of oatmeal you owe me," he said.

CHAPTER THIRTY-EIGHT

In the Tree

They stared up into the tree. The wind scattered golden leaves and light. As he climbed the tree with his eyes, Andrew felt the gnarls of the branches in his joints. A sinewy warmth spread from his knees, as familiar as sunlight. He wondered if Cameron and Olivia could also feel it in their limbs. He wondered if, somewhere in their childhoods, there had also been forests where the same feelings had taken root. But the question that Cameron asked, the most obvious thought of all, had escaped Andrew altogether.

"What if the person who left the boot prints is still up there?"

Cameron's whisper was even quieter under the tree. There came no answer from the branches above them, nothing but the wind.

Suddenly Olivia shouted,

"Is anybody up there?"

The wind itself was taken aback, slashed by the sound. Nobody moved.

Cameron mumbled in a furious breath,

"Are you crazy? You're going to get us killed!"

She began to clamber up the tree, wrapping her arms in their navy wool sleeves around the trunk.

"I'd recommend that you stay on the ground then," she replied without looking back.

The only option more unacceptable to Cameron than going up with her was staying behind. He reached for a branch above his head and slowly lifted himself. It was the first time Andrew had ever seen a justification for his disheveled hair.

Andrew lowered his eyes to the sloping trunk before him. His chest expanded with a draft of timber and soil. His shoes pushed off the grass one after the other as he pulled a branch, and then another, to himself. He saw the earth fall away below him. Instantly, he was certain that there could be no one else in the tree. The tree could never belong to anyone in the world but him.

It was a thick, gigantic tree. It was a forest on its own. It had its own clearings and thickets, and paths for strolling and getting lost. Andrew had always felt that a good tree can be explored, but the best trees are places to live in. He reached the top with the browsing eyes of someone who wants to stay awhile. He lodged his foot in the crook of a branch and drew a long, happy sigh. He felt the palms of his hands tingling from the ruggedness of the bark. Though his skin and his hair were crumbly with dirt, and though the taste of the tree had crusted on his lips, he couldn't remember the last time he had felt so clean. He wanted to rub his back against the trunk until his blazer turned brown. He wished that he could bottle the cold air and the sunset in his body. He closed his eyes and watched his eyelids glow. He breathed out once more and opened his eyes, and then he turned towards the Surway estate. He had known that he would see it, that from the top he would be able to look out over the fence, over the wide expanse of lawn all the way to the House. Even so, he gasped.

He saw a span of wall four stories high, framed by trees on either side. That was all he could see of the House. But the awe he felt spilled far beyond this wall. It crashed over it and flooded every corner of the House behind. He had never seen a wall of stone like this, and yet somehow it was almost familiar. It wasn't particularly ornate or forbidding. It was, in the end, only a wall. But it was also what he had always thought it would be, what he had known it would be, since the first time that he had heard of the House. It had exactly the texture and shade of a castle in a story. It was a place where kings lived. And even though he had never seen it before, he felt that every child in the world could picture it, because every child had imagined it.

He became aware of a stillness below him where there had been sound.

"Cameron?" he said. "Olivia?"

A few seconds passed before there was a reply.

"We can see the House," said Olivia. There was a bend in her voice that he had never heard before.

"Can you see it?" Cameron asked him. Rising from somewhere slightly lower in the tree, his voice carried the same reverence and wonderment as Olivia's.

"Yes," Andrew said, and he could hear himself smiling.

The three of them could see it, and there was nothing more to say. The sunset gleamed on the wall and blazed in the squares of the windows. Its color dazed them and everything around them.

But then Andrew felt something. He didn't know what it was. He felt it mostly in his mind, but also in his body. It came from below, prickling its way into his consciousness. It wasn't a sensation. It wasn't even a thought. It was only a bristling of instinct, for someone who had climbed many trees. He looked down. The feeling came from his right leg—more exactly, from the toes of his right foot. Was his foot about to slip? Was the branch under his foot unsteady? Or was there something below his foot, something below the branch, something so close that he could almost weigh it without touching it? He craned his neck. There was a denser scrap of darkness there below him in the leaves. Was it a shadow? Was it the shadow of a branch? Did it move in the wind? Or was it the only thing that was still while everything *around* it moved? Andrew leaned out further. The branch under his foot gave a creak.

"Can you see the whole thing from up there?" came Cameron's voice. "I can only see a couple of floors. It looks pretty amazing."

Andrew didn't answer. He shifted his foot down the branch. Again the branch shook—more freely this time.

"Maybe I should try to get up there for a better view," Cameron said. "Andrew, what do you think?"

And because no answer came,

"Andrew?"

Andrew hugged the top of the tree trunk. He knew that the branch under his foot was about to give way. Still, if he could only go a bit further, if he could only get a bit closer to that shadow below him... He drew his hands closer to his body and pressed them under his chest against the bark. He shifted his weight and looked down. The branch beneath him cracked. The shadow moved. Did it move in the wind? It was still. Was the shadow a shadow? Or was there a shadow beneath the shadow? One final question came into his mind, making everything else silent: did the shadow move *against* the wind?

The branch snapped more quietly than it had creaked. Andrew fell. He fell down the tree in a blur of red foliage, and the hissing of the wind faded the screams of his friends. He collapsed on top of another branch. He looked up, and the air gurgled in his throat. There, just a few steps down the branch, poised against the trunk of the tree, crouching, leaning back, leaning away from the place where Andrew had fallen, was a man. He had a mustache, and he wore a bowtie. He appeared to be from another time, from the top hat on his head to the boots on his feet. The only thing Andrew understood, the only thing he could interpret, was the expression on the man's face. It was a look of grief. There was intelligence and compassion in it. It was the face of someone who had considered every alternative and found no other way. With graveness, with resignation, and even, it seemed to Andrew, with something resembling regret, the man reached to his side and picked up an iron rifle. It was only then, when he lay down on the branch with the muzzle of an archaic rifle in his face, that Andrew began to hear the voices of his friends below him. They were asking where he was, if he was all right, if he could hear them. He didn't reply. He just turned over and rolled down into the air. The crash of a gunshot exploded above him.

He grabbed a branch with both arms and stopped falling.

"Andrew!" came the screams from further down. "Andrew, what's going on?"

Another gunshot burst overhead. A powder of wood blew into his eyes as he hung from the branch. He spat, and twigs dribbled out of his mouth. He knew the danger was above him, but suddenly he was terrified of losing his grip and tumbling down the tree. He hoisted himself over the branch, hugged it, and looked down. He couldn't see his friends. He couldn't see the tree trunk. He couldn't see the orange moss that was the surface of the earth. He spat out again, and a word inched up his throat. He tried to push it out as another gunshot rang. Soil spluttered from his mouth. He snorted dirt from his nose. Then the word blew out of his lungs, as broad and clear as any word he had ever spoken.

"Run!" His voice chafed against the branch. "Get off the tree and run!"

Another gunshot blasted over his ear, trilling across his brain. *Now get up*, he said to himself.

Lying down against the branch, he raised his elbows and tried to push himself up. The veins of his arms throbbed. He breathed in puffs that made him dizzy. Slowly, his weight lifted off the wood. The air rushed beneath his chest. He no longer felt the branch pummeling back his heartbeat. Another bullet zoomed past, this time more distant, eerily wide, and he shrank back in horror. A black shape dangled in front of him. One boot slapped down on the branch, and the man carrying the rifle gently raised himself before him.

The voices rose again from below. They were wild and raspy. But they were steady—they came from the ground. Cameron and Olivia had escaped from the tree. Andrew fixed his stare into the eyes of the man, eyes that narrowed, turned, and disappeared behind the rifle. The man took his aim. Andrew jumped up and knocked his fist into the man's leg. Another gunshot rang and ripped through the leaves far above them.

Andrew fell sideways and hit the branch with a bang of his forehead. He twisted his neck to look above him, to turn away from the pain. The man was standing on top of him. His boots were just able to fit over the branch on both sides of Andrew's legs. One by one every thought, every observation drizzled out of Andrew's brain. He felt the air draining out of his lungs, and his arms flopped down from his sides. There were no springs left in his body, no blood left in his muscles. There was nothing left at all, nothing inside of him or around him, nothing but this drowsy vision of a man outside of time in a forest of gold, under a sunset that would never end. There was nothing at all except the trust he felt in this man, as the man bent down to a crouch, coming down over Andrew, the trust that they both felt in his finger against the trigger.

And then, suddenly, a pause. The moment had ended. Was it *the end*? Andrew opened his eyes. He didn't remember having closed them. The sun had set. What had happened? The man no longer held the rifle to Andrew's face. It dangled, forgotten, over the man's knee. He was staring away into the distance, staring at something outside the tree. There was no expression on his face. His mouth was open without a sound, without a word in any language. Wobbling with the effort, Andrew turned his head. He saw the wall of the House. And in the highest window he could see, a light appeared, then disappeared, then continued to flash on and off. A figure passed behind the glass. Too far, too fast. It was featureless and colorless—except for one feature and one color: a single blot of red at the height of the neck. Then the light was gone. The window was black again, as black as all the other windows around it, and nothing more could be seen inside. Andrew felt himself screaming, but there was no voice in his body. Neither he nor the man with the rifle made a sound.

The scream smothered in Andrew's throat clawed at his chest. The spilling daylight seeped into his blood. His eyes darted back to the man who hovered over him on the branch. Andrew wrung every vein in his leg and hurled his foot behind the man's knees. The man fell without a sound.

Andrew turned aside and began to climb down the tree. He went slowly at first, then more quickly. As he stepped down each bough, every weakness shed from his bones. Every pain slipped from his skin. He almost smiled. He remembered how much faster it was to go down a tree than to go up. He leapt down from one branch to the next, and he felt that his movements wiped the light from the sky. He bounded to the ground and felt the cushion of grass under his feet. Two voices came to meet him, two voices so dear that his hands reached out for them before he could answer. But the voices came from above.

"Andrew!" they cried out. "Andrew, are you all right?"

Cameron and Olivia scrambled down the tree as fast as they could, their breathing louder than their steps. They almost collapsed on top of him, and he locked them in his arms and pushed his head between their shoulders.

"Why did you go back up?" he shouted. "We need to run! We need to go!"

They had barely started running when a gunshot burst at their side. Olivia screamed but kept going. None of them stopped. They sprinted over the path, over the cooler, darker ground where the daylight was gone. Only Andrew looked back. Evening gathered over the tree, over the sinking torch of the tallest branches.

He saw the man with the rifle running after them.

CHAPTER THIRTY-NINE

In the Woods

Down the path they ran. Andrew heard the footfalls of his friends slightly behind him on each side. He would run as long as he heard them. He tried to lighten his feet as he ran. He tried to fly over the ground, to avoid touching it altogether, as if the surface of the earth were an electric current. He kept waiting for an explosion to ring around him. But there was none. He glanced over his shoulder and saw a shadow skid across the twilight. It veered from the path and disappeared behind a bush. Andrew stopped. Olivia and Cameron stopped beside him.

"Don't stop!" Andrew cried out. "Keep going! Run!"

They stared at him, heaving, and they looked at each other. There was nothing on their faces but exhaustion. But they started down the path again. Andrew remained where he stood.

His eyes were fixed on the bush. The man had vanished behind it. No other movement came from it, no sound, as if the dusk had swallowed the man. But suddenly something quivered. It wasn't visible. It was hardly audible. But it shoved Andrew's heels into the ground. It began to grow. It became a rumble, as Andrew had known that it would. He knew what it was, and it twitched in his ankles as he stared at the bush. And because he knew what it was, he was too frightened to move, though he knew he must run. He stood completely still as a long black car appeared from behind the bush and swerved onto the path.

It was an old car, a vintage car, a shiny *automobile*, classic and beautiful. And it had no roof. Carefully, slowly, the man rose over his seat, still wearing his top hat, keeping one hand on the wheel. With his other hand, without stopping the car, he lifted and leveled, over the rim of the windshield, the needle of his rifle.

Andrew spun around. His feet churned over the grass. He ran without thinking, without evaluating distance, as if it was still possible to make up for the time he had lost. He ran feeling in his calves the rolling of the car flattening down all sound behind him. He ran until he caught up with Cameron and Olivia, and he had to restrain his arms not to reach out and push them onward.

"Faster!" he shouted. "Keep running!"

There was another command in his chest, one that he didn't dare say out loud, because he knew they would immediately break it. *Don't look back*, he cried without speaking. *Don't look back*, he silently implored them and himself as he ran.

A gunshot burst at their side. *Stop screaming*, Andrew shouted at Olivia in his head. But he treasured her scream. It continued to rush alongside him for a second past the gunshot, telling him that Olivia was all right, that she was still running, that she didn't even look back. *Just keep running*, he said to himself. *Just keep running*, he prayed to Cameron and Olivia. The rest of the universe hung on the other side of that sentence.

Another gunshot puffed behind him. This one was much closer. He felt its dust lifting in his feet. Could he still hear Cameron and Olivia? Yes he could, he told himself. He had no choice but to think so. He had no choice but to keep running. Another gunshot exploded, and he stopped thinking altogether.

The path narrowed in front of them. The lawn along the fence tapered to an end. They had reached the gate of the House.

The twilight was brighter in front of it, where an avenue bordered with trees sloped down to the river. Andrew looked down the avenue and saw the valley bowing to the House in the copper of dusk, across the water and up the mountains on the other side. But the avenue was too wide, too exposed, and too steep. Andrew continued down the road. He passed the two stone lions, and he imagined as he ran that they growled at the man behind him.

The car's rumble continued in his ears. It grew. It resounded more broadly at the top of the avenue and then narrowed again as it followed them down the road.

Suddenly, Andrew turned around. He flung out his arm as Olivia and Cameron hurtled towards him.

"Into the woods!" he shouted, and he pointed towards the trees across the road from the fence. They plunged under the branches and disappeared. The spark of a gunshot glanced at their feet, over the curve of the road, but they were gone.

Andrew turned towards the trees when the lights of the car racing towards him drew his eyes. He was paralyzed. He couldn't see beyond those lights, too big and round for a modern car, their sheen dully reflected over the arches of the wheels. He couldn't see those arches. He couldn't see the wheels, or the windshield or the driver. But the white lights swelled towards him. Their flare filled the world, spreading over the road to the tops of the trees, and everything behind them was black. He stared into those lights, those eyes that would merge and consume him, and he felt his own eyes widening. He couldn't move his feet, and he couldn't look away.

Andrew, move, he said to himself. The voice in his head was strangely calm. It was fearless and firm, though his right calf was shaking. *Take your leg in your hand. Reach down and lift your leg.* He leaned down and a bullet whirred over his shoulder. *So that's what bullets sound like way up close.* Then he dove into the woods.

He fell rolling over the forest floor. He tumbled over the soil, scratched by leaves and slapped with mud, and he heard another gunshot ring above him, far away across the air, on the other side of the earth. Then he heard nothing but the clatter of his skull over the ground.

He came to a stop, and he thought his neck was broken. He raised himself on his hands and knees because he thought that he couldn't, and he shook the dizziness out of his head. His face ached. He pressed a foot down on the ground and drew himself up. He looked around. Night had fallen in the woods. He couldn't see anything in the forest, and he heard no more than he could see. Even the wind had slipped away from him. There were no gunshots, no screams. The air was empty of the car's drone. How far was the road? He listened. Odd and obtuse, the rise and fall of police sirens passed in the distance, then faded. Little by little the quiet noises of the woods grew distinct in his ears.

Then another sound rose. Or was it a sight? Was it a light? He peered into the darkness, down the slope of the forest. It *was* a light. Or rather, it was a break in the blackness, a pale stripe across the night. It was a road. He had tumbled almost all the way down to the edge of another road.

And then there was something else. This time, it was a sound. Maybe it had been a sound all along. Maybe the light and the sound had both greeted him together. Relief pooled in his chest, almost in his eyes. He listened more closely. *Was that…?* The sound rose towards him from below, from somewhere further down the woods, but not as far down as the road. He heard it again and it flushed his face. It was Olivia's voice, whispering in the darkness.

"Andrew," she said. "Is that you?"

"Yes," he answered. His voice scraped his throat.

"Are you OK?" he asked. "Where's Cameron?"

"We're both fine," came the boy's voice from the same direction.

Andrew felt a sudden urge to run down and hug them. But he still needed to think clearly. His voice came out a moment later, still hoarse, but steady.

"You see the road down there?"

He couldn't tell which one of them whispered back,

"Yes."

"We need to go down to that road."

There was no answer.

"We can then head into the woods on the other side," he said. "If we keep going down the woods, eventually we should reach the river. And then we can follow the river back to Spring Forge."

There was another silence. Then a final whisper came back. Again all it said was,

"Yes."

This time, Andrew recognized Cameron's voice. But he knew the word came from the two of them. There was nothing left to say, nothing left to do but what Andrew had said. He bent his knees and took a step towards the road. A soft crunch in the distance echoed his movement, as Cameron and Olivia began to make their way down.

Andrew paused. He pricked up his ears and tried to silence his breathing. Was there another sound in the woods? He turned around. He could see nothing above him. The denseness of the night had deepened around him in the forest. He turned back towards the road and took another step down the slope.

Again, he heard something above him. He turned around once more, and this time he saw it. It wasn't the man. It wasn't even the man's shadow. It wasn't even the man's rifle. Instead, it was a tiny blade of light. It cast off a glow from the sky, perhaps the moon. It wasn't even the light that caught his eye; it was the straightness of it and its motionlessness in the forest, where nothing else was straight, and nothing else was still. It stuck out of a hollow in the darkness. Andrew considered the moonlight. He hadn't realized how much time had passed since he had jumped off the road. He began to run when the light twinkled and extended, and the barrel of the rifle tilted down.

"Run!" came his shout down the forest. A gunshot blasted. The bullet shook the leaves at his feet as he tore down the slope. He continued to rip through the trees, through the skeletons of their branches, and the bright strip of road went on tottering before him. Two shapes sprang onto the road, two beautiful, colorful shapes that stopped running and turned towards him. When he reached them, the sudden concrete under his shoes almost wrenched off his knees.

"He's behind me!" he cried, as another gunshot rang overhead.

But they didn't move. They only stared at him. Their eyes were fastened so securely on his face that they didn't even jump at the next gunshot. There was nothing he could tell them, nothing he could say against the sound of the rifle and the tramping boots. The woods on the other side of the road went on towards the river, but the three of them wouldn't go far with the rifle at their backs. The man had stopped shooting. It was pointless for him to slow down now.

Andrew turned away and stared into the distance. His eyes broke down the darkness. His mind unraveled the road. Instantly, he saw it rising and descending over hilltops and hollows, along stillness and peace. In the flash of a second, he saw it coursing away, gliding over the miles, cleaving into the night.

He jumped. His stare tightened over the road. He glanced down one side of the pavement, then the other, looked up at the trees on both sides, and again down the road, as if seeing it for the first time—not seeing it: *recognizing* it. He knew where they were. He knew the bend further down the road, the rise followed by a dip, and the light waiting at the bottom, at the intersection with another road. There was a gas station there. He blinked hard. There was a diner.

He turned around. There was no fear in Olivia's eyes. Her mind had let go of every idea except one, and that idea was Andrew. He grabbed her shoulders.

"Come with me."

Cameron's eyes had never left him. Andrew gave him a nod before glancing at Olivia again. Then he jumped into the woods on the other side of the road. They went after him under the trees.

CHAPTER FORTY

In the Earth

Andrew clenched his body under the earth. He clasped his arms around twisting roots and clamped his legs around fragments of rock. He knew that he wouldn't fall very far if he let go. He knew that the only way further down the hole was to force his body through the cracks, through the jagged gaps in the soil. But still, he was afraid of slipping—not of hurting himself, but of startling Cameron and Olivia below him, hiding in the crevices of the hole. He had let them go in first. He wasn't sure why, now that he was curled up above their heads. The tunnel lay below them—the tunnel that led to the treasure. They had stopped only a few feet above it. Even without moving, they might have been able to glimpse it, if they had known it was there.

But then Andrew remembered the man. He remembered the danger that had driven them underground. And he felt the same impulse all over again, the impulse to let them in first, and to watch over them as they went down. The secret was safe, Andrew said to himself. If they ever made it out of the hole again, if they ever asked him how he had known there was a hole there, he would just tell them that there were holes like this everywhere. He would tell them it was an animal's den. He would tell them that all forests had them. He could tell them whatever he wanted. They would believe him.

First, let's make it out of here, he said to himself. *Everything else can wait.*

And so he waited, and they waited. He listened below him for a word from Olivia or a whisper from Cameron, or a shudder that would mean they had fallen or gone further down. But no sound came from below. The only thing he heard came from above, just a few inches above his ears, and it made him coil his body even more tightly, as if to squash out his own heart.

The man's boots stalked over the soil, just a few steps from his head. Andrew felt the dead leaves crackling through his bones. He heard the curling of the wind around the man's body. The man paused, surveying the woods. He took another step and drew closer. Again he stopped. Andrew could hear his stillness. He could almost hear the shifting of his eyes as he examined the forest. The man was standing by the slanting tree, the tree that rose over the stub of rock that marked the entrance of the hole. But to the man, the tree and the rock were just a tree and a rock. Andrew told himself, he begged himself to believe, that he would have known if they had meant something more to the man. Somehow, Andrew would have heard a difference in the soil. He would have heard it in the heels of the man's boots. But he heard nothing. The world above him was silent.

Then the man took another step, and he came even closer. Andrew stifled his breath. He could feel the man's boot a few inches from his hair. The dried leaves under the sole almost tickled his ear. He listened for the man's breathing and he couldn't hear it, and what terrified him most was that he was surprised not to hear it. He realized that he could feel the weight of the man's body almost exactly on top of his head. The man didn't move, and Andrew closed his eyes.

The seconds passed. Maybe minutes. The man might have taken another step. Andrew didn't know. He thought he heard police sirens once more but he couldn't be sure, and the sound was of no help. He was assailed by the sounds in his own head. He felt his skull reeling. The only thing he could do to quiet his head, to push the nausea back down to his stomach, was to focus his mind on the silence below him, Cameron and Olivia's silence. He reached out in thought for their hands. He squeezed his fingers around the idea, and he felt their warmth on his skin.

The darkness deepened. The night was growing denser above. The earth around him began to stir. He was suddenly aware of a heavy stillness that had just ended. How long had it lasted? He couldn't tell. By the time he dared to tilt his head back and peer into the open air, his face was wet. A patter of raindrops fell over the leaves. He heard their pelting with the outsized senses of an animal. The soil around him began to crinkle and rustle, and he knew the man was gone. He drew a hand out over the surface, pressed down with his foot, and lifted himself out of the hole. Then he turned around and looked down.

"Cameron? Olivia?"

His voice wriggled down the passage. No sound came up in return. Nothing moved inside the hole. But then the blackness quivered, and he pieced together Cameron's face. Andrew lowered his hand and pulled him out of the hole. Then the two of them helped Olivia out.

They sat in silence on the forest floor. It was too dark to run, too dark to stand up, almost too dark to see one another's faces. They couldn't even see the rain, though they could hear it and smell it all around them. Olivia tipped her hair over her shoulder and held out her hand in front of her. She stared at it for a long time. Andrew made out her face, and he knew that she was trying to make sense of the baffling notion that someone had just tried to kill them. She made a great effort over herself, lowered her hand, and gave a pout.

"Next time, could you please come up with a slightly less *dirty* way to save my life?"

Andrew felt a spasm of laughter, but the feeling hurt across his chest. He tried to lay aside his own shock. He was out of breath. His throat was raw, and every joint in his body ached. He nudged Cameron with his shoulder. The boy was staring vacantly ahead, his hands wrapped around his knees. Then, without looking, without moving, in a tone that was like a wax mold of his voice, Cameron said,

"I wish we could have killed him."

Olivia smiled. Andrew rubbed his hand over Cameron's hair, the hair of a polo player thrown off his horse into a puddle of mud, but Cameron's expression didn't change. Slowly he shook his head.

"They warned me that high school would build character."

He was the first to get up.

"Let's get the hell out of here," he said, looking at Andrew. "Then Olivia and I can safely say that we owe you our lives."

The night was dark and cold, and the rain, however light, showed no intention of moving on. They began to walk. But just before making his way back to the road, when his friends had turned around, Andrew shuffled the leaves over the hole with his feet.

He hurried back to Cameron's side when the boy reached over his shoulder, leaned into his ear and said,

"Thank you."

They came upon the road again and stopped. Cameron and Olivia turned to Andrew. He looked in both directions. The way that led to the gas station and the diner was not an option. Someone might recognize him.

"This way," he declared, though he had no idea where this other way led. "But let's stay in the dark, off the road. We can follow it from the woods."

He wondered if they knew that he was also afraid of coming across the police. He was ashamed of the thought. But Cameron and Olivia did as he said without a word.

No one spoke as they walked. The shadow of the man seemed to lurk behind every tree. They thought they heard his footsteps over every creak in the woods. Skinny branches became his rifle. His hat swung in swaying leaves. They saw themselves in his eyes as they walked. They felt his hands reaching for their ankles. The rain grew sharper and thicker. The drops they saw in the halos of streetlights became fatter. But still, they could barely feel it over their faces, though their cheeks were flushed and wet.

Andrew was beginning to wonder if he had chosen the right direction when they came across a house at a fork in the road. It was a sturdy-looking house. It appeared to be old, and it was un-impressed with the rain streaming down the shingles of the roof. But what drew them most to the house wasn't its roof, its gables, its porch, or the green shutters around its windows. It was the light from inside. It was a warm, wholesome light, and Andrew thought, with a rush of excitement, that it waved like fire.

The three of them went up the steps of the porch. On a hanging sign outside the door, they read by the light of the windows,

Oliver Chucks

Established before you were born.

They heard voices inside, and they looked at one another. The rain gained force just as Andrew's hand rounded on the doorknob. It began to batter down the roof of the porch. He opened the door and they went in.

CHAPTER FORTY-ONE

Unexpected Encounters

The room erupted into applause the moment they walked in. It took them a few seconds to realize that it was directed not at them, but towards a corner in the back where an old man sat on a stool with a guitar in his hands. The man gave a smile that buried his eyes into his wrinkles. Swiveling his seat was the closest he came to bowing. As the applause dwindled, he stood up, picked up his mug from the empty stool beside him and marched off quietly from the spotlight. Conversations resumed around the room, and the three newcomers shuffled in from the door.

They felt as if they had entered someone's house, though it didn't look like any home they had ever seen. Clusters of people were hunched over mugs around wooden tables, and there was a bar along one side of the room. But the place gave the impression that no one came there for an hour or even for a day. It was a place to lie back in, a place to grow old in. Life happened there. The atmosphere was a comfortable mess. The walls were adorned with a hodgepodge of pictures and objects that were almost interesting or almost pretty. The people in the room all seemed to know one another. Some conversations spanned tables. Other tables didn't even need words, because the people around them knew one another better than any language. But most of all, what made the place feel like a home was the sense that it cared only about the people inside. The rest of the world could be shrugged off like the rain. A tall, burly woman bustled from table to table, with the gentleness, the might, and the indestructible jeans of a lumberjack, alongside the gruffness of a mother. Assisting her in caring for this place, across the room from the bar, was the fireplace Andrew had hoped for.

"Come on in, grab a seat wherever you like," came the woman's husky voice as she saw the three newcomers walking in from the door. "I'll be with you in just a second."

They sidled down to a table in the corner next to the fire. They could have called the police. They could have cried out across the room that a man had just tried to kill them. But Andrew saw Cameron and Olivia's faces, and he knew that, like him, they wanted nothing more than to huddle quietly behind the menu.

They had barely sat down when the woman strode over to their table.

"What can I get you folks?"

She carried neither paper nor pencil as she towered over them, waiting for them to speak. Nobody answered. Burgers and sandwiches beckoned from the menu, as well as soups, pies, and cakes scribbled on a chalkboard against the wall. But they all knew this was a place for drinking. They were still wearing their school uniforms. Andrew glanced at his friends, and he saw his own panic in their eyes. The trouble they could get in for being at a bar was almost inconceivable. They looked down. The woman lowered her eyes and saw their blazers.

"Damn it, I'm sorry—I'm getting blind serving pints every night."

The three of them shuddered.

"You folks are soaked!"

She turned towards a row of hooks on the wall.

"Here, hang up your jackets to dry. I'll grab a bunch of paper towels for your faces."

When she returned a few seconds later, she was carrying not only paper towels, but also foamy mugs from a nearby table, a pile of puckered newspapers, and a giant pepper mill. She smiled over them while they wiped their faces. Cameron's was the first to emerge, flushed and dry, under his rumpled hair.

"So tell me, honey," she said, "what would you like?"

The boy peeked uneasily across the menu.

"You guys still need a minute? You take your time with that menu, and if you need anything, my name is Sharon—just shout out for me anytime, or for that beautiful man over there, OK?"

She pointed to a tall young man with a pencil behind his ear who was standing over another table. Then she was gone, bustling among the other customers as if all of them were children who had straggled in from the rain. Cameron held up the menu in front of his face and motioned Andrew and Olivia towards him.

"We're in a bar," he mouthed the words. His eyes were open so wide that they pulled back his ears. It struck Andrew as funny that there was no notion left in those eyes of any greater danger.

"I know," Olivia replied. "But it's fine as long as nobody knows we're here. We'll just order food and some coffee and we'll be on our way as soon as the rain stops. Nobody here has any idea who we are."

Suddenly, a strangely accented voice rang out across the room.

"Well, I'll be damned—Miss Gladys, Mr. Day, and Mr. Renfrowe? Ha, talk about a surprise!"

They turned around, horrified, to see the jolly, goofy figure of Jesse McGallender bumbling over to their table.

"My three favorite freshmen—here at Oliver Chucks! Why, it's like having a surprise birthday party in here—on a random night!"

They felt themselves slipping from their seats.

"We just came in here to dry off from the rain," Andrew mumbled. "We're going to head out in just a—"

"Is it still raining out there?" Jesse broke in. "Is it coming down hard?"

His eyes fell across the soggy, muddy paper towels crumpled in a heap at the center of the table. He gasped as if they were all in casts from the neck down.

"Man alive, what happened to you three? Where've you guys been?"

Andrew had no idea how to respond. But he had learned that there was little need to talk when he was with Olivia.

"We were just going to order some coffee," she said.

Jesse snapped his fingers with a definitive air.

"Don't worry about a thing. Let old Jesse take care of it from here."

He spun around to examine the room, and he called out to the young man with the pencil behind his ear.

"Hey Owen," he said, "bring three mugs of yer hardiest cider for my three friends here."

Cupping a hand around his mouth and winking, but in no way lowering his voice, he added,

"And be sure to add a shot of yer best whiskey. It's raining hard out there."

The same thought bounced across their three faces. *This is it,* Andrew heard himself thinking. *A life of crime.*

But the man named Owen simply gave an impassive nod, swung a napkin over his shoulder, and disappeared behind the bar. Jesse turned back to the table and noticed the students' uncomfortable looks. He lifted his chin with a knowing air.

"Don't ye worry about a thing, my friends," he said, and they were sure he understood their anxiety. But then he added, addressing a table that included the daughter of the billionaire mayor and the heir to the Wimbley fortune,

"It's all on the house."

He whirled around towards the bar again and yelled,

"And three plates of the McGallender Special!"

Somehow these final words, which sounded like food, loosened the tension around the table. A smile broke on Olivia's face, spreading to Cameron and Andrew.

Jesse observed the effect. He raised a magisterial finger into the air and said,

"The McGallender Special is a highly secret burger. Very few people are allowed to taste it, and absolutely no one is allowed to talk about it."

They needed no further explanation. They exchanged excited glances among themselves.

"This is the best place in all of Spring Forge," Jesse continued. "The best food, the best drinks, the best people. It's been around for a long, long time."

All at once he slapped his leg, as if struck by an epiphany. He turned to Andrew.

"This is the place I told ye about, Mr. Day, that day when we were talking about breakfast! The waffles here are the best in the whole valley. There's really no better place for breakfast in all the state!"

"We've been looking for a place to grab breakfast before classes," Cameron said. "This is perfect!"

Jesse smacked a hand on the table.

"Phenomenal!" he cried out. "A new tradition for ye three, then. Trust me, ye won't regret it. And lunch is great too, and brunch, and dinner! I'm here almost every night. And I'm not even biased! Though there's something ye should know..."

He peeked over his shoulder at the young man with the pencil behind his ear, who was stepping out from behind the bar with three mugs in his hands.

"Ye see that handsome fellow coming our way? His name is Owen, and he's responsible for all the food around here, and much of the drinks, too. He's a fine, upstanding lad. He has a genius for grilling and a heart of gold."

His chest swelled. Andrew thought that he hadn't seen Jesse so proud even when speaking of his ancient clan in the Highlands.

"That's my brother," he said.

Jesse's brother had indeed splashed their cider with his best whiskey, and it warmed their hearts in secret. But they relished the secret of the McGallender Special even more; they devoured their burgers without a word. And when their plates were all empty (Olivia's first), they upheld their vow not to talk about it. The rain still pattered against the tiny window behind their table, and the window was dug so snugly into the wall, within a nook of faded curtains, that they couldn't see anything outside. One by one they settled more deeply into their seats, lulled by the tapping of the rain and the crackling of the fire, and they trailed their sleepy eyes across the room.

Jesse had gone back to the bar beside his brother. Andrew wondered, as he watched them, how two brothers could be so different. Strapping, agile, and quiet, Owen was the exact opposite of Jesse (and in the few words he spoke, he didn't have a trace of his brother's accent). The only trait they appeared to share was an affectionate awareness of each other as the evening drew on.

They moved around each other without a word, without a fuss, Jesse on his stool at the counter, Owen in and out of the kitchen behind the bar. There was another person, Andrew thought, who seemed acutely conscious of Owen's movements. Olivia's eyes shimmered when she glanced at him. After setting the burgers down on their table, he had wiped his hands on the apron he wore below the waist and he had shaken hands with each of them. Andrew had seen dozens of smiles on Olivia's face in the brief time he had known her. But the smile she gave, when she looked into his eyes and said, "I'm Olivia," was one he had never seen.

The evening advanced inside the tavern. Those who were expected to leave had left, and those who stayed were supposed to stay; their mugs and their chairs had taken root. Sometimes one of them asked for more beer. Sometimes Sharon refilled their pitchers without asking. But mostly every table remained as it was. The hours of action had ended. The world outside was asleep. The only things left were companionship and comfort; conversation was just an occasional consequence. Even Sharon busied herself with shelves and cupboards instead of people. Even Owen was able to rest his arms over the bar, his napkin still flung over his shoulder, his pencil still poised over his ear, and it made no difference whether his brother talked to him or was silent. Through the windows beside the door, Andrew, Cameron, and Olivia could see the rain in the darkness outside. Like the patrons of Oliver Chucks, it had found its place for the night. Andrew had told the Brandows, hours earlier, that he would be working late in the library. Olivia had told her bodyguards before sneaking out. And Cameron always went with Olivia. Andrew gazed groggily around the room. Perhaps it was the effect of the whiskey and cider, but he felt that there was nothing left to be done in the world.

Suddenly he started. His eyes were fixed on a black-and-white picture on the wall. It was the picture of an old road lined with old, unremarkable houses. The look of the houses and the nature around them hadn't changed: it was somewhere near Spring Forge. There was nothing extraordinary about it, nothing in the picture that warranted a closer look, nothing except for a sign on the street, a sign that Andrew could barely make out. He called Sharon as she walked by.

"What can I get you, honey?" she asked.

"I was just wondering, where was that picture taken?"

Sharon bent over the wall with a squint.

"That says Widener Street," she answered slowly, "here in Spring Forge." And she began to wipe the empty table next to theirs.

"Where is that?"

Andrew scrunched up his eyes to hide his agitation. He knew there was no Widener Street in Spring Forge. He had looked. The only place where he had seen the name before was somewhere deep below the ground. Sharon looked up at him and smiled.

"I'm afraid that isn't anywhere anymore. There *was* a Widener Street in Spring Forge, not far from here, actually. But a bunch of those roads were cut off or rearranged, and almost all of them were renamed, back in the fifties and sixties. That was a really wealthy family, the Wideners. The streets used to be named after all the old Spring Forge families back in the day."

Her face was as rough as her emotions were gentle, and her smile looked like a frown. It made Andrew nervous when she added,

"Before your time."

She lowered her eyes to the table again as she continued,

"Before mine too, to be fair! You can find lots of memorabilia of old Spring Forge here on the walls, lots of historical stuff from the early days."

After a pause, she concluded,

"From the days before the House."

Her arm gave a final sweep over the table and she walked away. Andrew looked at his friends. They smiled at him meekly like well-mannered children. They were too tired and too peaceful to listen. He turned away and saw something else. But he saw it in his mind, as clearly as he had seen it from the tree at sunset. He said nothing.

He kept on seeing it. Its shadow fell over his brain. It moved across his eyelids every time he closed his eyes. He could sense it staring back at him, like the picture of old Widener Street, the street that no longer existed except in places without color. It was a wavering black figure with a red blur around its neck. It came and vanished in a second, within the frame of a single window. It was the figure of a person inside the House. He had glimpsed it from the tree, when the man with the rifle had stood over him. The window had lit up. Someone had passed behind it. The sight had distracted the man with the rifle and saved Andrew's life.

Who had this figure been? Who was inside the House? Was it the person who had sent the letter? Was it the person who had claimed the fortune? One question above all others made Andrew's hands clench over the table, so that he wouldn't slide down to the floor. Was it the person who had left the crown for him in the cave?

He struggled to think through his exhaustion. The person who had left the crown must have been at the BNC ball. Who had been there? Where had he seen a red scarf? One thought came to him. It rose in him like sleepiness or sickness. It made him lightheaded but he couldn't fight it. Even more than the chase through the woods, more than the patter and bite of the rain, even more than the cider, the whiskey, and the McGallender Special, the thought dissolved his brain. It was the only thought he had left.

Mia Renfrowe, Cameron's mother, wrapped in her red shawl.

CHAPTER FORTY-TWO

Forgotten Pages

That night Hoss sat down at his desk and wrote the following letter:

Dear brother,

It has been a long time since I have written to you. I have thought of doing so several times over the past few weeks. More than once, I reached into my desk drawer for pen and paper. But each time, something came about to distract me. Each time, something turned my attention away from writing; something covered the emptiness and gloom that had driven me to write. Not tonight. Tonight there are no distractions and no escapes. Tonight I am truly alone with my own shadow, alone with my own thoughts, which means I can be alone with you.

Yes, I turn to you once again because everything around me is dark, because everything inside me is blacker than night. But when I look out the window over this City that I rule, that our father once ruled, and that never held much interest for you, it isn't darkness that I see. It isn't even my own shadow. No, I look out across the glass and I see you. I see your laughter and our childhood. I almost smile. You always become the only thing I remember, every time that I write to you. But do you still remember me? My dear brother, have you forgotten me? I know you haven't. I pray you don't. My dear brother, I feel better already. Every time, the moment I start speaking to you, the next thing I have to say is thank you. Thank you, my dear brother. The thought of you makes the sight of this City at night wonderful for me, as it is for everyone else.

He gazed out the window. The rain had stopped. It was after midnight. Banks of mist from the downpour drifted over the City, veiling and unveiling its lights. He looked up, and the sky was so black that he could no longer make out the lines of steel in the glass wall of his office. But the shadows of these lines fell across the room, and they made it less empty.

He looked down again over the City where he could see, this City that they called the New Rome. There was the universe. There were the stars. They were all below him, not above. And then he felt it all at once, the unreachable bliss. *Letting go.* No longer caring. No longer fighting. Just enjoying. Just leaning back in his seat at the table of the kings of the world. Savoring everything that life had given him. It was a bountiful platter. *Giving up.* He smiled at the vision. He knew he would never attain it. He knew that it lay even further from his reach than the treasure he had chased for so long. Nothing at all, in the City outside his window, in the ocean that rolled beyond it, in the galaxy that hovered around it, nothing was further from his grasp than this vision of letting go. He could never let go, as long as he lived. He was incapable of doing so. It wasn't his fault. The dream lingered beyond his reflection, and he bade it farewell. He brought his eyes back to the page.

I have been beaten. I am almost certain that I am defeated. No one knows how I feel. Hardly anyone even knows what I am after. You were always the only other person who knew everything in my life. You were the only other person who knew everything I've done and everything I am. I've never asked for your sympathy; I've never had to. And though

I've always deserved it, I've never had to dread your judgment. I've asked nothing of you. I've never expected anything from anyone. I had one request, one goal, one wish for myself and my life, one object for my hands to reach. Tonight, at last, I have learned that my wish is denied. Maybe you've heard, from where you are, that the rightful person has returned. I don't know if such news reaches you. Even if it did, could any interest you have in me produce an interest in this matter? The question is meaningless. In any event, this person has returned. I have been told. Everyone, except you perhaps, has been told. This person spread the news wide. But I wasn't sure. I needed to be certain. And so I sent a man to determine beyond a doubt, the man I trust most for such affairs. I sent him to hide by that place and watch, and I asked him to remove anyone who caught him watching. Tonight he came back, and he told me what he saw. It appears the news is true.

Hoss laid down his pen and closed his hand around his forehead. There was someone in the House. The crazy rumors, the tales of sightings, had been true. There *was* someone there. The Gentleman had seen someone. The Gentleman always saw correctly, and he always spoke the truth. The Gentleman wasn't the common and credulous man. He wasn't hysterical. He wasn't irrational. He had no superstition and no loyalty, at least to anyone above the underground where he lived. And he had seen someone in the House. Besides, there was also the other proof, proof that was more indisputable perhaps than what the Gentleman had seen. There was the phone call. But Hoss's thoughts kept away from *that* thought. It was too uncomfortable, and he didn't need it. The Gentleman's proof was proof enough. There had been someone inside the House. For how long? The Gentleman didn't know. And Hoss didn't know how to find out. But what did it matter? The doors of Surway House had opened for someone who wasn't Hoss. It was all over. He had lost. Sometime during Hoss's plotting and devising, during all his contemplating and contriving, someone else had quietly won. And now that it was all over, Hoss didn't even know if this other person's victory had happened yesterday or the day before, or last week, or last year. He didn't even know who this other person was, or where this other person had been all these years. Now that his plans had all failed, now that all his expeditions had proven fruitless, now that his networks, armies and stratagems had come to nothing one after another, it occurred to Hoss that the best thing he could have done was simply to stand outside and wait. He could have waited, day and night, to see the person who would defeat him, to see this person walk past him to the gate and go in. He let out a deep breath. His face pushed lower into his hand. He lifted his head and looked out the window again. Once again, beyond his own face, he saw his brother, and he saw himself beyond the memory of his brother. He picked up his pen again.

Where did you go? Where did both of us go? Are they gone so far, the days of our childhood? Is there nothing in our power to bring them back? They're just a few decades away; and every decade is just a handful of years. Is it possible, when I consider the vastness of the sky before me, that such a minuscule fragment of time, less than a second against the ages of the planets, can carry such worlds inside it? I don't understand. How can I be so powerless? And there we were growing up, being told by everyone around us that there was nothing we couldn't do. There was never any wisdom inside of anyone we looked up to.

The only wisdom was yours, my dear brother. Yes, I was the fast one. I was sharp. I was witty and ambitious. Our instructors grinned when they looked at me. They cocked their heads and they said 'just like his father.' And I'm sure they had other thoughts that they shared among themselves, things they didn't share with us or with anyone in our family. Of course they perceived how ruthless, how relentless I was.

Most likely they never told you how much wiser you were, how much more thoughtful and more gentle. You and I looked nothing alike, and we were even more different inside. Yes, I was the smart one. But I was never a thinker. You were. You pondered things. You weighed things. You understood things in time, instead of charging ahead, as I did, after everything they tinkled before us. That is why everyone preferred you. You were every one of our teachers' favorite, obviously. You would have even been Father's, if he had cared to like either of us at all. For this reason, I should have hated you. But even I couldn't help but love you. Even I could see nothing in you but good.

What did you see in me? I know what you saw later, because I showed it all to you, as I showed it to myself. But what did you see then? Did you already know what I was, before I knew it myself? When you saw how badly I wanted to be the best, could you already see the worst? Did you know that I was all bad? In your face, as I remember it, I now see recognition from the very beginning. I see it in your eyes in the face of a child. Maybe my remembrance is distorted. And yet I think I can see you clearly, even as a little boy. Perhaps the greatest fortune of my life was to know someone, from the start, who was able to know me completely.

And then you left everything. You left it all to me. You said you had no aptitude for it, and nobody disagreed, at least not sincerely. But people far less capable than you have fought to claim much less. You simply didn't want it. You had no desire for any of it. To you, it was all Father's doing and Grandfather's doing, and you didn't see what you could do for it, what you could do to gain any more of it. You let go of the business, and it all came down to me. There was your foolishness, and there was your wisdom, both evident for all to see. I should have thanked you for your decision. I should have been grateful for the madness—or the opposite of madness—that drove you to it. But instead, I was afraid. I was afraid that you would leave me too. I was afraid that you would leave me as you had left everything else and that you would go far away. And now you are gone, and we are both grown, and my fears have grown with me. They have multiplied, and they have also focused. They have extended and they have narrowed, and I am all alone. You did leave me, in the end.

But while you were here, you stayed with me. When we discovered, almost at the same time, that I had a hunger in me that was quelled only by other people's pain; when a fury rose in me whenever someone had something I didn't have; when the story of the Surway fortune, of the vanished wealth that exceeded our own, crept into our lives and took hold of my mind; at every step you gave me comfort, and you never turned away. I was always a brother in your eyes, even when you knew you were looking at a monster. You always looked at me that way, as no one else could. Yours was the only face a monster could love.

Hoss fell back in his chair. A smile, full of sadness, came over his face. He turned his head again towards the window. A grayness was rising over the rim of the earth. It was paler than the mist after the rain, wider than the exhaustion behind his eyebrows. He watched it through the great circle in the middle of the wall of glass, and he felt himself floating over the world from inside his enormous window. What time was it? Soon another morning would begin. Another day. *And I will still be here to greet it.*

The notion of monstrous children lingered in his brain. The image was itching him. It would have distracted him, but it was linked somehow to his torment. Slowly he remembered. The children the Gentleman had seen outside the fence. The schoolchildren from Saint Clemens. Little children come to explore, curious schoolchildren out on some adventure. And they had found the Gentleman. Hoss could hardly believe it. The Gentleman had seen them, and they had seen him. The Gentleman, who was never seen, had even felt compelled to kill them. He had pursued them through the woods, and he had chased them in his car. Hoss chuckled. Even in his dejection, the picture made him laugh. The man in his clothes from a century ago, with a rifle in his hand, at the wheel of a vintage car. How shocking and how odd. How terrifying and inexplicable! Hoss laughed out loud as he rubbed his eyelids.

Too bad. Their deaths would have cheered me up.

But the children had disappeared. The person inside the House had protected them. Again, Hoss thought of the phone call, and he gave such a shudder that he was embarrassed though he was alone. The children had run away. The Gentleman had tracked them in the forest. He knew where they had gone past a clump of trees beside the road. He had followed them as far as a slanting tree they could have climbed. But they weren't there. They were gone, in the darkness of the night. *Vanished*, Hoss had been told. Vanished in that tiny corner of the world where everything seemed to vanish. Vanished near a bend in the road that wound through the woods. The word gave him a sudden thrill. *The woods.* The place where nightmares came true, where fairy tales turned grim, where children of every time and every nation had always been told that evil lurks in the darkness. *The woods.* Why hadn't the Gentleman killed them in the woods? The thought of their dying there was so innocuous, so comfortable in Hoss's mind that he had to believe it would be painless for everyone. No one could begrudge it. *The woods.* The image appeared before his mind. It took form and color in his eyes—three children from Saint Clemens lying dead in the woods. He envisioned their bodies lying crumpled on the moss, their hair tangled with twigs, their fingers coiled around blades of grass, the flaming dragons on their blazers spouting rivulets of blood. The thought exhilarated him. It took sail on his sorrow. He was almost driven to feel that those pools of blood were his due, just like the treasure he had lost. But someone had called the police. Someone had seen the children's danger and called for help. Who had made this phone call? Who had looked out for them? And where had they gone? To think of those children's escape from the Gentleman, to think of their vanishing in the forest, where no trace of them was left, where not a single one of their bones had been crushed, made him resentful. Did they know who had called to save them? Did they know the person who had called from—

The thought that he had fought so hard to keep down bubbled up to the top of his brain. He let it boil over his mind, let it steam out of his eyes till he wished that he could tear off his scalp to let it spill over the whole City, and he knew that he wouldn't even bother to keep the story out of the papers. There was the final proof that he had lost. Someone had called the police. Someone had said over the phone that a killer was hunting three children. And the call had come *from inside the House.*

Hoss felt the bottom of his chest quivering, and he let his fist crash down on the table. The cap of his pen hopped, skidded noisily across his desk, and dropped to the floor.

Hoss reached a hand between his shoes without looking. The cap wasn't there. He lowered his head, peered beneath his desk, pressed his cheek against the surface of the table, and groped as far as he could around his feet. But the cap still wasn't there. He looked down. He inspected the colors of the rug, scanned its intricate lines, bent his neck to see further, and looked up beyond the desk. His eyes followed the rug across the room. And there, beyond its fringe, on the sliver of wooden floor along the opposite wall of his office, was the cap. He gave a groan. He frowned at the object—not even an object, just part of an object. How the hell had it vanished from under him and resurfaced all the way across the room? He pressed his hands over the armrests to get up.

He stopped halfway through the movement. Without un-
bending his knees, without unclenching his shoulders, the tips of
his fingers still grazing the scrolling armrests, he stared into the
air. His stare flew over the desk and fell to the floor, where it
rolled all the way to the cap across the room. His eyes fastened on
the cap, and he felt lightning through his body. Still he couldn't
move.

After a moment, he straightened his back, turned aside, and
stepped out from behind his desk. He didn't pick up the cap. He
didn't even go near it. Instead, he walked over to the old window
set against the wall. He unlocked the window and entered the
elevator that appeared behind it. He rode down to the marble
room beneath the tower, and he strode over to the door across
the landing. He walked into the study and to the bookshelves
against the wall. The bookshelves shot up when he reached for
One Thousand and One Nights, and he stepped into the chamber on
the other side.

The binder was still open on the table. He didn't sit down in
front of it. He leaned over the back of the chair and immediately
began flipping the pages. He leafed as fast as he could through the
blueprints, through the secret plans of the House. The towers
and the floors flicked before him, the halls and hidden levels, and
beneath them the years of his life that it had taken to secure
them, to find them and enclose them within the plastic protectors. Those protectors were of no use to him now—they only
made it slower to turn the pages. He skipped across the dividers,
over the House and the Main Gardens and the other Grounds
and all other possessions, never pausing, never reading, until he
reached the final tab. *Spring Forge and Local Area.*

He felt his heartbeat throbbing in the walls of the chamber.
He tried to quiet it, tried to ignore it, and strained his memory
for every detail in the Gentleman's narrative. His fingers came to

a stop near the end of the binder. He looked across the page, along the winding line of road that broke the crosshatch of the forest. He ran a finger down the page, and just as quickly he took it off, so that nothing could hide beneath it. Rounding his shoulders over the binder, he dug his eyes into the map. He felt the rest of his body going to sleep around the tightness of his stare. And he looked.

Within seconds he saw it. He could no longer see the page, or anything around the page. Everything ceased to exist, even the room in which he stood, even the tower above the room, even his fountain pen, uncapped, left to dry out in the light of sunrise on top of a letter he would never finish—everything except for a tiny cross on the map, the tiniest cross Hoss had ever seen, a letter X inside a square, inside one of the hundreds of tiny squares of the crosshatch that meant the forest, about the width of a finger away from the curving line of the road.

CHAPTER FORTY-THREE

Waffles

Andrew went to bed with a thousand thoughts and woke up with one. He was going to tell the Brandows everything. He was going to tell them everything that very day. He wasn't sure how the idea had come to him, how it had managed to brush away all other thoughts while he had been sleeping. It had jostled in his dreams past the shadow of a top hat, past the point of a rifle, past the headlights of a classic convertible, past a figure wearing a red scarf, and past the eyes of Cameron's mother, under the stars, inside the House, and in a cave deep under the earth. Nothing else remained in his mind as he looked out the window into the clear morning. He saw nothing in the pale sky but the steadiness of his plan and the steadiness of the Brandows themselves. He even smiled and said to himself, *never underestimate the magic of sleep.*

He would have to wait until the end of the day. This wasn't something he could tell them over breakfast. Besides, he wasn't even staying for breakfast: he was expected back at Oliver Chucks. Cameron, Olivia and he had decided to start off their new tradition right away. They had settled the plan within seconds last night, in a gust of rainy air, just as Andrew had hopped out of the taxi in front of the Brandows' house. The memory sprang him out of bed. Downstairs in the kitchen, his bag already strapped over his back, he muttered an excuse to Mrs. Brandow about a project he had to finish before class.

"You've been working so hard," she told him, looking confused and a little concerned.

He almost changed his mind. Seeing her standing in front of the stove, the spatula in her hand still gloppy with pancake batter, he almost took the backpack off his shoulders. He almost bade farewell to Oliver Chucks—and to Cameron and Olivia themselves. His fingers crept up the straps of his bag. But he stopped them.

"Things should calm down after today," he heard himself say.

He tightened his grip on the shoulder straps. He would tell her the truth in a few hours. There was nothing to do but leave.

He sighed as he pulled the door shut behind him. It was lucky that Oliver Chucks was famous for waffles. He would never in his life eat any other pancakes than Mrs. Brandow's.

He expanded his chest with the cold air. His breath seemed to shake the rustling trees. *A new day.* The thought set him off down the path to Oliver Chucks. It was different from his usual walk to school. It went through the road with no name, the road that was deserted—or almost deserted: he came across the abandoned shop sign on the sidewalk. This time, it didn't startle him. He even dipped his head in salute to the chef. He even watched himself glide across the mirror that stood for the face. He even mouthed the words on the tray. *What's mine is yours.* He knew it all. He was a regular. And he thought to himself, *no better way to start the day.*

He stepped into Oliver Chucks, and his eyes turned to the corner where they had sat the night before. Cameron was already there. He smiled at Andrew and pushed out his chin in greeting. Sunlight streamed in between the curtains of the little window behind him. The fireplace was out, but Sharon still bustled around the room as if she had never gone to sleep. Many of the patrons were the same, arming themselves with coffee against the day instead of whiskey against the night.

As he walked to the table, Andrew thought of Cameron's mother. Suddenly he recalled her face perfectly. He almost stopped in the middle of the room. Her smile took form before him. Had she known who he was? Had she known what he had done? Was his secret hidden in her eyes? He couldn't be sure. But whatever the answer was, he was certain of one thing as he continued to the table: Cameron knew nothing. His expression was as natural as ever. And Andrew, who had wondered along the way how to behave around his friend, found it as difficult as always to meet Cameron without smiling. The words flew out of his mouth before he sat down.

"Your breakfast is on me today," he said. "I owe you a bowl of oatmeal."

But another anxiety came over him as soon as he had finished the sentence. How was he going to pay? Would Cameron even let him? He caught sight of the stranger's initials inside his second-hand blazer as he threw it on the bench, and he nervously flipped it over. Cameron only smiled back at him and said nothing.

"Good morning honey," came Sharon's rough voice from behind. "Can I get you a cup of coffee?"

She didn't appear the least surprised to see Andrew again so soon. He wondered if she didn't remember him, but more probably she couldn't conceive that anyone who had ever entered the establishment could ever have breakfast anywhere else. He stared at the fat pot of coffee that looked like a plaything in her hand, as he secretly calculated what this new breakfast tradition might cost. Since it was taking him some time to reply, she went on,

"And if you want tea instead, just help yourself to whatever you need over on that shelf. No need to be formal honey, OK?"

And she went away so quickly that Andrew was convinced she could read his thoughts. He got up and made himself a mug of English Breakfast. It was only after taking his first sip, and quietly congratulating himself on the wedge of lemon he had thrown in, that he let himself settle down into the worn cushion of his chair. Then he asked,

"Where's Olivia?"

Cameron shrugged.

"She's usually very punctual," he said. "At least for meals."

She walked through the door right as he spoke these words. She strode over to their table, plunked down her bag on the floor, and plopped into her chair. Her eyes were already scanning the menu when she airily wished them a good morning. Aside from ordering, there was little to be said before breakfast.

The waffles, it turned out, were delicious, and Cameron found a "perfect constellation" of toppings in his oatmeal. But not even the copious *Oliver's Morning Feast* could draw a word or a smile from Olivia. She ate in silence and stared vacantly into her cup of tea. Her eyes only brightened when Owen McGallender stepped out of the kitchen to deliver several jars of jam that she had asked for. But her face dropped again as soon as he was gone.

Andrew didn't want to ask her what was wrong. He hardly dared to look at Cameron for fear that Olivia might catch his glance. But he couldn't help wondering what was on her mind. Was it the lingering terror of the day before? Was it a fresh understanding in daylight of the danger they had barely escaped? Andrew didn't think so. She hadn't shown the least bit of concern after the BnC ball. Fear didn't seem to last on her; it didn't stick. She had spent too many years without knowing what insecurity was. This was something else. It almost looked, from her expression, like some stubborn, dull ache, something partway between a problem and a sorrow, something that wasn't new and wasn't going away. Whatever it was, she appeared to be well acquainted with it, almost comfortable with it, though he had never seen it on her face. It was something ordinary, something routine, though she was the least routine, the most extraordinary girl that Andrew had ever met. As she silently ate her breakfast, it almost made her look like everyone else in the room.

At some point she must have decided that she had had enough of it. Perhaps *Oliver's Morning Feast* (and a spoonful of oatmeal, and a tiny bite of waffle) was too scrumptious, or the room was too cozy, or Sharon's presence was too comforting. Perhaps the nearness of Owen was too exciting. She gulped down the last of her tea, slammed the mug on the table, wiped her mouth with the back of her hand, and gave a sharp, final sigh.

Then she flashed a smile at her friends and said,

"Man, I love this place."

They smiled heartily in agreement. Cameron asked for the check, and Sharon's reply was as unexpected as it was beautiful— one of the most unexpected and beautiful sentences Andrew had heard in his life.

"We're not gonna charge Owen's family."

The time came to go out into the cool autumn morning.

"Be well," Sharon shouted after them just before the door slammed shut.

And as they stood on the porch, just a step away from the sunlight, breathing in the leafy air, their bodies warm and full, it seemed impossible *not* to be well. But a road, like music or sleep, does what it wants with a person's mind. By the time they reached the first turn, Andrew felt that the shelter of Oliver Chucks was lost forever. Olivia was gloomy again. Her silence became theirs, and it weighed over Andrew. The figure of Mia

Renfrowe reappeared beside him. He pulled away from his friends, so that its shadow wouldn't fall over Cameron. Whatever business she might have had with Andrew, it had nothing to do with her son. There was just one last thing Andrew had to do that required Cameron. Somehow Andrew had to find out where Mia Renfrowe had been yesterday afternoon.

All of a sudden Olivia said,

"My dad was in Spring Forge yesterday."

CHAPTER FORTY-FOUR

The Red Scarf

Andrew and Cameron stared at Olivia. She didn't meet their eyes. Her face was as blank as her voice.

"What do you mean?" Cameron asked.

"He was here yesterday," she said. "Turns out he got here in the afternoon, and he stayed until about midnight. He had a meeting in the City early this morning."

Andrew grasped at her words. They were difficult to hear beyond the din in his head. She lowered her eyes as they walked.

"I missed him," she said. "He was gone when I got back. He wanted to surprise me and take me out to dinner. He left me a note."

Her voice turned even emptier when she added,

"They told him I was working late in the library."

Cameron attempted,

"There's no way you could have—"

"It was the first day back at school." She cut him off without force, as if she hadn't heard him. "The day that school reopened, after BnC. He was so worried. He told me over the weekend that he would never stop worrying after what had happened. His note said his afternoon had unexpectedly opened up, but I don't believe it. He must have cancelled his meetings to come check up on me."

She made a grunting sound that Andrew had never heard before, like an upside-down chuckle. He kept his eyes on the ground. The shadow walking beside him had changed. It was no longer Mia Renfrowe. It had never been Cameron's mother. It was larger, and harder, and as he felt it reaching under his footsteps, he was astonished to see how recognizable it was. He felt an impulse to run.

Olivia went on,

"And there I was sprinting through the woods. Dodging gunshots. Almost getting killed. Hiding in a hole in the ground and then laughing about it over a mug of cider and whiskey. While he was waiting for me in my room, too worried to go to work, the mayor of the City. Waiting to surprise me, and take me out to dinner."

She sighed. The sound clove through Andrew's thoughts. He marveled at how phenomenal the Morning Feast must have been at Oliver Chucks for her to have been able to eat with such a sigh inside of her.

But then she tugged at the strap of her bag, lifted her chin, and declared,

"Oh well, another day, and we're still here. I still have the rest of my life to make him happy."

And she went on walking without another word.

After a moment, Cameron ventured,

"I guess that's the downside of having the mayor as your dad— he's never that far from the City!"

She gave a weak laugh. Andrew didn't make a sound. He could hardly see where he lay down his feet. He began piecing together thoughts, to hear what they might sound like in his head. His eyes wrote down invisible ideas over the blank space of the ground. Mayor Gladys had been in Spring Forge yesterday afternoon. He had cancelled his meetings. He had told his entire staff he was leaving. He had told all his bodyguards that he was going to spend the rest of the day with his daughter. He had gone to Spring Forge. And he had waited alone, undisturbed and un-observed, in Olivia's empty room, all afternoon. The busiest man in the busiest city in the world. All alone. All afternoon.

He *lived* alone, now that Olivia was at Saint Clemens. And be-cause he was so busy, so famous, and so powerful, he could al-ways be wherever he wanted to be at a moment's notice. He could always claim to be *somewhere else*. He could be anywhere, at any time, just as long as he was never *that far from the City*. Just as Cameron had said. Never more than an hour from Spring Forge. Andrew almost stopped. He almost fell a full step behind his friends. He almost gasped as his eyes narrowed over the pave-ment. He felt blinded by the words that no one else could see.

Mayor Gladys is—

Why had he kept his identity secret? Why had he covered his face when he had delivered the letter to the newspaper? Why had he hidden his name from the world? The answer was obvious. To protect Olivia. Olivia, his only family. Olivia, the greatest treas-ure of all, and the unknowing heiress to the largest inheritance in history. Mayor Gladys, Lord of the City, was—

What had Mrs. Brandow said about him? He had been in business before going into politics. He had made himself a bil-lionaire before becoming the mayor. He had ascended both sum-mits, one after the other. How? Where had he made his fortune? How had he built his power? The questions mounted in An-drew's mind. They multiplied and melded. How long had he been Lucian Baker? He came from nothing, Mrs. Brandow had said. How long had he known about the treasure? And the most petrifying question of all: how long had he known what Andrew had done?

Mayor Gladys had been at the BnC Ball. Andrew had seen him there. And he was in Spring Forge yesterday. He could even have seen the three students outside the fence. He could have seen them in the tree from the window of the House. He could have seen the man in the top hat trying to kill them. He could have flashed the light to save their lives. To save the life of his daughter.

A memory sliced through Andrew's mind. He could picture it. He could hear it so distinctly in his head that his hands jumped to his temples. The mayor had spoken to him after the ball, when Andrew and Olivia had returned. The mayor had said something to him, when he had shaken Andrew's hand and gazed into his eyes. *I've never said these words to anyone the way I'm saying them to you*, the mayor had said. *Thank you.* The words rang out in Andrew's head. *I owe you everything I have.* And then, before Andrew had had a chance to consider the words' meaning, the mayor had said one last thing.

Olivia is everything I have.

There was only one question left. Without caring any longer if he sounded suspicious, Andrew simply turned to Cameron and asked,

"Cameron, where was your mother yesterday?"

And just as simply, Cameron replied,

"She was in London, giving a lecture."

But then his face lit up, and he turned to Olivia.

"She's flying back tonight, and she's promised to bring back some Cadbury's chocolates!"

Andrew closed and reopened his eyes. And since the three of them had just come out onto the main street, his gaze fell across a newspaper rack and upon the headline of that day's paper, which none of them had seen yet.

Police Receives Phone Call from Man Inside Surway House

Lucian Baker was a *man*.

Lucian Baker was Mayor Gladys.

Andrew stopped walking. What he felt at that moment wasn't fear, or relief, or even the calm of conviction. It was exhaustion. His feet had carried him into cars and buses, into trains and planes headed for places he had never seen, across fire and gunshots, and deep into the earth. But on a corner of the main street of Spring Forge, they halted. And from there forward they would not go.

"I'm sorry," he mumbled. Cameron and Olivia turned around. "I just realized I forgot something."

They stared at him.

"I need to go back," he said, trying to steady his voice. "I forgot something back at the house."

Cameron and Olivia exchanged glances. Andrew looked down, as if they could read his mind through his eyes.

"Is there anything we can do?" Cameron asked.

"No," Andrew said. The word came out too hard as he tried to keep himself from stammering. "It's just something I forgot. It's no big deal. I'll just run back and get it."

There was nothing more to say.

"I'll see you later," he muttered, and he turned around.

He hurried away as fast as he could without running. Only when he had gone a few blocks did he allow himself to slow down and look back. They were no longer there. There was nobody behind him or in front, nothing but Spring Forge itself, the perfect little town in which so many mysteries and secrets settled, as if they had drifted into the wrong storybook.

Slowly he breathed out. He was alone. He didn't need to hide his thoughts anymore. He realized that he didn't need to think at all. He had carried too many thoughts in his head. Now he could set them down and rest. When the time would come to pick them up again, he would share the load with the Brandows. He would share everything with them: what he had discovered beneath the wardrobe, what he had taken from the cave, what he had found when he had gone back—even what had happened with the man in the tree. He would tell them about the chase in the woods. He would tell them about the mayor. He would tell them everything he knew, everything he had done. And tomorrow the world would be normal, and he would be normal, and he would wake up and go to school, and he would attend all his classes, and he would leave the adult world to adults he trusted. For now, all he could do was go back to their house and wait for them to come home. He would stay inside as if he were sick, and drink tea all day, and lay his head down on the couch. His head would be much lighter by the time they returned.

And since those hours now extended before him, since the sun was just peeking over the rooftops and the trees, and the whole day lay ahead, he took his time walking down the street. He even stopped in front of the shop where he had almost bought cuff links for the BnC ball. He peered into the window. The two mannequins were still there, still wearing their pocket squares and their tie clips, as comforting in their silence as old friends. He lost himself in the sight, not because he wanted anything they had, but because he could stare at them without thinking of anything else. Then something caught his attention. One of the mannequins wore a scarf. The other one no longer did. Together, when he had first seen them, their scarves had made him think of

Christmas. Now there was only one. The one that was left was green. And the other was—

"You're not looking for cuff links again, are you?"

He jumped and turned around.

Standing beside him, in front of the window, was the man he had met in the store. It was the man who had convinced him not to buy cuff links, the man who had told him there were cuff links in every house. He still wore his long black coat. Back then, he had complained of the cold. But now there was a warm red scarf around his neck.

CHAPTER FORTY-FIVE

Missing Things

The man watched him intently, in the same strange manner as before, at once polished and blunt. His graying hair was still ruffled. His beard still bristled, untouched. The fall weather had caught up to his coat, which no longer seemed too warm. But nothing about him had changed, as if he had never left the shop, as if he had stood guard there since they had first met, or Andrew had imagined all that had happened. The only difference was the red woolen scarf that he wore around his neck.

Andrew's mind went empty. He saw all his solutions, all his deductions about Mayor Gladys and Lucian Baker fall into nothingness. He had never solved anything, he had never had any evidence, and now he had no more thoughts, except the conviction that he knew nothing. He felt stupid, and almost resentful, to see that life was just a jumble of meaningless facts that looked like clues.

But the man wore the red scarf, and his eyes didn't move, didn't shift from Andrew's eyes. Andrew tried hard to remember what the man had just said. Something about cuff links. A question. The effort to remember steadied his heartbeat. He forced a reply from his throat.

"No."

He felt that there was nothing more he could say, now that he had given the man his answer.

But the man carried on, as if they were having a perfectly normal conversation.

"Good. I trust you found what you wanted."

His eyes were almost malicious. He seemed to grin in secret as he spoke. And then, all of a sudden, Andrew realized there was no reason to pretend. The man wore the red scarf. He was the figure inside the House.

As Andrew remained silent, the man took a breath and said,

"I'm not looking to get you in trouble, I promise. But shouldn't you be in school right now?"

An ordinary question. Andrew felt himself trying to breathe more smoothly. If the man was still pretending, then perhaps he could keep on pretending as well.

"I forgot something," he said. "I have to go back and get it."

The man nodded and lowered his eyes. For a few seconds, Andrew almost believed that he would turn around and leave. But then the man looked up again, and there was an unmistakable smile on his lips. His voice almost had the tone of a joke.

"Then I wish you well, Mr. Day."

Andrew stepped away from the window and started down the street. But then he stopped. His heart no longer pounded. His breathing had leveled. He was certain that the man was only taunting him, that he knew what Andrew knew, and that the only thing Andrew should do was get away as fast as possible. But there was a question on his mind, a single one among the countless many, that he knew he couldn't let go. It wouldn't let *him* go. Perhaps it was a matter of pride. He turned around.

The man never lifted his eyes from Andrew. Somewhere, near the top of Andrew's skull, somewhere off in a corner, a buzzing began. He fixed his eyes upon the man, the man whose name he suddenly remembered, the man whose name was Elder.

"How do you know my last name?"

The man shrugged.

"You told me when we first met."

"No I didn't," Andrew said. His voice, so forceful against an adult, sounded foreign in his head. The buzzing in his skull, barely audible, went on.

The man tilted his chin, as if pondering the question.

"Ah yes," he said at last. "I read it in that notebook of yours, when I first saw you in the store."

Andrew made no reply, keeping his eyes on the man's face.

"Your name is written on top of the first page," the man continued. "Do you remember?"

"Yes," Andrew said. The buzzing in his head became less faint.

The man looked away, squinting, as if grasping for a thought. His eyes shifted back to Andrew, from the corner of his face.

"That notebook," he said, "is that what you forgot?"

Andrew paused before answering.

"No."

"Are you sure?" the man asked him.

The buzzing became a drone, low and distant, but clear.

Again Andrew waited a few seconds before replying.

"I'm sure. It's in my bag."

Again the man asked him,

"Are you *absolutely* sure?"

And even though it was a question, his voice dipped instead of rising. He lowered his face over Andrew.

The droning drew closer, and Andrew's skin began to tingle.

"Yes I'm sure," he answered again. His voice was raw. He heard himself. He sounded angry. "It's right in here." He dropped to his knee. He pulled his backpack out in front of him. His hands shook as he fumbled the bag open. He was startled to feel the sting of tears in his eyes.

"It's right in here," he said again almost shouting as he yanked out his textbooks, his binders, his ruler and his pens, and underneath them the ridiculous lump of the pencil case he had been given, anything that had ever belonged to him in that school—except for the little black leather notebook. Suddenly, he gasped. He fell back on the sidewalk. He saw it. The notebook lay on the floor. Right on top of the gridded floor. The floor paved with gray-green, perfectly arrayed paper rectangles. The floor from which the Founding Father, Benjamin Franklin, looked on without ever blinking. The notebook lay on the floor—on the floor made of money. Andrew had dropped it. It had slipped from his hands when he had seen the BnC crown. He had taken the notebook out of his bag to add up what he had spent. And it had slammed to the ground. He remembered the noise. It had echoed in the darkness and then faded into the silence, and out of Andrew's mind. Now the sound burst across his head. He had left the notebook in the cave. And on top of the very first page, now that he could see it again, at the top of the first leaf as the cover swung open, for the eyes of Benjamin Franklin, and for the eyes of anyone who might ever visit Mr. Franklin below the ground, a name was written by hand, a name promising *Gratitude! + 1 dollar*, the name of the intruder.

Andrew Day.

Andrew sat silently on the sidewalk. He was no longer aware of the drone growing over his head, making the hairs on his arms shudder. The man staring at him spoke again.

"It appears you forgot your notebook."

Andrew didn't move. The droning grew louder.

"But I'm hopeful you'll find it again."

Still Andrew made no sound. And still the sound in the air grew louder.

"But while we're on the subject of missing things..."

Something rose then in the man's voice that drew up Andrew's eyes. Though he couldn't pull himself up to his feet, though his thoughts carried no words for him to speak, Andrew couldn't help but look up, because he knew from the man's voice that something had changed in the man's face.

"I have something else with me," the man said. "Something else that you may have been looking for." And with these words, he opened his hand, and in his palm Andrew saw a golden cuff link in the shape of a lion.

At that moment the drone over their heads became a rumble. It boomed over the houses and the treetops. It tore across the wind from the direction of the City. They both looked up. Immediately they saw it, so much closer, so much lower, than either of them had known: a small plane flying down over Spring Forge. The rumble grew louder over the silence of the street, rustling the leaves in the trees and then hushing their rustle. Then it shifted in tone and began to dwindle again, as the plane passed over them and away towards the mountains. A message trailed behind it, in a pale, shivering script that Andrew had seen once before.

LUCIAN BAKER I KNOW WHERE IT IS

The man turned back to Andrew. His eyes were wide with fear.

"The notebook," Andrew gasped.

And before he could realize that his voice had returned, that his whole body was his again, he was back on his feet with his bag on his shoulders.

"Andrew, wait!" the man shouted after him.

But Andrew was already running up the street towards the mountains.

CHAPTER FORTY-SIX

Lucian Baker

Down the street Andrew ran, past the shops, past the houses, and off into the roads sloping upwards from the town. Upwards he ran, up the streets that rose from the valley and onto the foothills of the mountains. He didn't have time to think of what had happened. He didn't have time to think of the red scarf or the cuff link. He didn't have time to ask himself, to tell himself, who Lucian Baker was. He didn't have a second to spare for anything that lay behind him. The only thought he had left was the notebook in the cave, the notebook he had forgotten. He had to get it back, he had to take it away, before the man in the plane, the man who set fires, could find out his name.

He didn't pause to imagine that the man had landed the plane, that the man had just leapt out of it and sprung into the woods, past the trees and the empty roads to the rock that marked the entrance. On and on Andrew ran, as if his body were lighter without thoughts, as if there were no reality left in his life but his legs, and the hard stretch of pavement that they pummeled as they ran. On and on he went, until he turned into the street that became the Brandows' street, and up into the driveway that climbed up to the Brandows' door. He yanked the doorknob and went into the empty house. Then he stopped having any thoughts at all.

He hugged the wooden wardrobe. He pushed his whole body against it. He had no conception that the man had just found the rock, that the man would have kissed it, if he could have waited a second longer. But the man immediately threw himself to the ground and began scooping out the forest floor. His skin wasn't used to the earth, but he couldn't feel the soil seeping over his knees.

The wardrobe gave a jerk to one side, so hard that Andrew almost fell. But it didn't turn all the way. Andrew leaned back and reached down to the base. He pulled as hard as he could. He groaned and his fingers shook. The wardrobe shifted, skidded, and scraped aside. The outline of the hole appeared in the floor.

Hoss clambered into the earth, through the roots and the leafage and the dirt that crusted his fingers, that ground under his fingernails and crumbled in his hair. He could taste it in his throat. And yet he smiled as he climbed down. He smiled because it was perfect. He smiled to think that at last he would crawl down to find it himself. The darkness tasted sweet to him, and he swelled his chest with it.

Down the steps Andrew went, one by one, two by two, as fast as he could without tumbling down the stairs. They kept on winding before him, beneath the house and into the earth. His heels could feel the hollowness of the tunnel below. But the stairwell went on, and his footsteps became stomps. He kicked the steps for descending so much further than he remembered.

He reached the final step. The ground no longer dropped before him. The floor became steady and wide, or at least wider than his body. A wall barred his passage. He had known it would be there. He also knew he could swing it aside, no matter how heavy it looked, almost without a sound. His shoulder pressed against the wall, and he came out of the stairwell. The wall swung shut behind him.

He took a few steps down the tunnel. There was no one else there. There was no sound at all. The light fell in slanting rays from the ceiling as he remembered. But he had never seen the tunnel in the daytime. It was almost bright. At first he didn't go far. He hardly breathed. He wondered why it was so difficult to convince himself that there was no one else in the cave. He closed his eyes and tried harder to make himself believe that he was alone.

Suddenly something stirred. A sound reached his ears. Not quite a sound, it didn't quite reach inside his head. It was a trembling of the skin right over the curve at the top of his ears. The wave of a movement had traveled to him in the close unmoving air of the underground. The tremor dropped from his earlobe and trickled down the curve of his jaw, down the line of the bone, and spread over his body. His knees began to quake. He looked at his legs and started to run.

He ran towards the movement, following the arrows on the floor. He ran until his footsteps drowned out the ripple of the movement in the air. He knew that whatever had made the movement was running as well, and he had to reach the cave first. He ran with such force that his head ached from the smack of his shoes.

Hoss couldn't hear him. The white arrows glowed no less brightly for him, and he raced down the tunnel where they guided. He couldn't hear anybody else, and yet he knew he wasn't alone. He could feel it in his joints, in the strain of his knees. Day after day he had searched for this tunnel. Night after night he had dreamed of it. And as he hurtled through it now, he could almost see it from above, he could almost draw the maze in his mind. It was vast, and it was clear; but though he saw nothing and no one, he knew it wasn't empty. It held a bounty that didn't belong to him. *Not yet.* The thought pumped the blood in his legs, made him wrathful and ecstatic. There was only one more obstacle left in his way, one more person under the ground; and he would scratch out this last obstacle with his nails.

But Andrew also ran, and his legs also surged with blood, and the arrows and the walls and the maze spoke to him also. He could feel the other presence. There was a force on the other side of the stillness before him, a force that was as frantic and relentless as he was. And so he ran even faster. And when he thought that he had reached the end of his speed he pushed further, against this unknown force that ripped through the sky and the earth. Arrow after arrow down the tunnel he ran, turning from one corridor to the next, past the street signs and the crossroads and the sloping shafts of light. He didn't even need the arrows as he ran, he knew everything already, as if he had always lived alone among the thoroughfares and passageways and street names of this silent city.

Suddenly he stopped. He dropped his hands to his knees. He tried to draw a long breath and his lungs whistled. But there was breath left in him still—he hadn't stopped because he was tired. He steadied his gaze over the wall. He squinted. He took a step closer. The wall was covered in shadow. He was standing about halfway between two shafts of light. At night, the wall would have been completely black. There would have been nothing there at all, nothing but a smooth plane of darkness down the side of the tunnel. But in the daylight, there was something, something that had caused him to stop.

It was a street sign made of metal, like all the other street signs throughout the tunnel. But this one was different. The others all had names he didn't recognize. But this one he knew.

LUCIAN ST

He read it out loud.

"Lucian Street."

The syllables burbled in his mind. They wobbled in the silence and the shade, like the call of a trumpet under water. *Lucian Street.*

He couldn't make sense of it. *Lucian Street?* Where was that? Where could that be? And as he considered the question, he began to wonder: why did it matter? Why did it matter to him even more than his notebook, even more than the presence of another person in the tunnel? How could this street sign have more power over him than his terror and his haste?

Silence. He commanded everything around him and inside of him to be silent. Everything except one thing. *Lucian Street.* He ordered every other thought to fade away. *Lucian Street.* He closed his eyes. He breathed in. *Lucian Street.* The sounds of the name flooded in and out of his chest. Images and echoes puddled into his mind. One echo. One image. Another street. *Widener Street.* An old road, with old houses, a bygone place that now existed only in black-and-white photographs. *Widener Street.* An ancient name, pronounced only in memory. The echo rose in his ears, the memory of a memory. *There was a Widener Street in Spring Forge*, the echo said. *A bunch of those roads were cut off or rearranged, and almost all of them were renamed.* Roads cut off or rearranged. Places renamed. Sewers redirected. Gradually, slowly, one detail at a time, he remembered the story. *The roads rerouted. The streets renamed.* His mind grew slower with each thought. Lucian Street. *Widener Street.* The will of one man had altered them all. One man's plan had recut them. To make room for himself—for his house. A house, spreading out over what had once been a road. Widener Street. One house, where there had once been many roads. *Lucian Street.*

Suddenly the image came to him. The image, not in black-and-white, but in color, the sound no longer an echo but a rustle, the murmur of the wind blowing through a tree, sweeping leaves over his face. The road cut off by the stone wall. The shortcut to town. His eyes cast off the wall, down the length of the tunnel, and all of a sudden he knew where he was, he knew that he was standing right underneath the road, he knew that the underground corridors and the street signs all around him represented the old streets above the ground, the old streets and their names from the days before the House. He was standing in the middle of Lucian Street, under the span of road that used to be Lucian Street, under the nameless stretch of road that Lyndon Surway had once called Lucian Street, before changing its course. Now there was no Lucian Street left above the ground, nothing but a deserted shred of road. And there were no houses left around it, no shops, no sign at all of the old street, nothing at all except the trees that swayed in the wind, and perhaps even the trees had forgotten it.

And then, all at once, Andrew remembered it. He saw it distinctly in front of him. He would have reached out for it in the half-light, if the vision hadn't transfixed him, if he didn't feel that it would flash through his body like electricity if he touched it. There *was* something left above the ground. There was something left of the old Lucian Street. A sign. A figure. An old wooden shop sign in the shape of a man. In the shape of a chef, wearing an apron and a tall white hat. A chef with no face, a chef with a mirror for a face, a chef with Andrew's face as he stared at it, a chef who looked at him with his own eyes. And as Andrew saw it again, as his body dropped under the shock, he saw the hands sticking out of the figure, the hairy hands curving out on both sides, and the tray the hands held, and the loaves on the tray. A *baker*. A chef who made bread on Lucian Street. The *baker* on *Lucian Street*. And Andrew's thoughts wandered in the darkness to the shadow of another figure, a man in a black coat, a man who wore a red scarf, and he fell upon the words that the man had once said, the first time they had met. *I can only watch*, the man had said. *You're the one who has to act. I can only watch.* Only watching. Watching and waiting. And on the other side of these words, a faraway place appeared, over mountain ranges and forests, across thousands of miles, the place where Andrew had been found, the place where he had lived before, and from where he had been chosen inexplicably to come here, when no one else had ever been chosen. Over train tracks and valleys, over rivers he had never seen, Andrew had been summoned to the oldest house on the street, the house that had already been standing in Lyndon Surway's time, the house with a spare bedroom on the second floor, a yellow bedroom where no one else had slept, where there was a secret stairwell under the wardrobe. And there was a shortcut from that house to town, there was a road that was empty, that was entirely empty except for a chef made of wood, holding a tray that carried loaves. And there his mind stopped, because there was something written on the baker's tray, in faded letters that Andrew knew, words that had been left behind decades ago, left by someone who could no longer speak, words that Andrew could read as clearly as he could see his own face in the baker's face, in Lucian Baker's face. *Lucian Baker*. The name wavered in the shadow as the words rattled on the tray. The name flickered in Andrew's eyes over his own face in the mirror. *Lucian Baker*. Andrew heard the name as he saw his face, until the words on the tray, the words that had called out to him from across a continent, at last resounded in his ears.

What's mine is yours.

A chill blew over his back, and he took off his jacket. He took it off because the chill was inside him, because the shiver had nothing to do with the cold idle air of the tunnel. He took it off because he trembled to feel it, because it seeped into his body like a fever, because he felt hot, in spite of the cold, and he was sticky with sweat, and he needed to check even though he already knew them: the initials of another name, in a jacket no one else had ever worn.

L. B.

There was no Lucian Baker. He was Lucian Baker.

Something burst across the tunnel. A sound, a real sound this time, a sound that reverberated outside his head. It came from further down the tunnel, from the direction of the other person. And before Andrew had stopped shaking, not in fear but in fury, before he could puff up with anger at the thought of this other person, of this intruder in the tunnel, who was coming to take what was Andrew's, he picked up his backpack, which he had thrown on the floor, and started running again. He started running down Lucian Street, under the old, severed Lucian Street and down the other streets of old Spring Forge. He shot past the white arrows and the street signs, and he acknowledged them as he went, he saluted them, he greeted them, he smiled at them as he ran. He would never need their help again. He could see where he was going, and he could see the end in his mind. It was no longer the notebook, or the floor of money beneath the notebook. It was no longer the cave, or the opening in the brick wall that led down to it. It was all of it together. It was everything that was his. He was running to get there first, to arrive there before the other person, the other person who was also running after what belonged to Andrew. The notion drove into his legs, more deeply than anything he had felt before.

The light of the underwater chamber appeared in the distance, around the final corner. He heard a clatter behind him. He had known to expect it. *The other person.* The other person was behind him. Andrew felt the other footsteps in the walls even more than he heard them. He was only a few steps ahead. He could picture his own shape in the other's eyes, flaring in the shafts of light. But he didn't look back. He had no time. All time lay ahead. Everything he could ever have imagined lay ahead.

He arrived under the ceiling of glass beneath the water. Sunshine streamed through the river. It danced in golden coils around the walls and bored into the glass pillar at the center. He sprang across the room and jumped against the wall. The footsteps in the tunnel grew louder as he climbed. With each tug of his limbs, he wanted to throw his head back and scream. He reached the top of the wall with a cry. He drew himself up, though his legs could barely stand. He was almost fully upright when the other person appeared in the chamber below him, the other person who was a man, a man Andrew had never seen. He was a handsome, elegant man. His face was distinguished, still young beneath his graying hair. He wore a suit that was impeccable in spite of the soil and mud smeared over it. There were twigs in his hair but they'd been unable to ruffle it. Most remarkably, the man was calm. There was a sharpness in his eyes that seemed almost at home underground. But he was also astonished. For a moment, the two of them looked at each other without moving. Nothing moved under the water but the waves of the river's reflection.

Then the boy, instead of straightening up all the way, began to bend his knees again. Slowly he lowered himself, and he picked up one of the massive, jagged rocks at his feet. He lifted the boulder with both hands, stretched himself upright, pulled it back over his head, and hurled it as hard as he could into the glass pillar in the middle of the room.

"No!" cried Hoss, louder than the shattering of the glass. The ceiling smashed down as the pillar crunched under it. The river thundered down into the room. It burst against the floor and sliced across the walls, leaping and slashing against the stone. Earth and water crashed down before Andrew. The riverbank toppled in front of him. He fell to the ground and dragged himself backward to avoid tumbling into the water or getting crushed by the rocks. He covered his face, and the last thing he saw was the back of the man's leg as the man ran away, back the way he had come. Rocks and mud piled up to the ceiling in front of Andrew, and he saw nothing more beyond them.

CHAPTER FORTY-SEVEN

Only Time

Andrew stood up. A wall of rocks had formed in front of him. He heard a dull rumble behind them. They were wet when he touched them with his palm. But they closed off the passage from the water on the other side. He turned around. The abandoned sewer stretched before him. To the side, he saw the break in the bricks that led down to the cave. He almost smiled to see it so plainly in the daylight that filtered down. But he didn't walk towards it. He was after what lay at the end of the tunnel, where the daylight grew brighter, slanting from the ceiling in droplets, then in trickles, and further on in streams. He began to walk.

He walked down the passage without hurry, without fear, with hardly a thought. He didn't know how long he would have to walk, but he knew where he was going. He knew it so clearly that he couldn't remember a time when he hadn't known what lay at the end. He went on walking as the light filled up around him, as gardens and meadows replaced roads on the surface above, and the sun rose higher over the world.

At last he reached the foot of a wide curving staircase, with only a few steps. There was a round door in the ceiling above them, a door made of stone. He was surprised only by how easily he could turn the wheel that opened it. He pushed the door and came out into the sunlight. Surway House stood before him, and a cold wind blew over the grass. He was standing in the middle of a fountain. And even though there was no water in it, he could feel himself floating.

"Andrew," someone called out. He knew the voice.

"Elder," he said, and he fell into the man's arms. His tiredness surged and receded over the warmth of the man's coat and the softness of his red scarf.

"Andrew, are you hurt? The man in the plane—did he find you?"

"I'm all right."

Andrew caught himself shaking, though he wasn't cold and he was no longer afraid.

"I broke the ceiling under the river. The water, the rocks, everything came tumbling down... He stayed on the other side."

The man gripped his shoulders and stared deeply into his eyes.

"Did you see what happened to him?"

"He escaped," Andrew said. "I saw him running away. He must have made it out of the tunnel the way he came in. But everything must be under water by now—everything up to the sewer. The sewer was walled off."

The man looked away, and his hands let go of Andrew. For a few seconds he said nothing. His eyebrows were still creased when he turned back and asked,

"Is the treasure safe?"

Andrew smiled, and his smile overtook the man's face. It seemed to spread over the lawn and sprawl under the sun.

"The rocks that came down closed off the sewer. The cave is safe."

Andrew nodded as he spoke, and the man nodded in return. Only then did Andrew feel that he could speak in a steady voice.

"You're the person I saw. You were the man in the House."

"I was," the man said. "I was the man in the House. I've been the man in the House for some time. Since before you arrived. I was watching, and waiting. I was waiting for you all this time. Waiting for you to come here, to Spring Forge, and to find your way to the cave. I waited outside the school when classes started. And I waited in the House. I didn't know when you might get there, when you might enter the tunnel, when you might take that first step under the wardrobe. Finally, on the day of the ball, I knew the time had come. I knew that night would set in motion the events that needed to happen. I wanted you to find the single cuff link in the wardrobe, and to look for the other one. I knew that looking for it would lead you to the stairs. But then I saw you step into that shop—I saw you were thinking of buying a set! And so I knew I had to talk to you. The time had come to greet you at last."

His face lit up.

"You had no idea then," he said. "But now you know. Now you know there is no Lucian Baker. There never was a Lucian Baker. There was simply an idea that Lyndon Surway had, an idea for his legacy. An idea and a task. The idea was his, but he gave me the task, to fulfill when he was gone. My task was to wait for his heir, to look out for you and protect you, and to guide you in secret to this place.

"And above all," he added gravely, "to watch over the fortune."

Andrew peered into his eyes, as if he might read all the secrets inside.

"It was you who wrote the letter to the newspaper."

The man bowed his head.

"Yes, it was. There were other people to protect, too. I was the only one to know the secret. With that knowledge came responsibility, much more responsibility than I had thought, maybe even more than Lyndon Surway had known. Maybe he and I had both underestimated the power of greed and of madness itself. Evil rose before us, harming innocent people, and there was no other way to stop it. I had to tell the whole world that the fortune was claimed. No one else could, because no one else knew the truth."

"So you made it all up, everything in that letter?"

"On the contrary," he said, "almost all of it was true. I really did know Lyndon Surway, and I meant every word I wrote about him. I also meant much of what I wrote about myself. The one lie was the signature. I wasn't Lucian Baker. No one is—except you. My own story is quite simple. Lyndon Surway gave me a mission many years ago. He knew it was a mission almost no one would uphold. He knew that, once he was gone, almost no one would stand aside and defend a treasure without an owner, a treasure no one else could claim. Almost no one would resist the temptation. But he knew that I would. He had reason to believe that I wouldn't break his trust. And so he gave me the mission. I didn't realize, at the time, that this mission would be my life's work. Now I know it is."

His eyes had clouded for a moment, but they brightened again. He cocked his head and said,

"Only you can determine whether it has been a worthy mission!"

Andrew said nothing. He had the odd feeling that he had slipped into another person's life.

"You see, Andrew," the man continued, "I have been watching over you for a long time. Ever since you were a boy. It was I who anonymously created the Saint Clemens scholarship. It was I who purchased the house where the Brandows live; they are my tenants. It was I who set it all up. I watched you grow up from a distance; I watched you learn and become strong; I watched you stand up, from afar, against loneliness and sadness year after year. I watched you learn how to fight and be peaceful, how to be tough and be happy. I watched you learn it all so well that sometimes it seemed you were preparing yourself for the incredible fate awaiting you. Of course we never met, but there were times, difficult times, when I was tempted to reveal myself. I was tempted to step out and help you, and to tell you what the future held. You had difficult times. Everyone does—you were alone. But I knew I had to wait. I knew that the best thing to do was just to carry on waiting. You would have been too young before. You had to grow up just a bit more. You had to be old enough to know yourself and to consider right from wrong. Old enough to see your life not as something you receive, but as something you build. Old enough to travel the country and be a student in this town. What kept my resolve in those difficult moments was the thought of the day when the wait would be over—when you would finally know that every step had been worth it."

Andrew looked away. His eyes fell across the Surway House.

The man went on.

"And so I continued to wait. I waited for years—even for a few days after you arrived here."

Suddenly, he started laughing.

"But once I'd met you in that shop, I couldn't restrain myself any longer! The risks I took... The crazy things I did! I even snuck into the BnC Ball, just to see the cuff links you were wearing! That night I could have given up the whole secret just to take a peek at your wrists. What would I have done if I'd been recognized? What would I have told you, there in public, if you'd run into me? And you *did* run into me! You ran straight into me outside that tent, down on that pathway along the river, do you remember? It's incredibly lucky that you were so concerned with your appearance, with your fancy tuxedo, that you didn't even look up as I tried to help you!"   .

Andrew giggled with amazement as he remembered tumbling into someone, someone whose face he hadn't seen, someone who had instantly disappeared from both the pathway and his memory.

"And when I saw your diamond cuff links, I knew it was done. I knew you had found the cave. The knowledge, the notion... The joy almost made me lose my mind. I thought I might splash my head in the water. The gift I had fought so many years to protect, the gift Lyndon Surway had entrusted me with for so long, was delivered at last. There was only one thing left to do. I had to find you. I had to talk to you. Later, in private. I had to tell you that everything was yours, that the fortune belonged to you. But then midnight came. The attack. I lost sight of you. I had no idea what had happened to you until I caught a glimpse of you as you were escaping. I saw you were safe. And so I ran. But I took something with me, something that might serve as a message between us after that night, something that others wouldn't understand."

"The crown!" Andrew exclaimed.

"The crown," the man repeated. "I didn't want to leave anything in writing for fear that someone else might find it. And after what had happened, I knew I wouldn't have the chance to talk to you again for a few days. I knew you would spend every moment with the Brandows. They are wonderful people. I knew they wouldn't leave your side all weekend. And I didn't want to involve them, especially after such violence. Of course, I went by their house a few times. Of course, I tried to see if there was a way to find you on your own. But there wasn't. And then I knew I had to go to the City. I had to deliver the letter to the newspaper. And so I left the crown in the cave. If I couldn't go to you, then you would come to me. I knew you would go back. I was almost certain that you would return the money. And I wanted to leave you a message. I wanted to tell you that it was all yours, that the entire treasure, just like the crown, belonged to you."

"But I didn't win the crown," Andrew said.

"Of course you did!" he beamed. "Of course you did. I saw the results—that's why I took the crown! Of course you're the BnC King! I don't know why you're so shocked, and why you were evidently shocked in the cave—shocked enough to leave your notebook behind!"

Andrew jumped. Once again he had completely forgotten the little black notebook.

"Your name was right there on the first page!" the man went on. "I couldn't believe it when I went back. What if someone else had found it? I had no choice but to take it. It's been with me all this time! You didn't even need to run after it today when we saw the plane. I tried to tell you! I shouted and ran after you but you couldn't hear me."

Andrew caught himself laughing, laughing for no reason. The thoughts he tried to raise one on top of another kept toppling over. All he could do was carry on listening.

"I continued to watch over you after I picked up the notebook, and I continued to wait. I knew it wouldn't be long then. I knew that the only thing left for you to do was to finish piecing the answer together. I thought you were already close. It was only a matter of going to the end, of realizing that there was no Lucian Baker; that Lucian Baker was a bogus name, taken from that sign on your path to school; that you were meant to find the stairs, that you were meant to find the treasure; and that what was Lyndon Surway's—what is Lucian Baker's—is yours.

"But when I saw you in that tree, under the barrel of that man's rifle, I realized I couldn't keep on waiting. I heard the gunshots from the House, and I ran over to the window, and the only thing I could do was flash the lights to distract your attacker, to give you a chance to run away, and then I called the police. That was all I could do. But I realized then that things had gone too far, much too far, on their own, that the time for waiting was over. I realized then that I must go and tell you myself, that I must go and bring you here for good.

"That night I couldn't find you. You came back late, and in a cab. You ran into the house before I could catch you. And the next day, today, you didn't go to school the usual way. You must have met your friends somewhere this morning—you were with them when I finally found you. I went up to you the moment you were alone outside that shop. I was about to tell you everything. I was just about to tell you when that plane appeared."

A shadow came over his eyes. He bent his head and his face slipped out of the sunlight.

"There is evil outside this fence, Andrew. No iron in the world can hold it back. There is evil we have seen and evil we haven't met yet. There is evil outside this place far beyond anything we can plan for. In ten thousand years we couldn't conceive of every danger a second holds. And with the size of one's fence grows the danger to be kept out. The dangers you face are immense, and your enemies will be many."

With his next words, his face lifted again.

"But I will help you on your way. I will stand by you at every step. There is only one thing you must promise."

He set himself squarely in front of Andrew, and he tilted his head to stare more deeply into Andrew's eyes. Bringing down his hand over Andrew's shoulder, he said,

"You must promise me never to reveal your secret to anyone. No matter how much you trust someone, no matter how much you love them, you must never tell them that you are Lucian Baker. I will help you begin your new life. It can take place in this

House if you want. I will go back to the cave with you, and I will help you rescue your treasure. The passage is walled off for now, but every wall can be broken. We will bring out the treasure—we will even get help for it. Today. Tomorrow at the latest. We don't even need to hide it anymore. Lucian Baker has returned. We can bring out your treasure and tell the whole world where it was. No one will find a path from the tunnels under water to the Brandows. You will be Lucian Baker, and you will be safe. All that is yours and all that you care for will be safe. I will do everything that can be done to secure your identity as Lucian Baker. The world will want to know of Lucian Baker. It cannot be helped. The world will claim Lucian Baker as its own. But you can hide behind what the world sees. You can build an entire existence to cover who you really are. You can be both Andrew Day and Lucian Baker, so long as no one knows that those two people are the same. No one can know. Protect yourself, Andrew. Protect those around you. You have already glimpsed the fury your fortune can provoke. You have already glimpsed the madness and the rage. Believe me, what you have seen is nothing. The man who flew that plane—what you have seen of *him* is nothing. That man, and his whole clan. His family. You don't know any of it. All that fury will come after you. After Lucian Baker. And so no one can know Lucian Baker is you. No one can know you are a child. Do you understand? Promise me, Andrew. That is the only thing I ask of you."

He looked away. He seemed almost apologetic.

"I suppose you have a choice—I realize I never asked you. Do you even want any of this? Do you accept what you have been given? You don't have to. You don't have to take the fortune. You don't have to hide your name and lead a double life. You don't have to do anything. But if you accept any of it, then I ask that you accept all of it."

Andrew steeled his eyes, and he held up his head under the man's gaze.

"I accept," he said.

"Good," the man replied, and he let go of Andrew's shoulder. He smiled once again and looked away across the lawn.

His name suddenly resurfaced in Andrew's mind—*Elder*. This gave him the focus he needed to ask his question.

"But Elder, why me? Why am I Lucian Baker?"

Elder turned to him again and gazed at him in silence, with a smile that was too peaceful to be broken with words. He had to shake it away gently before answering.

"Lyndon Surway didn't know when he would die—at least I don't think he did. But he knew that he would die without an heir. And the thought of having no one to whom he could leave the gigantic fortune he had built almost made it all worthless in his eyes. He didn't know whom to choose. He didn't know whom to find. And so he asked me to find someone. He died decades before you were born. But before he died, he told me his plan. It was highly elaborate, and he devised it in secret. All his wealth would be preserved. He would leave it all intact for someone, someone to whom he even gave a name. He set everything up perfectly. He settled his accounts one by one. He arranged all the proper entities—all the documents to prove Lucian Baker's claim and his identity, all of which are in my possession. He laid out his will. He hid away his treasure, and he gave me control of the house that led to it. There was only one thing left to do: find the person who would receive everything. That was my task. When Lyndon Surway disappeared, the search for Lucian Baker began. Everybody searched. But nobody could find him. Nobody but I. And for years, I looked.

"At last I found you. You were everything he had asked me to look for. You were at the dawn of life. You were nothing. Nothing was expected of you, and nothing was set aside for you. But I thought you could be something more than what you were. And I was right. You grew up to be hardworking and brave. Every day you rose a little higher than the little you had. You could look at what you were and still see what you could be. The world belongs to people like you. And it was Lyndon Surway's idea that someone like you should have everything."

Andrew couldn't hold back a thought, and he didn't know if he was speaking for Elder or for himself, in gratitude or in reproach. Perhaps it was just a question.

"But you could have chosen someone else."

Elder looked away again. He was squinting.

"Maybe there are no choices, and only things we find on our way. But there was a specific reason that it had to be *you*, Andrew Day, and not just someone like you. In you I saw the memory of someone else, someone who would be proud of you."

Andrew almost reached out to turn the man's face towards him.

"You knew my parents? You knew who they were? Is it true they died a long time ago?"

Elder smiled at him sadly.

"I wish I could tell you otherwise, but they are gone. I didn't know them."

Andrew felt lost for a second and was almost angry.

"Who was the person whose memory you saw in me?"

"There are things I can't explain—at least for now. Maybe someday I can tell you more."

Andrew lowered his eyes.

"What about Lyndon Surway? How did he die? What really happened to him?"

Elder shrugged.

"That I truly don't know. He took off in his plane and never came back. It happened decades ago. And I'm afraid what happened exactly is as much of a mystery to me as it is to everyone else."

The sadness in his smile widened before fading at last.

"But there have been revelations enough for one day. All you need to know for now is that the fortune is yours. It has waited for you a long time. It is a good and honest fortune. It was rightfully built and it is yours by right. It belongs to no one but you."

Andrew followed Elder's eyes as they edged past him towards the House. And at last he let his own stare wash over the towers and the domes, the terraces and the windows, the monumental sweep of stone and the luster of marble and glass, over the walls as grand as a city at the end of a traveler's road. It wasn't the first time he had seen the House. But he stored up that moment's image into his lungs, into the pit of his stomach, into the caps of his cheeks, almost as if he were saying goodbye. He knew that no building in the world would ever be so beautiful again in his eyes.

"It's all yours," Elder said, and his voice seemed to come from within Andrew's mind. "Everything you see here, and much that you cannot see. Everything inside the cave, of which you've only seen the surface—you've only seen the sliver of bills at the very top, at the top of a mountain that goes deep into the earth, made mostly of bars of gold. And much outside the cave that you've never heard of—stocks, bonds, real estate holdings, corporations and their subsidiaries, factories, farms, railroads and mines, acres of land in any climate you can envision. All held in trust over the years, accumulating wealth over the decades. All waiting for you. All of it is yours, and from now on your only constraint will be time. Every other resource that you can possess, everything else that you can ask for, you will have. The only thing that will diminish is time, time that will dwindle for you just as it does for everyone else. Be wise in what you do, Andrew. Use wisely of what you have, and always remember that money begets money, and there is always more to be found. But time, once spent, is gone forever."

His smile bent his voice.

"But you are still very young," he said, "and you have time as well in abundance. Go now, then, to what is yours. No one is better suited for it than you are."

As Andrew turned again towards Elder, he remembered other words he had once heard, words he had heard at the end of his first day in Spring Forge. He could still see the House when he looked at Elder; he could see it in Elder's eyes. Now he could also see it in the words he remembered, words Mrs. Brandow had once said, when the House had been nothing to him but words. *All we need is someone who can make something intelligent out of something fortunate*, she had said. And he nodded a silent vow to himself, and to Mrs. Brandow, and to Elder, and to all the Benjamin Franklins, and to the enormous House itself.

"I almost forgot," Elder said, and he reached into the pocket of his coat. His smile was already so familiar and comforting that Andrew could hardly believe he had once been afraid of him.

"I have a few things that I've been carrying around for you for some time. The first is your missing cuff link. Now you can have the complete set. Sure, it's not made of diamonds, but you should give it a chance—for sentimental value!"

And with a grin that made him look at once younger and older than he was, he plopped the tiny golden lion into Andrew's palm.

"And there's something else."

He handed Andrew a white envelope, in which Andrew felt something rigid and something loose. Before he could open it, Elder had turned away towards the long shaded avenue that led to the gate. But he stopped at the edge of the fountain and looked back.

"Oh, and one last thing," he said.

He leaned over the stone floor and picked up a little object that Andrew hadn't noticed.

"By the way," Elder said, "you owe me a dollar."

Andrew didn't open the white envelope until he was alone again in the Brandows' house. He hurried upstairs to the yellow bedroom and tore it open with his finger. The rigid object in the envelope was a legal document. It was surprisingly easy to understand, even though Andrew had never seen anything like it before—a property deed.

The loose object was a key.

CHAPTER FORTY-EIGHT

The House

Andrew asked himself to wait just one more day. It turned out to be a busy day, fast and dense with laughter and work. He could have told himself that his schoolwork no longer mattered. He could have avoided Cameron and Olivia, since he couldn't tell them his secret. But he wasn't able to give himself much guidance that day. He wasn't able to weigh the importance of what he did or the significance of what he said. All he could do was marvel at what a day in life could hold, and he excused himself from all other thoughts. It was the prettiest day he had seen in Spring Forge yet, at the golden cusp of two seasons. He had lunch outside again, by the river with his friends. As they ate and laughed together about nothing at all, he discovered that the three of them could never run out of things to say to one another, even if he didn't tell them everything. He even stopped looking at the river after a while. There was no change in the water that he could see, no trace at all beneath the stream of a small break in the riverbed further up the valley.

In the afternoon, he spotted the Principal across the lawn. Andrew ran over the grass.

"Principal Clare!" he called out.

The man turned around. The lawn was full of students. They fell silent and looked.

"Principal, there's something I've decided to give back to you."

The man eyed him suspiciously, as Andrew lowered his backpack to the ground and reached for a large, shiny object inside.

"Thank you for giving me the good news—and for giving me this," he said. "But out of respect, I don't think I can accept it this time around. There's always next year!"

The principal was as red as the crown Andrew placed in his hands. If the students all around them hadn't applauded the BnC King, Andrew might have almost heard the steam rising off the man's head.

Unfortunately, Andrew never came across Jesse that day. But he spent much of his day trying to picture Jesse's face the moment he would open his locker. There was a box waiting for him there, a box that came from a store in a neighboring town. And there was a note on top of the box that said:

I still think yours are nicer, but here is a backup set I know you'll like.

Other faces drifted through his mind as the day passed, and the faces he loved most filled him with sadness. The night before, Andrew had told Mr. and Mrs. Brandow over dinner that he was leaving their house. Something different had come over their faces at that moment. It was unfamiliar to Andrew, like the puddle of silence left by his words. His only answer to those faces and that silence had been the explanation that living with classmates would make things easier for his schoolwork. He had authorization from the administrator of his scholarship.

"When?" they had asked him. He had never known how much pain eyes without hostility could inflict.

"Tomorrow night."

The two of them had looked at each other and smiled at him. Mr. Brandow had even given his shoulder a friendly shake. But running back and forth between their faces, Andrew had wondered if he was crazy for leaving them, crazy for imagining that anything in the world could be worth more than what he had at that table. This notion made itself at home in the kitchen; it was still there in the morning at breakfast. All were present— pancakes obviously, but even Mr. Brandow, who had stayed home later than usual; and Andrew had unhesitatingly declined Oliver Chucks. The question lingered on. Why was he leaving this house that had started to feel, in just a few weeks, like the only home he had ever known? But he was already gone too far to turn around. And perhaps the path that lay before him might someday allow him to give back to the Brandows as much as they had given to him. He carried their faces with him all day long, as he knew that he would for the rest of his life.

The hours passed at school, and he did something that afternoon that he had never done: he read the *Spring Forge Gazette*. He was looking for a specific story, and he quickly found it. It was a slightly sinister story, though the writer's tone was light. A single-passenger airplane had been spotted flying over town the day before. A message was floating behind it, a message that might have reminded people of recent local events. But the whole thing had been a prank, and the paper provided no details on who was behind it. The memory of that face followed Andrew as well, but he had no clue of who the man was or where he had gone. Elder had told him the man would come after him, the man and his clan, the man who had unleashed a masked army on Saint Clemens and perhaps also sent the shooter in the top hat. But Andrew knew nothing more about the man or what Elder had called his family. The only thing Andrew could do, as he read the little paragraph over and over, was imagine the man lying down on the forest floor, the nameless man in the perfect suit, bedraggled, exhausted, soaked with sweat and muddy water, as the river rushing beneath him flooded the secret tunnel forever.

There was another incident in Spring Forge that day, but no one mentioned it anywhere. In all likelihood, no one even noticed it. There was an empty road not far from town, a deserted road where there had once been a street. Nothing was left of the old street, not even a sign showing its name, nothing except for an abandoned wooden figure on the sidewalk. For many years it had stood in silence, a sign for a shop that was no longer there. That day, the sign disappeared. And nothing remained of the old street but the speechless memories of the trees.

The day came to an end. Dinner with the Brandows was unexpectedly merry. Mr. and Mrs. Brandow were so kindly, so eager to describe all the excitement coming Andrew's way, that even his sadness felt warm in his chest.

"I'll come back for sleepovers!" he blurted out between two bites. "I'll miss you so much."

And when they hugged him at the end of the evening, he knew those words were the only part of dinner they would remember. He made his way up the stairs, and as he went he began to wonder if the best part of the life that lay ahead, the life of promise and possibility that he had dreamed of for so long, hadn't already begun. He wondered if perhaps he had been wrong to think that his life would begin with mythical deeds and turns of fate. Maybe the truth was that life happened at the kitchen table, asking Mrs. Brandow for more hot chocolate, or by the fire at Oliver Chucks, trying to guess if Jesse's brother had looked back at Olivia. Maybe the greatest destiny of all was secretly made of such moments. He had picked up as many flowers for Mrs. Brandow on his way back from school as he could carry. And when he had given them to her, it had crossed his mind that he could never ask for anything more than all the flowers his arms could hold, and Mrs. Brandow to give them to.

He had told the Brandows that he would be gone before they woke up. He was so determined to come back soon that he didn't even pack a full suitcase, taking only the clothes that would fit in his backpack. He had a few hours still. He turned off the lights and lay down in bed. But he couldn't sleep. His eyes wandered back to the wardrobe in the darkness. He needed to hold it in place with his stare, to secure it with his hands over his blanket. But nothing moved in the night. More surprisingly, he fell asleep. The sky was gray when he looked out the window.

He sat up on the side of the bed. The rest of the world was still sleeping. The time had come. He put on his school uniform, tightened his backpack on his shoulders, went down the stairs as quietly as he could, and walked out the front door.

Morning was just beginning to push off the horizon when he came to the gate of the House. He pulled the key out of his pocket and pushed it into the lock. He bowed his head to the stone lions and stepped in through the gate.

The avenue before him bent and rose into the distance, as if sagging under the shadows of the trees on each side. He looked past the trees at the lawn on his left. The sky turned white as he walked, a shade of white that held inside of it all the colors of the day. A tree in the middle of the lawn caught his eye. It was enormous. He couldn't even see the top of it from where he was. But he could understand the tree. It was the first notion he could grasp. This tree belonged to him. He could climb it, he could paint it, he could cut it down (which he never would), or he could build a house inside of it. He could raise a flag from the summit. It was his tree. And the other trees around it were also his, and the leaves on their branches, and the grass at their feet. They all belonged to him, as nothing had ever belonged to him before. He walked across a bridge that spanned a hollow in the grass that he knew was meant for water, and he carried the thought of the tree with him.

He had to keep thinking about the tree when he entered the House, when he first stepped into the entrance. He immediately felt that the marble floor beneath his shoes was cold, though the air in the hall was warm. He had to keep thinking about the tree when he tried to fathom the space in which he stood, a space that seemed too wide for walls and too tall for a ceiling, though he was no longer outside. He had to remember the tree when he took his first step on the staircase. He had to remind himself that the tree was his tree before he could be persuaded to touch the sculpted stone of the railing. And as he went up the stairs, he had to picture the tree just to convince himself that the staircase was also his, not only the right side he had chosen, but the left side as well, that the railing was his, that the chandeliers were his, and the curtains and the arches and the paintings and the windows, and the gardens beyond them, and the pathways in the gardens, and the statues along the paths, and the towers and the bridges over which the sun would rise soon, and all manners of things that he couldn't even conceive, and multitudes of things that he couldn't even name.

And then, suddenly, he stopped. He narrowed his eyes. There was a round table in the middle of the landing in front of him. He couldn't tell if the table was big or small, as big as a pond or as small as a pie, because he couldn't understand the proportions of anything around him. But he saw something on the table's surface, something whose size he could grasp. It was a letter. It was folded over. He stepped closer to the table. He could feel his arm reaching for the letter, reaching for the golden initials *LS* that had been engraved in it long before he was born. And even before he unfolded it, even before he touched it, he knew the letter was for him. He picked it up and smiled, as he read the single word written inside.

Welcome

Author's Note

Updated for the sequel's release, fall 2019

I will finish here as I began—and as I did when I wrote the first Author's Note in 2016—by thanking you.

In 2016, I had thanked you for taking a chance on this book, which I had published myself because I had more hope in you than in any publisher. Now I thank you again, but my gratitude has extended and deepened with time, like a beard.

Thank you for reading this book. And thank you for your Amazon reviews, which have been the markers of this book's adventure in the world. They have been both its box office and its critics' score, and their words have been more thrilling and more fantastical to me than any sentence I could ever write. Your support came after years of rejection, and I might have loved every minute of those years if I had known they would lead me to you. I've been wishing for you upon a star since I was far younger than Andrew Day.

In return, I have a sequel, Someone in the Walls, *which is now available on Amazon as an ebook and a paperback. Whether you pick it up or not, please know that it is written for you and because of you. It took even more years and more tears and sweat than the first book (still no blood), and I'd gladly spill them all at your feet again just to say,*

Thank you.

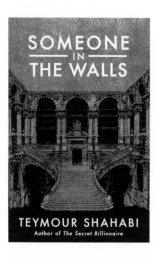

Andrew Day looks like any other student.

At the Saint Clemens boarding school, nobody knows—not even his two best friends Cameron and Olivia—that Andrew is one of the wealthiest people in the world. No one knows that he has inherited the fortune of Lyndon Surway, the legendary tycoon, who disappeared decades ago and was never found. Nobody suspects that Andrew is the new master of the Surway House, which lay uninhabited through the years.

But as life returns to the stairways and ballrooms of the magnificent home, as Andrew ventures through forgotten passages and unmapped doors, strange things start to happen, almost as if someone were watching him, as if someone had expected him. And as he learns more about the people he loves, as he journeys into dark places where no one goes, Andrew begins to wonder:

Who is hiding inside the walls?

Book Two of The Surway Fortune
Now available on Amazon

Acknowledgments

Chronologically, with one exception

It is fortunate and fitting that I should first thank my sister Maryam, who, along with her husband Nikolaj, kindly let me write this book in their beautiful dining room. For the snacks you left, for the home you provided while these characters' home was under construction—and for the lifelong home you are to me, thank you.

I uncovered a treasure in my own adventure, in the form of Judith Henstra, of bookhelpline.com. Through Judith, I had the pleasure and privilege of working with Ginny, whose brilliance makes me feel sorry for Andrew Day's cuff links. And if there is a more insightful and thorough editor in the world, I will classify that distinguished figure alongside Santa Claus and the Tooth Fairy.

Anyone reading this book will already have witnessed the breathtaking artistry of Kerry Ellis's book cover. But I must thank Kerry, in addition, for her tremendous kindness, warmth, and vision. Her picture of my book is worth many times 100,000 words. She raised the bar for this book—and raised the book with it. Her cover is the first impression the book makes; if I could make such a first impression upon meeting anyone in the real world, I would hop around from stranger to stranger all my life.

I made the journey from Kerry's cover to this final page hand-in-hand with the early readers, reviewers, and supporters of this book and of my online updates on YouTube and other platforms: Adam Boretz, Andrew Walker, Brian Pike, Heidi Angell, Jeannine and Salar Saleh, Kent Deron, Shahnaz Radjy, Sushant Sawant, Tara Turner, Tony Parsons, and Nicole from Arizona. Thank you for your tips, your guidance, your heart, and your help—in everything from the book's cover design and font to the preferred spelling of towards (with an *s*). A special thanks to Ian Nichols, not only for being the greatest friend on earth, but also for advising me on the physics of underground and underwater situations. Many of you affected the final form of this book with your feedback and counsel. All of you make me feel fortunate and blessed. Thank you for turning something terrifying into an act of friendship. Whatever happens from here, we've made it together. *What's mine is yours.*

On the subject of tremendous fortune: I've never been prouder (or more relieved) than during the two phone conversations in which my parents gave me their reviews. Thank you to my mother and father, Roya and Khosrow. My whole life, they have surpassed every author who's ever lived, by making everything possible.

Finally, I break with chronology to thank my brother Cyrus, who read the book chapter by chapter as the first draft was being written. Maybe it was because Cyrus saw something good and strong in this book that I found the fearlessness to share it with the world. In all things, as in this, he is my guide. And he is wiser, kinder, and greater in my estimation than any hero in history or fiction.

About the Author

Teymour Shahabi was born in Paris of Persian parents and moved to the United States to study Comparative Literature and Mathematics at Harvard University. He lives in New York City where he still spends time with both words and numbers, alongside people imaginary and real respectively. *The Secret Billionaire*, his first published book, is not an autobiography.

www.teymourshahabi.com
www.facebook.com/TeymourShahabiWriter
Instagram: @teymour.shahabi

Made in the USA
Middletown, DE
07 March 2020